The Intruder

Gillian Tindall lived in Fra[...] in London with her husban[...] to travel widely. Among her best known novels are *Someone Else* and *Fly Away Home* (which won the 1972 Somerset Maugham Award). She has published a critical biography of Gissing, a book on the urban development of London and one about Bombay. Over the years she has been an occasional contributor to *New Society*, the *Guardian*, the *Standard* and the *Sunday Times*.

Gillian Tindall

The Intruder

published by Pan Books

First published 1979 by Hodder and Stoughton Ltd
This Pavanne edition published 1983 by Pan Books Ltd,
Cavaye Place, London SW10 9PG

ISBN 0 330 26926 7
Printed and bound in Great Britain by
Collins, Glasgow
Filmset in Monophoto Times by
Northumberland Press Ltd, Gateshead

Author's Note

All the public events alluded to in this book did actually take place, in approximately the way and at the dates described. My grateful thanks are due to Mme. Albert Vulliez, for reading the manuscript for me and correcting, from her own experience and knowledge, some technical details of life in Occupied France.

It may be objected that no such event as I describe eventually taking place in 'St Laurent-la-Rivière' actually occurred in the Berry. This is true – but something similar took place further south, in the Limousin, and there were analogous events in other parts of France too, notably in a village near Lille. I would not like anyone to suppose that this is a book 'about' a nameable place or identifiable individuals: it is not. It is a book about ordinary people, and about war.

Gillian Tindall

Part One

One day in the early 1970s Jane returned to St Laurent-la-Rivière with her daughter Diana.

For years she had not meant to do so. This idea of a return to that place, that place had, long after 1944, been out of the question – or so it seemed: at any rate no one had suggested to her that she might ever go back. It was accepted by the family (by her parents, while they lived, by Diana's father, by her younger sister and *her* husband) that a return there would be unthinkable. Had she actually broached the possibility, they would probably have dismissed the idea as 'morbid', for that word was still in fashion then and all things had not yet become discussable.

No one had even questioned her, much, after the first tale was told, for after all what was there to ask, or even say? There are stories so simple in their abrupt conclusion that, once the first shocked reaction had been voiced, those who have reacted find themselves falling silent again, standing round as if with empty hands, shifting from one foot to the other, waiting to find something further to say which will be adequate to the situation. But there is nothing to say, nothing that can be found to bridge the gap between the ordinary and the inconceivable, no way of cutting Evil down to manageable proportions except by a retreat into unthinkable callousness. Gradually, on the edge of embarrassment, the listeners turn away, begin to talk again to each other in subdued tones about more normal, compassable subjects. Presently ordinary conversation is resumed, and the teller of the unordinary story must recover her composure and take her part in it, if she does not want to be shunned. It is not that any of the assembled company are unsympathetic to her, or even uninterested – but they have been made afraid.

They do not want to remain for long in that condition.

In any case there was no need for Jane to tell her story, for 'everyone knew' about it. That is to say, the name St Laurent-la-Rivière became public property. Paradoxically it acquired a permanency, a settled image that could not be affected, as living places are, by time and chance. Like the names of certain other places over the surface of Europe, it served not only as an informative notice board but also as a high wire fence round the event concerned, warning visitors not to blunder there unthinkingly. Beyond the fence, as 'everyone knows', is an expanse of scorched and blackened earth, dangerous with sharp fragments of metal, bones, mines . . . You, the intruder, stand still in silence a moment before the place, hat in hand or head reverentially covered, according to creed, making a formal recognition of its existence. Better stop short of actually entering it.

Jane, finding herself profoundly exhausted, mentally and physically, by the last few years, acquiesced to public opinion. The late 1940s passed for her with unreal swiftness, perhaps to make up for the weight of experience that had dragged upon the years just past. Several times she went briefly to Paris (at that time still the airy, ingenuous city she remembered from 1939) but although these visits, and the people she saw, awakened memories for her, they were old memories that hardly related to the central experience of the War.

For a time she had nightmares, in which she saw, repetitiously, the culminating events at St Laurent which, in reality, she had not actually seen. But the nightmares were imprecise, confusing, even unconvincing like a bad film, and by and by did not seem to be taking place at St Laurent at all. She recognised the sense of generalised, formless dread – she had lived with that intermittently for several waking years – but not the houses. It was as if the events which her intellect knew really had taken place at St Laurent, her dreaming self insisted on situating in another place which meant nothing to her. She was, after all, like everyone else, she concluded: her imagination refused to accept what had really happened. Her exceptional experience had not made her different. Perhaps it was false and sentimental to believe that experience made people different?

Occasionally she wondered if she was taking the coward's way out, cutting herself off from this whole section of her life which had been so momentous, cravenly respecting the barbed wire fence and warning notices put there by public opinion and – apparently – by a censor inside her own head. But perhaps it was better so. Even if the four years of the Occupation had taught her nothing else of use in her resumed life in England, it had taught her that courage is only an equivocal virtue. *Humankind*, said a quoting voice in her head, *can only bear so much reality*.

Skimpily educated, she had no idea who had written that or to what it had orginally referred, but she found herself repeating the phrase as she lay in bed in 1950 in the nursing home where Diana had been born and she herself had just had her fortieth birthday. She was thinking not of the drug-blurred birth, which had passed like an uncomfortable dream in a crowded railway carriage, but of how fortunate she was to have a new baby, now, a new life to raise further barriers against the past and to protect her through the years to come. A child, she recalled, forces you into comforting rituals and at the same time keeps you moving; it prevents you from thinking too much. A child is the great excuse for leaving other matters alone. Her son, Mark, had saved her during the War. Now this baby would save her again, in another way.

Sometimes, during Diana's childhood, the family of three passed through France on their way to holiday in Switzerland or Italy, but their route never took them anywhere near St Laurent-la-Rivière or indeed through the centre of France at all. It is fortunately a large country: whole regions of it remain undiscovered even to those who believe they know it well. Diana's father knew it to some extent: he had been there with the Army in 1940 and again in 1944. He spoke a fair French, and undoubtedly – as Jane remarked to him once with a distant amusement – knew much more about the actual political events of the War in Europe than she did herself. But she understood that he did not want to accompany her to that place, that place, which was nothing to do with him; nothing to do with anyone any more.

Several times, over the years, a restaurant or hotel keeper had admired aloud Jane's fluent, idiomatic French, wondering where she might have learnt it? She never told them the truth, for questions aroused in her a fear which brought the automatic reflex of a lie. It was irrational, she knew, but she was afraid of being unmasked, afraid that her false identity of ordinary English tourist would be penetrated. In the same way she had, for years, lived with the fear that her assumed character of French citizen would be revealed as a sham.

In any case, she told herself through the 1950s and '60s, the French didn't want to hear any more about the War. It had hardly been a glorious episode in their history. The only French people she ever encountered who were eager to reminisce about it were those who insisted loudly on their own part in the Resistance, and such people had become a sour joke already within a few years of the Liberation. To hear them talk, you would suppose that the whole of France had risen behind de Gaulle by 1944 except for a minority of well-defined, easily recognisable collaborators. Like many other people who knew the truth to be different, Jane remained silent on the subject.

It was not until the end of the 1960s, when she had been recently widowed and Diana had grown into a large, handsome girl with plans to become a doctor, that a desire after all to revisit the centre of France stirred in Jane. She ignored it for a while, telling herself that she should have done this years before if she was going to, that such a visit would now be at best (or worst) a meaningless gesture. But the desire persisted.

Though long out of touch with French life, she presently became aware that others beside herself were touched by the urge to visit this particular territory of the past. There were new books now about the period, and films appeared which documented or dramatised for the first time aspects of the Occupation which had not been exposed before. Evidently, it had all been buried too quickly and fearfully in the years after the War and in the two decades in which France had been busy turning herself from an old-fashioned, demoralised country into a modern and prosperous one. Now, the buried material had to be exhumed and re-examined, before it could be laid to rest in history.

Such, at any rate, was the view propounded by Diana, when her mother eventually confided in her. (Diana, by way of relief from memorising anatomy for her first MB, was taking an interest in psycho-analysis.) It was quite clear, she stated authoritatively: if her mother wanted to go back to St Laurent-la-Rivière then she ought to.

"I half want to."

"Then you still ought. If you don't, you'll always be a bit sorry you didn't."

How strengthening it is, thought Jane, when your own children's opinions become as valid as any other adult's – indeed, often more valid. For the first time in many years she remembered with true recollection, instead of approximately, the morning when Mark, aged fourteen, had said to her:

"Maman, you *must trust* me. I really am a better judge of this than you are. For both our sakes, you must let me go."

For years, she had not been able to recall that day and that decision except in a way that was deformed by the memory of overwhelming dread, as if the picture in her mind had been defaced and cockled by the chemical strength of the emotion in which it was fixed. Then, for many more years, she had not thought of it at all. But now, she found she could remember safely, even nostalgically, as if the passage of time had eventually transformed this buried, grisly remnant into something different. This must, she thought with amusement and recognition, be the sort of thing people mean when they speak of the blessings of old age.

So it was that Jane and her daughter found themselves, one day in the early 1970s, driving down through the centre of France, past Paris and the great plains, past the Loire, past the Cher – where, for several years, the German frontier had been, and so into the bucolic, gently undulating country towards the mountains.

"Pierre used to say that St Laurent lay just at the point where one half of France meets the other half," Jane remarked, as she and Diana sat drinking a cup of coffee in a small market town not very far from their destination. "It's a bit higher than this – just off the edge of the foothills of the Massif Central. This is still the plain." As Diana did not reply, she went on gaily, though uncertain now of her daughter's attitude,

"Pierre meant that St Laurent is exactly at the point where the earth on which you can still grow vines and melons merges into the upland where the bracken and heather and Spanish chestnuts begin. You can almost stand on the exact spot where fertile France gives way to mountainous France."

Diana jerked her head, flopping her hair back into place. Even Medical Schools these days, it appeared, didn't mind girl students with impractically flowing tresses. She said a little brusquely,

"You've hardly ever said anything about Pierre."

"Well . . . It seemed natural not to, I suppose. Particularly while Daddy was still alive."

"But Daddy must have *known* –"

"Well of course he did, silly." (Really she was so young still in some ways, after all.) "But in a marriage one doesn't talk about one's previous husband or – or whatever. Any more than Daddy talked to me about Margery, his first wife –"

"The one who was killed in the Blitz?"

"Exactly. Believe me, when two people both of them with – with sad things in their past, come together, they don't sit talking over the past much. They're just happy to have found each other and to get on with life."

"Yes, I suppose so." Diana did not sound as if she entirely approved of this idea. She said after a minute, "But it's me who's asking you now about Pierre. Not Daddy."

"Yes. Yes, I know ... But darling, I don't know what to tell you. He was a young man – I showed you a photograph of him once, I think, when you were quite small. He'd be an older man now, almost as old as me. But I've never managed to imagine him old."

"You – you weren't actually married to him, were you? Officially, I mean."

"No, indeed." (I wonder when she guessed that?) "That was part of my problem, all through the Occupation. As a matter of fact, though it seems funny to think of now, I suppose that for some of that time I was still legally married to my first husband – to Mark's father."

"Did you ever see *him* again – Mark's father I mean?" said Diana doggedly.

"Not after 1946 or '47. As I never asked him for alimony, I didn't know for years if he was still alive, but then I ran into him a couple of years ago at the theatre, and he looked quite jolly. Disgustingly fat, I thought, but quite in command of life."

This was the consciously flippant way she had spoken of her first husband ever since 1939. Diana laughed, relieved at the release of tension.

"You have had a complicated life, Mummy," she said, sounding vaguely envious. "People my age always suppose that your generation was awfully innocent and straight-laced, but they're wrong, aren't they?"

"Yes, quite wrong. At least –" Jane frowned, trying to isolate a truth. "It's not true that we didn't get up to whatever people get up to today – of course we did. At least – people like your aunt Susie didn't, frightfully, but people like me did and there were lots of us. But – yes – there was a difference. I think that because everything was more under-cover we were more *desperate* about it. Once you'd burned your boats then – you'd really burned them. Don't forget there was still a very large body of people in those days who were genuinely shocked by divorce and so forth, and you couldn't keep one foot in their camp, so to speak, and do what you liked with the other as people can today ... You had to choose, more. And I think that – perhaps because of this – love was very important to us. Being In Love. The idea of it, I mean, was simply the feeling. If you justified your actions by being In Love then you jolly well stuck to that and didn't give up easily."

"Were you – were you very much in love with Pierre?"

"Very, very much." She knew that to be so, though the feeling itself had been long irrecoverable.

"More then ever with Daddy?" Shyness at the unfamiliar topic was making Diana sound prim, her mother thought.

"Oh darling, what a question! Surely you've discovered by now that you can't quantify these things?"

Diana muttered into her coffee cup that she supposed so. She herself was seeing and, Jane presumed, sleeping with, a fellow student, a nice, rather ordinary boy from Durham. On reflection, perhaps Diana never *would* discover the impossibility of measuring different loves. For all her gloss of modern freedom, she was in many ways like her aunt Susie, her mother thought with relief. She said firmly,

"If you love someone very much and then – for some reason beyond the control of both of you – he is lost to you, there is no way of knowing how the relationship would have developed with time. And Pierre and I never had what you might call a normal life together. Always, there was this sense of time pressing on us – of living on borrowed time – which I suppose heightened emotion. Yes. But I know I did genuinely love him very much and he loved me. Yes."

"So that was how you came to be in France during the War at all?" Diana persisted.

"Of course."

"For love."

"You could say that, I suppose, yes."

"Wasn't that always unwise?" Diana in her stern-sensible voice, rejecting the romantic intensity of which her mother had spoken. How could her generation understand such an emotion, surrounded as they were by a luke-warm bath of general tolerance, Jane thought with sudden disgust? But she agreed meekly that, yes, with hindsight, her presence in France then did seem unwise.

"I mean, there was Mark," Diana continued.

"Quite. But you must remember that, in 1939, people thought that England itself might soon be invaded, or at any rate bombed to bits. In fact people were more pessimistic in England at that time than they were in France. Odd as it may seem, the Fall of France was not foreseen."

"So it didn't seem silly to take a child there?"

"On the contrary. Indeed Pierre's view was that we would be safer there than in an over-populated island like Britain where everyone would soon be starving."

"How interesting. I never thought of that."

"It could very easily have happened. Actually James – Mark's father – thought so too. It was about the one idea he and Pierre had in common."

Diana's right, in a way, she thought, but I'm not going to tell her so. I *was* a silly thing in those days, though not quite in the way she is suggesting. I was brave because I was so ignorant. I thought myself so independent and emancipated, a daring bohemian, almost a feminist – reading Vera Brittain, going (well, once) to a lecture about women in Russia – but what could have been more clingingly feminine than the way that, almost as soon as I'd left James, I attached myself to Pierre? Poor, dear Pierre ... I wonder what he saw in me? Perhaps he was taken in by me too, at first, in a way. He was escaping from a conventional background also.

They decided to pay for their coffee and go. Under a baby-blue sky of spring, the market stalls were beginning to shut for midday. Diana hastened off to buy some fruit to add to their picnic lunch. When she returned, she said with false casualness:

"By the way – what work did Pierre do? I don't think I've ever known."

"Oh, didn't you know? Well, he was a doctor actually!

Barely qualified when we first met." Across the coincidence mother and daughter smiled at each other.

As they drove, Diana careful at the wheel, along the road towards the hills which, by twists and turns, was becoming intermittently, stirringly familiar, Jane was aware of an emotion she had not expected. She felt nervous, frightened even – but also happy. And not just with a happiness of today, but with a reflection from the past also, as light is reflected from below the horizon.

Hereabouts, in this landscape, she had suffered and despaired. But here, too, she had been very happy, and not just in 1939. Later, even much later, there had been moments of joy. She had forgotten, but knew now that it was so. If she recovered nothing else on that journey, she would have salvaged that.

Part Two

Jane quarrelled definitely with her husband James in the month of Munich, though not, as it happened, about that. Afterwards, she would have liked to have thought that it was James's declared support for Chamberlain and Peace in Our Time which had finally convinced her that he and she would never see eye to eye about anything, but an innate honesty compelled her to recognise that, as a young woman, she had been the last person to quarrel with anyone over a political principle. True, James was infuriating, with his refusal to take foreigners seriously, and his apparent conviction that God and Chamberlain between them had arranged matters expressly in order that James and his kind should continue to live – but she was hardly eager herself to go to War for the sake of Czechoslovakia, wherever that was exactly. When James, who was at Lloyds, told her that the odds there were quoted at 32-1 against a War at present, she felt craven relief. But she did wish James and his friends weren't so *smug* about it, and so convinced of their own superior judgment. It was, she felt, all very well for people like Daddy, who'd been all through the Last War and seen their brother killed and so on, to feel that anything was better than a repeat performance. But James's naked self-centredness in the guise of wisdom was another matter.

However what they actually quarrelled about was something far more English. Mark, their only child, was now eight, and James maintained that it was high time he was off to prep school, preferably James's own old school – horribly known as Slaughter from the name of the village where it was situated – but, if not there, then to almost any other boarding prep school, before many more terms passed. James had an absolute conviction that boarding school from the age of eight, or eight-and-three-quarters at the very latest, was essential if Mark was to develop in a desirable direction.

"– After all, Jane, he'll have to go at fourteen anyway."

"That's different, fourteen's quite different from eight. Though, come to that, I don't see why he *has* to go away from home even at fourteen. Not everyone does. On the contrary."

"Don't be so devious, Jane. You know quite well that everyone of our sort does."

"Not always they don't. Look at the Montague-Smiths, they're sending their boys to St Paul's as day boys."

"The Montague-Smiths live in London –"

"Well we could move to London; I'd like –"

"– And *any*way people like the Montague-Smiths don't quite belong to the same . . . Naturally St Paul's is full of rich Jewish boys. But Mark is to go to Winchester, you know that perfectly well."

"I know you want him to go there, and I can understand that, I know it's a good education and so forth. But I won't have you making these lofty claims about boys like Markie *having* to go to boarding school. It just isn't true. Particularly at eight."

"They all go at that age. You know that perfectly well."

"Only in England."

"We're talking about England."

"No one else does it like that. Foreigners think we're cruel."

"Then it just shows," said James with an edge to his voice, "how bloody wet they are."

There was a more specific reason for James's tone than generalised xenophobia. For by then Jane had met Pierre, and though James was not going to admit that he knew about him he did know and was very much disturbed. It had only recently dawned on him that his marriage might really break up – that Jane, instead of just fighting him as she had done for several years, and which he found exhilarating in a way, might really leave. The blow to his self-esteem was acute.

In fact, though neither of them knew it at that moment, Jane had already left: the conversation was conducted on the downs near Rottingdean, where she and Mark had been spending the summer holidays with her parents. She never returned to the large, comfortable house near Henley into which she and James had moved as a young married couple nine years before: James and Jane, such a romantic young pair, exhaustively equipped with silver, glass, linen, toast racks, coffee tables, napkin rings and no less than two ice-cream makers, a credit to everyone. Instead, she remained in Rottingdean all the autumn, sending Mark temporarily to the tiny village-school, to the consternation of her parents who wondered to each other if their daughter was turning Red. Then at Christmas she moved herself and Mark to London. Her younger sister Susie had just married a doctor and vacated a flat in Marylebone High Street: Jane took over the lease.

Her parents seemed almost as distressed by her move to town as by the break-up of her marriage.

"Darling, *is* it wise? All on your own with a child . . . And what are you both going to live on?"

"On the money you and Daddy very kindly settled on me when I got married, of course."

"But that was hardly meant to be more than a dress allowance! What about Markie's education? Jane – you're surely not going to send him to an Elementary School *in London*?" Most districts of the town had, Jane's mother understood, 'gone down' since her girlhood there: she had images of foul-mouthed, ragged urchins as her grandson's only companions. Although a kind and fair person, she was imbued with the rural-snobbism which, between the wars, almost reached the level in England of a national obsession.

"No Mummy, I'm not. *Do* stop fussing, I do know what I'm doing, honestly. I've thought about this for ages. I know I'll manage. As for a school for Mark I'm sick to *death* of the subject, but as a matter of fact the last letter from James's solicitor said that, for the time being, James is prepared to pay any bills relating to Mark. So."

"Darling, I think that is really quite decent of him, you know. In the circumstances . . ."

"Oh so do I, so do I. Incidentally the letter also says that he doesn't want to divorce me 'at present'. Which isn't so decent, but there's nothing I can do about it."

"Oh dear, oh dear ... And I suppose you can't divorce him?"

"No, Mummy, I can't. Not unless he commits adultery in Brighton and sends me the bill. Come to that, he could conveniently drop the bill in here while he's passing, couldn't he? But he won't, so that's that."

Her mother looked disapproving, but whether at the word 'adultery' or at her daughter's determined levity, Jane was not sure. Presently she said:

"Well the matter will have to be settled eventually, one way or the other, won't it Jane dear?"

"Of course. James is just being bloody-minded. He might have seen this was coming years ago, but he simply didn't want to recognise it . . . He'll come round in the end. When he meets someone else, if not before."

Looking more disapproving still ('I'm not a prude, but really, this modern cynicism and so forth –'), her mother said:

"I think you may be misjudging him, dear, I really do. As you know, we've always liked James – though I do see now that he's not been quite the right husband for you – and I think that very likely he's still hoping that your marriage may be saved: I mean that you'll go back to him; Jane, don't look at me like that! No wonder he's in no hurry to start divorce proceedings."

"Yes, Mummy. I'm sure you're right. But it won't happen, you know."

"Darling . . . It would be so much better for Markie. For you to be living again as a family, I mean."

"Mummy, you know quite well that the main reason I finally left James was to prevent him from sending Mark away to school. Some family life – when the poor boy would only be home for a month here and a month there!"

"He means well, dear," said her mother in the evasive tone of one enunciating a principle rather than a considered opinion. She added after a moment, in a different tone,

"Daddy did tell me to sound you out on the subject of leaving Markie here with us for a while when you go to London. Just to give you time to get settled in and look around, I mean. He's such a dear little chap, we'd love to have him. But, as I said to Daddy, if your main aim is to keep Markie with you, I don't imagine you'll agree to that either."

"No, you're quite right. Mark and I will stay together for the moment, of that I'm absolutely determined. Thank you, Mummy, I know he'd be quite happy here – but no."

Her mother said rather shame-facedly:

"Oh dear, it is rather a relief to hear you say that! I had awful visions of our being left in charge of Markie, and then James turning up to fetch him and us not knowing where our duty lay –"

"You wouldn't have let James take him?" said Jane, shocked.

"Well, darling, he *is* his father . . . It is rather worrying, Jane; you do realise, don't you, that if James does divorce you rather than the other way round the Courts might award him custody of Mark? So Daddy thinks. If James should decide to fight about the matter, I mean."

"Oh – I don't think James would actually do a thing like that," said Jane slowly. "It would be too – unEnglish, if you know what I mean. Not at all an Old Wykehamist thing to do." But, in spite of her words, the fear was sown in her mind, strengthening her resolution to keep Mark as far from James as possible, even carrying him off abroad if need be.

It was also in her mind that when it came to the point, as it must, James would amost certainly rather go through the conventional farce of letting her divorce him rather than aim for a less gentlemanly truth; and that this was just as well, considering the existence of Pierre. But she did not say this to her mother. Her mother had no idea at that time that her other daughter, good, honourable little Susie, had unwittingly been the means of introducing Jane to Another Man. Had she known, she would have been sincerely shocked and would have had far less sympathy with Jane.

In fact, Jane had not left James for Pierre. But once the knowledge that she really was going to leave her husband had surfaced in her consciousness, she began to see Pierre in a new light. She had first met him at supper at Susie's flat the previous spring, and then later at the party that Susie and her husband-to-be, Geoffrey, gave as a farewell to their London friends (as they artlessly put it) just before they retreated to matrimony and a country practice. Pierre had qualified in Paris and was spending two years as a Registrar at the French Hospital in Shaftesbury Avenue, where (according to Geoffrey) a strange, antiquated, Gallic medicine was practised, alien to anything known in Britain and dependent on leeches, homeopathy and other even less mentionable remedies. Geoffrey and Pierre had, however, met at a conference and formed a friendship on the common ground of minor surgery, where their mutual interests lay.

Some time afterwards, Jane realised that she had probably condescended to Pierre slightly at their first meeting, and asked him if she had. He said she had.

"You were very much the charming married lady. Being kind to the young foreigner."

He was, in fact, a little younger than her, but the next time she met him he talked perseveringly to her about his training in one of the poorer hospitals of Paris and the eighteen months' Military Service had spent in an Army Hospital in North Africa, and by the end of the evening her view of their respective positions had changed. That night, a boredom and self-disgust which had been accumulating quietly for years within her finally broke through to the surface of her mind. How on earth could she ever have imagined, even at nineteen, that being married to James would be an occupation in its own right? How on earth, she asked herself, had she stuck it so long? – sitting in Henley watching Mark's Nanny take him for walks and waiting for James to come home and eat the evening meal prepared by the cook-housekeeper? Was this spacious vacancy, padded out with a little golf and tennis, for neither of which she had much aptitude, to be the sum total of life forever? Seen in these terms, the prospect was clearly intolerable. Hedonistic, energetic, a little spoilt and profoundly inexperienced, she set to work with her new-found clarity of view to construct her personal indictment of James and of the world to which, as his wife, she had been consigned. The indictment was a damning one.

"You married too young," said Pierre, the first time she let him take her out to dinner. "It frequently happens. France also is full of women who have made the same mistake. I have seen it all around, and sometimes in the consulting room also."

"But I suppose most of those were pushed into it by their families. I mean, arranged marriages are still usual with you, aren't they?"

"*Des mariages de convenance? Bien sûr*. But the fiction is usually maintained, you know, that the young couple have a deep affection for one another, and so often they believe it themselves. The romanticism of youth on the one hand and family pressures on the other. A fatal combination."

"There isn't that excuse for me," said Jane sombrely. "No one was trying to push me into it, I just dived in of my own accord. I ought to have known better. I suppose that James seemed so much the sort of suitable, good-looking, amiable husband that girls of my own background dream of while they're bored schoolgirls, that it simply didn't occur to me that we wouldn't really do for one another."

"It was his fault too, perhaps?" suggested Pierre politely. "He was, after all, older?"

"Yes. Oh yes. You know, that never occurred to me. I suppose he should have married a fluffy little thing who thought he was wonderful . . . Poor James. But how silly of him too. I mean, I wasn't all that – fluffy – even at nineteen. I don't *think* I was anyway." She made the remark uncertainly, hoping that he would say she could never have been fluffy, but he just laughed and said,

"You don't look fluffy – is it? – to me, anyway?" There was a slightly self-conscious pause between them. Then he sighed, and said: "One must, after all, approach marriage like any other serious decision – I mean, with great caution."

"I suppose so," she said. It sounded very foreign and rather dreary, put like that.

"I myself at this moment," said Pierre, beginning to play with the salt cellar, "– am busy with caution. Do you say that?"

"You could. Are you really, though? You mean –?"

"I mean," said Pierre deliberately, "that for the past several years there has been someone my parents wish me to marry. Once I have established myself, that is."

"And are you going to?" she asked, trying to sound matter-of-fact while a horrid weight settled within her.

"I am not sure. Not entirely. It would of course be an advantageous match for me. The girl is, or will be, quite wealthy. And she is a nice girl too – don't think I would consider it for a moment if she was not. She is a pleasant person, I have known her for most of my life. (We are vaguely related on my mother's side.) But –" he raised his hands and let them fall again.

She said briskly, feeling that now she couldn't bear this conversation much longer,

"But you're still not entirely sure you are going to marry her?"

"On the contrary! You misunderstand – I do not make myself clear. When I say I am not entirely sure, I mean that I am fairly sure I am *not* going to marry her. But I have to be certain before bringing myself to explain this unpleasant fact to my family or hers."

"And to her. Poor girl!"

"No. No, thank God not. Matters, you understand, have never been so much settled between us. There have been no letters – no rings or promises or even kisses. It's merely been something generally understood between our families, which in a way makes it the hardest of all . . . You look surprised."

"I am, rather, because I thought that, whatever other

French families did, yours had a modern ourlook. Your father's ideas and so on –" She knew that Pierre's father was a doctor too, and that he was a free-thinker (whatever that might be exactly) and a believer in the League of Nations, and that it was partly to please his father that Pierre had come to get experience in England.

"Yes. But 'modern' is a relative concept in France. Anyway it is mainly the mothers who arrange these things."

After a pause Jane said self-consciously:

"You know, Pierre, it's not my business, but the longer you hesitate the harder it will get, not easier. I know this because I've hesitated for years before leaving James when I knew really that we were no good together. I've only managed to leave him just recently, and I wish now I'd done it years ago."

She stopped, a little disconcerted, because Pierre didn't seem to be listening. He had called the waiter and was asking for more bread. Then he turned back to her. He looked bright-eyed, yet his eyes – black in a rather pale, bony face – were opaque at the same time, like those of a small animal. She could not read their expression, but he was smiling.

"I have just decided," he said.

She travelled back to the South Coast that night in a state of intense private excitement. Ordinary objects – the upholstery in the carriage, the lighted windows past which the line ran – seemed imbued with an extraordinary hyper-reality like objects seen in a film. She felt exultant like someone who has managed to break miraculously out of the confines of their own existence and into a new one where the old fears, constraints and calculations have no meaning.

Pierre had accompanied her to Victoria and sat with her in the carriage till the whistle blew. The newspaper placards still spoke of 'Peace', of 'Pledges' and of 'Honour' – words from which the meaning was, year by year and now month by month, evaporating. It did not occur to her till afterwards that her own words to Pierre on how the longer you hesitate to destroy an existing situation the harder it is, could equally have been applied to Britain's position under Chamberlain.

When she did think of this, the neatness of the analogy and the linking of her own personal destiny with that of Europe, pleased her greatly.

By Christmas, she and Mark were settled into the Marylebone flat, and in the New Year she sent him to a boys' day-preparatory school. He had not, she had to admit, learned much at the Rottingdean village school during the autumn. Now, initiated into Latin and Maths and school uniform, and rugger on Thursdays in Regents Park, he set off each morning with a new air of purpose. It was, she thought, delighted at his resilience, as if he too was enjoying the freedom and logic of their new existence. Any images she had had of a sad little boy 'cooped up in a London flat' (her mother's annoying phrase), mourning for the social nursery life of Henley, were dispersed. He soon acquired new confederates at school, including a polite, ginger-haired child who had no visible father either and whose mother (to Jane's pleasure and interest) was a moderately well-known actress.

He did not appear to miss his own father at all, partly perhaps because he had always been in bed anyway by the time James got home in the evening, but more, Jane thought, because James had had absolutely no talent for fatherhood anyway. His manner towards his son had tended to be peremptory, his ideas inflexible. He had bought Mark an expensive train-set when he was too small for it, Jane recalled with undimmed indignation, and then was cross when Mark mistreated the couplings on the coaches and had forbidden him to play with it alone. Then there had been that ghastly time last summer in Cornwall when James had insisted on trying to teach Mark to swim in a rough sea, and eventually a blue, choking child had to be wrapped in blankets and given hot tea by a sternly disapproving beach-guard ... In memory, the case against James intensified. Her parents' hints that a boy 'needed his father' fell on unreceptive ears.

James wrote briefly and coldly to say that he had no objection to the school she had chosen which seemed 'not unsuitable for the moment', but that of course the general situation was entirely unsatisfactory and that he still counted on Mark going to Slaughter in the near future. He had put his name down for September 1939, by which time he trusted that Jane would have come to her senses, and he remained hers ever, James.

Jane tore the letter scornfully up. She lived those months without a trace of guilt or regret and it was this, among other things, that led to her great happiness.

She and Mark enjoyed a series of child-sized treats for two: they sometimes had tea in a shop after school, they went to News Theatres where they saw goose-stepping troops, and films, which Mark rather preferred, about the life of badgers and otters. They rode on London buses all the way to their destinations, and Mark became obsessively knowledgeable about the Tube system. She enjoyed it almost as much as he did. Looking back over her happy but too-quiet, too-protected childhood, her early marriage and the years that followed it, it seemed to her as if in her whole life till now she had been marking time, waiting for the real thing to begin, and now it had. Only afterwards, when this time was over, did it occur to her that it had not been real life, far from it, but more like a long, delightful holiday.

Pierre was a regular visitor to the flat, but a circumspect one. Jane had now learnt enough about the divorce laws to know that, if she eventually managed to push James into giving her a divorce, it would be essential that her own life should appear respectable.

"Doesn't the King's Proctor know that people sometimes make love before eleven o'clock at night?" Pierre enquired mildly, arms behind his head, as he lay gazing at the ceiling.

"Apparently not. It's all too silly. Oh my darling, it's after half past ten – oughtn't you be thinking about getting up?"

Pierre had a room for the nights he was not on duty, somewhere east of Gray's Inn Road. Her imagination would follow him in his walk home across the wastes of London as maternally as if he were Mark. He used to look so tired, sometimes. If she had ever, long ago, yearned over James in this way, she could not remember it. The very idea seemed absurd. Compared with James's alien flesh, with its reddish freckles and copious hair, Pierre's smooth body seemed as akin to hers as was her child's. These two physical presences now formed her world; nothing else counted.

Remembering that year afterwards, when there was too much time – time to wait, to think, to watch the night fall – it seemed to Jane that during 1939 eleven o'clock at night was always coming. Of course. The whole year was the eleventh hour: this was the classic view of it.

Had it not been, would she have embarked on life in London with Mark, with Pierre, so easily, jettisoning all considerations but the present? She never knew the true answer to that.

It amused her to sense the different reactions her new life provoked. Her sister Susie, returning to London for a day's shopping for maternity clothes, was patently sorry for her, too tactful to say so outright. To Susie, now ensconced in a marriage for which she had waited loyally for years while Geoffrey completed his qualifications, it seemed awful that Jane should be having her life back to front in this way. When still a schoolgirl, Susie had admired her married sister's life-style, and found it extraordinary now that Jane should have willingly exchanged 'all that' for a belated dive into the life of flats and corner delicatessens and cheap restaurants and notes left out for the milkman because no one was going to be in. She did not see the charm of Jane and Mark's bacon-and-egg high teas with the wireless on; she felt that her sister had declassed herself. When she found that Jane had got a part-time job in a bookshop, she was genuinely upset for her. It *sounded* intellectual, but it was really just being a shop girl, wasn't it?

Jane found Susie's unvoiced concern more touching than irritating. She was, however, less amused by the attitude of a semi-friend from Henley who dropped in one day for tea and who, having heard 'on the grapevine, my dear', of Pierre, clearly considered the whole thing deeply and almost improbably romantic.

"But people *do* go around with people to whom they are not married," said Jane shortly.

"But sweetie, a Frenchman! And I hear he's frightfully good looking –"

"He's about an inch shorter than me," said Jane, "and as for being good looking, he looks like a rather unhealthy squirrel with black hair. If you call that good-looking." She was extremely annoyed to have her unique Pierre treated as a twopence-coloured exotic lover, a glamorous Maurice Chevalier stereotype. Or no, worse than that: an almost pornographic sex-object in English terms, a *French doctor*. "I hear you have a French doctor in tow," James had said at their last meeting, with the suggestive distaste of one referring to a french letter. He had also added that foreigners weren't gentlemen in the English sense of the term, whatever their profession, and that Jane had better watch her step.

She was more upset when she realised that her father was inclined to distrust Pierre for the same reason. But a carefully arranged dinner with Pierre and her parents went off well, and her father seemed reassured. Her mother was predisposed to like the French anyway. Jane and Susie had had a French nursery governess for several years, an amiable Protestant girl from the Cevennes who had been so useful with the household sewing ... She herself had happy memories of six months spent with a family near Tours when she had been eighteen. The house had had wisteria on it, and she had played a lot of tennis dressed from neck to ankle in white piqué.

"What a nice boy, Jane," she said kindly afterwards. "Your father and I expected him to be older, somehow ... Mark likes him, it seems?"

"Oh yes. Pierre's very good with him. They go on the boats together in Regents Park.'

"*That's* a good thing. I have been so worried about you, darling, but perhaps things will turn out for the best after all?"

In March, Hitler occupied the rest of Czechoslovakia. The next week, Jane heard from friends that James had joined the Territorials. Obviously his views on the prospect of war had changed. Was it too much to hope for a change on other subjects also? Unfortunately Jane knew from experience that James regarded stubbornness as a virtue.

Pierre was due to return to France after Easter, his contract in Shaftesbury Avenue fulfilled.

"Come back with me," he said.

"But – there's Mark . . ."

"I mean both of you, silly girl. It will be very nice for Mark to learn some French. We can stay for the summer at a cottage in the Berry belonging to my uncle and aunt. I have already written to them about it."

"It sounds too lovely for words, but I thought you would have to look for a new hospital appointment when you get back to France, Pierre?"

He raised his hands, looking, as always, as if he were holding an invisible object in them.

"Normally, that would be the case. But these aren't normal times. I've saved a little money – what is the point of my looking for a permanent job, now, when by next New Year I shall probably be mobilised."

"You mean, in the Army?"

"I do mean that. As an Army doctor. It is the young ones like me who go. Of course."

"Is war really coming, Pierre?"

"I'm afraid it is, my darling. In spite of your Lord Beaverbrook and the Anglo-Nazi Friendship League."

"Oh dear, I don't know anything about that. Politics just don't seem to rub off on me, I suppose I don't try hard enough . . . Will it really be like it was last time, do you think, with everyone dying in the trenches?"

"Jane, it is the same war – just the next edition of it. The Prussians attacked us in 1870, they attacked again in 1914. Now it is time for it to happen again. It has been coming for years – it's unavoidable."

But English people to whom she talked did not think it would be the same. They spoke gravely of a completely different type of war – of the mass-bombardment of

London, of the near-certain death of vast numbers of civilians. They said 'if', not 'when', but she could see that they too knew it was coming.

Her father, who was recently retired from the Home Office, told her 'in strict confidence, Jane – this is to go no further', of emergency plans, of large stocks of cardboard coffins already held by the Government in a secret place, of mass evacuations already worked out on paper. He seemed to anticipate Armageddon –'the possible destruction of society as we know it, Jane'. Secretly she did not find the thought of this as distressing as he did. Almost the contrary.

"Then you think," she said, her mind running in a parallel but different channel, "that, if it happens, Mark and I would be safer in any case in the countryside somewhere –?"

"My dear child there's no doubt about it. You *must* not stay in London with Mark if war comes. You know you always have a home with us. I don't approve of your leaving your husband, as you know, but in the circumstances . . ."

"James will join the Army at once," she said.

"Yes, I expect he will. Quite right too. Er – has anything else happened about this divorce business?"

"Yes. I heard from the solicitor last week. He's decided not to be a gentleman after all. He's going to divorce *me* because I won't play ball with him over Mark's school. I'm glad, really, it's much simpler, and truer come to that. After all, I did leave him."

"He's going to divorce you – for desertion?"

"Yes."

"Well, that's something, anyway. My dear child I do hope you know what you're doing. You young women today seem to think there's no such thing as public opinion."

"I can't help it, Daddy; I *won't* have Mark sent away to beastly Slaughter! If little boys of barely nine didn't still need their homes, God would have made them quite differently." She was quoting Pierre, whose orthodox French opinion was that the British boarding school system was cruel and stupid and turned out perverts.

"Well, you being the guilty party does rather put you

in a vulnerable position. I only hope, as I have said, that James doesn't decide to take charge of Mark."

"I'm making sure he doesn't have the chance to."

"Meaning what, exactly?"

"Pierre and I are thinking of spending the summer in France, Daddy."

'Well I can't possibly advise you for the best in this sordid situation," said her father at last in his coldest tone. But he looked so sad that she took his hand and said:

"Poor Daddy ... Would you hate it if I married Pierre?"

"Not at all, my dear. If that is really what the young man has in mind."

"I promise you it is. He's written to his family about it."

"Well, I shouldn't think they'll be very pleased, will they? I thought Catholics didn't believe in divorce in any circumstances."

"Pierre says his family aren't particularly religious – his father's by way of being anti-clerical – but that in any case the Catholic church doesn't recognise a Protestant marriage ceremony, so that from the point of view of his Catholic aunts it will be just as if I'd not been married before."

"But you have a child!"

"Apparently that's no great problem."

"Good God," said her father in mild British disgust.

At the end of April conscription was announced in England for young men of twenty and twenty-one. The following week Jane was packing to leave. The flat was being sub-let till the autumn; a German Jewish family, known to the owner of the shop where Jane had worked and newly arrived in Britain, had been grateful for the opportunity to take it over.

"It seems so illogical," said Jane, "that they've had to leave the Continent just when we're going there."

"They're from Germany. We're going to France. It's a very different matter."

"Yes, I know really ... How long do you think we can borrow this cottage, Pierre?"

"The whole summer – why not? It's empty. My uncle and aunt's *garde-chasse* used to live in it, but they've sold a lot of their land recently and he's gone elsewhere, it seems. What is *garde-chasse* in English?"

"Game-keeper, I should think. It sounds awfully grand."

"Not at all. The French country middle classes aren't nearly as grand as the British ones, you'll see. Anyway, as I said, my relations had to sell their land. Not a bit grand, that."

"Is it near a village?"

"On the edge. Down a little green path. With the road in front and some woods behind and my aunt's property on one side and the beginning of the village on the other. I always wished I could stay there when I was a boy, rather than in my aunt's too-big house where there were too many things I mustn't touch. You'll like it, I'm sure."

"I'm *sure* I shall ... You don't think the King's Proctor will find his way there?"

"Oh, I don't think the King's Proctor has ever travelled abroad, you know. To India, perhaps, in one of those hats, or just possibly to what you English have traditionally called 'Gay Paree' –but not to rural France. The Berry is rather remote, you see. But in any case surely now it is not you the King's Proctor is interested in but your husband? Since he is now the one supposed to be without a stain?"

"So it is, how silly of me, I was forgetting. Well, well, poor old James! Let's hope the King's Proctor doesn't get to hear about that brave little widow I hear he's got tucked up his sleeve now in Marlow."

"Really, this *hypocrisie britanique* ... But Jane, darling, one small thing: have you actually told your husband you're taking Mark abroad?"

Jane looked stubborn.

"No, I haven't. I don't need to. He's been on my passport ever since Mother and I took him to Switzerland when he was three, after he'd had bronchitis."

"Is that wise? Not to tell, I mean."

"It would be most unwise *to* tell James, in my view. He might try to stop me."

"In that case, won't he be angry when he finds out?"

"He probably won't find out for ages – if at all. I carefully haven't told our plans to any of the people I know who might conceivably see him."

"But if he tries to see his boy?"

"He won't. Haven't you noticed? He hasn't *once* tried to see Mark since we left home. Not to take him out to tea or anything. *All* I've had is fuss about his schooling."

"No, I hadn't really noticed that – though now you mention it . . ." Pierre looked, for once, inexpressibly shocked. After a minute he shook his head, as if in total incomprehension. Jane was reminded of her father's reaction to French Catholicism, and was obscurely amused.

After a minute, Pierre said,

"You did tell me where Mark was this afternoon, but I have forgotten."

"Having his swimming lesson at the Porchester Baths. Mrs. Sullivan – she's the mother of that little Jeremy – she and I agreed that the boys ought to learn to swim this holiday and so she's escorting them there one day and me the next."

"I see. I hope Mark is happy at the idea of the summer in France? It will mean leaving his new friends again . . . When I mentioned the subject to him, he just talked about how you'd promised him a bicycle."

"Yes, that's looming large in his imagination. Don't you think it's a good idea?"

"Of course! A splendid idea. We will all get bicycles. There is already, I think, an old one in my aunt's garage. Oh, I suppose that at his age one lives in the present."

"After all," said Jane, busy sorting Mark's clothes into piles – she was talking to Pierre through the doorway of Mark's bedroom – "After all, he knows he'll be coming back to the same school and seeing his friends again in the autumn."

"And will he?" said Pierre.

"Oh God, Pierre, *I* don't know." She came to the doorway and stood looking at him. "You know I don't know. Nor do you. If by then the War seems to be coming –"

"If I am mobilised –"

"If *James* is mobilised, you mean, and out of the way –"

"If your divorce is continuing all right –"

"If, if, if – Oh Pierre it isn't just Mark who lives in the present now, it's me too. But what else can I do?" Having said it, she wished she hadn't. It seemed too much an admission of something she would rather hide from herself as well as Pierre: the fragile and temporary supports upon which their relationship rested. She avoided his eye.

"What else, indeed, can anyone do?" said Pierre quickly, as if he would rather not analyse their situation too far either. He came and wrapped his arms round her, resting his chin on her shoulder.

"I am very tired this afternoon," he said inconsequentially. "I had too much Case Notes to finish writing at the hospital . . . Why have you put all those wool-things in a box? Are you going to take them all to St Laurent-la-Rivière? It will be rather a lot to carry."

"Goodness no, those are all the things I am planning to leave here, in store."

"I see. But Jane I strongly advise you to take some warm clothes for Mark, and for yourself too. You English think that it is hot all summer in France, but I tell you, the village can get quite cold at night. It is over three hundred metres of altitude."

"Let's see . . . How high is Marylebone High Street?"

"About two metres, I should think, judging from the fogs that appear in it. Never have I seen so many cases of respiratory ailment before I have been in London. No, seriously Jane, take a really warm jersey for each of you, and for yourself a pair of trousers."

Jane hesitated. She did possess a pair of blue corduroy slacks, as they were then called, cut like the Oxford bags of the 'twenties, which were fashionable again that year. Shopping in Marylebone High Street in the early morning, she felt that they looked smart in the right sort of way, but she suspected that they would look odd in a village in the middle of France, and she very much wanted to make herself acceptable there. She said so to Pierre, but he was adamant that she might need them. He also insisted that she bring an expensive tweed coat and skirt, which she had had made several years before for a holiday with James in Scotland but had never much liked.

"But it makes me look matronly, Pierre. Or *feel* matronly, anyway."

"In that case, unlike the trousers, you need have no fears about wearing it in St Laurent. It looks to me very suitable and warm."

"You'll be suggesting I bring my fur coat next."

"Well perhaps you won't need that. It might look a little opulent anyway in the game-keeper's – right, game-keeper's? – cottage. 'Opulent' – yes? You see, my English is perfecting itself!"

"It's really very good," said Jane truthfully. "I wish I could say the same for my French. I think I was better at it when I was six, with Mademoiselle Chabanac. But I suppose this summer will improve it a lot. We must start talking it together, Pierre. That will be fun!"

In the years that followed she was to be thankful many times over that Pierre had insisted on the blue trousers and the tweed suit. And she was to regret the fur coat.

They crossed via Dover one bright chilly afternoon. Mark, who did not remember having been on a Channel boat before, was gravely appreciative of it. There were gulls and chains and men in jerseys who shouted to one another, and then the water beneath the screw which looked like Fox's Glacier Mints, and then the long mahogany bar where he was, for once, allowed to sit. For him, the ship was an ocean liner: he was disappointed to hear they would be getting off again in two or three hours.

"You should have gone to America instead," said Pierre.

"Can we?" She felt childishly excited and free herself.

"One day. Look, Mark this is called a *grenadine*. It's for you to drink. Taste it – it's good." Jane loved him for the way he urged food or drink on Mark, wanting him to enjoy it. The English, on the contrary, seemed more concerned to stamp out 'greediness' even before it manifested itself. The English, she thought with a sudden access of ex-patriate scorn, forgetting for the moment all the love that had surrounded her in childhood, are *beastly* to children.

"There are the while cliffs of Dover disappearing," she said derisively; she was delighted to see them fade.

"They're not very white," said Mark disparagingly, spitting out his straw and getting down from his seat in order to survey them better.

Later, on deck, Jane timidly asked Pierre a question she had in her mind for several days, but had not wanted to raise till they had actually left.

"Won't your aunt and uncle in the country think it rather funny us living together before we're married? I mean," she went on hastily, as Pierre's face did not lighten for once as she spoke, "won't they mind about what the village people think and so on? I know it sounds silly, but . . ."

"It isn't silly," he said, lighting a cigarette, "but I have to admit something to you." For a moment she felt horribly afraid, knowing so little as she did of Pierre's background and therefore of his real obligations, wondering if perhaps she did not know him at all and was embarking on a terrible mistake, but she relaxed again as he went on:

"I have given my family to understand that we are, in fact, already married under British law. I don't mean I have told direct lies but I have referred to you as *ma femme* and have left them to draw their own conclusions. I thought it better, for reasons you will come to understand, to present them with a *fait accompli*."

As she said nothing, relieved but a little amazed at this information, he continued:

"For a while I have thought that perhaps we really will be married by this time. I did not understand that divorce will take so long. My compatriot, you see, all think that divorce is a mere formality among the immoral Anglo-Saxons – *qu'on divorce pour un oui, pour un non*."

"I see . . . But Pierre, they won't consider us properly

married without a church service, will they? You said –"

"No, they won't. But they will recognise that we are half-married, and that there's nothing they can say about it. Later, when we have really completed the formalities to satisfy the law of both our countries, we will arrange a nice church service. Hardly nuptial mass perhaps, but – *quelque-chose de convenable* to which we can invite my aunts. Then they'll forgive me. You'll see."

"Oh dear, I do hope so. I should hate to be the means of estranging you from your family."

"Well, you may meet my parents tonight. When we get to Paris I am going to telephone to them and see if they can have dinner with us."

"What about Mark?"

"Mark too, of course. You know that in France we don't believe in putting children to bed early."

"His Nanny still used to put him to bed at six when he was six years old. I did think that a bit much, it was one of the reasons I got rid of her. James was frightfully cross."

"Just because you asked the Nanny to leave. Ridiculous! You had a right to, surely. Mark was not a baby any more –"

"No, it wasn't just that. I – I think he was furious because it was then that he really understood that I meant it about him and me not having any more children. He kept saying two was the proper number and that everyone had two, and I just got obstinate. I suppose the real reason I took against the idea was that I knew by then that I might one day leave him, and he picked that up too. Oh, but you don't want to hear about James."

"On the contrary, I find him fascinating. (You must ensure that I never meet him: that would spoil the monstrous image I have of him.)"

"Well that won't be difficult to arrange for the time being." Looking at the bright sea she thought flippantly: I know why I'm so glad to leave England. Because it contains James. About ten million Jameses, very likely. All laying down the law and doing the accepted thing and wanting cooked breakfasts and watching their step about things. At least he *can't* want me back, now, not after what I'm doing. The idea exhilarated her. She was imbued with the strength of behaving disgracefully, and knowing it and not caring. It occurred to her only now that Abroad was the traditional refuge of the English who had done something not entirely respectable, and in her present mood the thought amused her. Discreet Italian *pensiones* . . . Louche boarding houses in Brussels, like in *The Constant Nymph* . . . But no, not really like that at all, she decided firmly, for to Pierre it was presumably France, not England, that was the reality, the permanent place. He was really the one risking everything by taking her there. She wished passionately for it to be a success.

Pierre suddenly said,

"Jane, I hope your decision wasn't definitive."

"What? Which decision?" He kept giving her these shocks.

"To have no more children, I mean. I should be sorry . . ."

They agreed that afternoon on the ship to try to start a baby as soon as it should seem convenient, forgetting, in their pleasure at the thought, that babies are never convenient.

Paris was just as she remembered, which, she knew, was what it was supposed to be, though it held as yet no nostalgic charge for her. Picture-avenues dwindled in vistas of lamps, like perspective shown in a stage set. Taxis with open fronts hooted incessantly and the voices of newspaper sellers cried *'Voici l'Intran'*. There was a now-remembered smell in the streets of foreign cigarettes and pungent dust. She even felt the same mixture of elation and nervous exhaustion that she had felt on her one previous trip here with James. It had been a long, tiring day.

"Is my bike here?" asked Mark, half asleep but intent on what was important.

"Darling, this is Paris, not the country. We're going to spend the night in a hotel. Rather fun!"

Pierre told the taxi an address on the opposite side of the river. They were given rooms with brownish wallpapers that seemed to Jane as old-fashioned as the city. From their windows they looked out over darkening plane trees and clanking trams. Wallpaper, trees, trams and sounds all struck her as dauntingly foreign.

"This is home to me," said Pierre gaily. "I spent years in this quarter, at Medical School. My family lives this side too, but a little further over, in the *septième*, which is quieter and duller. We'll see if my father and mother can meet us at the Brasserie Lipp – you'll like it, and it's not far by foot."

She and James had come to Paris on their honeymoon (James's concept of the proper place to go) and had stayed at the huge Hotel George V. The first night James had got drunk and it had not been a success. Nor had the second, third or fourth nights, she realised some time afterwards, though James himself had seemed unaware of the fact. Possibly he had simply been covering up. It had rained a lot, all her shoes had got soaked, and James was bored by art galleries but would not admit that either. By and by she had had a bad attack of home-sickness which had (perhaps understandably, she thought now) annoyed him a good deal. Yet it had been on that honeymoon here in this city which she had never had the opportunity to get to know and love, that Mark had been conceived. It seemed to her now as if, in that anxious and formless time, the future had already been making its imprint, casting not its shadow but its brightness backwards.

"Pierre," she said, absorbed in cosmic calculation, "do you believe there is a pattern to life?"

"Naturally," he said in a tone of polite agreement with this commonplace question, so that she could not tell what he really thought. He was trying to fix a stud in the collar of a clean shirt.

"No, really, I mean. Do you think that, in the past, this time we are having now was in some sense already there, waiting to be revealed?"

"Ah." He conquered the stud, put on the shirt and pulled his braces up. "What you are asking," he said at last, "is whether I think *our* future is already there now?"

"Yes, I suppose I am."

"It is not a question I really like to ask myself. It goes against our pride, doesn't it, to believe that we are just like those trams down there running inevitably to our destinations? And yet in a sense I do believe that the future is already there, yes. Particularly during this year."

"Perhaps," she said slowly, "it is not so much a question of *the* future but of a series of alternative ones. They are all already there, like – like tramway termini, if you like – but we have a choice as to which set of rails to take. Or a whole series of choices." She was pleased with this image, seeing momentarily the toy trains she and Susie had had as children, the legacy of their father.

Pierre looked happier now, but perhaps this was because he had got his collar fixed. He said,

"I remember when I was a child I used to wonder about the word 'destined'. As when you say 'destined for the Church' or 'destined to become a great man'. People like my aunts used it. And yet it seemed to me quite contradictory to what the Church also teaches about Free Will. I now see it as an example of people's words showing that their deepest ideas are really quite different from what they themselves believe – or think they believe. And I used to wonder about *le soldat inconnu.*"

"Who?"

"You know. At the Étoile. You've got one too, in Westminster Abbey."

"Oh yes, the Unkown Soldier ... You mean, you used to wonder if Fate had somehow got him marked down from the beginning?"

"Exactly. Was he really just an ordinary man once, indistinguishable in every way from others? When he passed by the Étoile before the War – if indeed he was a Parisian – did he not feel the faintest sensation, the slightest shadow? Indeed were all those who were killed in the War just exactly as ordinary as all the ones who were not. Now, as an adult, I know that they were. But as a boy I *felt* that they were not."

"Perhaps they weren't," said Jane. "Perhaps the rational

view is actually the false one. Maybe the people whom Fate strikes *are* different from the others." The thought fitted her ambivalent mood. She felt chilly and thought: this room isn't heated properly; not realising that she was fighting off depression.

"No, that is not so," Pierre said determinedly, sounding annoyed. "To think that is merely childish. We want to believe that those who have suffered have been somehow different from ourselves all along, because that would be proof that what has happened to them will not happen to us. But it is not true. I have seen that in hospitals."

For five minutes he seemed withdrawn and silent, but then became cheerful again. He wet and combed Mark's hair into approved neatness.

"Nanny used to put kirby-grips in it," said Mark. "Ugh."

"Ugh, indeed. Really, we French may have our complexes about our mothers, but you have them about your nannies. I am sure your mother was right to decide to bring you up herself. Now we are going to eat! And we are going to meet my mother and father and you must say 'Hallo' to them very nicely and shake hands."

The three of them walked down the boulevard together hand in hand. But when they reached the cut-glass interior of the Brasserie Lipp only Pierre's father was there to meet them. He was a grey-haired man, larger than Pierre. In spite of his formal affability Jane felt intimidated, and feared that her precarious command of French would slip from her. She had practised a little with Pierre but the language she had absorbed in the nursery from Mlle. Chabanac was hardly adequate, she feared, to conversation on adult subjects.

"Where is Maman?" Pierre asked his father, trying, Jane saw, to conceal his own tension.

"Unfortunately she has a headache," replied Dr. Leparde smoothly. Pierre rapidly asked something which Jane did not quite catch and his father answered. After a pause Pierre turned to Jane and explained lightly that his mother did sometimes suffer from migraines 'in spite of being surrounded by doctors in the family'.

It was a nerve-wracking evening. The food was excellent and Dr. Leparde senior seemed, after his first reticence, to be putting himself out to be agreeable. He and Pierre explained to Jane that the original Lipp had been a citizen of Alsace-Lorraine, now French again since 1918 but before that German for several decades, and that this was Strasbourgeois food they were eating. Dr. Leparde also added that in fact Pierre had been born in Strasbourg, where he himself had been spending a year as a young, newly-married doctor.

"Goodness," said Jane to Pierre. "So you were actually born in Germany?"

"In theory, yes. But fortunately of an impeccably French father. I don't think I'll find myself being called up to assist Hitler, somehow."

"Oh dear, I do trust not," said Jane, trying to sound flippant but fearing that she just sounded feeble. Dr. Leparde kept plying her with well-informed questions about England which she would have found hard to answer in any language. He was entirely polite, yet she felt she detected in him a Gallic mirror-image of that mild contempt for all things foreign which she knew in her own father and in James; the French, she remembered, had a long history of disliking the English, and they thought English women both dowdy and immoral. The spotted silk blouse and hat with a matching ribbon which had seemed pretty and suitable when she had put them on in the hotel, now felt schoolgirlish: Pierre had said that day-clothes would be right at the Brasserie Lipp, but she wished she were wearing a dull but impressive black dress and fox-fur like most of the other women in the restaurant. She wished her French were better, and she wished too that Mark would sit up straight and chatter and gobble up his food like he usually did, instead of slouching uncharacteristically on the plush-covered seat with black rings round his eyes. Poor little boy, he looked like a panda and no wonder: they shouldn't really have brought him out to dinner; perhaps the English were occasionally right after all.

Back at the hotel, when Mark had at last been put to bed, grumbling faintly, she wept in Pierre's arms.

"It's no good, they don't like me. Your mother wouldn't even meet me, and now your father thinks I don't know anything. I should never have come." Even as she wailed, she could hear the self-indulgent note in her own grief, and stopped, disgusted at herself. 'Now he really will be sorry he brought me,' she thought in panic.

But Pierre stroked her hair and remained calm. He did not say that she had got everything wrong, as she had half been hoping he would. He just said that naturally these things take time; his parents had to get accustomed to the idea of her as well as get to know her. "Don't forget that for many years they hoped I would marry my cousin Louise."

"As if I could forget! I was thinking about her all the time we were with your father. They must think I'm some sort of adventuress who has stolen you away from her."

"They'll change their minds."

"Then they *do* think that?"

"Naturally, for the moment, they don't know what to think. But you mustn't worry, my darling, really not. I know my father, he is basically a very fair man. He'll come round to you – does one say that? – yes – come round to you, and then he will convince Maman. In the end, everything will be all right, Jane, I promise you. I know my family, and they know me."

Later, as they lay in bed, the headlights of cars turning from the boulevard slid through the slats of the shutters and across the sheet. Pierre lay asleep on his back; the skin of his neck and shoulders was white and delicate. His eye-lids and sockets were purplish in the intermittent, travelling beams of light; he looked, she thought, with a spasm of guilt for her own self-preoccupation, exhausted. She knew that he was not physically, very strong, but his nervous energy normally concealed the fact. She vowed to try to look after him as he needed and deserved. Accustomed to the idea that he was more experienced than herself, she only now, watching him sleep, reflected that he was a simpler person than he sometimes seemed.

She herself lay awake too tense and overtired to sleep, listening to the noise of engines and motor horns that still rose from the street. Did people never sleep in Paris? She sat up on her elbow to look at Pierre again. He had not moved; he looked dead, his face a skull. In a sudden panic she shook his shoulder, speaking his name urgently till he mumbled and groaned.

The next morning was sunny and, having slept late they were all three themselves again. Pierre was inclined to suggest that they should spend another day or two in Paris so that he could show things to Jane and Mark, but she was anxious to reach their destination. Suspended like this between one life and another, she felt unreal; and she thought she would find it easier to get used to Pierre being the one who was at home and knew everything when they were in a quieter place. It was agreed that they would make a trip to Paris later in the summer.

In the early afternoon they caught a train going south from the Gare d'Austerlitz. Pierre tried to interest Mark in the relative significance of Austerlitz and Waterloo, but Mark said they hadn't done that bit of history yet at his school; he was more intrigued by the luncheon-basket with its complement of strong-smelling cold meats, which they had bought on the station. They changed trains at Châteauroux where they had an hour or so to wait. That May afternoon its outskirts were already dusty under a warm sun. They went for an uncertain walk; it seemed to Jane a dull town.

"It is," said Pierre. "There's quite a good cathedral, but otherwise the town is archetypally dull. A place made to wait in between trains."

"Full of old ladies in veils and grey cotton stockings?" This was one of Pierre's set images. He had professed himself surprised by the relative lack of these people in the streets of London.

"Absolutely. Such is the nature of the provincial, *petit-bourgeois* existence here in France – you can't call it 'life'. But, you'll see, Châtelet-le-Lys, our market town, is much nicer and more amusing. Smaller and less full of *des gens biens* and altogether different."

"What a lot of château-places."

"Dozens. This is a country of châteaux. The English built some of them. I suppose you do realise, my darling, that you are coming to the part of France where the English ruled for generations?"

"Oh – yes, in the Middle Ages." She tried to remember. "The Hundred Years' War, was it? Henry IV – no V, perhaps . . . Joan of Arc – that sort of time?"

"That sort of time, approximately. For us, *Henri IV et Charles V*. So you see, for you this is really a return."

From the window of the branch-line train which trundled slowly through the landscape, following the sun, veering east and then west again to wayside stations, she tried to visualise her journey in this guise, but everything was unobtrusively but persistently strange to her eyes: the unhedged fields where you could see the sides of the young green corn, the white dust of the roads disappearing into the flat horizon, the architecture of the halts through which they passed, the wooden seats in the carriage, the quality of the light itself – and surely those must be vines, those inconspicuous rows of greenery covering the sunlit plain? Her previous brief forays Abroad had always been to established tourist-centres, and accomplished in express sleeping cars which diminished distances and protected their occupants from the irrelevant other worlds through which the hurtling train passed. Now she felt intimidated by the sheer sense of a different type of life from her own going on here quietly and persistently for centuries without her knowledge. But gradually the countryside changed, the engine began to steam up and down small hills, there were more woods, the fields became smaller and hedged themselves almost as in Berkshire or Sussex, there was ivy on the tree trunks, and sudden glimpses of lakes and rivers. She really did feel that she was arriving somewhere that might conceivably be home, in spite of the two old ladies in black, exuding garlic and camphor, who clucked together in a rolling dialect further up the carriage.

Pierre put an arm round Mark, who had been quietly watching the scenery for some time.

"What are you thinking of, Mark?"

"I was thinking about my bike. I was wondering what colour it is."

"Darling, we haven't actually bought it yet," said Jane. Oh dear, was he expecting it to be waiting at the station? "I thought it would be fun to go and buy it together."

"But to him it already exists as an absolute reality," put in Pierre gently. "And of course in a way he is right. It *does* already exist – in some shop. It is just that we don't know it yet."

"Oh dear, we seem to be having that conversation about the future again."

"*Tch, en effet, toujours de la metaphysique* ... Let's avoid that just now. What colour would you like it to be, Mark?"

"Green, I was hoping. Of course –" he made a visible effort to accommodate himself to adult fallibility, "– if it's blue or red or even just black I will still like it. But I do hope it's green."

"I feel almost sure," said Pierre earnestly, "that it *is* green. And it will be one of the first things we will attend to."

The size of the station at St Laurent-la-Rivière surprised Jane.

"I thought it was just a small place."

"It is. It is also over a kilometre from here. The station itself is quite big because another line – not the one we have just been on – passes through it; it carries a lot of merchandise – what do you call it? goods – from the south to the north west of France. Look at those big buildings over there. A lot of cattle from the Limousin are loaded here. One hears them from the village in the early mornings."

"How do we get down to the village?"

"We leave all our baggages here with Monsieur Bernard

the station-master: my uncle and I will fetch them later with the car. And so we arrive in the village by foot with our hands in our pockets."

Jane was to arrive at St Laurent many times – by train, on foot, by bus or by the carrier's cart from Châtelet, by bicycle – but she never forgot that first time which was the rehearsal for so many others. The village was suffused with an odd, pinkish light, a pre-sunset light, which made the grey buildings look warmer than in the strong daylight, and which etched the leaves of the oak and apple trees against the deep blue sky as if they had been trees in a primitive painting. There was a smell of woodsmoke and cooling earth, and a cracked bell was chiming in the belfry of the church at the far end of the long, single street that curved down and eventually reached the river.

She would have liked to follow that bell, to go right down past the lighted doorways she could see in the distance. People came and went in the street, a car drove slowly down the middle of the bumpy surface sounding its horn. She saw a sign saying 'Café-Restaurant' and wished they could eat there instead of going to meet more of Pierre's relations. But just after the pitted, blue enamel sign that marked the village's beginning and name, Pierre stopped.

"This is my aunt's house."

A high wall with ivy on it, a pair of locked iron gates, a view of lawn and clipped hedges within becoming black silhouettes with the coming dark, a bell that jangled when Pierre pulled it. She felt touched, like a physical chill, with a sense of the defensive privacy of French family life, and waited soberly at his side, squeezing Mark's hand in hers.

"But there already," Pierre said gaily as the sound died away, "is my uncle coming to open for us. He must have been watching for us from the dining room window."

It was more than a week before Jane realised that Monsieur and Madame – or rather Mademoiselle – Yrieux were not Pierre's true uncle and aunt but some sort of cousins of that generation on his mother's side. Nor, in fact, were they husband and wife but brother and sister.

"Didn't either of them ever get married?" Jane wanted to know.

"Uncle did – his wife is dead. But poor Tante Madeleine had *une deception*. She's never quite got over it, you see."

Jane thought guiltily of Pierre's unknown cousin Louise, wondering if she were now a Mlle. Yrieux designate, a deceived spinster. But by and by it dawned on her that *'deception'* was merely the usual French word for a disappointment and did not necessarily imply perfidy: in fact Mlle. Yrieux's fiancé had died of fever in Africa. A large photograph of him ornamented her dining room, along with a stuffed wolf in a glass case also containing real bracken and a real dead tree stump.

Pierre said that there were still a few boars up in the hills near at hand, but that the wolves had all gone. Madame Audibert, the Yrieux's elderly servant, claimed to remember as a child having seen a woif coming down into a narrow valley, seizing a lamb and disappearing into the mist, but it wouldn't happen again: the wolf here in the glass case was apparently 'the last one shot in the region'.

Mark was greatly struck by the wolf, whom he seemed to imagine to be not dead but petrified: if its glass case was opened mightn't it just possibly come to life again? Jane thought it a surprisingly small and moth-blown creature: was this really the beast that had terrified rural populations for centuries and formed the basis for innumerable tales?

There were many other things in the house to interest a little boy. In one of the upstairs bedrooms there was a lot of late nineteenth-century children's books, including some English ones given to Mlle. Yrieux and her sister by an English governess when they were children. (Jane communicated this piece of information to her own parents, knowing that it would reassure them as to the social desirability of Pierre's family connections.) There was also a whole cabinet of lead soldiers of the same period, the property of Mlle. Yrieux's other brother who had been killed at Verdun. Perhaps because she still thought of them as her younger brother's, or perhaps for some other reason, Mlle. Yrieux did not want to unfasten the cabinet to let Mark touch them: she remarked that they were precious, almost antique ... It was Monsieur Yrieux who said, "Nonsense, they were made for children to touch; let the boy take them out for a little, it will do them good to be played with again."

Monsieur Yrieux had been a professional soldier when young, but for many years seemed to have had no particular occupation. He had come south to live with his sister after his wife had died. Pierre explained to Jane that, under the French laws of inheritance, he had in any case inherited an equal share in the house at St Laurent-la-Rivière – "and my aunt would have found it impossible to get an equivalent sum of money to give him instead."

"Suppose they hadn't got on well together?"

"That would have been too bad. France is full of families who do not really like each other but are obliged to live with each other from financial considerations."

Jane suspected that Monsieur and Mlle. Yrieux were not, in fact, particularly well-suited to one another, but had made the best of it. Mlle. Yrieux was pious. The village Curé, a dull-eyed young man, was a frequent visitor; she held classes in Catechism for the village children.

"Do the village people like that?" Jane asked Pierre.

"Not particularly, but they know it is good for them. Anyway it is what they expect of *ceux qui représentent la bourgeoisie* in the district. I'm sure villages in England have ladies in them just like my aunt, who play the same rôle."

"Mmm, sort of, but not exactly. They wear tweeds, not black silk, and they do the Girl Guides rather than Catechism classes."

"It's just the same thing."

"They also live in cottages together and raise Angora rabbits."

"Ah, that my aunt would never do. No rabbits. And she

would never live in a cottage however poor she might be. She doesn't really like the country much anyway – she goes and pays long visits to her sister in Paris – and she thinks it most peculiar of you and me to want to stay in the gamekeeper's cottage."

"I've noticed," said Jane.

Monsieur Yrieux never went to church at all, and enjoyed teasing the Curé by asking him unanswerable questions. He was an agile old gentleman, with a fleeting resemblance to Pierre and a fine white moustache, like a cartoon-Frenchman. He had a collection of guns hanging on the wall of his study, ranging from eighteenth-century flintlocks and Napoleonic arms, through to the arms his father had used in 1870, the rifle he had used himself in the War, and the shot-gun he still used for hunting.

"When autumn comes," he told Jane, sounding vague as to when that might be, "I will take your boy out and teach him to shoot. He's just the right age to start."

Jane suspected that safety would not have top-priority in Ernest Yrieux's expeditions, but she thanked him warmly, grateful for his ready kindness and his apparent acceptance of her and Mark. By contrast, his sister seemed to her unwelcoming. Without being exactly rude to Jane, she managed nevertheless to convey the fact that she did not regard her as a permanent addition to the family. Nor, though Monsieur Yrieux had insisted on being called 'Oncle Ernest' by Jane and Mark, had she asked to be called 'Tante Madeleine'. Nevertheless they went to lunch there every Sunday, when Mlle. Yrieux plied Pierre with food and asked him a series of indirect questions about what he had had to eat that week, which made Jane fume silently.

"Does she think I don't feed you or something?"

"You know the French think that English people can't cook. You shouldn't take her seriously. She's just fond of me, that's all, because I used to spend holidays here sometimes when I was a boy. And she hasn't noticed that I'm not a boy any longer."

Sometimes, at Jane's insistence, she and Pierre managed

to invite the Yrieuxs to eat at the cottage, but for one reason or another these occasions were never entirely successful. The first time, bent on demonstrating the best of British cooking (she had, at her mother's insistence, been to cookery classes before her marriage), Jane bought a beef joint from the village butcher. Then, determined not to overcook it (Pierre had impressed on her that this was the *vice anglais* where meat was concerned) she went too far to the other extreme: she was not yet used to the wood-burning stove in the cottage, and the joint was uncomfortably raw. It was also tough; she had yet to learn that large beef joints bought in small French villages were always tough, because they were pieces from oxen who had already done several years stint at the plough. Monsieur Bonnin did his own slaughtering.

The second time she played safe with a chicken that had stewed for hours in wine – Pierre's favourite dish. Mlle. Yrieux could find no fault with that, but she did not seem to appreciate the airiness of the cottage that day, with its windows all open onto a bright summer sky; she enquired searchingly as to whether the brick floors were not damp. Finally she said to Pierre with a sigh,

"Of course, you are a doctor these days. I suppose you know what you're doing."

Jane loved the cottage, and did not care at all that its floors were laid straight over the earth of France. The walls were thick stone, the beams solid. It had probably been a farmhouse once, Pierre said; it was certainly older than the Yrieuxs' stuccoed, late-nineteenth century residence to which it now belonged. There were two other rooms beside the main kitchen-living room, and a large attic which they had cleaned out and which Mark had claimed as his own place. For the convenience of their game-keeper, the Yrieuxs had had electricity installed in the cottage when 'the line' had come to St Laurent a few years earlier, and the wood stove warmed the whole place on cold evenings. But Jane had been disconcerted, on arrival, to find that there was no sink in the kitchen, merely a stone slab without a drain in the lean-to scullery, and no water laid on.

"But we have our own pump right by the gate outside," Pierre pointed out. "It isn't as if we had to go down to the well to fetch water. My aunt and uncle had the pump put in at the same time as the electricity. You see – it's quite a modern one."

"In England, modern pumps don't exist! I didn't realise . . ."

"But my darling, what did you expect – in the country?"

"Taps, actually. And a proper sink. I expect it was silly of me. I'll get used to the pump. And to that little hut at the end of the garden."

"You will find that there isn't a house in the village with taps indoors, and certainly not a modern water closet."

"Not even at the Restaurant?"

"No, no. Madame Mouret has better things to spend her money on."

"But your aunt and uncle have a bathroom, I've seen it."

"Yes, well, I don't count them. Anyway that bathroom is supplied from a big cistern above the staircase into which water has to be pumped by hand from their well. My uncle does that first thing every morning before my aunt gets up."

"I think she's extremely lucky to have him living with her."

"Ah, don't be too hard on her. She was brought up under the old ways, in the expectation of being a wife and mother in a world of carriages and arranged marriages. Now she finds herself a not-very-rich spinster in a world where her nephews and nieces jump in and out of cars all the time – as she says – and even the boys and girls who look after the cows go to look at film stars instead on Thursday nights in Châtelet. Giving themselves, she is sure, the most shocking ideas which are not only immoral but also above their station."

"Well she can't say *we* jump in and out of cars all the time. Neither in nor out."

"Alas, no."

They would have liked a small car. It would have been the one thing needed to make them entirely happy that summer. But, having counted up their joint money, Jane and Pierre regretfully concluded that even an old car would strain their budget. And anyway there were the bicycles. Pierre had disinterred a machine from the Yrieuxs' coach-house, which he had used to ride as a boy. Jane acquired one from the restaurant-keeper, Madame Mouret, who said she was too busy to ride it any more and anyway felt that she was getting too fat for it. Jane wondered if perhaps it wouldn't have been good for the Mourets' daughter, a silent, pig-tailed schoolgirl whose figure already presented problems, to ride it instead, but apparently Jeanne-Marie Mouret was considered too delicate for strenuous exercise. Mark's bike, the green machine on which he had set his heart, proved more difficult to obtain. The proprietor of the village's one garage (who had no petrol pump, but supplied petrol in cans to the village's other three car owners) could offer them several rattling, second-hand bicycles such as the village boys rode, and which were clearly his conception of the suitable thing. But all these looked dangerously large for Mark: Jane insisted that he must have one more suited to his age. In the end one was ordered from Limoges, and was delivered one glowing evening by the carrier's cart. It was green, with a gilt trim; it was expensive – and it was a British model.

"Made in Northampton," Jane read from one of the labels. "Really, how silly! We could have brought it with us for less."

It was strange to her to think that Northampton was still there, functioning, along with all the rest of England: people going to work and coming back again in double-decker trams, people drinking strong tea, eating fish and chips and suet pudding and jelly and custard, reading the *Express* and the *Telegraph* and the *Star*, following the horses and snipping football coupons ... Other people planning divorces and worrying about the King's Proctor and writing letters to *The Times* and insisting that their sons went to one particular school and no other ... As one often does when one has only been in a new environment for a few weeks, Jane felt that she had been at St Laurent-la-Rivière for ever, and that all the previous twenty-nine years were rapidly becoming as unsubstantial as a dream.

She wanted to get to know the countryside, not just physically but in her imagination also. It bothered her that her concept of French history was so hazy; she had never done anything of it at her fashionable boarding school but the French Revolution, and had a general impression that up to that point all French peasants everywhere had worn rags and lain dying by the roads, stuffing their ravenous mouths with grass. (She tried, and failed, to imagine Madame Mouret and her daughter and various other comfortable villagers as the direct descendants of those serfs.) But even if this was nonsense she had no sense of the general shape of French history, since its main points of reference – the massacre of St Bartholomew's Eve, the reign of Louis Quatorze and so forth – were, she gathered, situated at different places from English ones like the reign of Henry VIII and the beheading of Charles I. She borrowed fat, out-of-date books from Oncle Ernest and set herself to learn. The books were heavy-going, and she actually acquired more facts at her fingertips by asking questions of Pierre, who seemed to her amazingly well-informed on a whole range of subjects unconnected with his own profession. (French education, she concluded with pleasure, was actually superior to English, and *that* was one in the eye for James, wasn't it?) But she liked the books for the atmosphere they exhaled of a whole civilisation of which she had, till now, been in ignorance. Like the sunlit fields of central France seen from the train, its history now seemed to her at once fantastic and accessible, alien to everything she had learnt up till then yet entirely relevant to her present life. And as an explorer in a new land, she would read, discover, turn herself at last, she thought, into a properly educated person.

"Hasn't the Berry got a local author?" she asked Pierre one day. "Like Dorset and Thomas Hardy?" Hardy was a favourite of her father's: he had read *Tess of the D'Urbervilles* aloud to her and Susie one summer holiday in Bournemouth when they had been schoolgirls.

"Of course. Georges Sand."

"Oh good, I'll read him."

"Her, for heaven's sake, her! Georges Sand was a woman who dressed in trousers and smoked cigars and ran after the well-known writers of the day such as Balzac."

"Oh dear, she sounds a bit of a bore."

"She was. A dreadful, dreadful, conceited bore. Do you say 'man-eater' in English? Yes, well, she ate Chopin, for instance. By the time they got him away from her there was nothing left of him but skin and bone, poor little man ... You must ask Oncle Ernest, he's very funny about Georges Sand."

"Are you being just a little unfair to her, you and Oncle Ernest? I do remember hearing about her now, so there, I'm not quite as uneducated as you think. She-paved-the-way-for-other-women-writers. It said so in my school History of Literature."

"Oh dear, I do hope not. A dynasty of Georges Sands would be awful ... anyway, if you want to read something which will give you the feeling of the French countryside you would do better to read *Le Grand Meaulnes* by Alain Fournier. It partly takes place in the Berry, but rather north of here, and partly in the Sologne next door to that."

"I've never heard of that book."

"Ah, it was *the* great book of my adolescence. Meaulnes, the central character, appears mysteriously as a pupil in a village school like the one here; later he becomes for a while almost identified with the narrator and we hear how he finds a château in the middle of the forest where a *fête galante* is going on and he falls in love (of course) with a girl. Later again, when he looks for the château, it has completely disappeared, yet the girl is real, she dies later having a baby. But you must read it, it is not a book one can describe. Full of the nostalgia for lost childhood, lost emotion ... And Fournier himself disappeared without trace in the Great War."

Jane did read the book; not then, but later, the following winter, when she found a copy in the bookshop in Châtelet-le-Lys. But by then Pierre was no longer with her.

The ease and simplicity of their life enchanted both of them. (Neither reflected that it is only in the short term that lives ever seem free, because it is only then that they have not yet gathered around them the carapace of responsibilities and habits which they will, with time, inexorably acquire.) Pierre was taking his first prolonged rest after many years of study and exams and an exhausting two years in a foreign city. He slept a lot, and lay in the sun, till his white skin turned brown and he looked like one of his Mediterranean ancestors from his father's side. But for Jane the sense of change was more fundamental. She felt as if she had, in the last year, shed several skins, fusty layers that had been encumbering her for years without her realising it, and had now at last emerged as a butterfly in the beautiful landscape. When, rarely, she thought of her life in Henley only this time last year and saw herself there – sitting in the drawing room for instance, trying to screw up her courage to tell cook that last night's pudding had not had enough sugar in it – she felt the amused contempt for an alien person that one feels when looking through a collection of very old snapshots of oneself, looking cross in the wrong sort of clothes.

It was a fine summer. Frequently they ate cold meat and cheese in the garden, or rode off on their bicycles to picnic down by the river, or farther afield to the wooden uplands where the heather was already bleaching in the heat, or to the ruined Sarracan castle several miles away where pigs snuffled and munched within a doorway carved with stranger beasts and a coat of arms.

"This was one of the furthest points north that the Sarracans reached," Pierre remarked. "I tell you, this region is the meeting point of France. Sarracans ... English ... By the way, have you noticed how many people called Langlois there are in the village?"

"Yes, I was going to ask you: that is the old French word for 'English', isn't it?"

"Yes. You must speak to Jean Langlois about it. He is sure that his ancestors were English lords here and that that is why his family are all tall with fair hairs. Actually, I think he is probably descended from people who were servants to the English lords."

The Langlois were an extensive local family who occupied two adjacent farmhouses at the far end of the village: it was some time before Jane got their relationships sorted out. A solid, rather shy young Langlois girl, Reine, came twice a week to clean the cottage and do the washing. Her uncle was Jean Langlois: he was, among other things, the Yrieuxs' gardener and he did the cottage garden as well; they had arrived to find it neatly planted with potatoes, cabbages, lettuces and French beans. He was a dignified man of about fifty who did not believe, as he explained to Jane, in letting good ground stand idle. To her and to Pierre he spoke in a polite, even elegant French. Pierre said that was because Langlois, like most of the peasant farmers in the district, spoke the dialect at home and kept proper French as a Sunday-best language.

Langlois's labours provided them with more vegetables than they could eat and they were prodigal with them, secretly throwing away what they could not manage to consume. "After all, you don't want to spend your evenings making soup," said Pierre. Frequently, indeed, they fetched the evening meal from Madame Mouret, who did a line in *plats à emporter*: one night it would be pork and haricot beans, another pigeon and peas, another time tripe. To Jane, used to London prices, everything seemed almost unbelievably cheap. Pierre would ride down there with their largest lidded saucepan slung over the handlebars, and return more slowly, balancing it carefully. Once he fell off his bike, avoiding a cat who suddenly shot across the road in front of him in twilight pursuit of a vole: the pot of *boeuf bourguinon* ended up in the ditch.

"The cat-population will be pleased anyway," said Jane. "To have the stew, I mean."

Nothing, really seemed to matter that summer, there was nothing they could not laugh about.

Often, on Thursday evenings, they took the bus into Châtelet-le-Lys to see the weekly film show in the Mairie, where the projector sometimes broke down. With a pleasant background awareness of participating in local life and relishing a simple pleasure, they saw Fernandel and the youthful Jacques Tati and (once, a red-letter evening) Jean Gabin. They saw a series of films by Raimu, which were then still circulating in the French countryside, and once a René Clair, but the box-office lady told them that such films of French daily life were less popular in Châtelet than the American cowboy films.

Mark went to sleep in the Raimu films, lolling on their laps. *His* great treat was the week when the show was *'Blanche-Neige et les Sept Nains'*.

On Saturday evenings there was sometimes dancing in the square near the church, to the music of a barrel organ and accordions. Each week the organ went to one or other of the villages in the neighbourhood, in rough rotation. When it came to St Laurent, extra lights were brought out and hung in the chestnut trees: the feet of the dancers made a loud shuffling noise on the tarmac. Jane liked to watch them dance; she liked the way all the young men did it in the same style, though one alien to her. They waltzed rapidly, very upright, turning their partners round and round; they wore their caps pulled well down in front and their black alpaca Sunday jackets buttoned up high, and the most stylish had a cigarette clamped between their lips. In contrast, their partners, except for one or two noticeably pretty girls, looked dowdy and uncertain. They giggled too much between dances, standing together in huddles, showing their bad teeth.

Jane would have loved to dance too, but for once Pierre seemed reticent and uneager to seize his chance.

"We aren't village people, darling. They don't expect it of us. It might embarrass them."

"Oh surely not. They're all so friendly . . ."

"Yes, quite so, but they expect us to keep in our place – just as we, in a way, expect them to . . . Anyway married people don't dance in villages, even the young ones, and we don't want them to think we're not married, do we? . . . Look, there's young Jean Langlois, the son, the one they call Jeanot, dancing with the girl he's going to marry: his father was telling me about her. She's from Ourlats – that's a hamlet a few kilometres away, you know, by the Bois des Pendus ... She's pretty, isn't she? Every week, apparently, they go together to wherever the dance is being held. Her father was telling me 'The young people may as well dance while they can: after the harvest they're getting married'. That's the attitude, you see."

So, instead of dancing in the square, they danced alone in the cottage, to the gramophone they had brought from England, and their feet made the same kind of noise on the brick floor. They danced, in the middle of France, to the music of Gershwin and Benny Goodman and Noel Coward; they danced also to Charles Trénet singing *Y a d'la Joie* and *La Mer*, and to Maurice Chevalier singing *Valentine*. The songs were fresh, then, and the records new.

In July, they went and danced in Paris. They had promised themselves this trip, and eventually made it to coincide with the Bastille Day celebrations. They had, of course, been planning to take Mark with them, but when he heard of their plan Oncle Ernest protested:

"But you don't want to be encumbered with a child. Let him stay here in our house."

Jane hesitated, feeling that this invitation would not be endorsed by Mlle. Yrieux, but Oncle Ernest must have talked to her for she raised no objection; she even remarked that it would of course be much healthier for Mark to stay with them than to trail about on railway stations. He could have the bedroom Pierre had slept in as a schoolboy.

"There you see," said Pierre to Jane. "She's softening towards us."

Jane loved him for the way he said 'us', not 'you and Mark', as if they were already his family and inseparable from him.

They both played with Mark a great deal because they felt they should. He and Pierre had a complicated card game they played together with much shouting, and Pierre made him bows and arrows and a target on the oak tree at the end of the short lane that led to their house. It delighted Jane to see Mark having the sort of relationship with Pierre which he had never had with his own father. She herself read to him every evening, which he still liked although he could read perfectly well to himself: they had brought a lot of Biggles and Arthur Ransome from England, and she found an English book about Robin Hood at the Yrieuxs which fed his current pretend games. But one day he asked her longingly,

"Are we going back to England soon?"

"Oh darling . . . Well, soon, yes, I expect, but not just yet. Oh dear, I thought you liked it here."

"I do. But I would like to see Sullivan and the others again. I've no one much to play with here – except you two, of course."

It was true. Encouraged by them, he had occasionally played ball or tag with the village children in the square, but as soon as she and Pierre tried to creep away he would come running after them: he wouldn't be left alone with the other children because he didn't speak their language and evidently felt a fool. Jane sympathised with him, but wished he would learn more French. Her hopeful belief that children acquired foreign languages with effortless ease had turned out to be mistaken. She and Pierre were giving him French lessons, and they frequently, now that her own French had greatly improved, spoke French together in front of him, but he didn't seem impressed.

"When you stay with Oncle Ernest and Mlle. Yrieux while we're in Paris you'll need to speak French," she told him.

"No I shan't," he said. "Mlle. Yrieux speaks lots of English. She just pretends to you that she doesn't. And I think Oncle Ernest secretly does too." He appeared to regard speaking French as a curious affectation, and to believe that almost anyone could speak English if they tried hard enough. Jane was dauntingly reminded of James. Or was it simply that Mark's whole world had been changed, not once but twice in the past year, and he needed to cling on to a few certainties? She felt a sudden access of guilt, an unaccustomed emotion to her at that period. He seemed happy enough and looked radiantly healthy, but had the freedom of a new life which had brought her so much joy brought him mainly insecurity? Would he really have been 'better off' (whatever that might mean in either the long or the short term) in an English boarding school with a hundred and fifty little Sullivans, learning to withstand institutional food and homesickness and the cane? She did not believe it, but she worried occasionally about him. The immediate future, which all that summer had been a haze, now began to take the form of an ominous cloud.

"I really shall have to take him back to England this autumn," she said, not reflecting for the moment how this was to be organised in terms of her life with Pierre. "I mean, his schooling . . ."

Pierre, looking sadder than she had meant him to, said,

"Well. At least we've had this summer."

It did not occur to her till later how he must have construed her remark, and by then he maintained that he had not said that at all.

They had their three days in Paris, and danced on the Pont Neuf on the night of the Fourteenth to a military band. They did not ask themselves, or at any rate did not ask each other, if there would be a Bastille Day next year. In fact it was not celebrated again in Paris till 1945.

Jane had hoped to meet Pierre's father again in Paris, and perhaps his mother too this time. But Pierre did not mention this as a possibility once they were there, and presently she gathered that the Lepardes were in any case already on holiday, in a family house in Normandy – 'the Rouen aunts'. Did anyone in France ever stay where they didn't have relations, she asked tartly.

"Certainly. They go to Biarritz and Cannes. We will too sometime, if you like. But not this year, I think."

Something equally tart in his tone made her hold her peace and feel ashamed of her question. The next day, as they were leaving the Gare d'Austerlitz, passing in the train between the grey canyons of houses with their shuttered windows, he said suddenly,

"I shall have to get back to work again soon. I'm a doctor; I ought to be doctoring, not sitting on my behind in the sun ..." Then he looked up, saw her face, and held out his hand to her. In a kinder tone he said: "Besides, we will need the money, won't we?"

In August they helped with the harvest at St Laurent: apparently that was allowed and expected. Even Mlle. Yrieux came down to the fields in a black straw hat, with a basket of small cakes for the children. In some fields a reaper-and-binder quivered and roared, gulching puffs of black smoke from its high chimney like an old-fashioned railway engine, but in others men still stood in a line six-deep, scything all day and into the light summer nights.

When the harvest was in, not only in central France but all over Europe also, Germany and Russia signed a non-aggression pact. A week later German troops marched into Poland. On September 2nd France declared war on Germany, and England did so the following day.

That week Jane received two letters from England. One was from her father. He seldom wrote to her – it was her mother who had regularly communicated a series of small domestic events to her and, in July, the birth of Susie's baby. She opened the envelope with trepidation.

After various preliminaries, her father wrote:

... I therefore beg you to return home while you still can. We are expecting the worst, but your mother has been laying in provisions all the summer and Killick has just ploughed up the tennis court for us: we shall plant potatoes. We have an Anderson shelter already installed in the shrubbery, this seems to me a wise precaution as we are so near the coast. Colonel Blake, Dr. Robinson and I are to organise the Local Defence Volunteers: I must say that it is almost a relief to feel that it has come at last.

I know that you have always been of an independent nature, and I would not wish you otherwise, but I do feel *most strongly* that at such times families should stick together ...

There followed a few lines more and then an affectionate superscription.

Jane gave the letter to Pierre to read. He did so, and then said,

"I am in entire agreement with your father about families sticking together in time of war. When families found themselves separated from each other by the front line in the Last War it was – not amusing. But we differ in our conception of family. To me, you are *my* family."

A little later in the day, as they were watching the last hay-loads brought from the meadows, he remarked apparently irrelevantly,

"You see what a rich countryside this is. Everything grows round here, every kind of crop except for olives. France can, if necessary, feed all her population without importing anything. But this is not the case in England. England is dependent upon what she imports – and totally vulnerable."

"Then Mark and I would be better off here, if –"

"Mark and you will be better off here."

Two days later another letter came from England; from James. It was short and directive. The Montague-Smiths, he said, were sending their two boys to America, and he had made arrangements for Mark to go with them. It was all fixed up: hosts had been found for them, the financial side was organised. They were to sail on the twelfth. Would Jane therefore at once, please, arrange either to bring Mark back to London herself or to dispatch him there from Paris with a suitable escort.

He concluded:

I realise that you have never had the slightest interest in politics, and therefore perhaps you do not realise the idiocy of what you are doing. Nevertheless there is not the slightest doubt in the mind of any intelligent person in England now but that children of school age will be better off in the States, and we are fortunate to have been offered a place for him while it is still possible to send him. If you reject this offer, I shall know that, contrary to what you have maintained, you have never really had Mark's interests at heart all along, merely your own, and I shall not have the slightest hesitation in asking the Courts for custody of him.

Pierre read this letter too. He said at the end of it:

"But he is completely idiot himself, this man. Does he really imagine that the British Courts of Justice are going to send an official to the centre of France to fetch Mark – now, with Europe mobilising? He can have absolutely no imagination: he pretends to believe that Europe will become too dangerous to contain his son, yet he speaks as if the usual formalities of peace-time life will nevertheless continue unimpeded. It is *une comédie* this business of sending Mark to America. He is just doing this to – to punish you."

"Oh I don't know. He does care about the *idea* of having a son, you know. It's really just as you say – that he has no imagination at all, and hasn't understood that he's got no power over me any longer. Poor James."

"What is it he says here? ... 'not the slightest doubt in the mind of any intelligent person' ... Does he really mean that half the population of England are currently sending their children to the New World?"

"No of course not. He just means that he and three other wealthy people he knows are thinking of it. James is like that. He's really quite weak, that's why he always needs to feel he's doing the socially approved thing."

"Well I prefer your father's view that families should stick together. One should never separate oneself from one's children, especially not to send them to America. Why, they would turn into little Americans. Impossible ... You won't even reply?"

More emboldened by his reaction than she showed, Jane agreed that she would not reply. She added, "I must write back to Daddy, though. I wonder if letters will get through now?"

"You can only try. The French posts themselves are very disorganised, so many men have already been mobilised. Did you notice that it was not our usual man who brought your letter, but the kind post-lady herself on her bicycle?"

Pierre's own call-up papers arrived, however, the following morning. He was to report to a military depôt near Rheims within eight days.

"What will they do with you there?"

"They will issue me with an officer's uniform – a doctor, I note with relief, is automatically an officer. And then they will send me to some hospital near the front line, wherever the front line is by then."

But the front line was still the Maginot Line, and, contrary to immediate expectations, it remained fixed there for months, indeed for the whole winter, apart from a few isolated confrontations. The War had come. And yet it had not come.

Afterwards, when Jane looked back on that first winter of the War, the time that the English called the Phoney War and the French *la drôle de guerre*, what she chiefly remembered were the evenings at the Yrieuxs playing two-handed whist and vingt-et-un with Oncle Ernest. She did not really enjoy cards very much, but it gave the old gentleman pleasure and the time passed pleasantly enough. Mlle. Yrieux did not like what she termed 'soldiers' games'. The only two-handed card-game she would play was piquet: she preferred bridge, but partners in the district were hard to find. Jane herself did not play: her refusal to learn had been one of the many minor points of dispute in the early days of her marriage – when the disputes were still minor. Occasionally an elderly couple from Châtelet came over; at other times, when Pierre had a few days leave, a local land-owner, a widower, would be called in to make a fourth. Mlle. Yrieux often lamented that they had no other members of their own family living in the district.

"Doesn't the Mayor of Châtelet or someone play bridge too?" Jane asked Pierre. "Surely there must be a few people living there whom your aunt would feel she could invite?"

"My darling, the Mayor of Châtelet owns a shop that sells irons and tin baths, and is in addition well known for his anti-clericalism. Tante Madeleine would as soon invite the Anti-Christ into her drawing room."

Pierre quite often got leave that winter: there was little action, few war-wounds to dress; merely, he told Jane, a trickle of men with enteritis, V.D. and bullets in their feet. He would appear unheralded in St. Laurent in the early afternoon, having travelled all night from the north-east of France, and depart again two days later. The moments when, while washing up the lunch dishes – always a slow process at the slop-stone – she heard his step on the gravel path and his voice calling her name, were the most beautiful of the year.

Twice, instead of arriving, he sent her a telegram telling her to meet him in Paris the following day. On both occasions Mark stayed with the Yrieuxs and seemed to enjoy himself; but the second time, on Jane's return, Mlle. Yrieux said deprecatingly,

"Of course, we are only Pierre's old auntie and uncle – and not even that in reality: mere cousins ... We can't expect to see him very often."

"But he has his parents in Paris!" said Oncle Ernest. "Naturally he wants to see them."

Very probably, thought Jane, he did. But she never met them herself. She did not ask why: the time they had together was too precious to waste on disagreeable subjects.

Long after, she was to realise that Mlle. Yrieux was torn between her affection for Pierre on the one hand and the views of the rest of the family, particularly Pierre's mother, on the other. It was a difficult situation of divided loyalties for her, where Jane was concerned. Part, at least, of her touchiness stemmed from that.

Jane and Pierre had sent Mark to the village school in St Laurent. A regular education of some sort was essential for him, and this way he would inevitably learn French. It had not been entirely easy to organise. Monsieur Picard, the schoolmaster, was a relative newcomer to the village, from the north of France. Pierre told Jane that frequently schoolmasters came from a different part of the country. It was, he said, an attempt on the part of the authorities to ensure that the children should speak proper French in school, not local variants. Monsieur Picard would not, Jane felt, have let anyone speak in dialect, even in Picardy. He had a sharp face and a polite but cool manner. At first he was inclined to say that French schools were for French children only – "Such are the regulations, Monsieur" – but when Pierre asked him what alternative he could suggest for Mark, he fairly readily consented to take him. Later, Jane was to discover that this was typical of Monsieur Picard: he would tell you the rules, not necessarily to enforce them but to make you understand that he was making an exception for you. He was Secretary at the village Mairie also.

"I don't much take to him," said Jane with apprehension. "I do hope he's nice enough to Markie. It's going to be hard-going at first for the poor little boy in any case."

"I think it will be all right. It is said in the village that Picard is a good teacher and fair and takes pains over the pupils he considers worthwhile. In fact the only reflection I've heard made on him is that he doesn't bother about the more backward boys – he just leaves them to sit at the back of the class getting larger and stupider every year."

Madame Picard took the girls and the smallest children, in one class. She was a pale, quiet woman with reddish hair who always looked tired. As she had three children of her own as well as her schoolroom duties, Jane was not surprised. She also suspected that Madame Picard was afraid of her own husband, and for this reason she, Jane, distrusted Monsieur Picard.

Mark was, rather to his own disgust, put with the youngest children at first while he learnt French. Monsieur Picard also set him special homework every night, which he and Jane struggled over together in the evenings, sometimes with tears. But it was worthwhile, for after Christmas he was moved up into the bigger class with boys of his own age.

"He is a bright boy, your son, Madame – a good worker. He should go far."

His words were a great comfort to Jane. At least, in this no-time, this *drôle de guerre*, when she seemed to do nothing but wait from one week to the next to hear from Pierre again, they had achieved something: Mark now spoke fluent, if slightly bizarre French. It was, she vaguely felt, a wise preparation against the unknowable future; like those other preparations that Pierre made on her behalf, sometimes almost against her will. One leave in Paris he bought her a fine gold chain in the Place Vendôme.

"But it's much more than we can afford!" she cried.

"Take it," he said quietly. "It's an investment." He said no more so she took it, feeling horribly disconcerted. She had supposed he was buying it for her because it was pretty.

Another time, when he appeared at St Laurent, he insisted on accompanying her to the village drapers and making her buy what he called 'real underclothes'. Jane, accustomed to the fashionable silky wisps of the time, and to what indeed were known in England as 'French knickers', which no one wore for warmth, was mildly disgusted by the solid, stockinette drawers and woollen bodices that Madame Marcelle showed her. (Her name was not really Madame Marcelle, but that was the name of her little shop, which was also the ladies' hairdresser's.) Jane would have politely refused them, but Pierre had paid for them and had them wrapped up before she had the opportunity. Outside the shop she turned to him.

"Pierre, what on earth –? This isn't a bit like you. You might let me buy my own knickers."

"But you haven't though I told you to three weeks ago, so I've had to. Darling – the country in winter can be very cold, you don't realise yet. And wars are cold too, and these things are beginning to be in short supply. You'll be glad of them, you'll see."

But Jane still felt cross: she had been rather proud of the economical way she and Mark had been living, not wasting money on unnecessary things. She had, for instance, dispensed with Reine Langlois's services, explaining tactfully – she hoped – that now that Pierre was away she had plenty of time to do her own housework. For the first time in her life she swept and scrubbed floors, deriving a kind of pleasure in it from the idea of how far she had come from her comfortable upbringing – immeasurably far, she thought.

As she was not yet Pierre's wife, she did not automatically receive the proportion of his military salary that would otherwise have been sent to her. Pierre had to send it himself, each week, in the form of a postal order, and sometimes it took as long as ten days to arrive. It was over the postal orders that she first struck up a friendship with Mlle. Bisset, the Post Mistress. Mlle. Bisset did not live in the village; she bicycled in every morning from Châtelet-le-Lys, where she lived with her widowed mother. She was a pretty young woman of about Jane's own age: her lips and finger-nails were red, her hair was softly waved – most of the village women, if they had their hair 'done' at all, had it crimped into squashed ridges or kiss-curls by Madame Marcelle in the style of 1919. She was always very sympathetic when Jane came to enquire if her postal order had yet come and apparently as delighted as Jane when it eventually did. If she was puzzled that young Capitaine Leparde should choose this unorthodox method of remitting his salary to his wife, she did not show it; nor, since she knew Jane, did she ever ask for proof of identity.

Jane wondered if Mlle. Bisset had guessed she and Pierre were not truly married. She didn't think that anyone else in the village suspected. They all enquired kindly, at frequent intervals, if she had news of her husband; some of them had husbands or sons away to the north too. It had even happened that a child would be sent running to tell her when Pierre was sighted descending the hill from the station, his hands in his pockets.

"*Y a vot' mari, m'dame!*"

'Il y a de la joie', indeed.

Mark had now found some playmates. He confided to his

mother that he didn't really like any of them as much as Sullivan, and Jane could understand that: these solid little Berrichan peasants were not quite like the companions to whom Mark had been accustomed. But there was an Henri and a Jean-Luc and a Jean-Baptiste who appeared regularly in his conversation and occasionally at the door of the cottage. They were, Jane learnt, the sons of the Mayor, the butcher and the garage-owner respectively. Evidently the boys who appeared on foot each morning from the outlying farms, with their thick accents, their cloaks and their clogs, still seemed to him very alien.

She felt a deep gratitude towards him for his resilient adaptability. Was this really the same boy, with his *devoirs* and his *parties de foot*, who, this time last year, had gone to school in a striped cap and been initiated into rugger in Regents Park? The only real scene they had had was over his *tabliers* – his overalls. It had not occurred to her to send him to school in an overall. He went in the shorts and jerseys (knitted by his grandmother the autumn before) that he had been wearing all the time. But after a couple of weeks a polite message came back from the school: they would be obliged if Marc (he had evidently become 'Marc') would conform to the usual practice and wear an overall, since the school could not be responsible for accidents involving ink on the clothes. Jane, at a loss, applied to Madame Marcelle. That kind lady, pinkly glad to be of service, demonstrated the standard black sateen overall, adding that it came cheaper if one made one's own. But Mark – momentarily 'Mark' again – looked mutinous. That was a *frock*. He knew the other boys his age wore them, but had not expected to undergo such an indignity himself. The girls wore them too: he objected strongly. Only gradually was his resistance worn down, and then he wouldn't wear black: Jane and he finally compromised on blue cotton, such as Jean-Baptiste's father wore in the garage, and even then he instructed June to take up an enormous hem on it so that it scarcely reached below his waist. It was months before he accepted overalls as a matter of course.

She still read him Biggles and Arthur Ransome in the evenings. But these books were beginning to seem rather like messages from another life. She could tell that, for him, meaning was bleeding out of the stories, and anyway they had read them all more than once. One evening he asked instead for *Oncle Hansi*, a French children's classic of anti-German fervour set in Alsace-Lorraine, which Mlle. Yrieux had given him for his tenth birthday. She began it, but presently he took the book away from her to read to himself. She didn't read well in French, he explained with wounding courtesy; the words didn't sound right somehow.

And yet England was not really far away. Her mother wrote to her regularly, and the letters seemed to get through, though with delays. Her father wrote occasionally: he did not ask her again outright to return to England, and she was grateful for his tact. But he told her that a skeleton service of cross-Channel ferries were still operating 'since things have, after all, been so quiet', as if he felt this information might be of interest to her.

"Really," she said to Pierre when he came on leave in March, "I almost think I might go back to London for a few days to get some more of our things. We could do with them – even though the winter's really over now."

"Do be careful, darling," said Pierre apprehensively. "You would get to England safely, I am sure. But the authorities might not let you back."

"Even though Mark was here?"

"Exactly."

Jane, appalled, abandoned all thought of a trip to England. Her fur coat would have to stay in store a little longer, she thought, shivering in the spring winds which seemed to blow straight out of the north-east, from Germany itself. And she would have to continue to read her way through the volumes of Dickens and Scott on the Yrieux shelves if she wanted English reading matter.

Her father also managed to send her some of her own money, which had been accumulating for her in England. At any rate, he said it was her own money. She was pleasantly surprised at how much it was. She put it in a post-office savings account, which reassured Mlle. Bisset:

"So nice to have something put by, I always say! One never knows, in these times."

In April, out of the blue, when the days were damp and the ditches full of primroses, she received formal notice that James had been awarded his decree nisi. The divorce had, after all, been heard in her absence without a demand on his part for custody of Mark: evidently he had got tired of waiting – or his brave little widow had, as Jane remarked sourly to Pierre the next time he came on leave. Pierre was delighted.

"This is very good news. Now listen: you must write to England for your birth certificate, and I will see about getting mine."

"But this is only the decree nisi, Pierre; it doesn't become absolute for six months at least. Maybe more."

"Doesn't matter, we can start getting our papers in order now so as to have them all ready when the time comes. Don't forget, I have to get my birth certificate from Strasbourg. As that's in the Zone des Armées now, it may take some time."

May arrived. May 1940. It was the month of Jane's thirtieth birthday, an event which, she thought, she would have minded had she still been stuck in Henley with James, but here and now minded not a scrap. She and Pierre had planned to celebrate it in Paris, if he could get twenty-four hours' leave. He obtained it, and they met at the Gare du Nord on May 10th. That turned out to be the day that the forces of the German Reich moved at last into Belgium, Holland and Alsace-Lorraine on their almost uninterrupted way into France.

All leave was cancelled: the station loudspeakers were announcing it ceaselessly as Pierre's train arrived.

"Oh can't we have just today together?" begged Jane. She had on a new, pretty hat, extravagantly bought that morning at the Galeries Lafayette.

"My darling . . . Really no. Not this time. It wasn't really my turn for leave anyway, and I couldn't forgive myself if . . ." He didn't finish the sentence. He left within the hour on another train going north, and Jane and her pretty hat went to eat a tearful lunch alone in a small restaurant near the Jardin du Luxembourg.

She began her own journey back later that afternoon, but it was not till early the following day that, travel-stained and bone-tired, she got out at the station near St Laurent-la-Rivière and heard the birds singing and the church bell tolling the hour. All railway services through France were disrupted by troop movements: she had had to travel on an interminably stopping train via Bourges and Montluçon, then into the mountains, then back to St Laurent in the other direction. The first train she had taken, from the Gare d'Austerlitz, had been packed with Belgian refugees. Vague memories of her early childhood, in the Last War, came back to her like a scent of human bodies or the snatch of an old song, as she stood swaying in the stuffy coach, mechanically reading over and over again the Instructions in Case of an Alert nailed above the seats.

She made her way straight over to the Yrieuxs. Mark was sitting up in the high bed, drinking his morning cup of chocolate brought to him by the indulgent Madame Audibert; he had some of the lead soldiers spread out on the sheet.

"Where are Mademoiselle Yrieux and Oncle Ernest?"

"They're in the kitchen listening to Madame Audibert's wireless. Where's Pierre? I hoped he might come back with you. France has been invaded, did you know? But luckily not round here."

The news that came over the kitchen wireless was not good. Nor did it improve as the days went by.

Of the two Yrieuxs, it was Oncle Ernest, Jane was surprised to see, who took the invasion hardest. He who was always so debonair and apparently disinclined to take the world seriously, now drooped, seeming to become physically smaller. Mlle. Yrieux complained that he wouldn't eat and kept moving about at night. The day at the end of May when Belgium capitulated and signed an armistice, Jane called as usual to listen to the news and found him sitting in his study, seemingly at a loose end, fingering a rifle: it was, he said, the one he had carried in the Last War. He showed Jane how it worked, as if glad of some distraction.

"I don't think Pierre has a gun," she said, for something to say. "I suppose doctors don't need them."

"Ah – Pierre. You've no news of him yet, I suppose?" asked Oncle Ernest, as if recollecting who she was. His mind really did seem elsewhere.

"If I had, I'd have come straight up to tell you. Naturally."

"You know," he said after a long pause, as if making an effort, "I'm so glad Pierre is a doctor – so very glad. The risk is so much less … Our brother was killed at Verdun, you know."

"Yes, I know."

"Such a brilliant boy, far more gifted than I. Such a waste … Did I ever show you a photograph of him?"

Jane had indeed been shown one already, but did not say so. Oncle Ernest brought out his wallet, and she found herself looking at a stiff officer cadet in full regimentals. Opposite it was a picture of a young, calm-faced woman with her hair looped and plaited at the back in the style of 1910.

"My dear wife," said Oncle Ernest, with unaccustomed sentiment.

She stayed a little while with him, encouraging him to talk about his brother and his wife, since he seemed to want to. But she felt that the conversation hardly touched the roots of his extreme sadness.

Mlle. Yrieux told Jane in confidence that she felt her brother was 'exaggerating a little'. "After all," she said, "it's 1914 all over again. If we survived it once we can survive it again, I suppose." Jane did not feel so sure that it was the same thing, but did not like to say so.

Meanwhile Mlle. Yrieux distracted herself – as in 1914 – with the Belgian refugees. By early June two railway coaches full of them had come to rest in a siding at the station, the engine that had pulled them having taken itself elsewhere.

They consisted mainly of women, children, crying babies and a sprinkling of old people. They had untidy piles of belongings with them, little money, and less idea where they were going. Frightened, bored and resentful in stages, they passed their time telling each other atrocity stories from the Last War and trying to find food in the neighbourhood. They did not have drinking water or even water to wash in: the cistern at the station ran dry within two days, and the copse and meadow adjacent rapidly became unsavoury.

There were ugly interchanges between the refugees and the villagers: the Langlois clan mounted guard day and night, Jane heard, over their potato field. The Mayor of St Laurent was beside himself. He was a rotund man with a pleasant manner and the improbable name of Marcel Marceau, and it was clear that nothing in his life hitherto had prepared him for coping with this situation. He hardly went near the refugees for fear of becoming too involved with their problem, but spent his time closeted in the Mairie attempting to communicate with the Préfet of the Department by letter, telephone or any other means: would *Monsieur le Préfet* please take the refugees elsewhere? – anywhere, by any means; St Laurent was not a suitable place for them. But evidently the Préfet had other things on his mind at that moment for the refugees were there for over a week.

Jane heard this disparaging account of the Mayor's activities from Madame Langlois, Jean Langlois's wife; she, together with various other strong-minded women of the village, and Mlle. Yrieux to give authority to the proceedings, had made themselves responsible for collecting gifts of milk from the surrounding farms and distributing it to the refugee mothers. Jane was struck then – and it was not to be the only time – by the combination of practical kindness and prejudiced dislike of outsiders that Madame Langlois and her fellows displayed. They spoke of the train-load as *les Belges*, although many of them in fact came from northern France itself, and there was a note of deep contempt in the term, just as when they spoke of the gipsies that occasionally camped down by the river. Despite their genuine efforts to help, they seemed to think of these people who had had to flee from their homes as some alien and inferior race. Jane was slightly shocked, though she could see why they felt like this. Dirty, mainly ungrateful, and suspicious, the poor refugees were hardly a good advertisement for the northern manufacturing towns from which they had come. Jane met two of the women one morning, holding their babies and sitting in a dejected way beside the road that led from the station, as if they had set off to take a walk but had been overcome by the extent of the peaceful landscape all around. She attempted a conversation with them.

"At least it's quiet down here . . . That must be a relief after what you've been through."

The women turned their lacklustre eyes upon her. They obviously hated the countryside. She tried again:

"I mean . . . there's plenty of space for your children to play."

"Oh, that –" said one of the women eventually. "The kids don't like it here, either. We're used to the town, we are."

Jane left them, feeling middle class and foolish. As she walked on, she heard one of the women say to the other:

"That was a funny way of speaking she had. Didn't you notice?"

So even people from another region of France, whose own accent was ugly and glottal in her ears, noticed that she was a foreigner. Proud of her now-fluent French, she had not realised her English accent was still so recognisable. That morning, really for the first time, a little spark of fear ignited inside her.

The refugees went elsewhere eventually, but the news continued to get worse. By the middle of June they learnt in shock and incredulity that Paris was now occupied. This hadn't happened last time, Mlle. Yrieux could hardly conceive of such an event. But Pétain and Weygand were now in charge of matters and she took a little heart: she had great confidence, she told Jane, in Marshal Pétain, the hero of Verdun.

Meanwhile other refugees were seen in the land. Not just train loads of Belgians or supposed Belgians but people from the north, from the east, from Lille, from Rheims, from Châlons-sur-Saône, from Bar-le-Duc, from Nancy, from Troyes, travelling in cars and lorries, in wagons and carts, on foot . . . The countryside seemed full of them. The main road south from Châteauroux was said to be busy with a stream of them day and night, and not just civilian refugees, it began to be murmured, but soldiers too, French soldiers fleeing in disordered and broken groups from the ever-advancing enemy. Jane had not seen them, for the road passed twenty kilometres away from St Laurent, but she knew. Everyone knew. And yet at the same time no one knew anything. What had happened to the great French army? No one seemed to know that, not even the wireless. It was said the Germans were at Bourges. It was said there had been heavy bombardment at Châteauroux. It was said that German planes had been seen machine-gunning running women and children on the road just outside the town. But no one knew for certain.

On June 22nd France signed an armistice with Germany. There could be no doubt about that: Marshal Pétain himself came onto the air to tell the people of France about the new arrangement and to explain to them that it was no dishonour. He was over eighty, and asked the French people to trust him as they would a father.

Early the next morning, Jane bicycled into Châtelet-le-Lys. She was hoping to pick up more news there than was available in the village, and also to buy herself a second pair of stout shoes at the big shop in the market square known as the Bazaar. Pierre's warnings about being well-prepared now came home to her with new meaning.

In Châtelet, as in St Laurent, old men stood about the streets talking together in muted voices. Most of the young men were absent. "Now perhaps we'll see our boys home again," said a woman in the Bazaar with transparent relief in her voice. Jane sympathised: she could not summon up any more noble reaction herself. When she reflected that this whole, vast, beautiful land of France, the largest and proudest in Europe, had capitulated to her arch-enemy, she felt merely numb: the fact was not yet understandable. Remembered scraps from History supplied themselves: *'Roll up the map of Europe, it will not be needed these twenty years ...' 'The lights are going out all over Europe, they will not be lit again in our time ...'* But subsequent events, she seemed to recall, had proved these prophecies over-extensive. Life had continued; even Europe and her separate countries had, after intervals of confusion, continued much as before. It would be the same this time; they would all just go on as they were. She felt sturdily convinced of that.

She bought herself some shoes and also, on impulse, a new pair for Mark because she saw them on the shelves. He had had some not long ago, and these were at least two sizes too large, but it seemed a wise precaution. She hesitated a long time, however, before spending the money. She had had no postal order from Pierre for well over a month. Most of the money from England, she was trying to keep 'for emergencies'. Was this one?

She had had no news from Pierre for over a month either, but took strength from the fact that most families had apparently heard nothing of their menfolk in the Army since the invasion had begun. No news was good news, she dared to believe.

Weighted with the shoes and with some meat she had bought – the village butcher's shop had been strangely bare the last few days – she cycled the six miles back to St Laurent.

At the entrance to the village she encountered Mlle. Yrieux, but hardly recognised her. That lady, ordinarily so correctly dressed, even to her hat and gloves, when she ventured down the village street to buy a reel of cotton or a small fruit tart, was hatless, dishevelled, violently tear-stained: like a black spectre she seemed to stagger on the road. She had, she said incoherently, been on her way to give Jane the news.

For one interminable moment Jane knew Pierre must be

dead. But then Mlle. Yrieux explained: it was not Pierre but Oncle Ernest who was the first casualty of the war at St Laurent.

His sister had found him when she came downstairs in the morning and, not hearing him about his usual morning duties in the house, had looked for him outside. He was in the vegetable garden, with one boot off and his rifle clasped to his breast. He had used his free toe to press the trigger. He was not a cartoon figure after all.

He had left no note. Mlle. Yrieux insisted to Jane, to the Curé, to the local police and for ever afterwards, that it was grief for France that had driven the mild old gentleman to such an end: that, and regret that he himself was too old to assist his country in her hour of need. But, thinking about it often afterwards, feeling that she owed it to him to try to understand, Jane inclined to the belief that Oncle Ernest's act had something to do with his brother, and with the realisation that he and so many others of his generation had after all died in vain.

Mlle. Yrieux repeated over and over again,

"If only he had had a belief in God. He would never then have done such a terrible thing."

Jane was not convinced that a belief in God was particularly relevant to suicide, but did not say so.

She would have liked to avoid telling Mark the whole truth about Oncle Ernest, but did so because she knew he would probably hear it in the village anyway. Mark did not say much. After a while, he remarked,

"He said he'd teach me to shoot . . . He never did."

Later, he cried. But he insisted with anger that it was because of a poor hedgehog he had seen squashed in the road. Jane wondered if that was true. Certainly *Mrs. Tiggy-Winkle* had been his favourite reading matter for a while when he had been a very small boy, and he mentioned the book now, regretfully, saying he would like to see it again. He so seldom cried these days, or showed signs of nostalgia for his former life, that she was struck by the incident.

After that, he hardly ever talked any more about the

books or games of his early years. He seldom mentioned Oncle Ernest either.

At the beginning of July, Jane still had no news whatsoever of Pierre. It comforted her a little that a number of wives and mothers in the village, including Madame Langlois, were in the same position. Jeanot Langlois and his brother Jules were both 'at the war', no one knew where. So was Henri Marceau's elder brother. So was the baker's son.

The Germans had retired to the banks of the Cher. St Laurent-la-Rivière and its region were therefore just within the Free Zone, theoretically under Pétain's own government, now established at Vichy. Jane drew a deep breath. Her fate, and Mark's had the Berry happened to be in the Occupied Zone, was not a topic she liked to contemplate. A reflex of confidence and security from her privileged upbringing made her imagine that perhaps the phrase 'English lady' might have struck some resonant chord of respect in the breast of a German officer, but a developing adult awareness warned her that this might be over-optimistic. She thought of the women and children said to have been gunned down on the road from Châteauroux, between the sunlit plane trees.

On July 3rd the British sank the French Fleet at Mers-el-Kebir, before it could be used against them. At the time, Jane did not appreciate the significance of this event. It was only after the War, in fact, that she understood that very many people in France that weekend, besides Mlle. Yrieux, had turned against England.

Mlle. Yrieux remained convinced that Pétain was right. In her desolation at her brother's death, she clung to that principle. She was furious with England for what she regarded as her treachery, and angry with Jane when she realised that their views on the Marshal differed. She also assured Jane repeatedly that England would now certainly fall before long; after all, if the supposedly unbeatable French Army had collapsed so swiftly, the British Navy would certainly follow suit.

"You think America will save you," she repeated (though Jane had not said a word on the subject of America). "But no, no, you are wrong – America doesn't care."

America, it appeared, didn't care. Jane wondered if the little Montague-Smiths had got there safely. One night she dreamed of them. They were wearing French overalls and looking cross. James was there too. He insisted that it was time they had her parents over again for the day. He had always been punctilious about things like that. She woke feeling sad about her parents, and guilty.

She wished she could have dreamed, instead, of Pierre. But, perhaps because he occupied her thoughts for so many of her waking hours, there seemed no room for him in her dreams.

Her great fear (which she naturally could not admit to anyone else), was that, because she was not really his wife, she might not hear news of Pierre if any did come through. It would be his mother and father, in Paris, who would receive the telegram saying he was a prisoner. Or missing. Or –

Mlle. Yrieux was trying to go to Paris too. It seemed to Jane a ridiculous decision. Paris was occupied and central France wasn't: surely the old lady would have done better to stay quietly in the village? But, now that things were settling down and some limited communications were being re-established, Mlle. Yrieux seemed absolutely intent on joining forces with her sister. It was as if, with Oncle Ernest's death, she had completely lost her nerve about the countryside, a habitat she had never really made her own in any case. One evening she confided to Jane:

"People look at me in the road now that Ernest has done that terrible thing ... Such a bad example to them ... I hate to go down to the village now. I feel so ashamed for him."

But, apart from that one occasion, she seemed to be avoiding Jane, and hardly bothered to be civil to her when they met by chance. It was from old Madame Audibert, who would remain there as caretaker, that Jane learnt that Mlle.

Yrieux had got her travel permit and would definitely be leaving for Paris.

Jane was much too proud to say "But Mark and I will be all alone, cut off from Pierre's family, once you have gone." Nor did she give Mlle. Yrieux any message for Pierre's father. She had an unpleasant feeling that such a message might not have been delivered in any case.

She did not really blame Mlle. Yrieux. The old lady had lent them the cottage, probably against her better judgement, and was still doing so. (Perhaps, with hindsight, it had been a little childish of them to borrow it from her in the first place, she thought now: the idea of it had been so attractive that they had not considered . . .) And Mlle. Yrieux had, in her way, been kind to Mark. It was natural that, so recently bereaved, she should want to be with her sister. As Jane's own father had said, families should stick together in time of war. But Jane did wish Mlle. Yrieux had been just a bit less preoccupied with her own problems to the exclusion of anyone else's. Still, at some level, she thought of people of Mlle. Yrieux's generation as 'the grown ups', and was disconcerted when they did not behave in a grown-up manner.

Nor did she forgive Mlle. Yrieux for shutting up the lead soldiers in their cabinet inside the house and not suggesting that Mark might go there sometimes to play with them. The soldiers had become his favourite toy. It seemed stupid that they should remain shut away, along with the books and the furniture and all the other things, in a house where henceforth, only Madame Audibert would unlock the rooms now and again to let in a little air.

This was Jane's first time of anguished waiting for news of Pierre. She knew that his hospital in Rocroi, near the Belgian border, must have been over-run in the early days of the invasion.

Some of the young men of St Laurent had by now reappeared in the village, part of the demoralised, routed French forces. Like thousands of others all over France, once their military positions were outflanked if not before, they had made blindly for their home-village. No one had asked them if they wanted to go to war in the first place. They brought with them some ugly tales – of officers deserting their men, of local administrators deserting their posts even before the advancing Wehrmacht arrived.

The Mayor's elder son reappeared. So did the younger Langlois. But Jeanot, who had married during the previous winter and whose young wife from Ourlats was already pregnant, was still missing.

The baker's son was dead. Jane happened to be in the square when the telegram arrived. That afternoon and evening the baker's shop was shut. But the next morning it was open as usual. To each customer, the baker's wife said shortly:

"After all – people have to have bread." With her, grief took the form of anger.

Then one day Jane received a letter from Paris in an unknown hand. Arming herself against whatever it might contain, she tore it open. It was from Pierre's father. Pierre, he said, had been taken prisoner; his family had just heard, through official channels. The letter continued:

My son gave me to understand, last time we saw him, that in fact you and he are not yet married even under English law. He was naturally anxious that, should anything happen to him, I should be aware of your predicament. I therefore take this opportunity of sending you some money while such transactions are still possible. It would be his wish, since I imagine you can have received nothing from him since the invasion and will receive none as of right while he is a prisoner.

At the same time, however, I must urge you with the utmost seriousness to attempt to return to your own country for the time being, if you can hear of any means of doing so. I am told that it may still be possible for foreign nationals to leave on small ships from Marseilles or Sète, and would therefore advise you to seek information on this matter. I imagine the former Staff of the British Consul in Nice, if you are able to find some of them, would be the people to advise and possibly assist you. If you remain in France, even in the Unoccupied Zone (so-called), your irregular situation is likely, I fear, to put you in grave danger, also your child.

The letter ended there. He signed it, formally, as he would have to any acquaintance, *'agréez, chère madame, mes homages respectueux.'*

The banker's draft contained in it was for a sum in francs then worth several hundred pounds. It was a substantial amount by any standards, but certainly by those of the low cost of living in rural France. Jane understood: the money was not intended to help her to live but rather to help her to leave. She might need to bribe people.

Pierre had always said his father was a fair man. Jane was not ungrateful. Indeed the firm, concerned tone of the letter even seemed to carry an echo of her own father's, two months earlier. But all the same she sat with the letter and the money-order in her lap and cried unrestrainedly for the first time in fear and loneliness.

The next thing that happened was that Jeanot Langlois walked into the village one wet Sunday morning. According to those who saw him arrive, he seemed to materialise out of the thundery rain, and stood there smiling in the square by the church, greeting people as they came running from church and café. By nightfall, everyone in the village knew the story. He had been taken prisoner at the beginning of June with half his regiment and had been supposed to be sent to Germany. However he managed several times to avoid being transported eastwards by the simple but shrewd device of not answering to his name at the roll-call. "I knew they wouldn't run round looking for me. There were hundreds and hundreds of us, and several Langlois, Lenglos and Lenglens besides me." Meanwhile, he had managed to procure himself some sort of civilian clothes which he kept rolled up under his tunic. One day, on some pretext or other, he gained permission to go beyond the camp gates – and duly returned. He did this twice, and then, the third time, having allayed the guards' suspicions, he made off. Without money, papers or contacts he had managed to get himself across hundreds of miles of unknown France to his own countryside.

"But how did he manage?" Jane asked his father admiringly. If a Jeanot Langlois could do it, then perhaps a Pierre Leparde might too?

"Why, he went across the fields all the time," his father explained with pride. "And ate what he found there, raw, like that. And every time a German patrol was near he pretended to be working among the potatoes or cabbages or vines or whatever was growing. Not that there were any vines in the north, he said."

"Didn't you get very tired of eating bits of raw vegetable?" Jane asked him a few days later, when he came to deliver a load of wood to the cottage. He was a well-built, pleasant-looking young man; it was hard to imagine that he had sustained himself for weeks on uncooked swedes.

"Yes, very tired. But sometimes I had a cooked meal and a good bed all the same. Some of the people I met in the fields were very good to me." He looked subtly amused at something, and none the worse for his ordeal. Later, when she got to know him better, Jane came to understand, without him ever telling her in so many words, that he had found a woman, or perhaps a series of women, who had helped him. He seemed like a young man who could have made his way in the world. It was odd to think that henceforth he would return to the life of a peasant farmer, his world limited by the horizons of his native village, working the land that his father and grandfather and great-grandfather had worked before him, till he was laid in his turn in the same cemetery on the rise overlooking the river.

She turned Dr. Leparde's advice over and over in her mind, but did nothing about it. She had no idea where to start making enquiries. The Berry was as far from the Marseilles coast as it was from the Channel ports – further, probably. But of course the Channel ports were all occupied. Was it really true that she and Mark could not, if necessary, go up to Paris, buy a ticket for the boat-train to Boulogne, cross to Dover . . .? She knew, of course, with her intellect that this was so, but her imagination failed her. It was as hard to believe that the Channel was now an impassable barrier, as it was to believe in field grey uniforms in the village of Rottingdean on the other side and foreigners in jackboots ordering people like her father about. Yet, by all accounts, that too might very well be true soon. And in that case would she and Mark really be better off in England than they were here? The old arguments revolved in her mind. Perhaps she ought to try, at least, to travel to Marseilles or Nice to find out the true situation. There might, as Dr. Leparde had intimated, be other English citizens stranded there: the idea was encouraging. But she could hardly go alone, leaving Mark in St Laurent (with whom, now, anyway?). And she flinched at the thought of taking him with her straight away on a possibly dangerous and very likely fruitless expedition. She knew of absolutely no one from whom she could ask advice. Monsieur Picard? . . . No. He wouldn't know. Why should he?

And then suddenly life changed all over again. For one afternoon at the beginning of August, Mark, who had been hanging about the village on his bike, came tearing up the lane joyfully shouting that Pierre had been sighted on the road coming down from the station.

As a doctor, Pierre had been released by the Germans on parole. This had been the most probable outcome all along, had Jane only known it. He had stopped briefly in Paris with his parents and then had come down to central France and Jane. He made light of any difficulties he had had in organising this journey. Jane was too innocent, at that time, to realise the improbability of a parolled prisoner being given permission to disappear into the Unoccupied Zone. Only later did she realise that he must have achieved a Pass by bribery or trickery, but did not want her to worry about it.

"My darling girl, how are you?" he kept saying. "Have you really been managing on your own?"

She showed him his father's letter. He read it carefully.

"Oh how glad I am," he said, "that you haven't already

taken his advice. I was so angry when he told me you might no longer be here. How terrible it would have been if I had returned here only to find you gone – like Yvonne de Galois in *Le Grand Meaulnes*. I thought of you all the time in that boring, dreary prison camp – all the time."

Jane was a little disconcerted to hear the prison-camp described as boring: she had envisaged it, rather, as terrifying. Pierre's whole manner seemed very slightly febrile and out of touch with reality: she supposed it was the long weeks of sequestration and the sudden release that made him like that. He plied her with questions about the events of June and July, not all of which she could answer. She told him, instead, all she knew about Oncle Ernest's death. He paused at the end of her account and then said, sounding more like his old self,

"You know, I am almost more sorry about that than about anything else to do with this filthy war."

"Yes. I feel like that too."

A little later, he asked:

"Have you been able to cash my father's cheque?"

"Yes, Mademoiselle Bisset arranged it for me. I've put it in the Post Office for the moment – that's the best place, isn't it?"

"As good as anywhere else I should think, at the moment."

"Pierre, it was good of him, I thought."

"Hmm," said Pierre, and she saw that he had meant what he said earlier; he *was* angry with his father. "Well, we'll pay it back to him by and by, I hope. Once I shall be working normally again."

"Do you know yet where you will be working?" she asked, longing to hear – for everything seemed possible that day – that he would be working in some town in the region, Châteauroux or Bourges or Montluçon. He said,

"I have to go where I am sent, and I am afraid it will be in the Occupied Zone, my darling."

"And can – can we come with you?" She knew from his face before he replied what the answer would be.

"It is too dangerous, Jane. You don't realise what northern France is like now. There are soldiers and control-points everywhere. Permits for everything. If – when – we are really married, then perhaps ... But, as things are, we cannot risk it. I am only parolled, remember; they can revoke my parole any time they choose. And you and Mark wouldn't even get past the frontier. Why Jane, you haven't even an identity card between you!"

"We've got our British passports," she said absurdly.

"You'd do better to burn those ... Seriously, we must get some identity papers for you, one way or another."

"Where from? The Gendarmes in Châtelet?"

"Don't be silly. We'll get it done somehow. Picard may be helpful. I'll find out."

Two nights later they lay talking for a long while. At the end of it, Jane said soberly that, if he was to be in the Occupied Zone and she had to remain in Vichy-France, and if the War was to last years as now seemed likely, she thought that perhaps after all she and Mark ought to try to get back to England – or indeed to America. The strain otherwise on all of them might be too great.

It was the hardest decision she had ever taken in her life, far harder and more conscious than the decision to leave James two years earlier. She felt responsible, and grown-up at last, and very sad.

She was partly comforted when Pierre said that he was not at all sure whether it was possible for her to leave now in any case. He would try to find out. But he did not attempt to dissuade her from her decision. Some things, evidently, were too serious even for love to sway the balance. She wondered bleakly if the love on which they had both been prepared to stake so much was, after all, a luxury emotion, which belonged with their old, carefree life and not with the present.

But the next day the carefree life came back again, briefly, as Pierre declared that, before making any further plans, they would help get the harvest in.

It was just like the year before in the fields; it was possible to believe that France had never fallen. Except that this time there was a shortage of young men to do the heavy labour, and a more serious shortage of horses. Every family or farm who possessed two horses had had one requisitioned by the Army. Plough oxen, which had been dying out in the Berry, were apparently much sought-after now and were fetching high prices. Jeanot Langlois had had the job, while a prisoner, of preparing captured French Army horses to be sent by train to Germany.

"Ah, that made me angry," he said. "Most of those horses belonged to the people, not to the Government. They should have been returned to their owners, or distributed, anyway. We won't see them again, our good beasts."

It was just as well, thought Jane, that the reaping machine devoured wood; at least there was no shortage of that. Petrol, however, was rapidly disappearing. Petitjean, the garage-owner, was said to have a can or two still at the back of his yard, but if so he was keeping very quiet about it. The Picards' small car vegetated in its garage, and so did the Mayor's. So did the baker's van, which he had only owned a year. Oncle Ernest's elderly Hispano-Suiza was already standing on blocks in the Yrieux coach-house. There was a rumour that the twice-weekly bus into Châtelet-le-Lys would be withdrawn.

Jane and Pierre were glad now they had never had a car, since there was nothing to miss. Most of the villagers indeed were indifferent to the petrol shortage, except to complain that goods were taking a long time to reach the drapers and the village's two small grocers. But they were vociferous on the subject of the guns: that summer in the Berry all privately owned fire-arms, including shot guns, had to be handed in to the authorities. It was said that the rule had been made because the Occupied Zone was close at hand.

"It's ridiculous," stormed the baker, who, like his wife, was not famous for amiability. "How are we to keep the countryside under control? The foxes and rabbits and game will devour everything – the wheat, the pea-crops, everything!"

"Do they think we are going to shoot Germans with the guns? There aren't any Germans here anyway. Thought we were supposed to be in Free France ..."

Madame Mouret, whose husband was a retired Gendarme, said that she thought the Vichy authorities were being 'unreasonable': "– Our local police in Châtelet wouldn't make such a rule if it wasn't forced on them. They know people need to be able to shoot. What am I to serve in my restaurant this winter, I should like to know? There's not much butchers' meat about –"

Pierre and Jane debated what to do about Oncle Ernest's guns. They were a museum collection rather than an armoury, yet some of them were undoubtedly still usable, and Pierre did not want Madame Audibert to get into trouble later. In the end, with regret, Pierre handed in at Châtelet the more recent models, including the gun Oncle Ernest had carried in the Last War and had used to end his own life, but not the more ancient arms.

Pierre was making his plans to go to the south, 'just to see', as he put it. This was not, even in Vichy-France, a matter of simply buying a ticket: trains were few, and a priority-voucher had to be obtained. He invented himself some aunts in Toulon, from where his father's family had in fact come – "though that, admittedly, was nearly a hundred years ago."

"Very old aunts, then."

"Extremely old. Delicate, unable to travel, and requiring a visit from their favourite nephew."

He would have to go soon, for he was supposed to report in Paris for duty in mid-September. But before going on his expedition he succeeded in organising for Jane and Mark a fictitious identity card each. This was easier than Jane had feared it would be. Monsieur Picard, in his capacity as Secretary of the Mairie, procured the cards without apparent difficulty when it was explained to him in confidence that unfortunately their marriage had never been registered in France ... The cards were fairly expensive (it was not quite clear why) but looked all right. Jane felt a strong and strange emotion at seeing her own familiar face looking at her from a card stating in a foreign hand that she was Leparde, Jeanne, *née* Framy, born at Roubaix.

This last detail had been Monsieur Picard's own suggestion. He could hardly put, he said, that she had been born in England – "that would be merely looking for trouble, no point in mentioning it. Bah, your accent is vaguely reminiscent of certain Flemish – let us say you are from the north, you and your son. Roubaix is in the Forbidden Zone, no one will bother to check and anyway much must have been destroyed in the bombardments; they have other fish to fry in Roubaix."

It was also at his suggestion that her English name Framlingham – actually James's name, but there seemed no point in complicating the issue further – should be shortened to give it a vaguely French look. So Mark became *Framy, Marc*. No father was mentioned on his card, which Jane found amusing rather than hurtful. With Pierre there, she could laugh at such things again.

"After all," Pierre said, "you won't have to show the cards in the village, ever. Everyone knows you, here."

Jane supposed that was true. She also had the impression that one or two people in the village looked at her as if she ought not to be there. Pierre told her she was imagining things.

He set off for Marseille early one morning. He had a complicated journey to make over the Massif Central, with several changes of train. He would be going via the town of Vichy.

"*Do* give my love to Marshal Pétain," said Jane.

"But of course. I'm sure he'll be happy to know you are now a good French subject, joining in the international fight against Bolshevism."

"Oh dear. Perhaps he *is* right, after all. What do you think, Pierre – really?"

"I think," said Pierre, "that at eighty-four years old, which is what he is, one is unlikely to have the clearest judgement in the world. France has been sold by old men, you know."

"But if it saves lives?" If, as seemed possible, the rapid armistice had saved Pierre from further danger –

"It won't have saved many lives in the long run," he said. "You'll see. Matters won't stay where they are. Contrary to what some people imagine, the War is not over. Far from it." But he didn't elaborate.

He set off, wearing the heavy country boots that were known as his 'hunting boots', and the cap that went with them. He wore his Army officer's cloak, and carried a few belongings in a canvas game-bag over his shoulder.

"I look like a country postman," he said.

"Yes, you do . . . Our postman's back, by the way. I saw him yesterday. The grocer-lady told me the Germans parolled him because he's the 'only support of a widow'."

"I am interested to hear that the Germans are so tender-hearted," said Pierre.

"I always thought he had a brother, actually?"

"Stefan-Postier? Yes, he has. But his brother is not quite normal. Has fits or something."

"What a shame."

"Not at all. A great advantage, fits, in these hard times. They mean you don't get called up into the Army."

"I don't think I've seen the brother. Or perhaps I have without realising it."

"I think you probably have. A very dark boy, like a gipsy, much darker than the other. He hangs around the village sometimes. You wouldn't necessarily know there was anything wrong with him, he's not idiotic or anything – though I daresay Stefan-Postier told the authorities that he was. Actually I'm sure he does have gipsy blood. Their mother is Marie Stefan who lives in the little farmhouse the other side of the wood, just under the hill."

But Jane did not know Marie Stefan then.

Pierre kissed her goodbye.

"I can't say just when I'll be back darling. It depends on the trains – and on what I find. But it'll be within the week, for sure."

After he had gone, she spent the morning washing all the

floors, determined not to brood. Obviously, if she and Mark were after all to spend long periods here without him, she must get used to the idea. The likelihood of their actually leaving France now seemed to her, on further reflection, slender. Would Pierre really be able to find them a boat, and, if so, what circuitous route would it take? She was rather inclined to hope, in spite of their decision, that no such escape was any longer possible.

The week passed slowly. She and Mark picked a lot of blackberries. Madame Langlois advised her to make blackberry jam, substituting honey, which was plentiful that year, for sugar, which was becoming scarce. But although Jane said she would take her advice, she did not do so. After all, perhaps they would be leaving soon.

When eight days passed, then ten, and there was still no sign of Pierre, she began to worry in earnest. Yet at the bottom of her mind she still did not believe that anything very bad could have happened. After all, she had been for over two months without news before, and yet he had returned. He would return.

The September days went by. It was now past the date on which he should have reported to the authorities in Paris. Could it be that he had got held up and had had to go straight up north without returning to the Berry? It seemed possible and she clung to the idea, hoping every day that a letter might get through from the Occupied Zone.

One day a letter did arrive: she almost snatched it from Stefan-Postier's hands. But, to her surprise, it was from England. It had been opened, and re-sealed with a Red Cross sticker.

"Looks like you've got news from your own country, Madame," Stefan-Postier remarked softly, looking over his shoulder as if the cows in the field might be listening. She didn't like Stefan-Postier much. His manner had nothing openly in it that her mother would have called 'disrespectful' but there was something vaguely intimate about it that was quite different from the unaffected friendliness of Jeanot Langlois or various other people in the village.

She thought it was tactless of him to make reference to her foreign nationality just now, and felt sure he was waiting inquisitively to hear who her letter was from. In fact it was from her father. She had received nothing at all from England since the signing of the armistice. It was addressed for the first time to 'Madame Jane Leparde' without mention of her real name: previously, her father had compromised with his own disapproval by putting both names on the envelope. She took it indoors to read.

My dearest Jane, I have no means of knowing whether this letter will reach you. I have written several times already since June, but very likely you may not have received anything: I was warned that there was no guarantee of delivery. I do not know exactly what arrangements you have managed to make, and hesitate to keep on writing for fear of compromising you. We must be prudent, and you know that our thoughts are with you even if you hear nothing from us. Acquaintances at the War Office assure me that if you and Mark remain quietly in central France you are probably safe enough; I try to believe them . . .

The letter continued in this vein, and ended with an urgent plea to Jane not to 'do anything rash'.

Her mother had added a postscript: 'Susie and Geoffrey have been staying with us last month, their dear little girl is fourteen months now. How I wish you could see her!'

It was a kind letter, a concerned and thoughtful one. Yet it left Jane feeling more remote from them than ever. Too many experiences, both personal and national, were already piling up between her and those who had once been her own people. She felt glad, for her parents' sake, that they had a new grandchild to fill the empty place left by her defection with Mark.

And still there was no word from Pierre.

Term began again at school. One evening, when Mark was occupied in the school-house taking part in rehearsals for a concert to be given on All Souls' Day, she was gripped by such an access of loneliness that she decided to go and have dinner at the Restaurant. Madame Mouret, short of customers this autumn since the usual shooting parties had not come to the Berry, welcomed her expansively. She counselled her in an undertone to have the 'special meal' rather than the set one, and served her with roast woodcock. When Jane came to pay the bill, she realised that it was considerably more than she had expected. Embarrassed, she explained that she would have to go back home and fetch some more money.

"Ah, pouf – pay me next time you're passing," said Madame Mouret. But she added, a little defensively,

"You understand, Madame Leparde, that for a good meal – I mean a *good* one, not the set one – I have to charge a little more because the tradesmen won't deliver any more. They say they've no petrol, or no horses – or no provisions, even. So my husband or I have to go driving round the countryside in one of Marceau's carts to get our provisions. And expeditions like that don't cost nothing, you can imagine."

As Jane was leaving, Monsieur Mouret emerged chewing from the kitchen and enquired politely after Pierre. He was a fine figure of a man, whose policemanly courtesy and dignified bearing concealed (Jane guessed) a simpler mentality than his wife's. Jane told him she had no news. No news at all. But she was unable to explain the extent of her anxiety, since naturally no one in the village outside the Mairie had been told particularly of Pierre's journey to Marseille: they supposed him to be back in the north.

"Ah dear me," said Monsieur Mouret comfortingly. "Yes, the mails are still very disorganised. But courage, my dear lady! At least you know now that he is not in enemy hands. Not like in the summer."

She was so eager to believe he knew what he was talking about that she felt strengthened by his words.

Mark came back from the rehearsal shortly after she had returned home herself.

"There's lots of schools joining in, Mum. The school at La Faux and at Ourlats and Bussières and – oh, lots. But we're having the concert in our school, because we're the biggest and because Monsieur Picard is organising it."

"Yes I know, he told me. What are you going to sing?"

"*Le Petit Navire* – with a mime. And *Trois Jolis Tambours* as a two-part with the girls. And then with the other schools we're singing *Il Pleut Berger* and *Trompe Ton Pain, Marie* – that's a dance too. And *Maréchal, Nous Voilà!* at the end."

"How does that go? I've never heard of it."

He hummed it. It was reminiscent of the Marseillaise.

"– Monsieur Picard says these are the new words. And right at the end we've all got to turn and salute the photograph of the Marshal that's in the schoolroom this term. Because the Sous-Préfet of the Indre may be coming."

Evidently, Jane reflected with some irony, Monsieur Picard believed in keeping all his options open. But she did not say so to Mark. She was not sure how much he really understood of the conflict taking place in the world beyond St Laurent-la-Rivière, and was wary of transmitting to him any definite opinion which he might afterwards bring out innocently in other company. She longed to confide more in him, but hesitated to burden him with the responsibility of adult knowledge.

And it was mid-October and still she had heard no word at all from Pierre.

Jeanot Langlois's young wife had her baby. Jane was touched to receive a verbal invitation to come and drink a glass of wine at the Langlois' farmhouse after the christening. She guessed that it had been issued on the spur of the moment: Madame Langlois had called to tell her husband something one day when Langlois was doing the cottage garden, and had obviously noticed Jane's despondent air.

"Come over Sunday," she urged her. "It's just the family, nobody from the town or anything, but you'll be very welcome, I'm sure."

Her manner suggested both genuine kindness and a degree of reserve. Jane understood that by 'nobody from the town' Madame Langlois meant 'no one else of your class'. Although Jane was now doing her own cleaning and washing, and lived in a house smaller than the Langlois' own, they continued to treat her with the slight ceremonial distance appropriate to a person from another sphere.

She found out from Mlle. Bisset that the proper thing to offer on such occasions was a cornet of sugared almonds – 'daintily wrapped up'. She bicycled into Châtelet in search of them and eventually found them at the third Pâtisserie she visited. They seemed very expensive, but she was bent on making the correct gesture. She told herself that, thanks to Pierre's father and her own, she had plenty of money – for the moment. Though, if Pierre's unexplained absence were to last a long time . . . She dare not, for the moment, give his disappearance any other name than 'absence'.

The Langlois' farmhouse kitchen had been newly whitewashed for the occasion and was full of their relatives. She was relieved to find (though a little surprised, considering the price) that a number of the other guests had brought sugared almonds as well. She was later to learn that people like the Langlois grew or obtained by barter virtually everything they needed in their daily lives except coffee and tobacco; it was therefore only at marriages, baptisms and First Communions that they indulged in the luxury of shop-bought articles, and then the conspicuous extravagance was part of the gesture.

Madame Langlois and her sisters must have been baking all the week; there was a great array of tarts, small cakes and *brioches.* The men stood around in stiff collars and shiny boots, talking loudly, with their caps on. The baby, displayed in its mother's arms, was swaddled, with a huge white bow tied round the middle as on a cake. She saw the Curé, who seemed rather surprised to see her.

"And how is your husband's dear aunt?" he asked presently. "You have good news of her, I hope?"

"Oh yes," said Jane firmly, "quite good news, thank you Monsieur." If he didn't even know Pierre had disappeared again, she wasn't going to tell him. Too late, she realised she should have called him 'Father'. It didn't matter. He wouldn't be any use to her anyway, whatever happened. A pity. There must, she felt, be plenty of better and more intelligent country priests, like in Bernanos's book which had been a best-seller the year before.

The lack of companionship of her own kind was beginning to oppress her, though for a while she did not like to phrase it to herself like that. She genuinely liked a number of the village people and felt that they liked her: it cheered her up, during her long, too quiet but strained days, to make an expedition up the street, and exchange words with obliging Monsieur Bonnin at the butchers or with Madame Mouret at the café or Madame Marcelle among her bobbins, front-lacing corsets and dress-preservers. But such contacts had started as just the normal interchanges of public life to which she had been brought up. ('One should try to take an interest in the village people,' her mother had used to say. 'They do appreciate it.') She could hardly pretend to herself that this was an adequate substitute for relationships with people of her own class and education.

There was Mlle. Bisset. In other circumstances, Jane was well aware, she would have considered the Post Mistress just 'a nice little woman', perhaps better educated than the rest of the community but hardly material for close friendship. Mlle. Bisset liked things dainty, she confided in Jane; one day when she invited Jane into the back room of the Post Office to admire some material she had just bought to make a dress, Jane indeed saw Mlle. Bisset's cold lunch 'daintily' laid out ready on an embroidered cloth. But she was warm and sympathetic and had seen a little more of the world than the Berry: she had even spent three months in Paris with a married sister, and Jane clung to her. Mlle. Bisset did not need to ask Jane if she had any news of Pierre: she saw all the letters that arrived, and so knew that no news could have come. One day, when Jane called just to say 'Hallo', she said comfortingly:

"They're bringing out printed cards now, for communication between one Zone and another. Cards on which you can transmit family news, and you cross out the words or the sections that don't apply. From next week all communication with the Occupied Zone has got to be by means of these cards, but you know, perhaps it's better that way, mm? At least, like that, one will know that the information is getting through. I expect you'll get one of these cards soon from your husband, and then your mind will be at rest."

"If only there was somebody else I could ask for news . . ." said Jane.

She knew virtually none of Pierre's friends, certainly none living locally. Once, in Paris, they had met another young couple for dinner and she had liked them, but of course she did not know their address. She told herself that the relationship between herself and Pierre had been too new, too intense and intent upon itself to admit of a gradually developing network of shared social contacts. They had had only the one summer really together in France, here in a place that was not even Pierre's home, and after that only snatched weekends . . . But she admitted to herself, thinking it over, that friends and social life were probably more important to her than they were to Pierre anyway. With him, the loquacious, sociable manner of the well-brought-up Frenchman, which she had at first taken to be his real self, in reality masked the rather secretive personality of the natural loner. He had been an only child, he was more comfortable in one-to-one conversation than in a group; it had seemed to be natural to him to settle down into a closed, family intimacy with herself and Mark, but he had not made many other friends in London. Perhaps, she thought suddenly, seeing their coming-together for the first time not as something unique and extraordinary but in the perspective of both their lives – perhaps he wanted to join us really because we were a ready-made family for him, and this is the way of life he understands best. I'm sure he was lonely in London before. And perhaps, she thought, it had been typical of him, too, to bring them here, to a kind of secret place, an idyllic retreat away from ordinary life.

But even if St Laurent-la-Rivière had been Pierre's boyhood home, Jane doubted if the surrounding countryside would not have revealed itself as being full of families like the Lepardes. Pierre had seemed to accept it as normal that a village should have almost no middle-class inhabitants: the Yrieuxs had indeed been, as he said, the solitary representatives of the bourgeoisie. But quite early on it had struck Jane how different this pattern was from that of the southern English villages she knew. An English village the size of St Laurent, particularly in such countryside and not in a totally inaccessible region, would have had a dozen or more middle-class houses. There would, she thought, have been a retired colonel or major and his lady, and a doctor, and maybe a solicitor with a practice in the local town, and several well-educated spinsters or widowed sisters sharing chintzy interiors; the Vicar would have had a wife and family, there would probably have been a 'gentleman farmer' or two, and perhaps even a writer or painter living in a cottage such as her own. From her own childhood, she knew that these people would have formed a cosy group distinct from the village, exchanging sherry together on Sunday mornings. In her present loneliness, she would gladly have joined such a circle, even if it had been faintly reminiscent of life in Henley. But in St Laurent it simply did not exist. The village was far more homogeneous and tight-knit than its English equivalent would have been. Initially she had found this charming; there had seemed to her a toy-quality about St Laurent that first summer, and the cottage had seemed a toy home, a place to play at married life together, not a serious permanent dwelling which would enslave them. But without Pierre, she saw it differently.

She supposed that Châtelet-le-Lys must have a sprinkling of what her mother had called evasively 'people of our sort, dear'. It presumably had a few doctors and lawyers and the Head of the local High School, if no one else. She had, come to think of it, even met one or two such people at the Yrieuxs. But, remembering them, she felt very alien to them, more alien in a way than to the village people. They would live in those large Victorian houses on the fringe of Châtelet, with high gate-posts and cement pineapples. They would go to Mass each Sunday and dress with an old-fashioned correctness that was uncompromisingly urban. In short, they would be versions of Mlle. Yrieux, and probably all Pétainist as she was.

... And even if they weren't, how was she to meet them? Doubtless none of them knew of her existence.

Did she have an existence, officially? Her identity card was a false one; it corresponded to no entry in a record anywhere. No one, literally no one, elsewhere in France knew that she was here, except Pierre and his father and Mlle. Yrieux and maybe one or two other members of his family, all of whom probably hoped she had by now taken herself off to England.

And the time went on, and Pierre did not return.

Where, *where* could he be? Her mind ranged again and again over the map of France, concentrating now on that region, now on this, as if by sheer strength of will and emotion she could thus somehow perceive his present whereabouts. Marseilles ... Paris ... Rheims ... ? Her imagination wandered like a lost spirit over the hundreds of kilometres in between. Somewhere, *somewhere* over that wide land, he too was thinking of her.

It did not occur to her that he might, by then, no longer be in France at all.

All Saints' Eve arrived, with the school concert. Jane, crushed into the audience of peasants in Sunday clothes, many of whom had received their few years of education in this same building, thought how nice the children looked on the whole, and how well they had been trained to sing, and felt grateful to Monsieur Picard for arranging it all even if it did end with *'Maréchal, nous voilà!'* Were those words, in any case, really more or less appropriate to life in general than *'Aux armes, citoyens'*? Mark, in the second-to-back row with the other boys of his age, looked perfectly at home, all the more so since she had sent him to the village barbers; he now had the same ferociously shorn head as all the rest.

The following day, November 1st, was a kind of supernumary Sunday. The smells of succulent lunches drifted from the windows along the street, and later in the afternoon small parties of people visited the cemetery to deposit drooping, mop-headed chrysanthemums or dead-looking wax wreaths on family graves. Jane thought, not for the first time, how odd it was that French country cemeteries should be so much less beautiful than the fields all round them: they were grassless places of dust and monstrous stones. But the view from this one was lovely, with the curve of the river and the woods below. How odd it must be to live in the village, and know beyond any doubt that one day you would lie here.

No, it was not odd really, now that she thought about it. On the contrary, it was her own life that was strange, dislocated and torn out of context. What had she done for the first twenty-nine years? What was she doing now?

There was Mark. She clung to that thought. His birth and upbringing at any rate gave a thread of coherence to an otherwise disjointed saga. But what violence had she done to him and his birth-right, by bringing him here?

That evening, she felt so wretched, and so desperate for some means of beginning to seek for Pierre, that she called impulsively on the Picards, who lived in the rather cramped quarters on the top floor of the school. They had, she realised with embarrassment, hardly finished their supper. Monsieur Picard was still masticating cheese. Their children, three little girls with Madame Picard's pinched, red-haired looks, stared at her. Madame Picard, after a pause, offered her a glass of wine and an apple, which she ate while they made awkward small-talk. She complimented Monsieur Picard on the concert; he replied that it was hard to organise such events in these times, but 'one must make the effort to encourage the children to take a proper pride in themselves.' Then suddenly he wiped his mouth with a napkin, announced that Jane and he would go elsewhere for their discussion, and shepherded her off downstairs to the schoolroom. Jane realised with embarrassment that he thought she wanted to see him on a school matter: she hadn't meant to exclude Madame Picard, and anyway the schoolroom was cold, the stove would not be lit again till tomorrow morning. Monsieur Picard gestured her towards a form and sat at his own desk, a situation hardly conducive to a discussion between adults, she thought.

"Was it about your boy? You've no need to worry about him, you know. As I've told you before, he's doing well – very well, considering the language difficulty he has had to surmount. He and young Petitjean are my best scholars in that year. His spelling needs much attention still, but I suppose that is normal with a bi-lingual child."

"It – it isn't about Marc, Monsieur Picard. I know he's doing all right, and I'm grateful for the special attention you've given him."

"Bah, it's my job ... Is it about your card then – your papers – do you need a frontier pass or something? If so, you should really come and see me when I'm in the Mairie, you know."

She said desperately,

"Oh please – I know you probably won't know any more than I do – but how does one begin to look for someone who has disappeared?"

He spread out his hands in the Gallic gesture which she had once imagined to be peculiar to Pierre.

"Ah – that. How, indeed. It's your husband you're talking about?"

"Of course."

"Mmhm. You know, I'm very much surprised to hear he is missing, very surprised indeed. That priority ticket he had in order to go to – wherever it was – was perfectly in order; I made it out myself for Monsieur Marceau to sign. Of course the police in Châtelet had to countersign it, but that was no problem either, Mouret sees to that for us."

She explained the real reason for Pierre's journey to the south, and also added her fears that he had had to re-cross the Zone frontier again with inadequate documents. His eyelids moved but he still looked unimpressed.

"Let us keep calm. People are inventing pretexts for journeys all the time. Naturally. There is no great danger, the authorities cannot possibly check up properly on everybody or even on a tiny fraction of them ... However, there is always the possibility that your husband has had the misfortune to be one of that minority. He could have been caught in a random scrutiny."

"Yes. I've been thinking that. He is a very careful person, but –" She left the sentence unfinished, suddenly wondering if it were true, anyway.

"There is another possibility. You say that your husband had it in mind to enquire about a means for you and your boy to leave France ... I do not like to put evil thoughts into your head, but I am wondering if he can by any chance have fallen into the hands of people who appeared likely to be of use but who have in fact betrayed him to unfriendly authorities."

"Are there such people?"

"Most certainly, there must be."

She looked at him sitting there so calmly in his grey worsted suit and his rimless glasses and had a horrible suspicion about him. But, if Monsieur Picard himself could not be trusted, it was far, far too late for her to withdraw trust from him. She could only continue along the way she had begun.

"Monsieur, if – if my husband *has* been taken prisoner again – had his parole revoked –"

"You will certainly hear this news sooner or later from his family, will you not? One is allowed to communicate that fact; I have seen the new correspondence cards."

She said: "His family would rather pretend I don't exist" – and burst into tears.

As if well-accustomed to women crying he patted her shoulder, exhorted her to courage, and even produced a clean handkerchief of his own for her. He did not, she registered as she sniffed and mopped, seem disconcerted by what she had just said. Evidently, she thought with pain, he had already drawn his own conclusions.

"Now let us see," he said, re-seating himself behind his

desk as if deliberately to restore the space between himself and her. "There are, of course, various agencies to which I believe one can apply for information concerning missing persons. The Red Cross, principally. Or, for the Occupied Zone, there is a German Police Information Bureau . . . You know, from what you tell me, by far the most likely is that he has met with problems in returning to the north . . ." He appeared to hesitate,

"Will you let me give you some advice?"

"Please do," she said, blowing her nose.

"If I were you, I would refrain from instituting any such search. Yes, I know this may seem hard advice. But if you start contacting official agencies to try to trace your husband you run a grave risk of drawing attention to yourself – and your boy. I am sure, I am quite sure, that your husband would say the same as I do. Your papers will not bear any investigation. Do nothing, Madame! Continue to lie low here. Who knows, one day – perhaps sooner than either of us imagines – your husband may walk down that road again from the station."

As she bowed her head over the desk in front of her, clenching her teeth and tautening her throat to keep herself from crying again, she had a sudden impression that he was smiling to himself. But as she looked up again sharply, she found him moving papers about on his desk.

As she got up to go, he said suddenly, almost in an undertone as if offering her something not on offer to everyone, like Bonnin the butcher with a leg of mutton,

"Would you like me to make certain enquiries on your behalf? I mean that I would contact the various authorities as if I were doing it on my own initiative – as the Mayor's Secretary in a small place making a routine check on the whereabouts of someone previously domiciled here. His priority-ticket must have expired by now."

"Oh yes!" she said. "Yes, please, *please* do."

"I'll let you know of course as soon as I discover anything. If I do."

"Oh *thank* you Monsieur Picard. Thank you very much indeed."

"Bah, it's just my job," he said with affected modesty. He escorted her to the door and bade her goodbye with a friendly hand-clasp. Not till he had bolted the door of the school carefully after her did it occur to her that her thanks to him would have been much less effusive had he not seemed, in the first place, so cool and unhelpful. It was almost as if he had beaten her down initially and reduced her to tears in order to raise her up again.

She washed and ironed the handkerchief and returned it to Madame Picard, who received it with a look of nervous surprise.

December came. The winter set in, colder than the preceding one had been. It seemed to Jane that her hope of suddenly hearing from Pierre ebbed and ebbed along with the temperature. The memory that she had once been happy was as distant and theoretical as the memory of a hot summer's day when one sees the same landscape gaunt and apparently dead under a winter sky.

One Thursday afternoon a fortnight before Christmas, when it was just over twelve weeks since Pierre had disappeared, Monsieur Picard knocked at her door. She rushed to let him in – his expression did not suggest that he had good news, but you never knew, with him. Pierre, she thought, oh Pierre! Extraordinary, now, to think how joyfully she would welcome even the news that he was back in prison, since that would be safety, of a kind, and an end to torturing speculation.

But Monsieur Picard had no news at all. That was what he had come to tell her. Everywhere he had tried he had drawn a blank.

"That still does not mean, Madame, that your husband is not in prison somewhere. It just means that his name is not on any of the lists – the list of the Deported, for instance. But there has been so much disturbance in France these last months ... The lists are rather approximate, I should imagine."

She said: "The Deported?"

"Yes. Deported to camps in Germany. That is normally the fate of prisoners of war, at the moment, it seems."

She had not realised that, and at once wondered why she had not. It was obvious, really. After a pause she asked,

"What – what other lists are there?"

"Well, the list of those still held in France. And, of course, the lists of those who have been shot, Madame."

"Shot?"

"Shot – executed." Monsieur Picard looked at her hard with eyes he seemed to be making deliberately expressionless behind his glasses. Then he added,

"But a prisoner of war is not normally shot, unless in exceptional circumstances ... Anyway, as I say, his name is not on any of these lists. So far as I have been able to ascertain. I have asked the offices concerned for a re-check, but one should not pin too many hopes on that ..." He paused, and then said smoothly, "I ought to tell you that the other day the Mairie also received an enquiry from his family in Paris, asking if he was in the district. Evidently they have been making the same search that we have. So do not fear, Madame, that he has abandoned you to return to his parents. It would seem indeed that he has simply – disappeared. You have my deepest sympathy."

She would not cry in front of him again. But after he had gone she went upstairs to the attic. Since it was the weekly half-day from school, Mark was there. He had his stamp album open beside him; he had brought it from England, but had not had the opportunity to add much to the collection since. He rarely got it out these days, it was part of his old, lost life; but Mlle. Bisset had recently shown Jane the new stamps that were being issued, and she had bought a set for him. The one-franc stamp for packets showed Marshal Pétain's saintly, grandfatherly face, but there was an alternative stamp you could buy for one franc plus five centimes surcharge. It bore the legend 'For Our Prisoners of War' and showed some French soldiers languishing inside a barbed wire compound, one of them seated and reading a letter.

She sat down on the floor beside him and clung to him, weeping passionately. He had never seen her cry like that before. At first, when he understood what she was crying for, he strained slightly away from her, like a dog or a cat that does not want to be fondled, eyeing her sideways with a mixture of consternation and aloofness. But presently, as if realising that she was not going to be the one to pull herself together, he seemed to change his mind, and put out a tentative hand to stroke her cheek.

"Ugh, you're all wet!"

"I'm sorry, I'm sorry . . . I can't . . ."

"Silly old Mum. You needn't cry. I'll look after you."

She had thought it was only in sentimental Victorian tales that children said this to their mothers. A moment later, he made his point still clearer by adding,

"You don't need Pierre so much as you would if you didn't have me." Funny, she thought through her distress; he always seemed to like Pierre so much and get on so well with him, accepting him as a new father, never a sign of jealousy . . . Yet now there was a faint edge of triumph in the boy's tone, almost as if he had witnessed the downfall of a rival. He was growing older, of course: it was probably to be expected.

But would an English schoolboy have reacted in this way? A boy kept in isolation from adult life and emotions, trained to think of nothing but cricket and football and Latin, brought up to regard home-life as an occasional treat and adults as distant, powerful people whose preoccupations were fundamentally different from his own? She thought not.

Perhaps, even now, it had not been such a terrible thing to bring Mark to live in France. Perhaps, after all, he and she would both gain something from this hard, cold time.

But the winter went on. And there was never any news of Pierre.

Part Three

The early months of 1941 turned out to be one of the hardest winters for fifty years, Jane was forced to recognise that Pierre had been right the year before, when he had made her buy warm underclothes. She was glad of her blue corduroy trousers and tweed suit. She occasionally thought regretfully of her fur coat, hanging unused in Debenhams' cold store, but it was more of a theoretical regret, a vague self-blame, than a keenly felt one. Debenhams and Selfridges and Marylebone High Street seemed unimaginably far away now. Even Paris seemed distant and unreal.

She worried more actively about how she would manage when Mark grew out of his present stock of jerseys and shorts. His thighs and wrists seemed more noticeable than they used to be. Fortunately the overcoat they had brought from England had been a new one with 'room for growing', but he was just eleven now and in another year or so would presumably begin expanding at a more alarming rate. New clothes, she had heard from Madame Marcelle, were becoming unobtainable, and even if one could find them a clothing card was necessary for the purchase, and she and Mark had none. She took a little comfort from the thought of a spare pair of Pierre's trousers – unfortunately not his thickest, those he had been wearing when he left – which were hanging in the wardrobe. Eventually Mark could wear those, if the War lasted so long.

Then, in a pang of self-reproach, she thought: what on earth am I doing feeling sorry that Pierre was wearing his thickest ones when he left? That means that at least he may have them on now, *now* at this moment, as I stand at the table peeling potatoes on the coldest, darkest day of the winter. It's one tiny thing to be thankful for. And his hunting boots and his officer's cape too.

Oh, God, if you exist, I don't actually think you do but *if* – please make Pierre still be wearing those warm things. Don't let Them have taken them away from him.

She kept the stove going day and night, but still she could not seem to defeat the bitter cold which came up from the cottage's uneven tiled floors, or rather from the earth immediately beneath them. Was the place damp? She feared it must be, thinking of the simple way in which it had, long ago, been constructed: great stones just piled up, one upon another, into thick rough walls, with plaster slapped straight on top of them. There were several stained, flaky places where the plaster never seemed quite dry, winter or summer, and one day when she was prodding experimentally at one of those a great hunk of plaster detached itself and fell crumbling at her feet like a piece of rotting cheese.

She plumbed her memory for what she knew of twentieth-century building methods, and came up with 'damp course' and 'cavity wall'. The first, presumably, had been unknown in rural France a century or more ago, but as for cavities the walls seemed full of them – the chinks and tunnels between the stones where they heard the field mice scuttling at night. Pierre had used to say that they undoubtedly had a whole town there, with steps, alleys, steep descents and habitations perched on ledges, like a Mediterranean hill town. She didn't mind the mice inside the walls, but wished they wouldn't venture so boldly into the kitchen at night. The dormice were the worst: they didn't seem to know that they ought to be in hibernation at this time, or perhaps the ever-burning stove had upset their natural cycles: she used to find their droppings and their footprints all round the scullery slop-stone in the mornings. They nibbled the soap and anything else they could find; she had to take to shutting all packaged food and vegetables away in the meat safe. One night, when they were noisier than usual, she woke, reeled into the kitchen and snapped on the light. Two plump creatures with decoratively striped faces and eyes like beads stared at her from the table-top, but did not move. Between them was a large crust of bread which they were evidently trying to drag away between them, like two porters with a steamer trunk. After a long, self-conscious pause she hissed and waved her arms and they ran away, abandoning their load, but she heard them return as soon as the kitchen was dark again. They returned every night.

The winter countryside, apparently so dead and drear during the short days, seemed in the nights full of a tenacious and slightly hostile life, like a hidden resistance force in occupied territory. Under cover of dark a horde of small destroyers moved in, gnawing away at wood and sacking, eating stored grain, sucking the insides from eggs laid down in preserving fluid, pillaging and despoiling. But these secret forces also waged battles between themselves: sometimes if she had to go down the dark garden path at night, she would hear the cries of some small animal meeting its end in a ditch. Twice she saw an owl flap and swoop low in the moonlight, and night after night another one, a screech-owl, made its strange sound in the meadow: she did not know what it was till Langlois told her. Close to, its slow screech was like a rasp of a saw across wood, but when it was further away it sounded like a person somewhere, stertorously breathing, with vague, all-embracing menace. She understood now the origin of some pretend-joke Pierre had had with Mark early on, about a giant in the meadow, and which had been supposed to be a secret from her.

During a particularly bitter week at the beginning of February, when a crust of half-melted and re-frozen snow lay on the roadside verges, she moved Mark's bed out of the bedroom and into the kitchen nearer the stove. She couldn't move her own, larger bed – it didn't look as if it would even go through the door – but she laid a padding of newspaper on the floor and spread her own mattress and bedding on that each night, taking it up again every morning. Mice or no mice, there seemed no point in forsaking a warm room at night for the freezing bedrooms.

At rare intervals she thought disbelievingly of Henley. She thought of the boiler stoked every morning by the cook before she herself had been awake. She thought of the radiators in the hall and dining room, and of the gallons of hot water always ready to fill the bath. She thought of the upstairs and downstairs lavatories, and of the big gas fire in the bedroom which was lit at six every evening. She thought of carpets and armchairs and bland, smooth cleanness.

She really did not regret any of it. If only – only – Pierre had been with them, or even if he had just been safe in some known place from which he could write her letters, then, she believed, she would have been perfectly happy here, in spite of everything. She had never cared much for physical comfort, as such. Sometimes she thought of the song *The Raggle-taggle Gipsies-oh*, which her mother had played on the piano for herself and Susie to sing as children:

What care I for my goose-feather bed
With the sheet turned down so dainty-oh –
What care I for my newly-wedded lord?
For I'm off with the Raggle-taggle gipsies-oh!

'Poor lord' Susie had used to say gravely. But Jane herself had been, as a matter of principle, on the side of the gipsies, and the woman who escapes from her comfortable life to join them. Perhaps that romantic nursery song had marked her life.

Huddling into bed on the floor near the sleeping Mark, wearing an old pair of Pierre's socks and a jersey over her pyjamas, she sometimes hummed the refrain to herself with a tiny amusement, then saying to herself in a Nanny's voice, 'What did I tell you? You've brought it on yourself?'

Sometimes, lying awake in the dark, hearing the screech-owl breathe in the meadow, counting the quarters chimed by the cracked church bell, she tried to reach Pierre. Not in her imagination but in her essential being, on some dark plane where time and space were both unmeasurable, a still centre of the turning world where everything went on existing for ever and 'then' and 'now', 'near' and 'far', were irrelevant, short-sighted concepts. Spiritually, perhaps, she told herself, he was so near to her at that very moment that, had his presence been translated into physical terms, merely by stretching out a finger in the dark she could have touched him ... At other times she thought of the night sky, and then of all the other night-watchers all down history who had looked on the vast, lonely space and had made it familiar and homely, populating the black vault with recognisable men and beasts: the Water-carrier, the Bull, the two Bears, the Seven Sisters, Orion. It was only with her intellect that she knew the sky to be a black vista of other worlds, infinitely remote and uncaring. Emotionally, she told herself, it was something quite other. A protective vault hanging near to earth, glittering more and more brightly the longer you looked at it; or something still closer and more intimate than that – a moth-eaten blanket right on top of you, through the many tiny holes of which you could glimpse an unchanging, heavenly light.

She would drift off to sleep uplifted and comforted. But when each morning came the vault was transformed into a low, grey, uncaring sky, and small flurries of snow blew against the black hedgerows as Mark set off for school. The stove smoked sometimes and the wind rattled the door, and all the morning and all the afternoon she was alone.

For several days they both had bad colds, and she kept Mark at home. She sent him to school again the following Monday, but he coughed so much that evening and looked so pale and pasty that on Tuesday she kept him at home again. On Wednesday he was wheezing and, though she had no thermometer, she was fairly sure he had a temperature. After a worried consultation with Mlle. Bisset in the post office, she decided to get the afternoon bus into Châtelet-le-Lys to see what the chemist there could recommend for bronchitis. There was no chemist in St Laurent. It was just as well this was the day the bus ran. Six miles there on a bicycle, on the icy road, and six miles back with the wind from the mountains in her face, would hardly have done the remnants of her own cold much good, she thought. She had never fussed before in her life about her own health (that had been something middle-aged people did) but she was uncomfortably aware now that she herself must remain well enough to fetch the wood, light the stove, scrub and peel the vegetables, cart the dirty water out to the ditch.

What, oh God what, she thought with a clutch of panic, would Mark do here if anything should happen to her?

She put the speculation aside as morbid and unnecessary. Almost as bad as wondering what would become of herself if Mark developed pneumonia, and –

Hush.

The bus, now fuelled not by petrol but by smouldering charcoal in a specially constructed box, trundled and wheezed towards the town as if it had bronchitis itself. It stopped in the square opposite the Town Hall and the war memorial, and as she made her way over to the main shopping street she noticed that the big house next to the Town Hall with a walled, private garden was a doctor's house: a brass plate gave the times when he saw patients. For a moment she hesitated, thinking: if Mark gets any worse . . . But she passed on. She could not get a sick Mark to town except on the bus, and that wouldn't run again till Saturday. She had heard that even doctors had very little petrol for home visits, and why should she suppose that this unknown one (*Faculté de Médecine, Université de Toulouse*) would be prepared to come all the way to St Laurent to visit a household he did not know? And there was in any case the basic, underlying fear which reasserted itself: it was not wise to make contact with a strange doctor in Châtelet, it was in fact dangerous. How could she be sure he would not mention her illicit presence in the area to what she thought of, in general terms, as 'the authorities'. Doctors were by nature conformists, inclined to uphold authority. All except Pierre, of course.

It was worrying enough in any case just going into Châtelet, where inevitably she came up against unknown shop-keepers who might be hostile. But at least the chemist in the market place had known her by sight for some time and seemed a pleasant old man. She went and consulted him on ailments of the respiratory tract, and eventually emerged with many francs worth of suppositories and inhalants and a strong recommendation that she make a hot flannel poultice for Mark's chest – and keep him very, very warm: the night air was particularly dangerous, there was too much oxygen in it for someone with a sensitive chest. She was grateful for his kindly interest, but could not help feeling that the proffered advice was terribly old-fashioned. Of course, French medicine was like that, as Susie's husband had said. The very first time she had met Pierre she had heard them have an enjoyable argument about it, with Geoffrey saying that the French seemed to be stuck in the nineteenth century and Pierre retorting that the British had a compartmentalised, mechanistic approach to the human body and appeared ignorant of the first principles of good diet. If only Geoffrey – for whom she had never particularly cared, rating him as a typical doctor and a little pompous – had materialised now in Châtelet, how warmly she would have flung her arms round him!

The chemist also told her that there was a modern drug which doctors had begun recommending within the last two years for acute pulmonary inflammation, but that he had none of it now and could not get any ('because of the situation, you understand Madame'). She gathered he meant M & B. A lot of medicines were in short supply now, he told her, including anaesthetics.

Because the price of medicines had shocked her, she did not even go to buy a cup of coffee to cheer herself up, but hung about in the part of the Bazaar where books and gramophone records were sold. This proved to be a false economy, for in a sudden fit of what was either madness or a profound sense that life ought to be more than warm underclothes and vegetable soup and essentials from the chemist, she bought a record of the main theme from Beethoven's 'Pastorale'. That would be something to nourish her in its own way, better than the well-worn records of dances and popular songs which she and Mark had now played too often.

Later, she was never to regret the money she spent on that record. But at the time she travelled slowly home feeling guilty and discouraged. Over twenty francs gone in one day. She must look at her Post Office book again, and do a serious reckoning.

When she got back to the cottage Mark was dozing, but woke and seemed better. He said that while she had been gone Mlle. Bisset had called and had made up the stove for him, and that later his friend Jean-Luc Bonnin, the butcher's son, had come, sent by his parents to enquire how the illness was progressing. They had also sent a piece of liver as a present. And Jane took heart again, and felt that this had, after all, *faute de mieux*, become their home, and that they were lucky to be there.

Mark presently recovered. But someone else died in the village during that very cold spell: Madame Audibert, the Yrieuxs' servant. Jane felt guilty that she had not even realised the old woman had been taken ill; it had all happened quickly. She first heard of her death when the Mayor stopped her by the Post Office and asked her what should be done with the keys to the Yrieux house?

"Perhaps someone else could be found to clean and air the house from time to time?" she suggested diffidently, but the Mayor looked dubious. He had no authority to arrange such a matter, he explained. In any case, few people these days had time to spare. And there were no arrangements for paying a new person ... In the end, faintly exasperated by him, she said that in that case she'd better take the keys herself, and he handed them over with expressions of gratitude as he had obviously been intending to do all along.

She visited the house that afternoon, telling herself that she had a perfect right to, in the circumstances, and was indeed doing Mlle. Yrieux a favour; nevertheless she felt like a trespasser or a burglar. The place seemed a mausoleum enshrining a way of life and thought so different from her own that it was hard even to remember that she had, for a brief period, eaten meals in this chill, dust-filmed dining room or played whist in the drawing room where now even the mirrors and pictures wore cotton shrouds. She had never been meant to come here, disturbing this life; Mlle. Yrieux herself had recognised that and had acted accordingly . . .

In what had been Oncle Ernest's study, the guns Pierre had handed in had left their ghostly marks on the wall. The ink had dried in the ink-well. A yellowed newspaper still lay folded on the desk: it might have been giving news of the Last War rather than this one.

In the end, after some hesitation in which was mixed an obscure distaste for the belongings of a family who had so rejected her, she took away with her a few of the books that looked readable. There were, she realised, whole shelves of pious works in various rooms, presumably Mlle. Yrieux's property, which repelled her. From the beds upstairs she took two thick rugs and, as an afterthought, two stone hot water bottles. From the kitchen she took the few tins of food and bottles of wine she could find – stocks seemed to have been run low – and also the wireless set. It was a cheap, poor quality set, but Mark would like to have it.

She stood for a while in front of the cabinet of lead soldiers, but she did not have the key to it. Anyway, she told herself, that might indeed have seemed more like stealing than like a sensible wartime borrowing of useful objects. In any case Mark, who had loved them so a year ago, was perhaps getting beyond the age for soldiers. So she left them sealed away behind their glass, with their motionless, raised spears and their tiny, silent drums, unwatched and alone. And she left the whole house alone again, shutting and double-locking its heavy door, abandoning it to small, scuttling things and to the slow, creeping damp.

In her own cottage, the dormice remained a problem. Opening a cupboard in which some spare bed-linen had been put away, she found a whole nest beautifully constructed from a chewed-up sheet. Madame Langlois, who had no sympathy at all with the rodent world, and no admiration for their skills, said that poisoned wheat might help, and she would get her husband to bring some over, but that dormice were that artful (as well as being lazy and dirty), they tended to recognise the wheat and not to eat it. The only thing that would really do the trick, she said, was a cat. Jane had refrained from getting any animal up to then, from an unspoken feeling that after all her tenancy there with Mark was not permanent or predictable. Might they not, one day, need to take a sudden departure ...? But now, cross about the sheets, she procured a yellowish kitten from a nearby farm. He was a fine, broad-headed creature with faint tiger stripes, as if there still moved through his small frame the blood of some wildcat ancestor, infinitely remote in the turnover of feline generations. She thought that as he was a tom she ought to have him 'done', remembering the pristine, domesticated pussies of her childhood, but apparently no one bothered to doctor cats in rural France; the people she asked seemed amused by the very idea, and she felt rather a fool.

For several months the cat thrived, keeping her company by the stove during the day and acting as mouse-scourge during the hours of darkness. Even if he did not catch many, he must have frightened them away, for the nightly scufflings ceased. He grew large and sleek and demanding, forgetting that he had been born a barn-cat of a half-starved mother. But when at last the spring came he took to going further and further afield and sometimes disappeared for whole days at a time. Jane and Mark decided that he probably had girl-friends to see, and hence duels to fight, throughout the neighbourhood and that it was no use worrying about him. But eventually he just did not come back at all. A few days later Jane found him by chance in the little copse near their house, where she had gone to pick bluebells. He had been killed, and partly gnawed, by some animal – presumably a fox – who must have been disturbed at his feast and abandoned it. Jane, horrified by this transformation of a soft, responsive friend into an object of bloody horror, buried him quickly. She did not tell Mark the truth, saying instead that Thomas had no doubt gone seeking bigger hunting grounds, greater opportunities for his obvious prowess, and that this was only natural and they must not mourn him. But she herself minded so much that, dormice or no dormice, she refused to get another cat. Why lay yourself open to further grief? It was better not to form the attachment in the first place. She had always, before, rather despised people who took that attitude to life, but now, for her, it seemed the only possible one. Why give further hostages to fortune when she was so heavily committed in that dircction already?

In any case she had other worries on her mind. Long before the late spring at last brought relief to the hard earth and to people's sore lips and fingers, the ration-card problem had presented itself. In theory, numbers of everyday things were now only obtainable in return for allocated coupons: butter, oil, eggs, milk, sugar, meat, tinned foods, wine, tobacco, soap (inferior now and gritty), coffee (also an inferior, ersatz powder) – these were all rationed. In practice, however, in a countryside entirely composed of small, mixed farms, the problem was to some extent surmountable, even by someone in Jane's position. Of the list of precious commodities, all forms of meat and dairy products were produced and sold around the villages of the Berry without any official apparently taking a close interest in the matter. So, of course, were vegetables, fruits and wine; people spoke with a pity that was almost disbelieving of the tales that filtered out of the larger towns of people queuing for hours for beetroots or cabbages. But the prices on this 'free' market were creeping upwards all the time, and in any case even the fertile Berry did not produce soap or sugar. In March, she was offered a kilo of honey by the old bee-man living down the road, and accepted it gladly, thinking that now she and Mark could have honey in their hot milk in the mornings, this giving it the semblance of milky coffee. And she could give him bread and honey when he came home cold and tired from school. But she was horrified to find that the asking price, which that time last year had been seven francs, fifty centimes, was now over thirty francs. And, since bread tickets were being introduced, what would she put the honey on anyway?

She went grimly to Picard at the Mairie, expecting him to say that it was extremely hazardous for him to procure false bread cards for her and Mark, which he did. But (as she had also expected, wise to him by now) he eventually produced two counterfeit bread cards, and did not even charge her for them. But he warned her that, in future, if checks on the number of cards being issued were tightened up, he might not be able to renew them. He suggested instead that she look around for a regular supply of 'real' false cards. There were, he explained, 'false false' ones, like hers, and 'real false' ones, which were genuine cards that had been issued through the normal channels to people who did not actually need them because they grew their own provisions. Quite a lot of people, he said, in a sudden access of frankness, had two cards for most commodities anyway – one really their own and the other illicitly acquired. After all, the strict ration was too stingy to support a healthy existence, wasn't it?

Confused by an English concept of fairness, Jane said,

"But – the people in the shops: Monsieur Bonnin and the baker and Madame Maure at the grocers and so on – they know everyone in the neighbourhood. So they must surely realise when a person comes in for a second loaf of bread or another thirty grams of meat when they've already had some?"

"Bah, of course they know – but why should they worry? The more tickets that Bonnin or Madame Maure have to give in at the end of the month to the distribution centre, the better, from their point of view: it means that their allocations for the next month will be that much bigger. The more that can be squeezed out of the authorities the better: we must protect ourselves. France is being bled white, with all the produce that is being shipped off to Germany."

Evidently, Jane realised, in an occupied country or even in the fictionally free land of Vichy-France, black marketing and the evasion of rules, instead of being disgraceful, unpatriotic activities, were normal and commendable.

After turning the matter over in her mind for several days, on the spur of the moment she approached Jeanot Langlois, whom she came upon carting manure. He genially asked her if she'd like some for her vegetable garden, as he was passing, and she accepted, but shyly added that what she really needed was a bread card 'if ever his family should have one to spare'. She knew that they grew their own wheat, and that Madame Langlois regularly baked.

Jeanot Langlois agreed readily, seeming quite unsurprised. He added that he could easily get her extra meat and fat cards too: she only had to say the word.

Awkwardly she said:

"Yes, fat cards *would* be useful. I've been buying butter from the people nearby, the Michards, where we fetch our milk, though they don't always have it to sell now that the cows are beginning to calve. But I hadn't really thought of getting us meat cards. Proper meat has got so awfully expensive. Recently, I've just been buying bits of salt pork or sausage – you know, the things Bonnin sells when he has them that aren't really part of the ration."

Jeanot looked shocked.

"You mean you've *no* meat cards?"

"No."

"But – can't Picard make you one?"

"He hasn't offered to."

Jeanot's face wore the expression of one who would like to say what he thought of Picard but was restraining himself. At last he said,

"But why did you not mention this to my father or mother already? Our family would have been only too happy –"

More embarrassed then ever, realising that, because he probably still thought of her as a rich lady from the town, he still had not realised her predicament, she said,

"I'm afraid I shouldn't really use our savings on buying *one* meat card, let alone two. Extra cards must be valuable things these days. Naturally I can't expect your family or anyone else to give us cards for nothing."

Still looking shocked and disapproving, he digested this almost in silence. Then he left, remarking to her over his shoulder that she could count on him.

That evening, as it was getting dark, he appeared again with his horse and cart in the road. He called to Mark who was, as usual, hunting for one of his tennis balls in the grass by the ditch. Standing at the cottage door, Jane saw him hand a couple of things to Mark, touch his cap, and then urge the horse briskly on his way.

Mark brought the objects to Jane. There was an envelope containing two bread cards and two fat cards with all trace of the owners' names carefully scraped off. On the front of the envelope was written one word *'Gratuite'* – 'Free'. The other thing was a large, unplucked chicken.

She supposed that Jeanot had probably conveyed the information about her newly-poor situation to the rest of the Langlois clan. Their respectful manner to her did not change, but they appeared, if anything, more often to see how she was getting on; Jeanot's father dug the vegetable garden over as usual and planted it that spring. It was odd for Jane now to remember the time when the superfluity of vegetables he had produced for them had been a source of mild difficulty and amusement to them, and Pierre had said "After all, you don't want to spend your evenings making soup." These last two or three months she and Mark had been practically living on the potatoes, carrots, leeks and winter cabbage from the garden, and she was looking forward impatiently to the first spinach, lettuce and bean crops of the summer.

She felt that she owed it to Langlois to make her position clear to him, and to say that she herself should maybe take over the gardening as she had the housework the year before. She had no experience of growing vegetables, but supposed that she could learn. But the suggestion seemed almost to offend him.

"I'm not worried about being paid, Madame. And I can provide all the seedlings out of my own garden – I always have plenty to spare. Monsieur Leparde will doubtless reckon up with me when he returns from the War."

She was grateful to him for his faith in this event. Indeed, partly from lack of firm information and partly to keep her courage up, she had not told anyone apart from Monsieur Picard and Mlle. Bisset that Pierre had disappeared. People supposed he had had his parole revoked for some reason. When asked a direct question she always said that he was a prisoner, and the questioner would look respectful and sympathetic and ask little more. She preferred it this way.

People like Madame Mouret, whom she had once seen frequently, she tended to avoid. Madame Mouret was, after all, a business woman whose job was keeping her restaurant going. Jane felt apologetic that she could no longer afford to eat there, much as she sometimes longed to. She also felt that, in Madame Mouret's eyes, she was socially derated. This time, it was not funny, merely depressing.

It was that spring that Jane first identified Marie Stefan, the mother of the postman and of his darker half-brother. She realised then that she had several times seen her, down by the river or up in the woods, or walking along some road a long way from the village, but each time had assumed she must be some nomad. Marie Stefan, whom no one ever referred to as Madame Stefan, was probably not as old as she looked; she had more white teeth still intact than many of the villagers, but her long, straggling hair was quite grey and her face was deeply wrinkled. Her clothes were a collection of black garments with a look of having been constructed for someone else, or for several different people. She was not offensively dirty, but dirty merely in the way people are who never indulge in anything but a brief splash in a rain water tub. There was a patina on her skin which made it hard to tell what its natural tint should be, and grime was etched into the folds and creases emphasising them as in a lithograph.

She did not often come into the centre of the village, but one day when Jane had braced herself to drop into Bonnin's shop to see if there was anything going, she was there with a sack over her shoulder. Jane gathered that she was trying to sell Bonnin something, but as they broke off their evasive conversation every time another customer came in, it was hard to follow the deal. They didn't seem to mind Jane's own presence, indeed Marie Stefan made room for her in the small shop and smiled at her as if she knew all about her.

"... And that's my last word on the subject. I've told you before, Marie, I don't want trouble at Châtelet," said Bonnin emphatically. "– *Yes*, Madame Pilot, and what can I do for you today? ... No, I'm very sorry, no sausages at all. No, none ... My dear lady, if only I *could* I would most willingly ... Yes, still, only thirty grams this week, I'm afraid ... Yes of course, if your family cares to hold their rations over till next week I might manage – of course I can't promise ... Yes. Yes. *Good* morning, Madame Pilot. My regards to the old man ... Yes, I'll certainly see what I can do ... Ah my God, Marie, you see what problems I have! *All day long* people are coming to me saying 'Oh Monsieur Bonnin, let me have some sausages', 'Oh Jacques, you surely won't refuse me a bit of offal' – What am I to do? I would willingly give everyone exactly what they want, but I can't. And now you come nagging me to buy pheasants off you which you've certainly trapped from somewhere near the town, for you know that if you go on taking them from round here Marceau will carry out his threat and report you ... Do you want to get me into trouble with Them in Châtelet?"

"You know I don't, Jacques, don't be a fool," said the woman amiably, setting down her sack on the sawdust floor to rummage in it.

"I tell you," said Monsieur Bonnin, wiping his face abstractedly with a bloody cloth "with all my problems I'm sweating, just standing here, *sweating* do you hear? Even with the door open."

Jane made to go, feeling that the meek enquiry about bones for stock which she had planned would be the last straw, but Bonnin stopped her.

"No, stay Madame Leparde! Who knows, I might have some giblets for *you* ... *Good* morning, Father, and what may I have the pleasure of – ?"

While he discussed the meat ration with the priest, Marie Stefan winked broadly at Jane. Evidently, in spite of all that Bonnin said, the deal was going through. Jane lingered, and presently saw three pheasants and two other game birds, soft, brilliant feathers and lolling heads, rapidly removed from the sack and stowed somewhere under the butcher's block. Some paper money changed hands and Marie Stefan left the shop, bidding Jane a polite good morning.

Jane got a little pad of giblets wrapped conspiratorially in newspaper, and thrust into her hand with a wink and a nod as 'just something to help fill the boy's belly. I know what boys are –' Emboldened by this kindness, she said, in a low voice,

"How does she kill the pheasants without a gun?"

"Shsh!" Monsieur Bonnin glanced anxiously round the shop, as if a high ranking Vichy official might be lurking in the cold room, or dangling from one of the meat hooks disguised as a side of beef.

"Her son's an expert with a catapult and with traps," he murmured.

"Stefan-Postier?"

"No, no, not him – the younger one. Sylvain. Ah, he's a deep one, he is! They say he's not quite all there, but if *he's* not all there then I'm a genius. He keeps ferrets, too, for the bunnies ... *Good* morning, young miss, and what did Mother want today?"

A few days later, when she had called at the Langlois' farmhouse to thank Jean Langlois for some planting he had done, and had been invited in for a glass of wine, she asked them about Marie Stefan. Was it true, as people said, that she had once been a gipsy?

"She must come from gipsy stock," said Madame Langlois shortly. "Stefan's a gipsy name. Thieves and rogues, the lot of them."

"I don't think she's a gipsy herself," said her daughter-in-law, "she's always been living hereabouts. Cousin Georges remembers her from years ago. He said she was the belle of the village then and all the boys fancied her! Maybe her husband was a gipsy."

"Husband, husband!" scoffed Madame Langlois. "She never had a husband. No one knows who fathered those boys. 'Twasn't the same man each time, that's for sure; they're quite different. Stefan-Postier's a decent enough fellow, I daresay."

"The other one answers polite enough when you meet him on the road," said Jeanot's wife. "I met him the other day when I was taking Baby for a little walk, and he spoke to her ever so nice. But they say he's a bit funny in the head, don't they?"

"He's a clever poacher," said Jeanot, who'd come in with his younger brother Jules and heard this part of the conversation. "But he has queer turns – you know: stands still all at once as if he couldn't hear you and didn't know where he was, and then he falls down unconscious. I remember, because I was in his class at school. Didn't happen often, but you never knew when it was going to. I don't know if he still does it."

"Shame, really," said his wife. "He's a nice looking boy too, for all he's so dark."

"He must be a bit daft, though, for I've heard the lads say he can't read," said Jules. "They never managed to teach him at school."

"They never had much chance to, for he wouldn't *stay* in school," said Jeanot. "He was away more often than he was there. Marie Stefan used to say he'd had another fit, but I don't believe he had 'em that often. We used to see him around looking quite normal. No, he just didn't like school. Didn't suit him."

"Didn't old Vollin threaten to have him put away in a boarding school if he stayed away too much?" said Jules. "Someone told me that."

"Well – he may have threatened it, I suppose. But none of us took much notice of old Vollin, did we?"

"Oh, Monsieur Vollin's bark was much worse than his bite," said Madame Langlois. "He was the old schoolmaster before Picard, Madame Leparde – I always thought he was too soft on these boys really; they learnt to get round him.

But anyway he would never really have sent a boy away to boarding school just because he didn't like his studies. He wouldn't have been so cruel."

After a pause Jeanot Langlois remarked that there were some real gipsies again down by the ford: he'd seen them from the hill field when he was ploughing. They'd had two wagons, so everyone had better look out for their own dogs and horses and chickens.

"No better than common robbers," said his father shortly. "Something ought to be done about them."

"Maybe something will be," said Madame Langlois. "I heard What's-his-name on the wireless yesterday – one of those Government men, anyway – saying that France is going to be cleaned up. One day we'll have no more gipsies, he said. And no more Communists or Jews either. So that will be a blessing, won't it? Our chickens will sleep easier on their roosts."

"I never heard tell that Communists or Jews go after chickens!" said Jeanot, making a joke as if to cover some embarrassment and glancing at Jane as he did so. When she left shortly afterwards he accompanied her to the gate, ostensibly to give her some garlic because she and Mark had finished all theirs. At the gate he said awkwardly:

"You mustn't mind my mother. She doesn't really know what she's talking about. It's different for me – I was with two Jews in the prison camp, and they were as nice boys as you could wish to meet. One was a wireless operator and the other was a bootmaker by trade. Just like anyone else. But people like Mother have never seen a Jew: there aren't any in these parts. She thinks they've all got two heads ... You mustn't mind her."

Jane wanted to say something which would show how much she appreciated his thoughtfulness, but, not finding the words, managed only to thank him effusively for the garlic. Jeanot at least knew that there were other worlds beyond St Laurent, and she felt warmly towards him for it.

*

Having once met Marie Stefan, Jane now kept seeing her. When the early summer warmth made the grass in their lane grow long and soft, she used to come and collect it in the evenings in her sack. It was for her rabbits, she said. She always greeted Jane politely, saying,

"You don't mind if I pick here, do you?" in her soft, surprisingly clear voice. Once or twice, thinking hopefully of future pheasants, Jane sent Mark out to help her.

Then one day she came at lunch time and stood by the open cottage door. Jane suddenly noticed her, and wondered how long she'd been there.

"Come in, won't you?"

But Marie Stefan seemed shy on others' territory. She glanced at her muddy men's boots and at Jane's scrubbed floor and shook her head. She made one or two remarks about the fineness of the day and how well Jane's peas were coming on, and then said,

"It was about the grass for my rabbits, see."

"You know you're welcome to take it from all round our garden. We don't need it."

"It wasn't exactly that ... I've got a lot of rabbits at the moment, see, and they need a lot of grass, and I haven't the time to collect so much. I've had a lot to do, these days; my boy's not been too good again ... Sylvain, that is ..."

"Oh? I'm sorry to hear that –"

But Marie Stefan did not seem keen to enlarge on Sylvain's disabilities. She said,

"What I was thinking was – if your little lad liked to collect grass for me each evening, regular-like, for a few weeks, then I'd give him two rabbits out of the new litters when they're big enough."

"Oh, I'm sure he'd like that. How kind of you, Marie Stefan."

"I'd let him have a buck and a doe, see. To start you off, like."

"Lovely," said Jane, not really considering the implications of this offer.

"I hope you didn't mind my suggesting it," said Marie Stefan, backing away, suddenly shy again.

"No, no, it's a very good idea ... Now that the evenings are getting longer ..."

"Then I'll leave this sack with you," said Marie, dropping it on the step. "Plantains, they like, tell your lad. And dandelions, of course. And nice soft grass, but not couch grass."

In fact, as Mark was given a lot of homework these days, and also liked to play football after school as the evenings lengthened, it was often Jane herself who stuffed the sack with the rabbits' evening collation. But for form's sake she usually made Mark take it on the saddle of his bicycle down the road and along the bumpy field path that wound round the base of the woods to where the Stefans' cottage lay, right under the hill where the crops met the bracken and heather. He reported that there was a dog there 'one of those French ones who are always tied up'.

"I know. It's a shame, isn't it?"

"Yes, *I* think so. But I think they're quite nice to this dog, actually. When I came last night they'd just finished eating, and Marie Stefan poured the rest of the stew that was left into her own plate and then put it down for the dog. Then it licked the plate absolutely clean – you know how they do?"

"Yes, I know."

"– And then Marie Stefan gave him the other plates and he licked them too, and then she just put them up on the shelf as if they'd been washed!"

"Mark, she *must* have been going to wash them later."

"I bet she doesn't. They haven't got a pump there, or even a well – I noticed particularly. They go down to fetch the water from that little stream that runs into the river. I've seen Sylvain fetch it."

From time to time Jane went there herself. The cottage was one of the few left in the district with thatch on it, but the thatch was untended and was falling away in places, patched here and there with sheet-iron. It was odd to think that the trim thatched cottages she remembered on the downs near Rottingdean ('delightful period residence ...') were the same type of dwelling; and odd too to realise that their postman, with his modern uniform his efficient and officious manner, emerged every morning from this lair.

She never saw him there. But Sylvain, with his ragged corduroy trousers and his rather long black hair that bore a fleeting, disquieting resemblance to Pierre's, was sometimes about. One day he showed her the rabbits with pride, in their complex of shanty pens beneath the overhang of the thatch. The original pair had been wild rabbits, he said, which he had captured in the woods, but then he had crossed the breed with a white one someone had given his mother. He stroked them appreciatively.

She could not decide if he were really simple, or not. His manner was a little childish and direct, but that might have been just the manner of a young man who had lived all his life in one village, hardly ever going as far as Châtelet-le-Lys. She couldn't imagine Sylvain putting on a tight best suit and escorting a giggling girl into town on the bus to see Greta Garbo or Fernandel. He did not seem exactly shy, but there was something slightly detached about him. She never, either then or later, sensed with him that slight edge of curiosity about herself which tinged her relations with most of the people in St Laurent. But then Marie Stefan seemed incurious about her also. She and Sylvain, unlike her other, inquisitive son, were private people.

But Marie Stefan seemed to like Jane. One day she gave her a freshly baked potato-cake. Reflecting that even if Marie Stefan's kitchen hygiene was non-existent the cake had at least been through a hot oven, Jane ate it. It was surprisingly good. There was an odd smell in the cottage, not fetid but slightly pungent, that reminded Jane of animal skins. Perhaps it was something to do with the goats Marie kept in a pen nearby, and with their milk that she made into cheese. Jane never actually saw a goat in the cottage's one room, but it would not have surprised her. The chickens from the muddy yard outside were allowed to wander in and out as they chose, and Mark swore that one evening a box of newly-hatched chicks had been ensconced on the bed, swathed in the grubby feather-quilt.

Occasionally Jane thought about that bed, apparently the only one. Could they all sleep in it together? She could hardly imagine Stefan-Postier in such a situation, but with Sylvain anything seemed possible.

Shc said one day to Mlle. Bisset, that 'Sylvain' seemed an oddly romantic name for such a family to choose, but Mlle. Bisset said that it was a traditional name in the Berry – all the peasants in the old stories were called 'Sylvain' and 'Solange'. Hadn't Jane read any Georges Sand yet? Oh, she must – she really must: Mlle. Bisset would bring her a volume or two sometime from the Town Hall library in Châtelet.

Jane tried to ask more about the Stefans, but Mlle. Bisset seemed less interested in them than she was in most people. Looking a little prim, she said that Stefan-Postier did his work correctly, she had no complaints about that, but that she really knew nothing whatsoever about Marie and Sylvain: they were hardly the type to come into the Post Office much.

Jane understood that the social gulf between Mlle. Bisset and Sylvain Stefan was profound and unbridgeable. Her earlier idea, that the village was a one-class community, was proving too simple. There might be a total dearth of people of her own sort of background, but she was coming to understand that the place did have its social gradations nevertheless, and that people like Mlle. Bisset, Madame Marcelle and her brother the Mayor, and the Mourets, felt themselves as distant from Marie Stefan as (in her heart of hearts) Jane did from them. Or so she would have once. Now, she was not sure. And in a strange way she sometimes felt nearer to Marie Stefan than to anyone. Marie Stefan was, so far, the only person who had treated her as an equal by asking for a service *from* her.

Many people were very kind, of course. Jeanot Langlois had several times, since their conversation about ration cards, left chickens or eggs at her door. Madame Langlois had given her several pots of apple jelly. The cross baker-lady had amazed her by sending a present of a tart on the day in May that she had heard from Mark was his mother's birthday. (Jane gathered that Mark had vainly tried to buy her chocolate in the village with money obtained at school from the sale of some marbles.) Monsieur Bonnin continued to be generous. But no one asked her for anything in return, and indeed what could she give them?

She longed to be something other than an object of charity, someone else than this pitiable outsider to whom one must be kind because, poor lady, her husband had gone, and because there was the child to think of ... Sometimes she wondered if many of the minor favours she received were really due less to her craven attempts to be nice to people than to Mark's solid, well-integrated presence in the village school. Occasionally, when she was feeling low, the constant obligation to make herself agreeable and acceptable to people, conflicting with the thought that they would just feel she was putting it on to get something out of them, was hard to bear. Harder still was the intermittent, terrifying thought that, if she and Mark failed now to keep on the right side of people – unspecified people, including those she scarcely knew – it might one day, literally, cost them their lives. It was said that the Germans were not going to leave Vichy-France in peace always.

In any case it was complicated, this business of receiving favours. It was inevitable, Jane supposed, that each family should consider themselves her chief benefactors and be wary of others. When the promised rabbits were brought over by Sylvain in one of the inevitable Stefan-family sacks, Langlois was there doing the vegetable garden, and Jane could tell that he was not pleased to see Sylvain appear. Perhaps he, like his wife, disapproved of the Stefans, or perhaps he just felt that the Langlois honour was impugned: perhaps *they* should have been the ones to supply the rabbits, if Madame Leparde wanted rabbits: she would only have to say the word ...

He set to work rather aloofly to make a hutch for the

rabbits out of an old packing case. Sylvain had not brought a hutch: Jane wondered if he thought the rabbits were going to hop about her kitchen? They were a grey buck and a grey-and-white doe with dark eyes. Mark named them Henri and Colette, which were apparently his favourite French names, and because they were handled a lot they became tame. Jane and Mark developed a fantasy about them – or rather Jane did, to amuse herself, remembering how good Pierre had been at this sort of game; while Mark, who had never been, to Jane's disappointment, a particularly imaginative child, listened appreciatively. The rabbits were a newly-married couple living in Châtelet-le-Lys in one of the new villas near the cemetery with wrought iron gates, and they were planning a daring holiday in Biarritz. They hadn't noticed there was a war on because they were always eating, and because they were too well brought up to talk to strangers.

Later in the summer they were separated into two hutches, after Langlois had warned Jane that, if Henri stayed much longer, Colette, despite her apparent gentleness, would turn on him; shortly after this Colette gave birth to seven babies. As these grew bigger, and were duly named after the Seven Dwarfs, it became quite an arduous job to find enough grass for them all, now that the autumn was here. One morning Jane was out hunting for stuff along the sides of the road when Stefan-Postier came along on his bicycle: he seemed to be in no hurry.

"Time you got rid of that litter," he said. "Didn't my brother tell you that?"

"No. I don't think he said anything about it –"

"You can't keep a whole hutch of rabbits in the winter. They'll eat you out of house and home. Time you sent the lot of them off to Bonnin."

Jane, who had vague thoughts of giving some away as pets to Mark's school friends, was shocked at his tone of brutal gaiety. She had known of course, she told herself, that people reared rabbits for the table, not just for their winning ways, but she hadn't for some reason envisaged the young rabbits' fate as that. She murmured something about preferring to let them go gradually.

"Oh of course," he agreed, "with meat prices going up all the time on the free market you might do better that way. You could take them into Châtelet in pairs on market day, people there'll pay more for rabbit than they will in the village."

She said, trying to harden her heart, thinking of good prices, of *money* – "Could I take them alive into Châtelet? Or would they have to be dead?"

"Dead's a lot easier."

"The thing is . . . I know it sounds silly, but I'm not sure how to kill them myself."

He stared at her in rude amusement, and she wished she had not allowed herself to be drawn into this conversation with him.

"Why – hold them by the back legs, of course, and smash their heads against a wall! Come on, I'll show you now with one, if you like. You'll be wanting to eat one or two of them yourselves, anyway."

She set her jaw, feeling a panic rising in her as if Stefan-Postier might have been likely to force his way into her garden and into the hutch against her protestations, while innocent, hopeful Sleepy and Dopey and Sneezy and the rest wiggled their noses at him.

"Not today, thank you. It's kind of you to offer, but I want to keep them all a little longer."

"OK, OK – let me know when you want it done. No trouble I assure you."

She was greatly relieved when he was gone. To her shame, when she gave the rabbits their grass, she found herself crying a little into Colette's soft fur with an emotion she dimly realised to be transferred from elsewhere, repeating senselessly "I'm going to kill your children, Colette. I'm betraying you." But, telling herself that sentimentality about animals was just one of the many luxuries she could not afford these days, she made up her mind to the young rabbits' fate and laid her plans. They should disappear in two lots, so that Mark should not have the shock of the empty cage all at once, and she would kill them herself if necessary rather than let that Stefan do it, or entrust them to anyone who might use his method.

In the end it was Sylvain who came and did it each time, by some quick punch on the back of the neck followed by a twist, a way that seemed less gratuitously brutal than the method recommended by his brother.

"I like rabbits," he said thoughtfully, as he stowed the warm corpses away in his bag. "Nice animals." He had offered to sell them for her too, and she had agreed gratefully. It was worth it, even if she didn't make so much that way.

He skinned and gutted one for her and Mark to have that evening. She made him take the head away, and discovered that once the body was reduced to familiar-looking joints it no longer seemed to be connected with the lolloping, furry creature of a few hours earlier. The hot-pot she made was delicious.

When Mark came home from school he did not ask after the exact fate of the rabbits, though his eyes went rather sadly to the depleted hutch. He only said anxiously, after Sylvain's second visit:

"We won't – we won't send Henri and Colette away, will we?"

"No, I don't think we *can* – do you? Sylvain did ask about Henri, but I said we wanted to keep both of them through the winter. I only hope there's not too much frost and snow, because that will make grass so difficult to find."

Later they were to have many more litters from this pair, but they never again made the mistake of petting the young rabbits or naming them. And rabbit meat became an important item in their diet, indeed almost the only meat they had.

And so 1941 drew to its aching close. The anniversary of Pierre's going came and went, and still there was no news of him and no word from anywhere.

*

On New Year's Eve 1942 Jane and Mark were invited to dinner in Châtelet-le-Lys by Mlle. Bisset. Jane found herself looking forward to the tiny celebration absurdly, as if to a party in London in the old days. Mark had no best suit that fitted him now, but she herself put on a dress she had not worn since she and Pierre had used to go and play cards at the Yrieuxs in that first, unreal, winter of the War. Had it really been two years ago? On the one hand it seemed far longer, a halcyon period irrevocably distant, and yet on the other hand it was hard to believe that all those days had really passed – days which seemed long at the time but which, filled with trivial physical tasks and material preoccupations, flicked by leaving little to remember them by.

Sometimes, at long intervals, an intimation would come to her that this was a momentous period for her, perhaps the most momentous that she would ever live. And yet she felt herself embedded, from day to day, in a long numbing littleness.

She and Mark, nervously armed with their identity papers in case of a stray police-check, rode into Châtelet on their bicycles under a clear, starry sky. Mlle. Bisset and her mother turned out to live on the first floor of a large, stucco building with wrought iron balconies, in the avenue that led to the station. Madame Bisset herself was in black silk with jet beads, and her daughter was in dark blue crêpe-de-Chine with a frilled neck which, she confided to Jane, she had only just finished sewing that afternoon: evidently Jane's own black wool frock with Pierre's gold chain had been the right thing to wear. Madame Bisset, who was fat and rather lame, seemed flustered but pleased to meet her daughter's new friends, and with a superfluity of tact made no allusion to Jane's nationality. "You see, we haven't invited anyone besides yourselves: you've nothing to worry about," said Mlle. Bisset to Jane in an undertone as they went through to the dining room. The room, a scaled down version of the Yrieuxs, was chilly; a small porcelain stove appeared to be heating only its own corner. But the meal, which began with eggs in cream and continued with roast pork with pears to follow cooked in syrup, was so large and delicious that Jane had great difficulty in not appearing nakedly greedy. Mark, who had no such inhibitions, ate everything that was placed in front of him, including a third helping of the pears.

"Mark, you'll be *ill*," said Jane in an anxious English aside.

"Oh please don't worry about him Madame," said Madame Bisset, evidently picking up Jane's tone if not the words, and smiling abstractedly at him. "Those pears are just good home produce – I bottled them myself. Take a little more wine, Madame; this claret is one my dear husband bought, just before he went." They launched into a conversation on the importance of bottling in these hard times, and the impossibility of buying new rubber rings for the jars. Although this was the sort of conversation Jane herself had interminably these days with Madame Langlois and various other women in the village, she nevertheless welcomed it now as a respite from the old lady's earlier conversation, which had been almost exclusively on the subject of her daughter, whose name proved to be Evangeline. Inhibited, no doubt, by discretion and delicacy, from enquiring into Jane's past and current career, Madame Bisset evidently felt no scruple about parading her daughter's life in front of them. She regaled them with a detailed report: how well Evangeline had done at school, what the teachers had said, what her dear father had said, how, when and where she had pursued her training in the Post Office service, how she had been appointed in charge at St Laurent when she was only twenty-six; how, when this terrible War was over, they both hoped she might get a still better job somewhere in the region, but not of course too far away since she had her home here in Châtelet and her old mother to make her comfortable ... Madame Bisset punctuated this amiably gloating recital with appeals to her daughter for confirmation – 'Didn't you, dear', 'Don't we, dear?' – and Jane thought that if she had been Evangeline Bisset she would one day, driven beyond endurance, have left her comfortable home for ever. But that kind young woman sat there, placidly agreeing with what her mother said (except to laugh off tales of her own scholastic successes), and from time to time unobtrusively fetching plates, clearing others and replenishing glasses.

"You see," said Madame Bisset in triumphant conclusion, "my elder daughter is married and lives in Paris now, but I still have my little girl with me. Yes indeed, I couldn't manage without Evangeline. My legs, you understand. But Evangeline is very patient with her old mother, aren't you dear?"

After they had at last, rather soberly, toasted the New Year in – Mark looking bright-eyed, haggard and a little unsteady on his chair – Madame Bisset retired ceremonially to her own room. Jane, unexpectedly exhausted, nevertheless stayed a little while, feeling that Mlle. Bisset would be disappointed if they did not. Mlle. Bisset produced for inspection a cabinet portrait of her sister, her sister's bald husband and her equally bald baby. She said suddenly,

"I do wish you would call me Evangeline."

"And you must call me Jane, of course!" said Jane. "I would have suggested it before, but I – that is – the French don't seem to call each other by their first names very much."

"No, I'm afraid we're very remiss about that," said Evangeline sadly. "We aren't close enough to each other – except in the family, of course. We aren't a friendly race, they say. It must be difficult for you at St Laurent, Madame Leparde, with only your son close to you –"

" 'Jane', please –"

"– Such a good boy, a credit to you, as everyone says, but you must miss your parents ... and Dr. Leparde, of course."

"Oh but," said Jane awkwardly, torn between a need to confide how deep her loneliness was and a desire not to sound ungrateful, "People are very kind. Look how kind you have been to us in inviting us here tonight. Anyway," she added, not quite truthfully, "I've always been rather an independent person ever since I was a child, and that's probably just as well. Come to that, if I hadn't been rather independent I don't suppose Mark and I would be here in the middle of France today." Even as she said it she became fully aware for the first time of a contradiction here, something false in the persona of semi-bohemian independence which, on leaving James, she had assiduously cultivated. Had it really been a sign of independence to leave one man only to attach herself at once to another, following him like a lamb wherever he went? Surely not.

She suppressed the longing to tell the whole story to Evangeline Bisset who, after all, could hardly be expected to take a tolerant, modern Anglo-Saxon view of divorce; particularly if she herself had never been offered the chance of marriage.

"You're probably much braver than I am," said Mlle. Bisset with a rather sad smile. "Sometimes I think I am too dependent on my mother, and she is on me. I know in my heart that this is really so. But what can I do? And she's not getting any younger, she will need me in earnest soon." She paused and then, as if reading Jane's thought, she added,

"It's no good my thinking of a husband and children for myself, you see. Poor Mother took it badly enough when my sister married, even though it was really quite a suitable match and there was no reason why not . . . My going would be catastrophic for her." And Jane, comparing her own life and contrasting it favourably, yes, in spite of everything, with the other young woman's permanent unfulfilled existence in this tiny provincial town, said with something like urgency,

"But Mlle. Bisset – Evangeline – how can you *bear* it? Just this – for ever. And one day your mother will be dead and you won't even have her."

As soon as she had said it she felt how rude she had been, and that the other would surely take offence, with reason. It is one thing to criticise one's own life, another for someone else to do it. But Evangeline Bisset did not seem offended. She said simply,

"Yes, at times I am tempted to feel like that myself. But at other times ... I manage to see things in a different light. I am very fortunate really, to be so loved; so many people have no one ... And of course I have my religion. It *is* a comfort, you see."

Jane mumbled something about being unable to comment on that side of things.

"No? Well these things are very personal, aren't they? I know that belief isn't given to everyone. And I suppose you are Protestant, anyway? I remember learning at school that the English are Protestant."

"Well, yes. But I'm really not religious at all you know." For some reason she felt a need to state the fact.

"No? Well, as I say, it doesn't suit everyone." She smiled again, with a touch of irony. "Oddly enough, I don't think that my mother really has any religious belief at all, for all that we go to Mass together every Sunday! Poor Mother isn't really a very happy person."

Lying in bed at last, with the night half over, after their ride home by moonlight, Jane went over this conversation in her mind. She had wanted to set the record straight and not be drawn into a false position with Evangeline Bisset, whom she now admired reluctantly for something to which she herself had never thought to aspire; in doing so, she had told something of a lie.

The fact was that, in spite of her modern agnosticism and a mild scorn for the sort of Gentle Jesusery that she had been taught as a child, Jane had recently taken to saying prayers. She had decided not to pray directly to God to save Pierre: that sort of whining, personal application made it seem as if God were a super-Pétain or a German officer from whom she wanted a favour. But she sometimes, in a ritual gesture towards Him, said a formal prayer when she had turned out the light, often the childish Paternoster she had learnt from her Nanny:

... Now I lay me down to sleep
And trust the Lord my soul to keep.

It was up to Him, she felt, to take it or leave it. She would remind herself that she had yet to be convinced that He cared anyway.

That same night, by the same moon which had lighted their road home, a British plane flew low over France and dropped by parachute two men who were to become the national co-ordinators of the Resistance. But Jane did not know that.

In the New Year she took stock of her position: it seemed necessary. Till then, in spite of her generalised economies and an even more generalised worrying, she had not really faced the future. The main reason for this was that she had not been able to envisage it at all clearly except to believe that the present state of affairs would not – surely could not – last. All through 1941, on both optimistic days and pessimistic ones, she had believed at some level that her situation at St Laurent-la-Rivière was only temporary. *Something* was bound to happen, she had felt irrationally, before the year was out. Either Pierre would suddenly reappear again, or she would have some word of his whereabouts and perhaps be able to make contact again with his family. She had a happy day-dream in which she occasionally indulged. In it, Dr. Leparde senior reasserted himself and extended to her further help, friendship, money or perhaps even an offer to her to join forces with them in Normandy, or wherever they were now . . .

She also had a less cheering imaginary scenario which for a long time she believed to be more likely, indeed almost inevitable according to what she heard from Radio-Vichy. England would be invaded in her turn and would capitulate: the War would then be effectively over, and however unfortunate this would be for both Britain and France it would be her personal deliverance; for presumably once hostilities had ceased she and Mark could come out of hiding, prisoners would be released and gradually everything would return to something like normal, or at least to a new form of normality. Jane felt that it was better to be alive, under almost any régime, than gloriously dead for one's country: she remembered having once had an argument with her father about this, and more recent events had only strengthened and confirmed her view.

But now it seemed that England was not, after all, going to be invaded, and the future began to extend for her in a dark, dreary vista along which she must take a nerve-wracking journey whose length was quite unknown. America had entered the War and so it might now continue for years and years, judging from the items of news which Monsieur Picard occasionally, conspiratorially, passed on to her when he chanced to see her: evidently his own wireless set must be capable of picking up the BBC broadcasts.

One day in January she nerved herself to do calculations on the money that remained to them, the hoard composed of the sizeable sum sent by her father during the first winter of the War and the other sum sent by Pierre's father to help her escape. Without these two windfalls she would have been destitute long before now. At first, the total they made had seemed to her a virtual insurance against total want: only last summer, one day when she had been feeling brisk and hopeful, she had reckoned that if she continued to practise their present rigorous economy, buying only what seemed absolutely essential for herself and Mark to keep them going, the money that remained would last another two years, or even three with extreme care – say, till the summer of 1944, if only prices would remain static. In theory they should, since the price as well as the ration of all staple goods was now fixed by decree. But in practice many things had to be bought, or supplemented, on the 'free' market, and prices there were inexorably rising. True, it was as yet only certain scarce things, like clothes or saucepans or honey, which had gone up inordinately, but even commonplace and fairly plentiful commodities were creeping up too. Meanwhile all salaries and pensions were frozen as well. Jane knew that she was not the only person in the village who looked on the future with financial foreboding. Even if she had been Pierre's true wife and in receipt of the

Government pension for the wives of prisoners of war, that hand-out itself had become inadequate by all accounts and was not being increased. But it would have been *something* coming in. For a while she became, inevitably, obsessed by money, and a fearful calculation of francs and sous seemed to dominate her waking hours and intrude upon her dreams.

It wasn't just their food that cost money. There were other things as well which they could not do without: soap (when it was obtainable), mending wool, bicycle and shoe repairs. She needed too to keep a reserve, in addition to their ordinary expenses, for any medicines they might need, for Mark's school books and writing materials and – most important – for the electricity bill. Far from being an unnecessary extravagance, as for a while she had feared it might be, the electric light in the cottage had turned out to be an economy: those without electricity, which was most of the village, were now having to spend a small fortune on candles and lamp oil, neither of which were obtainable through an official channel.

Feeling devious, she encouraged Mark to bring his friends, particularly Jean-Luc Bonnin, back to the cottage to do their homework in her good light. There was no harm in making their parents feel obliged to her, particularly when, as in the case of the Bonnins or the Petitjeans, this sense of obligation showed itself as under-the-counter sausage meat or a new inner tube for her bicycle produced from nowhere despite the rubber shortage. But she still had to pay for the tube, and it was not cheap. She had to have it. Everyone needed their bicycles these days, to range the countryside visiting this farm that had cheeses to sell, or that other cottage that would give you pickled eggs in exchange for rabbit meat.

Imperceptibly but steadily her standards crept down. To save soap, she washed herself and their clothes less often: Mark never wanted to wash anyway. There had been the day she realised that you didn't need shampoo to wash your hair, and the day when it came to her that heating clothes in plain water on top of the stove got the worst of the dirt out of them anyway. There was also the day when it occurred to her that most women in the village did not waste several francs a month on disposable objects when a few cloth towels would last a lifetime. Advised how to fold them by kind Madame Marcelle, she 'invested' in several of these Victorian aids to feminine hygiene. At the same time, perhaps glad to move onto a less intimate topic, Madame Marcelle remarked that she had managed to get a small consignment of knitting wool that week. It was rather poor quality stuff, she said, but, if Jane was interested, she should buy some now: goodness knew when there would be any more.

Jane confessed that she barely knew how to knit, without adding that this was because, in her teens, knitting had seemed to her a ridiculously fuddy-duddy occupation. But, seeing the wool, she thought of Mark's jerseys that were riding up over his middle, and of the socks which kept forming new holes over his toes, and after some hesitation she closed with Madame Marcelle's offer to do the knitting for her 'for a consideration'. There was evidently an understood rate which that lady, as a village knitter, mentioned without embarrassment.

So Mark had an ample if rather scratchy green jersey on his birthday, and two pairs of stockings to match. But her savings crept down and down, and she dreaded another illness, another puncture, another hole in a shoe. And suppose a real emergency arose: suppose she and Mark suddenly had to leave St Laurent after all? Suppose they *had* to escape. She dare not think about it.

The obvious solution to the immediate problem, which had suggested itself to her long ago, was to find some way of earning money. But what? There could be no question of her drawing risky attention to herself by taking a job in Châtelet, and what, in any case, could she have done? No one, now, was likely to want English lessons or to have their children looked after by an incognito English woman, and these were the only occupations for which she felt herself minimally equipped. There was no work for women in the village. Or rather, the women worked all the time, as she did, but at digging vegetables, cutting up windfall apples and drying them in the oven, patching and mending, and walking or bicycling about in search of ham, sausage, flour, a promise of some dripping ... She would gladly have scrubbed their floors for them if that would have earned a little money, but they all scrubbed their own. The memory that she had once, only two years ago, considered herself bravely unconventional for disposing of Reine and doing her own housework, now seemed ludicrous.

There was always Madame Mouret. The restaurant was the only place in the village that occasionally employed outside labour: Jane knew that Reine Langlois used to help serve there on Sundays and at wedding parties. In the end, screwing up her courage tightly, telling herself that it didn't matter what Madame Mouret thought if only she would pay her to do some washing-up or something, Jane went there. She entered by the usual door and Madame Mouret came out beaming, obviously hoping that Jane wanted lunch, or at least a cup of ersatz coffee. Jane, aware already that she was making a mistake, managed to utter her request.

Madame Mouret said little but her first reaction was one of obviously shocked embarrassment. After a few moments she collected herself sufficiently to apologise to Jane for being unable to help her; to say that, alas, with trade so poor, and set-meal prices fixed by law, she wasn't in need of much extra help. She said it several times in different ways. She also added that everyone had their problems these days, didn't they? – that there were several people in the village she was particularly sorry for but she couldn't help everyone, that was just the way it was ... She seemed to be defending herself against an unspoken charge. Jane could not help remembering that last meal she had had there, whose price had not been fixed.

As soon as she could, Jane left the restaurant. She should never have gone there. From now on Madame Mouret would feel guilty and resentful towards her. She might even decide she disliked her.

Evangeline Bisset listened sympathetically to Jane's problem but could suggest no ready solution. Couldn't Jane dress-make, she asked at last? These days some of the women in the town were turning out old curtains and bedspreads and the like, and someone who was clever with her needle would surely be able to pick up some work. But Jane, feeling useless and silly, admitted that she could no more dress-make than she could knit. 'I did do some embroidery at school,' she ventured, suddenly remembering acres of stem-stitch and lazy-daisy, boring but soothing and not too difficult. Her mother still had that cushion-cover at home in Rottingdean. Mlle. Bisset looked dubious; there wasn't much demand for embroidery, she thought.

However she must have had a tactful word with Madame Langlois, for that lady appeared at Jane's cottage a few days later looking self-conscious. Acting as unconvincingly as only a really honest person can, she said that she just happened to wonder if Jane knew how to embroider and had some time to spare? Her youngest daughter, Jeanot's sister, needed a First Communion dress. The dress her cousin Reine had worn was too small for Marie-Jo – they should have had the girl done last year! The only white material they could get was butter muslin, which seemed a bit plain and rough, seeing that some of the other girls had beautiful dresses passed down in their families. But if it could have something worked on it . . .

"I'd be glad to," said Jane helplessly, "but I wonder if I can get any silk or cottons to do it in? Everything's so scarce."

Madame Langlois triumphantly produced skeins of thick cotton thread from her bag.

"Left over," she said proudly. "From the days when we were girls and used to wear white cotton stockings on Sundays. I would be that grateful, Madame Leparde. I'd promised our Marie-Jo a nice dress, but I didn't know where to turn. None of us knows how to embroider – our hands are too rough, you see, and you have to have been to the convent school to have learnt that sort of thing."

Jane's own hands, after eighteen months of housework and firelighting, were hardly smooth. She had finished all her handcream long ago, also her vanishing cream, and had looked longingly at the pots in Madame Marcelle's hairdressing window without feeling justified in buying anything. But if the Langlois were going to pay her it would be worth investing in a tube of glycerine. On the other hand, the illogicality of them paying her to sew while Langlois himself did her garden for nothing, seemed to her too glaring to be passed over. She tried to convey this to Madame Langlois, who replied almost tartly that there was a going rate for this sort of skilled work, Madame Marcelle would know it, and Jane would of course be paid it. "It's nothing to do with any arrangements you may have with the Mister. This is just something between you and me – it'll come out of my egg-money. If you want to know, Madame Leparde, my husband doesn't much hold with my spending money on a dress for our Marie-Jo. He doesn't understand what it's like to be a girl.

Jane put in many hours of work on the butter muslin that winter by the light of the more-than-ever necessary electricity. The daisies and tendrils with which she covered the dress were rather uneven because she had to do them freehand, but they were surprisingly effective. She thought that probably the 'going-rate', scrupulously paid to her by Madame Langlois, had, by her, been fairly hard-earned: someone more used to the work would have done it quicker. But she was proud of her efforts, and enjoyed the unstinted admiration of the Langlois family.

Then, in March, Mark damaged his bike careering on it over a dry ditch in some wild game. He bent the back wheel and broke a pedal, and a substantial sum out of Jane's earnings had to be put towards repairing it.

She was angrier with him than she had ever been in her life, though conscious, even as she stormed about his stupidity and his inconsiderateness, how unfair she was being. He was only a child, it was natural that he should want to play boys' games, and indeed the way he spent so much time out with the other boys had always been a matter of pleasure and relief to her: it would have been awful if he had been lonely too. But all the same: he knew how precious and irreplaceable bikes were. And they weren't only things like that –

"– *And* there's your boots. You've only been wearing those larger ones since Christmas and already the right toe's all worn –"

"I can't help wearing out my boots," said Mark, his hands trembling slightly.

"It's not just ordinary wear, it's bloody football! How can you expect them to last if you're always kicking a ball with them? And what do you think you'll wear when you've ruined them? I can tell you, Mark, there *won't be any more boots after these*. There just aren't any proper boots to be had these days, on or off the ration, and if there were any we couldn't afford them. We can't *afford* for you to be thoughtless, silly child. You've bloody well got to grow up a bit."

Something, perhaps in his mother's tone rather than in what she said, got through to Mark. He looked stricken. Jane burst into tears.

She had been so careful, up till then, not to impose her own continual, minor burdens on him, thinking that if she did this would spoil his cheerful pleasure in life. She had been proud of the way she had not moaned and whined and nagged at him. The idea that one did not behave like that towards a child was part of her social inheritance. He knew in general terms of course that money was short, but what did this mean to him apart from having no pocket money? There was nothing much a child could spend money on these days, anyway. Very likely he still thought that 'can't afford' was just one of those things grown-ups said that nevertheless didn't prevent them from buying for themselves or their children anything that was really needed. He would have to learn now, have to understand –

She told him all her dread: the sinking savings, the

increasing need for money, the hopelessly indefinite future; once she had started it all came out, she could not stop. He listened in silence, occasionally nodding nervously, with that same dazed, slightly guarded look on his face with which he had met the fact of Pierre's disappearance. When she had finished, he said,

"I'm sorry about the bike, Mum. I really am . . . But it will be getting too small for me soon anyway, you know. The saddle and handlebars are right up now as far as they'll go."

"But if you manage to keep it in a good state we'll be able to sell it! Bikes are valuable."

"Will I ride Pierre's, then?"

"I – I think you'll have to. After all, you have to *have* a bike."

He thought a minute and then said with apparent effort, but with a kind of heady heroism,

"Mum, I don't *have* to. Not all the boys do. I could walk. We'll sell both the bikes if that'll really help – mine and Pierre's. I could always borrow yours – just odd times, you know."

"You can't walk into Châtelet and back every day," she told him, "and you'll be needing to do that next autumn. At least, I suppose you will?"

"To the High School?"

"Yes. Has Monsieur Picard said anything to you about that?"

"Not lately, I don't think, not to me. But if Jean-Luc and Jean-Baptiste and Henri go, then I should, Mum. I'm just as clever as them. In fact I'm a lot cleverer than Henri: he thinks he's good, but that's mostly because his handwriting's very neat."

"I'll have to go and talk to Picard about it," said Jane abstractedly, rubbing her wet hanky round and round her fingers. Mark hung about for a little, stroked her shoulder tentatively saying "Poor Mum. It'll be all right . . ." and then went out to play. But from that day on something changed in their relationship. She no longer tried to keep anything from him but talked to him as if he had been another adult, and he responded in kind. After a few months it seemed odd to remember that she had only lately regarded him as a little boy to be sheltered from the full reality of the situation. He was twelve years old now. He seemed to have grown up a lot, just as she had tearfully asked him to without expecting that he would do so. Indeed she noticed after a while that through listening to the wireless in other people's houses, he was better informed on the process of the unseen War than she was herself.

She went to see Monsieur Picard: he received her as always in the schoolroom, but this time he was trying to mend the iron stove. There was something wrong with the dampers, he said. He was in his shirt-sleeves poking irritably at it. A stench of soot filled the cold room.

When he understood what she had come for he laid down the metal implement he was using, and said,

"But Madame your son cannot go to the *lycée*, it is out of the question, I'm afraid."

"But I thought . . . That is to say, whenever we've talked about it you've always said he's a good pupil."

"So he is. One of the best I have had here, in fact. But I cannot enter him for the scholarship examination – in fact I cannot even recommend him for an ordinary place. Not in the present situation."

"But why?" said Jane, aghast. One of her minor comforts had always been that if Mark continued in the way he was going he would receive a full French education just as good, in its way, as an English one.

"Because, as a pupil, he has no official existence."

"But he's been attending your school."

"Yes, but only because I have connived at it and have sought advice from no one but myself: I told your husband that when, as a favour, I enrolled Marc. We all thought it was to be a temporary situation. You understand . . . I have not been receiving the usual allocation for him."

Jane took a minute to digest this delicate allusion. When she had done so she said dejectedly,

"Then we're already in your debt, Monsieur Picard. I'm sorry – I didn't realise."

"Bah, don't apologise. It is always a pleasure to teach a hardworking, receptive boy. But, you understand, I can hardly go to the Inspector at Châteuroux and say 'Monsieur: I have this boy who has risen from the ground and whom I wish to enter for the scholarship exam'. The district Authorities are not particularly accommodating – unfortunately. Perhaps it's because we are so near the frontier."

"But – our identity papers . . ."

"Forged papers like yours are to get you out of trouble in a tight spot. If you are stopped on the road, for instance, or on a journey, or if your ration card is challenged in a shop in the town. They can't be safely used to claim benefits that pass through official channels. We are a bureaucratic country, Madame."

"I've noticed."

After a minute Monsieur Picard picked up his implement again and stood handling it. Looking quite kindly for once, he said,

"Your boy will just have to stay here with me."

She wanted to cry out 'But it's not fair! Only the dull ones who are going to stay on the farms do that. He needs a proper education, and his best friends will be moving on.' But if Monsieur Picard was doing her a favour anyway she could not say that. She did not say anything.

"Next school-year I will have to organise the higher course for him myself," he said, beginning to fiddle with the stove-pipe again. She was uncertain whether he meant her to go now, or whether his unaccustomed informality meant that she was to stay. She said stonily, thinking oh God, the money, the *money* –

"You must tell me what new text books you would like me to get for him."

"Oh – as to that," he said easily, "it may not be necessary for you to buy any books. I have all my own old High School text books. I daresay we shall manage very well, he and I." A large gobbet of soot suddenly detached itself from the inside of the chimney and fell out of the ventilation-trap onto the stove's ornamental iron top. He stepped back with a mild exclamation of disgust, but then looked satisfied.

"Ah-ha, now we are getting somewhere, I think . . . Yes, books: you know I think I am quite going to enjoy taking Marc through the *lycée* course, as a challenge." His eyes glinted behind his glasses. Warming to him – he really was a decent man underneath it all, she thought; she could see why the boys got on with him – she said,

"It's a relief to hear he won't be needing many new books. I dread any extra expense now. You understand . . ." She had, she reflected in momentary disgust, become so used to dropping craven hints about her poverty to people that she hardly felt embarrassed about it any longer.

Monsieur Picard must have taken the hint, for after that Mark never again came home from school with a note requesting her to purchase a text or even a new exercise book. Instead, later in the year, Picard produced a lot of forms from the Mairie with blank backs and gave them to Mark to do his homework on. He also started lending Mark books of his own, mainly history books and historical novels with a pronounced republican flavour. "Later on, when Marc is old enough," he told Jane, "I have the complete works of Balzac. And all Zola in pocket editions."

She got the impression that the sense of possessing these volumes, and the cultural implications of this, were more important to Picard than the contents. But you never knew with him: he might be genuinely well-read. Meanwhile, she seized the opportunity to borrow Balzac and Zola from him herself. Balzac occasionally sickened her: the characters' near-universal preoccupation with money was too near her own; but in Zola, whom she found easier to read anyway, she could lose herself. She read a good deal that year. It nourished her mind, lifting her out of the grinding daily round, the endless minor variations on leek soup, carrot soup, potato pie, potato and leek soup, the endless trivial but arduous and time-consuming jobs. It was something to do while she waited.

Waited for what? At times she no longer even knew. Pierre had been gone eighteen months. At moments the pain of not having him and not knowing what had happened to him was still as sharp as if it had occurred the week before, an almost physical sensation which made her wince and clench her teeth. But at other times even hope seemed beyond her. Hope, and its concomitant of fear, were too painful to sustain continually. There were whole days now when she did not even think of Pierre, or thought of him only in the past tense.

Then, struck with remorse, she would have periods when she thought of him continually. For if she gave him up for dead might that not, in some terrible way, make just that edge of difference between his survival and his extinction? She understood, now, why some women, even when faced with the overwhelming probability that their missing son or lover had died in battle, refused to believe it and went on hoping, for years after a war had ended. They weren't being absurd, she thought sometimes: just unusually brave and determined. But she herself could not manage it. Not as a permanence. More and more she took refuge in the idea that Mark and his future were all she must concentrate on for now.

In June 1942 new laws came into force in the Occupied Territories concerning Jews. At the same time life for everyone became more tightly controlled in the part of France still called Free. Posters appeared in Châtelet and even in St Laurent, urging men and boys to volunteer for labour in Germany 'to facilitate the return of prisoners'. It was widely said that this was a trap, and that by and by the word 'volunteer' would be replaced by another. There were rumours and fears that even the nominal freedom of Vichy-France would not endure much longer.

Jane was vaguely aware that the Germans were oppressing France because they were not now having things all their own way elsewhere. She tried to be glad, that Britain was not invaded, that Russia was fighting back, that there were Allied victories in North Africa. But she was also aware that the better England and America did, the worse it would be for those caught in Nazi-dominated Europe. They were all in a cleft stick, but she more than most.

The RAF, it was said, had already made some bombing raids in the Paris region. Suppose, one day, they came over to bomb Vichy? What would be her situation then among the people of St Laurent?

One fine night in July, when the dark seemed only lightly spread over field and lanes, someone knocked tentatively at her door. This was an unprecedented happening. Most of the doors in the district stood open all day, except in the coldest weather, and callers were treated with an amiable lack of surprise. But when night fell everyone retreated behind their shutters, and to disturb them for a trivial reason was unthinkable. She hesitated several moments before opening the door. The cottage, after all, was a little way out of the village, the nearest house to it being the Yrieuxs' which was empty. There were tales these days of refugees ('Jews and Communists') roaming the countryside, breaking into farms and terrorising the inhabitants.

While she hesitated the knock came again: the tentative person wasn't going to give up. Looking round, she picked up the bread knife and held it unobtrusively against her skirt before she lifted the latch of the door. It had come to her that in any case it was probably only Sylvain. Twice already that summer he had called on her very early in the morning, before her shutters were open, and had seemed unconcerned and unnoticing when she had opened the door to him wrapped in a blanket. One of the times he had brought her two wood pigeons to cook, and the other a clutch of quails' eggs. Both times he had refused to take anything in return. She opened the door.

But instead of Sylvain with his sack and his rumpled hair, there stood a shorter, neater figure. It was a young man of about her own age whom she had never seen before in her life. He had a pale, smooth face, dark rather wiry hair, and wore a collar and tie. His expression, which she could see in the bright moonlight, was one of extreme nervousness and diffidence.

"I am very sorry to trouble you. I hope I haven't frightened you. I am a friend of Pierre Leparde's."

In a few minutes he was sitting in the cane armchair while she heated up the remains of the soup for him and cut up the last of the bread. His voice sounded light and musical in the quiet kitchen. It was, she realised, the first educated Parisian voice she had listened to since Pierre had left. You couldn't call Picard's northern intonation and prissy schoolmaster's turn of phrase 'educated', and everyone else, including Evangeline Bisset, had some degree of the rolling, local accent. Jane had always liked that accent but now, listening to Serge Beckman – for that was his name, he said – she felt almost as if she were hearing Pierre talk, and the memory of what she had been missing for so long came over her in waves that nearly overwhelmed her. Her hands trembled with excitement so that she could hardly cut the bread.

But she already knew that Serge Beckman did not bring the news that she had, for a wild moment or two, hoped: he had not come from Pierre. He did not know where Pierre was now any more than she did. He knew that Pierre had originally been taken prisoner, but had not heard of his release on parole or of his subsequent disappearance. He was in fact shocked when Jane told him of this. His own friendship with Pierre dated from the first winter of the War, when they had been stationed together at Rocroi. Like Pierre, he was a doctor.

"Yes," said Jane slowly, "I *do* remember him mentioning you now." She took the soup off the stove, poured it into a bowl and brought it to him. The dragging disappointment of the realisation that this stranger brought, after all, no news of the living Pierre, was nevertheless palliated after a few minutes by a certain pleasure and excitement at having such a visitor at all. "Eat," she said, "You're obviously very hungry." The first thing he had asked her when he got inside the cottage was whether she could give him something to eat. After a decent show of politeness ("But aren't you going to have some of this yourself?") he fell to and consumed the soup and the bread very quickly.

"You're on the run," she said.

He agreed that that was so. His neat, clean appearance did not suggest that he was a hunted man, but he told her that he'd been on the move for the last three weeks, ever since a notice had arrived at his home in a suburban district of Paris requesting him to present himself at the local German command-post for 'assessment'. He had left that morning and had been travelling ever since. He risked staying in small hotels in out-of-the-way towns, but since his papers were stamped 'Jew' he did not take a train anywhere for fear of being sent back to Paris in custody. In Occupied France Jews were no longer supposed to move about, even from one town to another. He had paid a boy with a rowing boat a large sum to take him across a deserted bit of the river Cher, where it formed the frontier north of Châteauroux. He had not had much to eat because you could only buy rationed goods at a place where you were registered and, in the Occupied Zone at least, he had not dared to use restaurants much.

He was making his way, he said, to Lyons, where he had an uncle, a watchmaker and jeweller, who would probably shelter him. He said 'probably' with the brave air of one determined not to reveal to the listener the full extent of his fear. He seemed the sort of man who hated to be a nuisance to people, and who found it degrading even to have to speak of his own problems. He kept apologising to Jane for having disturbed her, as if his call had been a sudden impulse, though she could tell from the journey of the last few days which he described to her that he must have been making his way steadily in her direction for some time. He had had her address, he told her, from Pierre, when it became obvious to them that northern France was being overrun and that their field hospital would shortly be either evacuated or captured. When the latter had happened, and Pierre and a number of other people had been taken prisoner, he himself had escaped in the confusion. He had kept the address, remembering Pierre saying vaguely that it 'might be useful' for him to have friends in central France. He had hoped these last weeks, he said – though not very confidently – that he would find Pierre there as well as Jane.

"In October it will be two years since I last saw him," said Jane quietly.

"Yes. I understand that now. I am so very sorry. I only wish that I could have brought you good news . . . So you've been alone all this time?"

"Yes. Except for my son. He's asleep just now in the next room."

"How old is your son?" asked Serge, stiffening. She told him, and he sat back again. She saw clearly the image that had momentarily formed in his mind – a fully grown-up son who might resent this late-night visitor, who might make trouble for him. Poor man, his nerves were on edge, he had clearly lived with fear continually the last few weeks. She felt terribly sorry for him.

She herself knew what mild, chronic fear was like. But at least in St Laurent, where everyone knew her, she felt reasonably safe, and she had as yet no reason to go anywhere else. How awful it must be to travel through a land where even your appearance put you at risk: Serge Beckman, she thought, *looked* so Jewish that no one with an interest in these things could possibly have mistaken the fact. Even so, this was supposed to be the Free Zone – Perhaps he was a chronic worrier; she rather thought Pierre had described him like that.

"At least you're much safer down here?" she suggested. "In Vichy-France, I mean. Jews aren't restricted in the towns here, and they don't have to wear yellow stars, do they?"

"In theory that is so," he agreed. "But in practice I am afraid that the Vichy government have been handing refugee Jews back to the Occupying Forces."

"How foul of them. I didn't know that."

"Haven't you heard of the argument there has been going on about this recently, since Laval took over?" he said, gently reproving, and she felt ashamed for having considered him neurotic.

"I really don't hear anything much here," she explained. "Just rumours. And the village people don't necessarily understand the half of what's going on elsewhere. I'm afraid I've become quite stupid, living here."

"It's entirely understandable I expect," he said after a pause. "That the ordinary people here shouldn't realise what is going on, I mean. After all – none of us realised just how Fascism would be implemented in France. People believed till this summer that if they were born French and minded their own business they had nothing to fear."

"That isn't so any longer, then? I didn't properly realise ... The wireless talks about 'foreign Jews' being deported and I suppose I thought that was what it meant – recent refugees from Holland and Germany and so on. I should have realised it might be a lie."

"'Foreign Jew' is an elastic phrase, we are coming to realise. And what happens today in the Occupied Zone may happen tomorrow in Vichy – here."

"Would they really have deported you from Paris if you had obeyed that notice and presented yourself at the Command Post?"

"Undoubtedly. As a Jew I am forbidden, since last month, to practise my profession. They would have sent me to do forced labour in Germany. Or possibly – this has happened to some friends of ours – I would have been sent to an internment camp. There is a big one at Drancy, just outside Paris. Conditions there are said to be – not pleasant."

"But why are they rounding up Jews and keeping them there?" said Jane. "It seems a bit pointless."

"No one is sure how many they *are* keeping there. It seems that some people are sent on from there – somewhere else. To the east, I suppose. Maybe to other camps in Germany. There are stories. People disappear ... But no one knows where."

In the thick silence, Jane said,

"Might Pierre have been sent to such a place?"

"Oh I really could not tell you: I do not think so, as he is not a Jew," said Serge hastily. He added, "I am sorry, you have troubles of your own. I shouldn't have spoken to you of these things. I feel sure that Pierre is simply in a military prisoner-of-war camp somewhere. There seems to me every hope for him."

Jane said thoughtfully, "If I – Mark and I – were in the Occupied Zone we might have been interned ourselves by now. Mightn't we? I'm not French myself, you see."

"I had," said Serge with a smile and a slight bow, "already noticed that fact. I'm afraid an English accent is never lost!"

"Mark has lost his," said Jane quickly, "At least, I think so. People say so. You must tell me tomorrow if you think he has."

"With a child, it is different. He is fortunate."

He stayed two nights, putting up a show of reluctance to bother her but obviously thankful for the respite. He spent much of the day resting and dozing. She washed and dried his shirt and socks for him, feeling happy. She urged him to stay longer, but he said that that might endanger her and Mark: someone in the village would notice she had a guest.

"They wouldn't mind," said Jane obstinately. "They're nice."

"Are you sure they're *all* nice? Of course not. Country people are always wary of strangers, and you're bound to get one or two people who are ready to run to the authorities and tell tales."

She hated his suspiciousness, but knew in her heart that he was right; or, if not right, at least justified.

She had made up a bed for him in the kitchen. On the first morning, after he had been introduced to Mark, he said to Jane in a nervous undertone,

"Your son won't mention me to his school-friends, will he?"

Jane retailed this to Mark, who said crossly, "What does he take me for?" – and set off to school before his usual time. But that evening he asked Serge searching questions about his life in hiding: the subject seemed to have a certain fascination for him.

Jane had bought eggs, produced the best meal she could, opened a bottle of wine. The wine, rough, red stuff, grown locally, was her one indulgence. Cheap as it was in the village, she would not have felt justified in buying any this year, but at the end of last summer she and Mark had helped with the harvest in the Langlois vineyard. They had spent four happy days at the job. She had expected perhaps a bottle or two in return, but had in fact been presented with the scrupulously calculated 'share' for the two of them: a cask of twenty litres. This she had bottled, under Madame Langlois's directions, and the bottles had provided occasional solace ever since. There was only one left now. She was looking forward hopefully to the next grape-harvest.

"Don't you like wine, Mark?" asked Serge, when Mark refused it.

"No," said Mark. "It's lucky, isn't it? Anyway, it's fair. Maman lets me have most of the jam we're given."

Jane did not enlarge upon their day-to-day problems: she was enjoying the evening too much. She and Serge (they were on first-name terms now) talked of Paris, of medicine, of his hopes for the future, after the War. Serge spoke warmly of Pierre, of his kindness and his wit and his professional capabilities, as if Pierre too would belong as a matter of course to the unimaginable post-War future. Jane came to understand that this serious young man had hero-worshipped Pierre, a little, who came from a different background from his own; and she felt herself included by extension in Pierre's aura.

She told Serge something of her own family. He listened attentively and took down her parents' address.

"If I ever get the chance," he said, "I will send them a letter – not mentioning your full name, of course, in case it goes astray – to say that I have seen you and Mark and that you are well. You never know: I might encounter someone with the means to smuggle letters out of France. I am told there is a network ... Some Resistance movements are beginning, you see." But he did not enlarge on the fact.

She asked him: "Are we – the Allies – really winning the War now, do you think?" She had not dared ask this question so far of anyone in the village. She never felt quite sure which people were all for Germany's defeat and which had adjusted to the idea of a quiet life under Pétain and the Reich and had no enthusiasm for seeing these arrangements upset by further bloodshed.

Serge paused a moment, then answered carefully:

"Yes, I think we, as you say, are winning now. But it will be a long struggle. And it will be worse, I am afraid, before it gets better."

Almost the only domestic subject they touched on during that evening was the dormice who, with the warm weather, had returned to the cottage.

"Like Persephone?" he suggested. "A sign of summer."

"Exactly! But Persephone only ate six pomegranate seeds, while these –" She was very cross with the mice: they had even chewed a piece out of a check wool shirt of Pierre's which she had been hoarding carefully for Mark when he should have grown still bigger. "I'm laying plans," she said. "Jeanot Langlois is going to try to get me a new sort of poison for them that he says a friend of his uses. You have to put it on bread, apparently, but I think it will be worth sacrificing a few crusts in a good cause."

Serge was visibly and genuinely shocked.

"But it's dreadful to kill things. The mice don't mean any harm, it's just their nature. Anyway if you poison the ones that you already have, more will just come. Can't you find some way of living in peace with them?"

"Not if they eat clothes, I can't."

"But they're such charming little creatures. I used to hear them running round inside the walls when I was alone as a child before my parents came to bed, and the noise always comforted me. Can't you decide which part of the house is for them and which for you?"

"Well, yes, I suppose I could – but how could I get them to stick to this bargain? I can't *explain* to dormice."

"What you should do is, you should leave food out for them deliberately in one place – the attic, perhaps – and then they will go there and not trouble you down here."

"I wish I could believe you!" said Jane laughing, but wondering if he could be right.

"It sounds like the division of France," said Mark suddenly. "Into different zones, I mean."

"Ah," said Serge, "but which of us is the Germans?"

"They are the Germans, taking our food and things."

"Are you sure? I'm not. I think perhaps that *we* are the Germans, the master-race, and the mice are the others ... Translating that back into human terms, we in France are now in the position of the dormice. We should therefore be very careful how we treat them."

The first night he had seemed to fall into an exhausted sleep almost before she had left the kitchen. Tonight, however, she sensed that he was not ready to sleep. Long after Mark had retired to his room and she herself had tidied the kitchen for the night, he remained alert in his chair.

Although she was tired herself, she did not want the evening to end. The thin, taut thread of sympathy and understanding between herself and Serge was precious: she dreaded to break it. And in the morning he would go.

"Are you quite sure," she said, not on a sudden impulse but from a conviction that she was making the right offer – "Are you quite sure you don't want to stay for a bit? I could explain to people that you are a friend of my husband's. They would understand ... And a doctor would be useful in the village. I've heard people say they wished they had one nearer than Châtelet. When Pierre was here he used to prescribe for people sometimes, or look at cuts and sprains and things when they asked him to." She had a superstitious feeling that this young man had been sent to her. If she sheltered Serge here, might not someone, somewhere, shelter Pierre?

Also, she longed desperately for his civilised, adult company. It would be all right, it must be; whatever nonsense the village people heard on the wireless about Jews they really, as Jeanot had once said to her, had no perception –

"No," he said gently. "You have been more than kind to me and I am greatly tempted – but no. I might get you into terrible trouble. And, on another level, it might not be good for your son. No, I shall set off again tomorrow. You have given me new courage. I too was feeling very lonely."

She said goodnight to him and went to bed, but could not sleep. The light was still on next door; she heard him moving about from time to time. When at last she got up again and went in to him, he was sitting wrapped in a blanket reading Monsieur Picard's copy of *Germinal*. He put it down, got to his feet, and came and put his arms round her.

In the darkness of her bed he seemed both like and unlike Pierre: the familiarity of the situation belied their essential strangeness to one another. Though short, he was heavier than Pierre, and very quiet – so quiet that it occurred to her he probably came from the sort of background where people, deprived of privacy, automatically make love quietly to avoid disturbing the rest of the family. She was afraid to speak, afraid to spoil things for him, in case he, like her, half wished to pretend that she was a different person.

After a while, he himself began to talk. There was a girl, he said, in Paris, whom he had wanted for some years to marry. No, she was not Jewish, though one of her grandmothers had been, but his family did not really mind: they kept few religious observances themselves and they liked this girl. Everyone liked her.

"You'll manage to get married," said Jane gently, thinking this was perhaps the real reason he would not stay with herself. "Perhaps she'll make her way to Lyons too."

No, he said, it was no good: in fact it was all over now. Her parents had turned against him and he could not blame them; no one in their senses would try to marry a Jew now. It was forbidden in Occupied France now, and by and by it would be in Vichy-France also.

"But when the War's over –" she said, offering him the one comfort she could offer herself.

"No," he said quietly. "No. I've lost her now. Wars change people, you know. Even her. And it's changing me too. I can feel it."

United in their separate losses, they clung together, as if each was trying to draw strength from the other's warm body. But what was a body, after all? Perhaps, she thought wearily, they were trying to put more feeling into their embrace than it could really bear. Yet that did not mean that the feeling, the wanting to reach one another, was not real. She hardly slept all night. As soon as the sky began to show pale at the rims of the shutters, he got up and began to dress.

"Your son will be awake soon," he said. He had a number of times referred to Mark like that, as if to use his first name would have been too much of taking-for-granted familiarity.

"Hardly, yet awhile. You've plenty of time."

"No," he said, "I must go anyway. If I hesitate now I shall be lost: I won't have the strength to leave you."

She wondered just what he meant by that, but did not ask.

When he was dressed, she said,

"At least let me make you some tea. It's not real tea, of course, it's dried herbs, but it's something."

"No," he said. "No, you'll have to light a fire to boil the kettle. I must be on my way now."

"Then take some bread with you. Take some chicory too. I wish I had some cheese to give you."

"No, no, I won't take your bread rations. The only thing I wondered was – I just wondered if you could let me have a little money? I'm running low on cash."

It was obvious how difficult it had been for him to ask this, but she must have looked aghast, for he said at once, retreating physically –

'Oh no, please don't if it is difficult. I just wondered … I shouldn't have asked –"

She explained her situation while he looked more and more concerned. He said: "I had no idea. I should of course have thought. But why didn't you tell me before?" He added almost reproachfully: "I shared my troubles with you."

"Oh – I'm so sick of the subject myself. It was a relief *not* to talk about it, you must believe that." She offered him the few francs she had in the house, but he said there was now no question of his taking a sou from her – "On the contrary, I ought to pay you for the food I have eaten."

"There is no question of *that*," she said firmly.

They parted affectionately in mutual guilt, with promises to try to keep in touch.

She heard nothing for several weeks. She often wondered if he had reached Lyons, but after a fortnight or so her sense of him began to fade. It was almost as if she had dreamed his brief visit and its culmination. He became simply an elusive shadow-body among those that intermittently populated her own body at night, imaginary comforters without force or daytime reality.

Then, one morning, Stefan-Postier brought her a small package. It was post-marked 'Lyons' and marked 'trade sample'. Inside was a ring with a pretty stone which at first she assumed to be paste. She was amused, but very faintly insulted by this apparently conventional gesture. 'Because he slept with me he feels he must give me something,' she thought. But then she read the note that accompanied it. In small, neat handwriting it said: *'This is an amethyst, so you will be able to sell it if you need to. I often think about you. Remember me to your son. Serge.'*

There was no address on it, so she could not write to thank him. She would have liked to do so but perhaps, as he would have insisted, it was safer not to. She wondered if he had been able to stay in Lyons with his uncle. She also thought at times about his parents, living in a city where they were forced to wear yellow stars and were not allowed to ride on buses or to join queues for food.

She was never to hear from Serge Beckman again. Long after

the War was over, it occurred to her that, if he were still alive, he probably assumed that *she* was dead, and might like to know she was not. After some hesitation, she asked an international organisation to try to trace him. They eventually came up with a Serge Beckman who had been arrested near the Swiss frontier early in 1944 and sent to Drancy, and of whom no trace had been found at the Liberation. He was from the Parisian region and approximately the right age, but they could not confirm that he was the right one. Beckman was not that uncommon a name and nor was Serge. There were others. There was another Serge Beckman who had emigrated in 1946 to São Paulo. He had a record as a collaborator. There were so many people. It was very hard to be quite certain about the ultimate fate of any one of them.

In November 1942 the English and the Americans launched a big offensive in North Africa, and Admiral Darlan ceded to them. On the eleventh of that month, on the twenty-fourth anniversary of the day when the guns had ceased in 1918, the Germans overrode the Vichy Government and formally annexed the whole of France. From now on, each provincial town would have its German garrison, and even places as small as Châtelet-le-Lys would have patrols.

There were new, more stringent regulations about journeys and letters, and about vehicles. All wireless sets were to be handed in. Jane, feeling that there was no point in breaking the law unnecessarily, handed in the old Yrieux set despite Mark's protest. She hadn't been able to get the Free French broadcasts on it from London anyway.

Picard, however, could get them on his set, which he evidently did not relinquish. One Sunday morning when she met him in the square he remarked quietly to her that she might care to come and listen some time. Then he passed rapidly and conversationally onto the subject of Mark's special lessons. But before he left her, raising his Sunday hat in that ceremonial way of his in which there always seemed to be a hint of sarcasm, he said, "By the way – forgive my mentioning it, but I heard you talking in English to Marc earlier outside the bakers ... I do beg you to take care. In view of the new situation, you understand."

"You mean, people might hear us?"

"Precisely. It does not matter perhaps too much in the village where you are known. But you never know, particularly on a Sunday, who may be visiting the church or the restaurant. And I think you should definitely avoid doing anything so imprudent in Châtelet."

"We do, of course," she said firmly, but he continued,

"In fact, I would advise you to avoid it at all times, for these things are a matter of habit are they not?"

Jane went home slowly. When she reached the cottage, she said,

"Mark darling, I think we ought to begin talking to each other just in French. All the time. Even here at home."

Part Four

That fourth winter of the War was another cold one. There also seemed to be even less to buy. It was said that the occupying forces were shipping more and more produce to Germany. Train-loads of cattle continued to pass through the stock-yards up at the station. Sometimes Jane heard them bellowing, and thought of those other, rumoured transportations northwards, not of cattle but of men and sometimes of women and children too. She also thought of Pierre saying that in wartime it was better to be in France than in England because France could feed herself. He had not envisaged that she would be feeding the urban populations of Germany.

Pierre seemed far away now, not just metaphorically but also as if she perceived her actual distance from him across the unguessable wastes of Europe. She felt an obscure, different pain, compounded by a sense of guilt and loss, that her original grief had lessened taking hope away with it. One dark night of beating rain she thought, soberly and very sadly,

I'll never see him again.

It was like a piece of knowledge that had been there for some time, but which she had only now put into words. Yet the words themselves disintegrated as she tried to hold them in her mind to test them; they slipped like a worn mechanism, evading meaning. What did 'never' mean? It was an intellectual concept, bleak but without force. You couldn't *feel* 'never' or touch it or see it. You could not even suffer it: you could only suffer piecemeal, one day or hour at a time, through a dragging expanse of years. 'Never' was just a melodramatic word for an absence, a lack of hope, for nothingness; and a life without hope was also without despair.

The mood passed and hope still, intermittently, returned to her, but it no longer seemed like something to cling to on principle. On the contrary, it was an indulgence, a happy daydream. Only now did she realise properly that, right up to last November when Vichy-France had been overrun, she could have sought contact with the Red Cross and a possible exit route for herself and Mark. It had not crossed her mind to do so; she had been waiting for Pierre to return. And now it was too late.

It was possible, she thought objectively, that Serge's brief passage through her life had in some way driven her further from Pierre. But she hardly ever thought of Serge either. Indeed it seemed to her that she did not think much at all these days. Even reading now often seemed too much of an effort. Nearly all her waking hours were devoted to the search for food: it was not a frantic search, but a constant, interminable, grudging one, like the labour of a man pushing a plough. There was no escaping from it; they had to eat. The toy cottage, the village and the surrounding countryside, the one-time landscape of freedom, had become in turn a prison. The place in which nothing mattered so much that you could not laugh about it had vanished as utterly as the secret château in *Le Grand Meaulnes*. Only rarely, in summer, did some nostalgic sense of it return to her, brief as a scent and as unsatisfying.

In the summer it had sometimes been hard to believe there could be any real problem about food, for the fertile countryside produced abundantly. In summer she could help with the cycle of pickings and harvests and be paid in kind. In the winter, however, the fields and gardens were almost bare. Then, what people had they kept for themselves. She found that she had to go further and further into the cold countryside, pushing her bike up the hills where the bracken lay flattened now in the ditches, to find the remote farms where – someone in the village would have told her – they would still sell you a bit of butter or a piece of salt pork. Often the trail would be a false one, and increasingly often too, if she did find the goods offered for sale, she would refuse them because the prices seemed so high.

Some farmers were whispered to be making a fortune out of selling to townspeople. Once or twice, after she had said flatly, "I can't possibly pay that. I just haven't the money", a farmer or his wife had reduced the price, as if realising that they had mistaken their customer. But more and more, as that winter went on, they tended to insist that what they had asked was the present 'free' rate and that there could be no bargaining. Madame Langlois expressed herself as scandalised at such profiteering, but Jane did not really blame the peasant farmers. She realised for the first time the true meaning of phrases often vaguely overheard in the conversations of people like her husband James: phrases like 'market forces'. If, for instance, eggs were in short supply, as they were in the months when the hens stopped laying, then eggs *were* valuable, that was all there was to it. She did not feel she could spare the emotion to get angry about it.

The only resentment she occasionally felt, which would flare at sudden, unexpected moments and then sink feebly down again like a spurt of heat from a damped-down fire, was a painful anger at the sheer fact of having to feel *grateful* – grateful to fate for this life of drudgery. She had told herself so often that she and Mark were very lucky really to be safe here in the depths of the country, that their situation and their experiences could have been far, far worse than they were ... so often, that the repetitive, dutiful reflection had begun to sicken her, and she longed momentarily to make some violent, irresponsible gesture.

But most of the time life seemed to have reduced itself down to a string of days, which were good or bad according to whether some quite small thing – like getting four eggs or not getting them – made her happy or dejected. A failure, or a slow puncture on her bike, or a brusque word from someone in the village, would send her home deeply discouraged, while a small success, or gift, or a happy encounter, would make her almost jubilant.

Sometimes, descending the hill into the village at the end of a weary afternoon, seeing the single street curving down to the irregular square before the church and then on, past the outlying houses to the river, she had an odd sensation of her own insubstantiality. She had come here by pure, unlikely chance and one day she would go again, but the village itself was far more permanent than she was, or than any of its present inhabitants. It had a long history, it had endured in much the same form for centuries, while conquerors came and went in the region. There was a house near the church with a carved sixteenth-century doorway, now lived in by the village tailor, and among the trees near the river were huge, hewn stones that were said to have been part of a castle destroyed by the English during the Hundred Years' War, when they had put the countryside to fire and sword, slaughtering men, women and children.

One day when she had been to see Picard at the Mairie to beg two new forged bread cards, he had shown her the old map of the district, which dated from the years after the Revolution and the setting up of communes. Though smaller than it was today, the place was entirely recognisable. There was the church, and the tailor's house and the mayor's, and others that probably (Picard remarked) were not the same that lined the street today, but which occupied the same sites. There was her own cottage, next to an empty field where the Yrieux house would later be built, and there was the Langlois property with its two farmhouses, and – yes, there was Marie Stefan's cottage under the hill side by side with other, now vanished buildings, as if there had been almost a separate hamlet there then.

There was no cemetery. Picard said that the dead of those days were buried behind the church, and pointed to the back-square where the plane trees were planted today and where the boys played football and the annual fête was held.

Beyond the village fields of the eighteenth century lay the forest, far more encroaching and enveloping than the broken tracts of woodland today. Through it ran the lanes and footpaths that still ran today as roads, criss-crossing the open countryside. But the main road several kilometres from the village, that led to Châtelet-le-Lys and eventually to Châteauroux, was not there. It was as if the village and its neighbouring hamlets existed then as a self-contained world, barely touched by events outside.

Afterwards, at night, sitting by the stove, she would think about the village before the road and the railway came; she could almost persuade herself it was still there, that quintessential St Laurent, and that, by effacing herself still more, by becoming yet more uncomplainingly part of the landscape, she could slip through the mesh of the present and evade its dangers. No German troops could come marching down a road that was not yet built: no effective orders could come from a country town many days distant over muddy, rutted tracks through deep oak woods, much less from a Paris immeasurably distant where people did not even speak the same tongue. In the past, lay safety.

The fantasy preoccupied her. There was no one with whom she could share it: Mark did not understand it. One evening, after he had gone to bed, she found she had sat for over an hour, her hands in her lap, lost in it. Is this what they mean by 'living in the past' she asked herself, with faint amusement? I must be becoming senile.

She did in fact feel stupid these days, sluggish and numb. Perhaps it was the cold, which seemed to be worse than it used to be, soaked deep into lathe and plaster and stone? Then one day it occurred to her that she was suffering from slight malnutrition. It probably didn't matter too much, and there was nothing she could do about it anyway. Nearly all the scant protein she could lay her hands on, she kept for Mark. He was growing fast, she reasoned: he must have priority or his mental and physical development might be permanently stunted. Most days she bought half a litre of milk, or a whole litre when the farm would sell her that much, and made Mark drink most of it. Milk was calcium: it had been one of her own mother's axioms that if you had plenty of that it didn't matter so much what else you went without. Her reward was seeing that he still looked sturdy and that his energy seemed undiminished. She became used to her own perpetual, vague craving for something other than mashed swedes or vegetable broth, and hardly noticed it any more. She couldn't help noticing, however, that her hair came out a lot in the comb and that her skin seemed unnaturally cracked and dry. Her hands were in a particularly bad state, with tiny fissures that bled at the slightest thing. She undertook to embroider a small child's frock for Madame Marceau the mayor's wife, but had great difficulty in completing the job. Madame Marceau made polite remarks about it and paid her for the work, but Jane knew it had not been a success: bits of the cotton were all frayed, where she had had to scrub it to get the bloodstains out.

Evangeline Bisset sympathised over the dry skin: it was due to lack of fats in the diet, she said. She herself had a milder form of the same problem. With her work at the Post Office, she could not go round looking for extra food during the day, and her mother's legs of course wouldn't permit *her* to do it.

After that Jane, smitten with guilt because she had thought of the Bissets as comfortably stocked with provisions, went looking for food on Evangeline's behalf. They would share the result, or Evangeline would give her something obtained in the town – a tin of sardines, or some sweets. Once, overcome by a sudden longing, Jane ate the sweets herself during the afternoon, instead of keeping them for Mark. Later, she was appalled at herself. How could she have behaved like that?

But she was not the only person, she knew, on whom privation and worry were having their effect. In January, the bread ration was cut. Because the coupons on the cards still looked the same, people seemed to have difficulty in understanding that each actually represented less bread: perhaps they did not want to understand. There were scenes at the bakers. Neither the baker's wife, who normally served, nor the baker himself who emerged from the bakehouse to arbitrate, were good tempered or diplomatic people at the best of times. Now, badgered for something they could not give and complained at for regulations that were not their fault, they both seemed in a permanent state of defensive fury. You would have said, from the way Madame Chauvin slammed the bread on the scales and then snatched it off again to hew further pieces off it, that she hated her customers, and some of them seemed to hate her.

One day when Jane was in there for her thrice-weekly share, Madame Chauvin banged the end-section of a huge load onto the scales and then hesitated. The lump weighed considerably more than the 350 grams to which Jane's various illicit cards entitled her, but much of it was hard crust – the bakeress obviously decided to let it pass, and was quickly handing it over when a voice behind muttered:

"Huh – so a foreigner gets an extra hand-out now while we wait."

There was an abrupt silence in the crowded shop. Jane, feeling herself grow pale, did not dare look round. She was not even sure who had spoken, but thought it was the cobbler's mother-in-law, a cross little woman.

"After all, Madame Leparde has a growing lad," said an old man's voice mildly.

"Growing lad," another woman grumbled. "Haven't we all got kiddies at home. We can do without outsiders coming in, taking the bread from our mouths.

Jane, taking her bread, passed through the shop like a shadow, though the people parted to let her through. In passing, she caught sight of one woman's face – red, suffused with what might have been either anger or embarrassment. Had she been the second speaker? Jane did not know her, she must come from an outlying farm. She walked away from the shop trembling, knowing that now that her back was turned the incident would be furiously discussed inside.

No one referred to it afterwards. But a few days later the baker himself served Jane, declaring as if to the world at large,

"I won't be told how to run my own shop."

A young woman with a toddler caught Jane's eye and

smiled sheepishly at her. It was clear that the previous scene had reverberated right round the village.

The lame man from the smithy speaking broad dialect said humorously,

"You'll have a heart attack one day over that oven of yours, Jules. You want to take a turn in the fresh air from time to time like I does."

"Fresh air be damned," retorted the baker. "What did fresh air ever do but get on people's chests and kill them? Ah, these bastards and their coupons – I'm up all afternoon pushing their dirty bits of paper about for them. I'd like to see *them* doing a decent night's work in a bakehouse."

And Jane left the shop that day thanking God that the baker's ready animosity was for Them, remote, unknowable Them, and not for herself. The same seemed to be true of most of the people in the village. But not, she now felt certain, for all.

Did terrible danger wait for her, in some innocent-seeming village house with oil-cloth on the table, in some remote farm where a man or a woman with a grudge might observe her narrowly and might even now be planning their visit to the police in Châtelet? Or not even to the regular police, who were said to be accommodating and to want only a quiet life, but to the new German-inspired police, the Militia? Or to the Germans themselves.

She could not know. It was simply a risk she knew she must constantly take; and this small, private knowledge was a further drain upon her energy and spirits.

Her savings were going fast. She sold the green bike to Petitjean, who said he had a buyer for it in Châtelet, and that helped, for bicycles were precious now. It was less than four years ago but it seemed in another life altogether that she and Pierre had ordered the bicycle specially and it had been sent all the way from Northampton. Mark, too, seemed a different creature from that little boy who had wanted the bike to be green, though she could not quite express to herself where the change lay. His cheerful personality was still the same; he and she were in some ways, partly from force of circumstances, closer than ever. He still liked to be stroked and hugged when she said goodnight to him. And yet she felt that he had, over the months and years, become such a different version of himself that between him and the child of nine he had been there was little connection. Most of his assumptions, attitudes and turns of phrase now were those of a French country boy, merely rather more intelligent than some. He liked birds' eggs and butterflies, and these now decorated the washstand in his room. He had made new arrows for the bow Pierre had long ago bought him, and had tipped them with the tail-feathers of a jay. He also had a catapult. Vanished was the child with the soldiers who said "France has been invaded – but luckily not round here", and vanished too the one who had cried and said it was because of a hedgehog he had seen crushed in the road. The killing of small animals – dormice, pigeons in the garden – was something he could now accomplish with a matter-of-fact professionalism that shocked Jane rather, though she had to acknowledge that it was right. She felt it might only be a matter of time before he took over as rabbit-butcher from Sylvain.

Speaking French at home with her, as well as at school, had perhaps finally divested him in these last months of his old identity. Only in his dreams would he occasionally speak out in English, and when she asked him about it in the morning he never seemed to remember. In his waking hours he did not appear to miss the language at all. It was rather she who, after he was asleep, would speak English sentences to the empty air, as if trying the words out to make sure they were still there. Though it now came naturally to her too to speak French, and she did not even know the English equivalent for some of the terms they used in their daily life, nevertheless she felt that there was, too, a loss in her life, something either blunted or missing, a further erosion of the self she had once been.

At least Mark could ride Pierre's old bike. Obstinately she refused to deprive him of that, and anyway it saved his shoes from wear. Or rather, *her* shoes, for his feet were now the same size as hers and she had given her only solid walking shoes to him. She herself wore wooden clogs, like many other people – they had been almost obsolete in 1939, but now two elderly clog-makers in the village were doing a thriving trade in them. They were heavy and cut into the feet till you got used to them, but were at least waterproof and surprisingly warm.

Mark's clothes had become a pressing problem. At just thirteen he had outgrown all his old ones except his coat, which had turned itself into a short-waisted, skimpy-sleeved jacket. But he was still too small for Pierre's grey flannels, and she hesitated to try to cut them down for him; at the rate he was going, in another year he might need them as they were now. She conferred with Madame Marcelle and Evangeline Bisset and, under their supervision, managed to turn the skirt of her tweed suit into a pair of knickerbockers for him, such as boys of his age wore in France. Their check pattern made them oddly smart, almost bounderish. That left her with no warm skirt, but Madame Marcelle declared that this was no problem; with a little effort one could turn an old piece of blanket into a quilted underskirt and wear it beneath a thin dress 'for a good appearance': this, she confided to Jane, was what she herself did, obligingly lifting up her black sateen skirt for Jane to see. So one of the Yrieux carriage rugs became Jane's principle winter garment. Lacking Madame Marcelle's skill, she had failed to turn it into a tailored petticoat that would fit under a summer skirt, and so wore it just as it was. She felt bulky and dowdy: blanket, she realised, was what Marie Stefan wore all the time; but it served its purpose and, she thought, all helped her to merge into the landscape. Who, now, seeing her walking or bicycling slowly along an empty road, would dream that she was anything but what she seemed – a farmer's wife in clogs, shapeless skirt, old jerseys, and a headscarf over hair snipped short for convenience?

Marie Stefan herself seemed to respond to the gradual transformation of Jane's appearance: she talked to her more readily these days, telling her where, in the winter landscape, she could find the plants the rabbits liked. She asked Jane if Sylvain were still getting her a good price for her rabbits in the market. Jane said that she had no means of telling, but that she didn't feel Sylvain was cheating her. Marie Stefan looked exaggeratedly shrewd.

"No, he won't cheat you exactly. But if he gets a bit over the odds for a plump one he might be tempted to keep the extra money to himself. I know that boy of mine . . . What did he get you for the last buck he killed?"

"Oh that one wasn't for market. I – I wanted us to have a good dinner for once. It was Mark's birthday. Mademoiselle Bisset came to dinner too, and brought Mark a cake." She felt a slight fool mentioning this modest celebration. Marie Stefan said nothing, but Jane suspected that birthdays were luxuries unknown to the Stefan way of life. She often felt divided, these days, between the desire to go on giving Mark what she had been brought up to regard as the irreducible elements of a good childhood, and the feeling that, in their present situation, such an attitude was frivolous indulgence.

The birthday had been a good day, when she went to bed feeling confident that the future was, after all, possible. But matters were, in practice, becoming desperate. Their stock of potatoes were almost finished, and the carrots were going mouldy and tasting of the earth. The few onions that were left had soft bits in them: it hadn't been a good year for onions. There would be no more rabbits ready to sell till the spring. Since one lucky strike with his catapult, Mark had had no luck at bagging wood pigeons. They had all but finished a sack of beans they had acquired, and she had had to open her last jar of chestnuts carefully salted away in the autumn. She used their money only for absolute necessities – for bread, for milk, for a few bones to make stock, for a little dripping. Once, she would have believed it impossible that spending reduced to this level should not make her hoard of francs last almost indefinitely. She had repeated to Mark several times the fact that eventually their money would just run out, but had not really believed it herself and therefore had not encouraged him to think the danger was as imminent as in fact it was. So when the day actually came that she must draw her last thirty francs out of the post office, she was too appalled to tell Mark or anyone else. The dilemma, unvoiced, was still not quite real.

Evangeline Bisset would have noticed and been sympathetically concerned. But she was away with 'flu, and so it was from an unknown young male supply clerk that Jane drew it. She had to show him her identity card.

"Do you want to close this account, Madame?"

"No. That is – no, I don't." She *must* get some more money from somewhere to replenish it. But where?

"In that case you must leave one franc in it."

She eked that twenty-nine francs out over many days, almost making a game of it. But the day arrived when she literally did not know how she was going to pay for the bread ration on the next one. Doubtless the bakery would give her credit – but credit against what, and for how long? And, apart from bread, she did not know what she and Mark were going to eat the day after.

That morning she gave Mark the last of the existing bread, and the milk. She told him she was not hungry, and believed it herself. She felt weak, but with a detachment of mind which she mistook for clarity. Time itself, which had crawled so for the last two-and-a-half years and yet had carried her so far, seemed to have slowed to stopping point. She was very conscious of small sounds, of bits of wood settling inside the stove, of a dog barking a long way off, of Henri and Colette shuffling in their hutch on the far side of the wall, even of the feet of birds on the frozen gravel outside.

She sat for some time with her hands in her lap. A sense of utter weariness possessed her. "I must do something," she repeated, formulating the words in her mind as if they were in themselves a substitute for action.

In the end, she put on her shabby tweed jacket and went out. The countryside was in the grip of a hoar-frost: each twig and leaf in the ditch was etched in white, petrified and still. Black ice filmed the stone slab beneath the pump. Her clogs rang on the road when she reached it.

She would hardly have been surprised if, on passing the oak tree, she had found the next plot empty and the Yrieux house gone – or rather, not yet come. She would have known then that the village had contracted with cold and hardship, reducing itself down to its long-ago self, far from any roads, lost among the oak forests.

Once, she recalled, with a brief, dim perception of irony, she had imagined the peasants of bygone days as antic figures in a child's history book. Unreal creatures, immeasurably alien from herself, they had lain by the roadside in rags, attempting to stuff their gaping mouths with frozen grass. Now, as she walked slowly and mechanically in the direction of the Langlois farmhouse, she glanced with dread at the empty verges, almost expecting to see there premonatory spectres – shadows not merely of the past but of her own possible future, and Mark's.

Madame Langlois was baking bread and greeted her kindly but in a rather preoccupied manner. She cut a slice from a finished loaf that was cooling on the side. Jane accepted it, realising now how hungry she was, but then, when she got the soft dough in her mouth, she could hardly swallow it. Madame Langlois looked at her curiously.

"Aren't you well, Madame Leparde?" she said after a while.

Jane hesitated. She had meant to lead up to the subject gradually, put her cards on the table before Madame Langlois, be matter-of-fact and sensible about it. But suddenly her longing to stay in this hot, bread-scented kitchen forever and relinquish her lonely struggle was so intense that she found herself near to tears. It was a confused and self-pitying account that she managed to give to the listening woman. It was coming out all wrong, she knew – it was awful of her to behave like this, like a whining object of charity. But she could no longer help herself.

Madame Langlois lifted a new pan of risen bread, tested it with her finger, and then stowed it away in the oven.

Finally, red in the face – but this might have been from the heat – she turned to Jane,

"Madame Leparde, we've always tried to do our best for you, I'm sure. There's my mister been doing your vegetables for you these two years past, and Jeanot fetching you wood and even sawing it for you whenever you've needed it –"

"Yes, yes I *know*. Don't think I'm not grateful. I *am* –"

"I've always tried to be neighbourly and been glad to help you out with jams and eggs and that when I can. And paying you to do that dress for Marie-Jo . . . What I've always said is, if we can't help each other out in this life then the world's a poor sort of place –"

"– You've always been terribly kind. And indeed I wouldn't bother you now, but I really don't know how –" Oh please stop.

"– But, when all's said and done, Madame Leparde, you're not my own flesh and blood. My own family's got to come first with me, hasn't it? Times are hard, you know, even for us people that grow our own stuff. Fact is, Madame Leparde, *you didn't ought to have come here*, so far away from your own kind, and your own people who'd look after you and see you right."

Madame Langlois turned sharply away after this speech and began adding more wood to the stove. Her whole stance expressed the painful resentment felt by an essentially kind and practical person who has nevertheless had a greater demand made on them than they had ever bargained for. Jane said nothing. What could she say? That she hadn't known the War was coming? That she hadn't realised how long it would go on or what it would be like? That she had led such a comfortable, sheltered life for her first thirty years that the danger of real hunger and want simply hadn't entered her imagination? She was ashamed to say any of this. She said nothing. But after some time, when Madame Langlois said nothing either, she ventured in a small voice,

"I'm sure you're right, Madame Langlois. We really ought never to have come, I see that now. But we are here, and – I just don't know what we are going to eat for the rest of this month. Or next." To her disgust, she heard her voice tremble again.

Madame Langlois turned back to face her. In spite of her hard words some sort of struggle seemed to have been going on inside her. Her face looked puckered. She said harshly.

"Haven't you got anything you can sell? Folks like you should have."

"I – I've got a gold chain. And a ring."

"Well, for the Lord's sake! Sell them."

"I – I was keeping them for a real emergency. For if Mark and I have to escape from the Germans. Or – or if either of us falls seriously ill." This had, all along, been her policy.

"But what do you call this if not an emergency?" cried Madame Langlois, hands on hips. In spite of her bullying stance her amazement seemed genuine. "You *will* be ill if you don't eat. You sell those things – yes, and your wrist-watch too – and live on the money from them as long as it lasts and *then* we'll see. I've no patience with people who cry poverty when they've something stuck under the mattress all the time. We had an old aunt like that – drove me mad, she did."

Walking slowly home again, Jane had to admit to herself that Madame Langlois was right. Or, at any rate, right within her own terms: those of a peasantry whose existence had been hand-to-mouth from time immemorial. It was she, Jane, who had been hedging and holding back. A few years ago, when she had left James and come here with Pierre, she would unhesitatingly and rather proudly have described herself as 'unconventional' and even – half-joking – 'turning her back on bourgeois values'. But, on reflection, what could be more cravenly entrenched in middle-class tradition than to refuse to spend your last reserve of capital on food when you were hungry? 'Eating into capital' was, she thought, the cardinal sin for her parents' generation. Her mother had always said that the trouble with the working class – 'splendid people though some of them are' – was that they would live in the present and take no thought for future emergencies that might arise.

Now she would have to live like this herself. Property, after all, was no real charm against evil, even though, for all her life, she had unthinkingly believed it was. Suppose she went on keeping the chain and the ring in reserve and one day a German patrol knocked on their door? The amethyst's colour and the gold's shine would do her and Mark no good then.

Clasped against her stomach and warming it was a loaf. Madame Langlois had thrust in into her hands at the door.

Later in the day, when she was washing up after the bean stew she and Mark had had for lunch, and he had returned to school preoccupied with some new algebra, Jeanot Langlois appeared self-consciously at the door. She saw him through the window and wiped her hands slowly before letting him in. For the first time, she was not glad to see him. Probably he had not wanted to come, probably he, like his mother, just regarded her as a nuisance and as a responsibility he should not be asked to shoulder.

It was true: people had their own lives to lead. She herself was an outsider, an intruder, just as the customer in the baker's shop had said. She had tried hard to integrate herself, to make herself accepted. But it was no use. She was not one of them. For a few hours or days in the summer, picking peas or grapes or bringing in the hay, she might feel herself to be a genuine villager, but then the happy interlude would be over and she would be alone again.

"I heard you'd been to see Mother," he said when she finally opened the door.

"Yes. I – we were talking about things. I've got a bit of jewelry I want to sell. I don't know quite how to set about it, but I expect I'll manage."

"In Châtelet, you'll find someone," said Jeanot abstractedly. He tilted his cap forwards and scratched his head. It wasn't about jewelry that he'd come to talk.

"Mother's a bit upset," he said suddenly.

"I'm very sorry if I upset her," said Jane, moving things around on the table. She didn't look at Jeanot face to face: she couldn't bear it if he turned against her too. He had always been so cheerful and friendly, and she had always felt more at ease with him than with anyone else, almost as if he and she had shared some unspoken area of experience which the others did not know.

"No," he said laboriously, "I mean, she's upset because she thinks maybe she wasn't nice enough to you this morning."

"Her advice was very good," said Jane dully. "I shall take it."

"Well ... I'm not just going by what Mother told me. Mother can be a bit sharp sometimes. And she's worried these days – Reine's been staying at our place because my uncle's house is full just now, and she's taken up with a lad over at Berjac none of us likes much and my aunt's saying it's Mother's fault. Mother's got that on her mind, see."

"I understand." Stupid Reine. She always was a simple-minded girl.

"She thinks she was maybe too hard on you. So do I. After all – you can't help the trouble you're in. I told her so."

"Please," said Jane, "Please don't let her feel bad about it." (Otherwise, she thought, she really will begin to dislike me.)

"I told Mother she ought to have said for you to come to our place to eat," he said suddenly after a pause. "Just till your own spring vegetables come on ... You'd be welcome, I'm sure, both of you. With a big family like ours you can always make things stretch a bit."

"Oh, I couldn't possibly expect that," said Jane hastily, though this was precisely what, in her lowest moments, she had longed for. "I can't impose on you all like that. We'll manage. We must. A lot of people are very good to us – besides yourselves of course. Marie Stefan and Sylvain bring us things sometimes."

It was not, she immediately realised, a tactful thing to say. Jeanot looked reticent. Jane went on after a pause,

"I know your family doesn't like them. They do lead rather a primitive life ... And your mother is so house-proud. I expect she thinks Marie Stefan is dirty."

"'Tisn't that exactly. None of the older women like her much. Reckon they think she knows too much about them all . . . She used to be the midwife, see."

"*Did* she?" The image that 'midwife' presented to Jane's mind – a commanding figure in immaculately laundered white, from the nursing home where she had had Mark – was so discrepant with Marie's dusky, sack-draped figure that she wanted to laugh.

"Well, in the old days that was, before they had to have certificates and that. Her mother was midwife before her, I've heard. But the new laws came and Marie Stefan wasn't allowed to deliver babies any more. It's our cousin, Solange Langlois who lives up at the Granges, who delivers them now. She did a training for it in Limoges. But for a long time Marie Stefan still helped people. Maybe she does even now."

"Helped?" said Jane vaguely, thinking of Marie's surprisingly gentle manner, her gift of rabbits.

"Yes." Jeanot looked highly self-conscious but evidently couldn't resist continuing now that he had started. He went on with meaning.

"She's a maker-of-angels. As they say."

The phrase was unfamiliar to Jane. Sedately he explained.

"Makers-of-angels stop babies from coming. They send them to heaven before they can be born. In a manner of speaking."

"Good heavens," said Jane weakly. "I never heard that word before."

"There are other words, I daresay."

"Yes of course."

He said almost casually, relaxed again now that she had understood: "Oh, every village has one. Or more than one."

"Yes, I suppose it must."

There was a silence in which they both thought their own thoughts. Into Jane's mind came the memory of a fear which, though brief, had been so alarming that once it was over she had put it right behind her and never recalled it till now. About three weeks after Serge Beckman's visit the previous summer she had thought, with a sickening lurch 'I haven't had my period –' But the next day she had known it was a false alarm.

Afterwards, she had genuinely forgotten all about it. It had gone away, become unreal, as so much else had become unreal: her childhood, James, Mark's early childhood, her old life in England, her parents, Marylebone High Street, the first carefree year at St Laurent, Madame Yrieux, Oncle Ernest, Pierre –

Yes, Pierre himself.

On an impulse, pierced with memory, she said to Jeanot, "I've sometimes wished Mark had a little brother or sister. But I suppose life would have been harder here with two children ... I really don't know."

"You're still a young woman," he said, with a quick, appraising glance of a young man who has been a favourite with the girls himself. "You'll have another, I shouldn't wonder. When your husband comes home."

"Not before, certainly!" she said, trying to turn this unbearably serious subject into a joke. She didn't feel like a young woman any longer. She felt heavy, old and worn, and sick with hopes of Pierre's return that had grown stagnant with keeping, but as Jeanot looked at her and fidgeted with his thumbs in his braces something stirred within her in spite of herself. She said self-consciously, aware of a submerged sequence in their conversation,

"I hear your wife is having another?" Madame Langlois had mentioned it that morning, saying something about mouths to feed.

He admitted that this was so. A moment later he added, almost moodily for him,

"She wanted it, and so did I, in a way, though I don't rightly know why. People like us, we have kids: it's something to have done. Something to leave behind you – someone to carry on, and maybe get further than you did. I can't explain myself very well."

"I think you do," she said encouragingly, and after a moment he went on,

"Sometimes I wonder if I ought to have left the land

and gone after a job in Châteauroux. Or Limoges or Clermont, or Paris even. There are opportunities ... A cousin of ours went. I used to think about it when I was in the Army and met people who'd had a better education than me. They weren't any cleverer than I am, though. I could have learnt what they'd learnt. But then, when I was taken prisoner, I used to sit and think about St Laurent and see it in my mind and when I escaped I came back here. I always did like the land, after all."

After he was gone she sat for a while by the stove with her chapped hands in her lap, thinking about him. She imagined his childhood and his youth and what his old age would be. She wished, rather, that he were not married. She knew he liked her.

She took the jewelry to the post office the following morning. Evangeline Bisset examined it with cautious admiration, breath drawn in. There were rules against selling gold these days, she said: she wasn't sure what they were, she would try to find out. There would surely be a way round them. About the amethyst there would, she thought, be no problem, and none about the watch – people always needed those. If Jane did not want to make herself conspicuous she, Evangeline, would take the ring and the watch to the big jewellers in Châtelet. Meanwhile, with the greatest circumstantial delicacy, she offered to lend Jane some money of her own against the eventual value of the jewelry: would Jane permit her – ?

Jane would. She certainly could not afford to refuse such an offer. The only thing that made her feel faintly guilty was that Evangeline seemed to have assumed that the ring, like the chain, was a present from Pierre, and was warmly sympathetic towards her for having to sell objects 'of such importance'. Jane's tentative suggestion that she should sell her wedding ring also was vetoed absolutely.

Jane had a brief, insane desire to say 'the ring came from my first husband for whom I have nothing but contempt, and the amethyst came from a recent one-night lover I never mentioned to you.' What on earth would Evangeline have answered? Would Jane have been cast out, out from the fold of people who were 'nice' and into the outer darkness along with the Stefans and those who hit their children and let them go about without shoes – the village criteria of bad parenthood? Or would Evangeline Bisset's Christian love have proved itself calmly equal to such a demonstration of spiritual abandonment after all? Jane could not guess, and did not dare put it to the test.

A few weeks later Evangeline Bisset called at the cottage on her bicycle in the rain with the news that the ring and the chain had been sold together to the jeweller and the watch to an 'individual'. The total came to over two thousand francs. Her cheeks were pink, and she seemed just as pleased as Jane herself. Considered as a sum of money on which to live for the indefinite future, two thousand francs was pitiable enough, but it was a great deal – a very great deal – better than nothing at all.

A subtle change seemed to have come over Jane's position. No doubt news had got round the village that she was now virtually destitute. People had adjusted to the idea that, from being a wealthy visitor, she had become like themselves, subject as they were to wartime shortages, but now she seemed to have passed some further barrier: she was recognised as a special case. She had become, officially, 'that poor Madame Leparde'. She was both humiliated and relieved to find herself thus singled out.

Her relations with some people underwent a change, not always for the better. Those who had always been kind, like Monsieur Bonnin and Madame Marcelle and the dried up little cobbler in his hutch near the church who was now having to re-sole shoes with wood – these people treated Jane with greater politeness than before, if anything, as if to dissemble delicately the fact that they now charged her little or nothing. "You've never made a nuisance of yourself, Madame Leparde, not like some I could mention –" Monsieur Bonnin would say, pressing a paper-wrapped lump of dripping into Jane's hand, beaming nervously and shooing her out of the shop before another customer should enter. But some people let Jane know all too clearly when they felt they were doing her a favour. When she tried to pay Petitjean for putting a patch on her front wheel, he waved the money aside with such a coldly patronising air that she felt she did not want to go to the garage again. She minded that a good deal. Jean-Baptiste Petitjean had, after all, been one of Mark's best friends at school, and had often visited their cottage. But Jean-Baptiste, like Jean-Luc, was at the High School in Châtelet-le-Lys now. Apparently he had ambitions to become an engineer, while poor Mark had had to remain in the village as Picard's solitary Advanced pupil. She told herself that Petitjean was a short-sighted man, who would one day find himself slighted and ignored in turn by his socially advancing son, but she burned with the injustice of it all.

She was also considerably put out when Madame Marceau, the Mayor's wife (and sister-in-law to 'Madame Marcelle') stopped her in the street and asked in a tactful but penetrating undertone if she would care to purchase any of Henri's old clothes for Mark at 'a very low price – much less than I'd ask anyone else, dear, seeing how you are placed.' Henri, she explained, was growing into such a robust boy, such an early developer, that he was much bigger than any of his contemporaries. The truth, as Jane perfectly well knew, was that Henri was over a year older than Mark. He was now Mark's main friend left in school, since his academic abilities had not proved up to High School standards. His parents declared loudly that they would not have wished him to waste any more time on study anyway, and in the summer he was due to start working in his father's carting business.

"I can't afford to buy Mark anything else just now," said Jane flatly, hating to have to admit what she felt was another injustice to him. "It's kind of you to think of me, Madame Marceau – but I can't, however cheap the clothes are."

Madame Marceau looked surprised and faintly insulted, as at a mild rebuff.

"But surely you must have *some* resources?"

"None, now. Unless I can find a way of earning some more."

Madame Marceau looked as if she did not altogether believe her. Jane was irritated and depressed by this encounter, but in her heart she knew that she herself, long ago in Henley, might have dismissed talk of someone having 'absolutely no money at all' as a manner of speaking.

In contrast, Madame Chauvin at the bakery said to her one day in her usual abrupt, grumpy manner,

"Are you interested in clothes for your lad? I'm giving 'em away, mind. I'm not going to sell 'em."

It was one of the first days in the year when spring seemed, after all, to be coming. The bakehouse, which all winter remained with tight-shut doors and windows, palpitating in its heat, was tentatively exposing its floury surfaces to the air. Madame Chauvin led Jane through it to a heavily padlocked storehouse behind. (It was rumoured that some village bakers had had their rationed flour-stocks plundered: by gipsies, nomads, refugees or – the word was a new, tentative one on people's lips – Maquisards. Resistance fighters.)

Among the precious sacks, once they were revealed, stood a tin trunk, which Madame Chauvin also laboriously unlocked.

"Our boy's things," she exclaimed drily. "They're yours, if you want 'em. They might as well do some good to someone. It's all the same to me." And she leant against the door jamb with a face of contorted unconcern while Jane eagerly looked through the shrunk flannel underwear and serviceable, mended shirts and Sunday suit and boots – boots, wonderful! – the clothes of the son who should have been the baker here one day too, but who had not returned in 1940.

With the spring other people too seemed to stir and reappear in Jane's orbit. She had not seen any of the Stefans for weeks: apparently there were quite long periods when Marie Stefan never came into the village at all, even to collect her rations; she must, the grocer-lady remarked darkly, have 'other resources'. But early one morning she appeared in Jane's garden and was even induced by Jane to come in and have a cup of coffee. (It wasn't real coffee, of course, or even the ersatz kind reputedly made from acorns which Madame Mouret and the proprietor of the smaller café served, but a little precious wheat, roasted on the top of the stove all night and then ground freshly in the coffee-grinder. It made a brew which smelt and felt something like coffee, even though it did not taste right.)

She had come, said Marie Stefan, to ask if Jane minded her picking the primroses and cowslips that were now showing in the ditches of the lane by the cottage. It was strange, Jane thought, that Marie Stefan had the reputation of a thief; she seemed, on the contrary, almost over-scrupulous about what might be another person's property. Possibly she was well aware of her reputation and was anxious to compensate for it.

"They aren't *my* primroses, Marie Stefan; we don't own the lane – at least I don't think we do – even though it doesn't lead anywhere but here." She had forgotten, as she spoke, that she didn't actually own the cottage either. She had become so identified with it that she felt physically part of it, in a way that she had with no other house she had lived in.

"But what do you want the flowers for?" she asked as an afterthought. It was inconceivable that Marie just wanted to stick them in a jam-jar on her own greasy table.

"Sell 'em in the market in Châtelet," said Marie promptly. "I always do that in the spring. Towns' people like the flowers then. Later in the summer, when they've got their own roses and that, they aren't bothered."

I ought to have thought of that, Jane registered. I could have made some money that way ... She was still intermittently humiliated by her own blindness and incompetence at making the most of what the countryside had to offer. It was, for instance, Mark who had first thought of cooking omelettes with the blown yellow mess from the insides of the birds' eggs he collected.

She said cautiously, wary of seeming to steal Marie's custom from her,

"Do you think people in Châtelet would buy flowers from me?"

Marie considered, head on one side.

"Well ... They'd wonder a bit. They'd hear you was a foreigner."

"I know. That's always worried me ... I don't even like going into Châtelet now."

"And you don't look like a person who ought to be selling flowers," said Marie candidly. "You look too much like a lady."

Jane, who thought that these days she looked very far from that, was amused and flattered. Marie Stefan seemed to be ruminating.

"Tell you what," she said suddenly. "I wouldn't advise you to share the flower-selling with me, no really I wouldn't. But I'll give you something instead."

"Oh but Marie I didn't mean it like that," said Jane hastily. "I tell you, wild flowers belong to the person who picks them."

But Marie Stefan repeated mysteriously that she would give Jane something. She drained her coffee cup noisily and seemed pleased with the idea in her head.

A few days later Sylvain turned up with a large, covered basket which cheeped and rustled. He set it down near the stove and raised the lid: a palpitating cushion of day-old chicks, yellow and fluffy as toys from Easter eggs, raised expectant bills. They had alert, bead eyes, and seemed impossibly unlike the plump, silly fowls they would one day become. Although Jane knew there must be a serious purpose behind their arrival, she felt rather as if she had been presented with some deliciously frivolous gift from Harrods Pet Shop.

"Mother says," said Sylvain as if repeating instructions,

"that seeing as you've got a nice warm place here and no cat or anything, maybe you'd like to rear these for us? Then, when they're pullets like, you can give half of them back to Mother and keep the others yourself."

"That's very, very kind of your Mother," said Jane warmly, though rather appalled at the responsibility fourteen chicks represented. They seemed so tiny: suppose they were all to die? And what did they eat –

"Mother sent a bag of feed – here. She says when that's gone you must get some more, but as soon as they're a month or so old they can begin scratching about outside for themselves and eat potato-peelings and that. It's just while they're so small they've got to be in the warm. Oh, and they need a lot of water. In a little bowl, like."

"I see . . . Should I leave them here by the stove?"

"That'll do nicely, yes. So long as you shut them up tight in the basket at night – see, it's got straps – so as the rats can't get 'em. Mind you –" he stared at her with limpid eyes, apparently feeling that he was repeating things she must surely know anyway – "They won't stay long in the basket, if you leave it open. Few days' time and they'll be hopping round the place. That's when you have to be careful not to tread on 'em. My brother's got clumsy feet when he's at home – he doesn't bother where he's putting them." He looked suddenly angry. "And there's the dog – he's a terror for chicks when he gets the chance . . . Anyways, Mother reckoned they'd be safer here with you. And then the ones you keep – by the end of the summer you'll have their eggs, like. You won't have to buy eggs no more."

Genuinely touched, Jane repeated,

"It really is very kind of your mother to think of us. First you and she helped us with the rabbits, and now this. We really are lucky to have you."

Sylvain looked exaggeratedly pleased, as one unaccustomed to compliments. "Mother likes you," he remarked. "She reckons you have a hard life, on your own like with your boy."

"Oh well," said Jane awkwardly. "I daresay life hasn't been easy for her either . . ."

"That's just it. She reckons you understand what it's like. Lots of the people in the village look down on us, see, because we're not their sort." He made the remark not with bitterness, but like one repeating a learned creed: indeed it crossed Jane's mind then that Sylvain and his mother performed, within the closed community of St Laurent, the useful, indeed necessary function of Untouchables, and that they were almost proud of the fact.

"– But Mother says you've always been that nice to her, just as if she was anybody," said Sylvain placidly.

"Well perhaps I'm not the same sort either as a lot of the people here – in a different way," said Jane. She felt a certain amusement at the unlikely comparison, but, when she thought about it, it did not seem so inept after all.

As if pursuing the same line of thought, Stefan suddenly said,

"Your boy – does he have a father?"

Jane paused before answering. It was impossible to take offence at a question so guilelessly put.

"He did once," she said at last. "But I'm afraid he doesn't now, no."

"Ah, I thought not," said Sylvain with an unexpected hint of worldly tolerance in his voice. He added after a minute,

"My brother used to torment me and that when I was little, telling me he had a father and I didn't and so I didn't have any right to be here. But I found out later that wasn't true. Anyway Mother says that my brother's father beat her and she was glad to see the back of him. She liked my father better, she says, for all he was a tinker and a traveller. Her own mother's people were travellers too . . ." He paused, and then said anxiously, as if just reminded of something.

"Did you hear tell they're doing away with tinkers and the travellers and that?"

"No – who's 'they'? Who's doing away with them?"

"Them. The *Boches*."

"Where did you hear this?" said Jane, a small, unpleasant tremor in her own mind responding to the dread in the boy's voice.

"The lads were talking about it in the café."

"Well, perhaps it's just talk. You know how rumours fly around these days ..." She thought of the spreading local rumours of a Resistance force organising itself in the hills, but decided not to confuse the issue by asking Sylvain about that just now.

"Mother met a traveller in the market in Châtelet," he said, staring at the floor. "An old boy what mends pans she knew from way back ... He told her the soldiers had raided a travellers' camp last month over Châteauroux way and had taken all the men and boys off."

"That's bad," she said cautiously. "If it's true."

"Bad ..." he echoed, shaking his head. He paused, then added with sudden energy. "I've got hideouts up in the woods what I use when I'm hunting. Mother knows that. I'm going to show her where they are."

"That would be a good idea, perhaps," Jane said soberly. She could see clearly his line of thought. Sylvain might be childish, as people said, but he had a common sense of his own. His hideouts up in the woods remained at the bottom of her mind, and she drew an obscure comfort from the idea of them.

The chicks absorbed much of her attention for the next few weeks. They seemed so vulnerable, and Sylvain's casual remark about the rats getting at them had alarmed her. They grew fast, however, doubling their size and weight in a week, and soon, as he had predicted, began escaping from the basket and wobbling about the room. She kept rounding them up to count them, but in spite of her vigilance one drowned in the carefully filled water bowl. She found its draggled body, like a sodden powder puff, when she came in one day from weeding the vegetable garden. Later, another mysteriously disappeared without trace, but that was when they were considerably bigger, growing feathers and venturing outside: she supposed some predator had got it. But the remaining twelve thrived, turning convincingly into chickens.

They still, however, hopped in and out of the house as they liked whenever the door was open, which it normally was in fine weather. Jane could see their point: they had been reared inside; in their tiny brains they regarded her – she supposed – as their mother; they certainly followed her around. No one had taught them that large chickens were not supposed to come into houses. The floor tiles were continually covered with their droppings. You got used to it, she discovered, and didn't notice it any more.

When Madame Langlois called, however, she did notice it, and her disapproval was clear. The appearance of Stefan-chickens in the cottage did nothing to breach the guilty constraint which now existed, on both sides, between her and Jane. Jane was sorry, but felt there was nothing she could do about it. The prospect of eggs in the coming year was much more important than the state of the floor, and everyone said that if you cosseted chickens and took trouble over them – as she was certainly doing – you could get them to lay at almost any season. She could not think, now, why she had not thought of acquiring some before.

It was made clear to her however that Jean Langlois also disapproved of the keeping of undisciplined chickens anywhere near a vegetable garden. The vegetables were fenced off from the plot that had, before the chickens came, been covered with grass, but the fencing was old and the chickens found a gap in it. Jane came out one Sunday morning to find Langlois, lips pressed tight together, arranging wire-mesh; always a man of few words, he was less communicative than she had ever know him. He simply remarked that it had always made him sick at heart to see good work undone, and those early lettuces weren't likely to recover.

After that, he came less often to do Jane's garden. He still provided her with seedlings, and would give advice politely when asked, but it was clear that he would rather relinquish control of it to her. Jane saw that this was perfectly fair. He had been more than good to her in the past, and she had now absorbed enough knowledge about growing vegetables to do it on her own. It shocked her now to realize how little she had known, about that or anything else it now seemed, only a couple of years before.

She minded her gradual estrangement from the Langlois family. Now that it was summer and she didn't need much wood, she didn't even see Jeanot often now. When Reine was married off, rather hastily, to her suitor from Berjac, they didn't invite Jane to the wedding. She would have liked to tell them that she still felt grateful towards them. But it was impossible to do so, for it was clear to her that their drawing away from her was the price she must pay for her virtual adoption by the Stefans, which seemed to have occurred on a different social plane.

Both Marie and Sylvain called frequently now, ostensibly to see how the chickens were doing but really, Jane thought, because they liked to see her and her cottage was a useful stopping point on their way from the village to their own lair. They were not demanding guests. Only rarely would either accept a cup of 'coffee' or a glass of wine and water, and then the next one to visit would always punctiliously bring a cabbage or a bag of last season's nuts. Often one or other of them, after a greeting, would merely sit in placid silence for a while on the bench outside the door, perennial sack on the ground, taking the weight off shoulders or feet. After the work-ethic of people like the Langlois, which she herself had unconsciously imbibed and which demanded that one must never be discovered quite unoccupied, Jane found their company strangely refreshing.

After a while she herself began making sporadic return visits to Marie Stefan. Quite often the thatched house would be deserted, the door open but only cooling ashes on the hearth and a chicken or two sitting on the rickety, cane-bottomed chairs, and the dog barking dolefully from his packing-case kennel. But when Marie was at home she always seemed happy, in her own noncommittal way, to see Jane. She would kick the smouldering log in the fireplace into a thin flame, and shoo a chicken away for Jane to sit down. Then she would just continue with whatever she was doing. Once, when Jane was there, she disappeared outdoors for so long that Jane, feeling that she could not possibly be wanted, went home. But that evening Marie appeared reproachfully at Jane's cottage,

"Why did you go? I was that sorry when I came back and you wasn't there. It's nice to have a bit of company."

Occasionally she would sit down on a low stool herself, shapeless skirts spread wide above her man's boots, and become abruptly communicative. Once she told Jane about the time a travelling photographer had come to the village and had taken a picture of her at her request – "I knew my boy's father then. I wanted the picture to give him, see."

"Sylvain's father?" asked Jane curiously.

"No, not him. The one what I had my eldest boy with." One of Marie Stefan's slight peculiarities was that she never referred to either of her sons – or to anyone else's relatives, come to that – by name, and this was a trick which Sylvain seemed to have caught from her. It made their conversation a little confusing. Long afterwards, Jane was to reflect that in consequence she never actually had learnt Stefan-Postier's first name. It was as if his obtrusive rôle as village postman had superseded any more intimate identity.

On this occasion Jane waited, knowing better than to hurry Marie, and presently a sepia photograph in an oval tin frame was produced for her to see. She had heard that Marie Stefan had been 'the village beauty' once but had scarcely believed it, taking the remark to be a vaguely moralistic one in the 'see where beauty leads you' tradition. But now, looking at the faded likeness, she saw the years stripped away and Marie Stefan's witch-like profile revealed as that of a handsome, aquiline girl. In place of the straggling grey hair was a fine show of black curls; and, where Marie's present eyes were embedded in wrinkles from too many years of going from the dark house into the bright sunlight and back again, this girl's eyes were black and fine. The girl wore a respectable, high-collared dress of the 1900s.

"Our Sunday dress," Marie remarked. "Me and my sister used to share it ... Really nice stuff, it was." She seemed to be admiring the dress and, by extension, her own youth and optimism, with wondering humbleness across the pit of years, yet Jane thought she saw a glint of irony in her eye all the same. In much the same way, she thought, she herself now regarded her own past self in England.

"Where is your sister now?" she asked quietly.

"Dead an' gone. Least, that's what I tell people. I haven't seen her these twenty years, and she'd have been back to see me, else ... She married a traveller who took her south, see. Out of Spain, he was."

"I wonder, you know Marie," said Jane, "I wonder that you've stayed in this one place yourself? I mean – Sylvain told me one day that your mother was a traveller too ..." She had understood that the Stefans disliked the word 'gipsy'.

"Her people were. They were Kashewaras" (or that's what it sounded like) – "But she married our Dad, didn't she, and he wanted to stop here. Like I thought I was going to marry our eldest boy's dad. But it didn't work out." Again that faint hint of self-mockery.

"Was *he* a traveller?" Jane asked, thinking of Stefan-Postier's light complexion and bossy, off-hand manner.

"No, not him. A soldier, he was – not from round here. He never come back no more after the Great War came, and good riddance to him," said Marie Stefan shortly, with a dark, brooding look that reminded Jane of Sylvain.

Another day she spoke suddenly of Sylvain's 'fits'.

"He don't throw himself about or froth at the mouth or anything," she said. "He just stands still a moment as if he was miles away – and then he comes to, like, and shivers and maybe cries a bit. He can't help it. People used to say it was because I'd dropped him when he was a baby or tried to do away with him before he was born, but that was just their nastiness ... I never tried to do away with him, though if I'd wanted to I could have." She fell silent, and Jane remembered what Jeanot Langlois had told her and didn't comment. Presently Marie continued:

"Mother – she only died about ten years ago, when the boys were quite big already – she used to say that it was in the family, that one of our uncles had had fits like Sylvain and it wasn't nobody's fault, just the way they were made. She used to make a stuff for him to take to calm his blood – all sorts of things go into it, plants and that, I still make it sometimes. I don't know if it really does any good, but he likes me to make it for him."

"You never took him to a doctor, I suppose . . ." said Jane tentatively. Marie cocked a sceptical eye at her.

"Nah – doctors don't know anything really."

Jane said nothing about Pierre being a doctor. She wasn't sure if Marie knew that, though she seemed to know most things. Presently Marie went on:

"Mother didn't believe in doctors and no more do I. Mother was cleverer than 'em anyway. See, there was this woman once – she's still in the village so I won't tell you who she is – when she was young and silly she kept coming to Mother and me to help her out, and we did. And then one day she gets married. But she'd weakened herself, see – weakened herself inside with all she'd been getting up to. For she couldn't carry that baby and she lost the next one too, and she kept going to the doctor in Châtelet – him that used to live near the school – and paying him money for this and that and none of it was any good. So in the end she came back to Mother again. And Mother helped her and gave her stuff to drink and at last she had a live baby, and another one to go with it. So you see, Mother was cleverer than the doctors were."

Something in Marie Stefan's tone reminded Jane of Sylvain's when he was talking in his turn about her. Evidently, in the Stefan dynasty, it was the mother and child relationship that counted and endured, while transitory husbands and fathers came and went. In that way, too, she began to feel somehow akin to Marie Stefan, though she was reluctant to admit it to herself.

When the warm weather came Marie Stefan made her a present of a she-goat. This time there was no pretence that Jane was being given it to rear or 'to do a favour' as with the rabbits and the chickens. Marie just said "I'd like you to have her." When Jane pressed her, she took in return, and after decent hesitation, Jane's spare bedding. Any day, Jane expected to see Madame Yrieux's other carriage rug re-appear as part of Marie's clothing.

So, by the late summer of 1943, Jane was better organised and equipped to manage almost without money than she had ever been before. The chickens were starting to lay, the goat was in kid and would soon be producing milk. Much time was spent escorting her up and down the lanes so that she could eat her fill, while Jane herself gathered sacks of grass for the rabbits. The vegetables were doing well. She had learnt by now to store and make use of every single piece of free food the countryside offered – windfall apples, blackberries, mushrooms, chestnuts, hazel nuts, even sorrel, nettles and dandelions – though the rabbits had priority for those. They had multiplied into a battalion that must be decimated again when the cold weather came. She had a plan afoot to get some bees, if the old bee-man could let her have a swarm, and was only put off by having a pig by the knowledge that they had to be fed on 'household scraps' and she and Mark left barely enough scraps to satisfy the chickens as it was. Mark was growing fast now, and eating more than ever. Pierre's old trousers almost fitted him. His voice was breaking, too.

He was restive that summer, for the first time. With the long, light days the realisation that his closest friends were now irrevocably established in Châtelet at the High School, seemed to come home to him. More and more, when they came back to St Laurent in the evenings, they spoke of lessons and people of whom he knew nothing: they were launched on a life from which he was debarred. There was a *lycée* Sports Club that held meetings in town after school on Thursdays and Saturdays, and Jane overheard Jean-Luc and Jean-Baptiste talking enthusiastically about 'their' football and gymnastic coach: she saw Mark's face become uncharacteristically shut and aloof, and knew that he had heard too. She was afraid even to let him know how much she minded for him, in case that should make it worse.

After his first pride as being Monsieur Picard's 'special' pupil, he was getting bored with his solitary lessons too. Picard, he confided to Jane, tried his best, but he just didn't know enough himself about the subjects he was now trying to teach.

"The Rhetoric and Logic and stuff, Maman – he does it all out of the book, and I know he's just one chapter ahead of me all the time. And he's no good at Latin either, he treats it as if it was equations or something. I really know more Latin than he does, actually, from when you and Pierre used to do it with me, ages ago, when you thought I might be going back to school in England."

"I thought you'd forgotten all about that," said Jane sadly.

"So had I, but it comes back ... Lots of things come back, suddenly, just for a moment, like smelling something – don't you find that too, Maman? Then they go again ..."

There were a number of boys scarcely older than Mark who were not at the High School, but, like Henri Marceau, were already embarking on their life as working adults. They milked and herded cattle, dug and ploughed and sowed, backed huge, fierce-looking horses between shafts with throaty masculine cries. When Jane met them in the lanes they would touch their caps to her as their fathers would, and in the evenings they went to the smaller café, the one at the far end of the street from the Mourets', where the labourers congregated. In a few years more they would be as gnarled and sunburnt as the elder men, and fathering children themselves. They weren't, Jane knew, Mark's chosen companions, but he knew them all and had memories in common with them of marbles and card games and birds' nests: it was inevitable that, in the absence of other friends, he should want to keep up with them. That summer, in defiance of both herself and Monsieur Picard, he began to work in the evenings at the farm where they got cows' milk. As soon as the school term ended, he began to work there all day.

"I hope the Michards realise this is just for the harvest season," said Jane warningly.

"Well I've said I'll still give them a hand with the milking, morning and evening, when autumn comes. They were pleased, they need another pair of hands now that that fat Louise has got married and gone to live down at Bussières ... Go on, Maman, don't be stupid, you know they pay me in wheat-flour and chicken barley and other things we need. We don't want to eat bloody swedes all winter again. Maman, I'm *thirteen and a half*. I can't go on not working – just sitting in school like a kid. What would people think?"

Jane had to give way and be grateful for what he earned rather than censorious. She doubted if she could have stopped him anyway: he had become very determined recently. She could not say that his attitude was an inappropriate one: he had simply adapted to his present life. Of course he had.

"You mustn't give too much time and energy to the Michards' cows that you ought to be giving to your school work," she told him, but without much conviction.

If he had stayed in England with James, this coming autumn would have been his first term at Winchester –

The thought presented itself to her mind, complete and revelationary in its brevity, like a telegram from another life. Or like a shaft of light, suddenly illuminating, cruelly, a dark place. Unable to bear the hard, white dazzle of the past, shc shut her eyes tight. The light went out again.

Other things were happening in the world beyond St Laurent that summer. In July, the Allies landed in Sicily. In the late summer Jane several times accepted Picard's long-standing invitation to go and listen to the wireless set he kept hidden behind a shelf of books. Hearing, over the muffling and crackling air, the French language broadcasts put out by the BBC, she felt the stirrings of emotion and excitement, as if the voices were not just bringing her the first news that a German defeat might really be on its way, but also re-awakening in her a sense of another life elsewhere, far from the confining lanes and endless small fields of central France. She had known in theory, of course, that it was there all the time, but had not felt it till then.

But she did not go very often to the Picards' apartment above the school for the atmosphere there was rather uncomfortable. It might simply be, she thought, that Madame Picard was nervous about the clandestine wireless and wished that her husband wouldn't listen to it; but it seemed to Jane that a degree of nervousness and coldness emanated from that lady which was less to do with the wireless than with herself.

"I expect Madame Picard's jealous of you," said Mark casually,

"Oh don't be ridiculous, Mark . . . I mean, she *can't* be? I feel in Picard's debt, of course, for several reasons, but we've never been exactly bosom friends."

"I didn't mean quite like that . . . I don't think she thinks you're carrying on with Picard or anything."

"Indeed I'm not," said Jane indignantly, oddly repelled by the idea but immediately wondering if something in Picard's own manner towards her – determinedly formal but with unnerving hints of intimacy – did suggest just that.

"Madame P's a funny woman," said Mark sagaciously. "Everyone knows that. She doesn't really like anything that her husband has much to do with. She doesn't like *me*, these days."

"She was nice to you when you first went to the school and were put in her class," said Jane anxiously. The suggestion of someone not liking either herself or Mark always filled her with obscure dread.

"Oh that was years ago, when I was a little kid. She doesn't like me now that Picard's been giving me lessons on my own this last year. It doesn't bother me. Why should it?"

But it bothered Jane, partly because she felt that, logically, Eulalie Picard and she should have become friends. Surely they might have had a few interests in common unshared by most of the villagers? She felt this even more strongly after an extra child appeared in the Picard's cramped household. She was said to be 'a cousin, visiting' but she had a sallow complexion and large dark eyes and Jane guessed that she was a Jewish refugee child, sent here into relative safety from the north. But when she tried, one day, tentatively, to ask Madame Picard about the child's origins, the response she received was so frigidly uncommunicative that she did not dare pry further.

"You shouldn't have asked her," said Mark, who, as usual, knew more of what was going on than she did. "Madame Picard didn't want to take a child. It was *his* idea."

"That was good of him, I think." She needed to feel that she could trust and admire Picard. Sometimes she needed to quite desperately.

"Bah," said Mark with a strong hint of Picard's own manner. "He's being well paid to do it. That's what people say, anyway. Picard isn't famous for doing things for nothing, you know."

"Mark how *can* you be so cynical? After all the time and trouble he's taken over you."

"Well, perhaps he thinks that when the War's over you'll be able to pay him."

"Perhaps he does," said Jane wearily. "Perhaps he does. And perhaps I shall. At the moment I just can't imagine it."

That September several more strange children appeared in the village, boarded out in various families. Picard seemed to be acting as a placing agent. Jane would have liked to make friends with these children, for Serge Beckman's sake and, through him, Pierre's. But they were all younger than Mark, and all girls except for one boy of four, and so there seemed little basis for her to get to know them.

She thought of taking a refugee child herself. But Picard did not suggest the idea to her, in spite of her hints, and she did not like to broach it outright for fear of a rebuff. He had always been so opposed to her doing anything at all which might lead to her identity being called in question.

And she supposed that he could not, in all honesty, have recommended her to any anxious family as a safe placement. Sometimes she wondered, with dim humour, if her occasional fantasy about her own insubstantiality was due to Picard's insistent suggestion that she should become as near invisible as possible.

The presence of the children in the village was a sign of other things happening elsewhere besides the events far off in Italy and Corsica and in North Africa. German repression in France was intensifying, it seemed. Stories came from the towns of deportations and executions, of hostages being taken at random and then shot in reprisal for attacks on German soldiers. And along with these facts, which the Germans themselves publicised as a warning through the official news channels, came persistent word-of-mouth news of a country-wide Resistance movement forming. Evidently Jane and Mark had not been the only people in France to get themselves better organised this year. It was no longer a matter of isolated groups of outlaws in the hills. Bands of Maquisards were sabotaging German dêpots, blowing up bridges; it was said too that they were organising rescue chains for other people on the run.

St Laurent-la-Rivière, like France itself, was divided as to the virtue of these activities. Some – the Bonnins, the cobbler who was known as 'the Red', Jeanot Langlois – spoke of the Maquis with guarded admiration, saying that their time was coming and that we should see France free yet. But others, including the Mayor and the Curé spoke of them with open contempt as 'bandits' and escaped convicts. Others again seemed unwilling to mention them at all, as if fearing that even to admit knowledge of their existence might draw down revenge from the occupying forces. Then in late September, a band who were hiding up in the sheep-country above Limoges mined a German troop train. The damage they did was not very serious, but forty men were rounded up at random in a small town near the line and shot. The shots, though fifty miles away, had echoed round St Laurent before the day was out.

"Stupid, bloody young fools," ranted the baker. "What did they think they are doing? Oh, they're very fine, these gestures, all very brave I'm sure – but who pays the price? Innocent fathers of families, that's who." Angry spit flecked his lips.

Public opinion in the village had veered, with reservations, on his side, though one or two of the younger men declared that such attitudes were cowardly and that the Germans had to be fought if they were ever to be beaten. It was said that the Langlois had quarrelled with their younger son about it, and that he was threatening to leave home and join the Maquis. It was said that Bonnin and Petitjean, the garage-owner, were no longer on speaking terms, and this was shocking for Bonnin liked everyone and everyone liked him. The atmosphere in the village was unpleasant, and Jane, for the first time, disliked going there. It seemed to her that some people went out of their way to seek her opinion on recent events, with a note of accusation or innuendo in their voices, as if they believed that she in her position might know something they did not.

Jane supposed that had she been another sort of person, she might by now have become involved in Resistance activity herself. Once, in the days when she believed herself to be a free and independent spirit, a breaker of conventions, she might have enjoyed fantasies, with herself as heroine, in which she sheltered English or American or Free French soldiers in the cottage before passing them on to the next hideout. But not only did she lack any information as to how to go about such an enterprise, nor whom to contact – the very idea, when viewed in the light of reality, made her feel almost sick with fright and a kind of squeamishness.

As a child, she had maintained stalwartly for several years that History couldn't possibly be true because it was too awful, and she felt the same panic-stricken impulse towards denial affecting her now. The thought of playing an active part in the War, however commendable in theory, and thus going out of her way to court brutality and perhaps draw it upon herself, was horrible to her. This was something beyond rationality: a perception that Evil exists as something absolute and powerful in its own right. Reared on a gentle, bowdlerised form of Christian morality with a mild leaven of twentieth-century enlightenment, her conditioning was to think in terms of human wickedness, however regrettable, being nevertheless to some extent explicable in terms of human selfishness, greed or fear – of folly and frailty rather than pure malevolence. But now it seemed to her that she had always really known, underneath, that pure Evil was true, it was real, and so terrible that even the knowledge of it was to be shunned, as people in former generations shunned the very name of the Devil or Hell.

She hesitated and prevaricated with herself. Sometimes, waking before dawn, she would attempt to comfort herself back to sleep, as she had done intermittently for years, with the idea that Pierre was, after all, alive and well and somehow in charge of his own destiny after all. Now it was inevitable that this belief should take the form of a fantasy about him as a Resistance-leader, too highly placed and important to risk incriminating her by making the least sign to her. Wasn't almost the last thing he had said to her in 1940 a cryptic remark about the War being far from over – that 'matters wouldn't stay as they were'? Was it remotely possible that even then his journey to the south was not just on her behalf but was connected with some secret organisation? In the dark, she wanted this to be true. But in full daylight, she usually shrunk from the idea.

Then one day news came through that some of those actually responsible for the mined train had been arrested, and had been hanged from the railway viaduct above Limoges. She knew beyond doubt then, from her own physical revulsion, that whatever Pierre might or might not have done the Resistance was something that she herself would do better to leave alone.

The bodies were said to have been left there by order, to be set swinging by each passing train. When she woke at dawn now, she saw them. After a while it seemed to her that one of them was Pierre.

I am a coward, she thought, *like most of the rest of them here, but with less excuse. I am a coward but at least I know it*. The dull, ignominious female courage of endurance she had had to muster over the last three years and more, she did not count. After all, she had had no choice.

Then, falling back on the thought that had been the excuse and the reason for everything these last years, and the one that Picard was constantly repeating back to her, she said to herself: it isn't as if I had only myself to consider. There is Mark, always Mark. How could anyone deliberately put their own child in danger?

She did not stop to reflect that Mark was getting older as each month passed. In fact he was hardly a child any longer.

Mark, less busy at the farm once the harvest was in, had made friends with Sylvain. They went fishing together down by the river, where the brown, transparent water had retreated over the gravel in the summer's heat and chubb and roach were trapped in a few deep pools. They went on other, less licit hunting expeditions too; one night when they returned Sylvain was carrying one of his ferrets under his torn jacket and Jane saw with consternation that Mark had the other under his jersey.

"Mark, surely ferrets bite?"

"Not these, they're tame and they've got used to me now . . . Feel how lovely and thick their fur is, Maman."

Jane put out a tentative hand. The creatures seemed as small and softer than cats, and timid too, yet with a muscularity that was not feline. Sylvain was obviously intensely proud of them, and Mark participated in this pride. The ferrets gave off a musky, pungent odour that, she now realised, she had often smelt on Sylvain when he had been standing near her: his clothes must be impregnated with it. After that evening Mark's jersey smelt of it also. It was as if Mark and Sylvain had become slightly confused in her perception.

"What do you talk about all the time you're together?" she asked Mark curiously. "Ferrets?"

"Yes, and other things. Fish, Birds, Animals – Sylvain knows a lot, you know."

"People say he's not quite all there. I've never really made up my mind about him."

"Oh, he's not stupid," said Mark authoritatively. "But – there's something . . . Being with him is more like being with another boy than with a man. He talks about his family sometimes, and about his fits. He hates people to laugh at him. His brother used to laugh at him a lot when he was younger. He doesn't like his brother, you know, and I'm not surprised. He says that one day he ran away from home because of that and tried to drown himself in the river, but it didn't work. It's more difficult to drown yourself than you'd think, he said. So he just set off walking. In the end the Gendarmes picked him up the far side of Montluçon. Mouret brought him home."

"Heavens, Montluçon. That's quite a way."

"He walks all over the place still. He knows the countryside better than anyone else, you know. He knows where the Maquisards are just now, up in the forest. The other Sunday he and Marie Stefan took them some food. He said that if they stay there he might let me come up too, next time."

His tone was excited and interested. He might have been talking, as years ago, about his green bike. Foreboding stirred within her.

"Oh Mark," she said. "Do be careful."

"It's all *right*, Maman, I don't even know the way there myself. *God* you do worry sometimes!"

"It must be age," she said, smiling painfully and fending him off as he tried to grab her playfully round the waist. "I never used to worry about anything once – not really *worry* – but now . . . Oh Mark, do leave your agéd mother alone!" She was only half joking. Her next birthday would be her thirty-fourth, no great age, but she did feel old, worn and made more vulnerable through being brought to a greater sense of reality. Growing up at last did not mean, as she had joyfully thought at thirty, being liberated from craven fears. On the contrary.

Term began again: the last of the summer warmth disintegrated into days of continuous rain. It soaked into the old walls of the cottage, making the damp patches near the floor show clearly again like the stains of old misdeeds; it hissed in the chimney so that when she opened the door of the stove a gust of smoke would eddy into her mouth and eyes. The hut at the end of the garden seemed particularly dank and chill, its wooden walls slimy to the touch; its roof had begun to leak and it was much visited by snails. She spent whole days indoors, watching the rain blowing like a fine muslin curtain across the deep grey sky and the deep green grass. Each time Mark reappeared, whether from school or from the Michards, his clothes would be wet again. She seemed to be eternally trying to get something dry, standing over the stove moving it about in her hands. For the first time she really appreciated the practicality of clogs, which at least did not get soaked right through – rubber boots hardly seemed to be known in the village, and the English pair from Daniel Neals that Mark had worn as a little boy had long been outgrown and traded with the cobbler against repairs.

They both caught heavy colds which they could not shake off. Mark coughed a lot at night and first thing in the morning, when he disappeared into the sodden mist to round up 'his' cows. She was fearful that he might develop bronchitis again as he had during their first winter alone. If he does, she thought, I shan't go to the chemist in Châtelet again: I can't, we've no money for that sort of thing – I'll ask Marie Stefan's advice: she's sure to know of something I can cook up for him to inhale, a herbal mixture or something. The thought of Marie Stefan's accumulated, inherited knowledge comforted her.

But Mark improved, and she forgot her fear again. When he complained of a pain in his face one evening, she was at first inclined to think it couldn't be anything much. The rain had abated at last, and in its retreat the weather had turned colder.

"You've probably been standing around in a cold wind

for too long with those damned cows," she said. "Is the pain near your ear? I'll fill the stone bottle with warm water and you can hold it against the place."

But the next day, though the wind had gone again and a cold sun was watching the yellow leaves moulting from the trees, Mark said that the pain was worse. At lunch he sat holding his face and would not eat. It dawned on Jane that he had toothache. He had not known what it was himself, for he had never had it before. As a little boy, he had been taken regularly to the dentist. Since 1939 neither he nor Jane had, of course, been near a dentist, but she had not worried particularly about this: she had good teeth herself and believed that he had inherited them, and no one could say that his diet, poor child, had contained too many sweets. But toothache he now appeared to have; in the night he woke several times crying with pain; Jane felt distracted at her inability to do anything for him. He had had their last two hoarded aspirins hours ago. At first light she herself got dressed and called on the Michards to say that Mark could not come to milking this morning. Though a taciturn family and not very bright – old Michard was rumoured in the village to have been up to something with his own dull daughters – they expressed a mild interest in toothache. One of them remarked that raw alcohol was the thing, if you had some – you put it on the tooth and that numbed it. Looking at their blackened and gap-toothed mouths Jane was not reassured that the advice was particularly sound, but she felt sufficiently desperate to go in search of raw alcohol, at any rate as first aid. She knew that the Langlois and several other families distilled their own rough brandy from fermented grape skins, and nerved herself to seek one of these families out and ask for a little as a favour.

As she was passing Madame Mouret's café, not yet open at this hour, she encountered Monsieur Mouret on the doorstep breathing in self-conscious gulps of fresh air. It had been months since she had even seen him: she had heard that he had returned part-time to the Gendarmerie in Châtelet-le-Lys; many of the younger men in the force were engaged elsewhere these days, people said meaningfully, and in any case the amount of extra paperwork the War had brought was snowing the local police stations under. Madame Bonnin had had to wait six hours to get a priority-ticket to go and see her sister near Cahors.

Jane greeted Monsieur Mouret with a diffident respect in which there was more than a hint of dread: his work must inevitably bring him into contact, however indirect, with Them, the unseen forces of oppression. She didn't see a tall, lantern-jawed man in his late fifties, a slow-moving country constable, limited and decent, but rather someone who was, for herself and Mark, a potentially powerful and dangerous figure.

But Monsieur Mouret evidently still saw her as Pierre's wife and Madame Yrieux's niece-by-marriage, and greeted her with deference accordingly. He enquired after Mark, saying what a fine young man he seemed to be becoming, and tut-tutted over what Jane told him. Warmed by his routine kindliness, she plucked up courage to ask him in an undertone – she rather hoped Madame Mouret wasn't anywhere near at hand – whether by any chance he could let her have a tiny amount of spirituous liquor for Mark, even perhaps real brandy?

Indeed he could, said Monsieur Mouret. There was still one cask in the cellar, and he would never see a lady worry herself for want of such a little thing. But oughtn't the lad to see a dentist? They weren't nearly such butchers these days, as they had been in years gone by – And Monsieur Mouret smiled encouragingly at Jane, displaying teeth whose many gold fillings were testimony not only to the existence of French dentistry but to the Mourets' relatively high social status.

When Jane explained about her lack of money – how often now, she thought wearily, had she explained this in an apologetic undertone to one person or another – Monsieur Mouret looked surprised and vaguely dubious: it seemed that, like Madame Marceau, he did not really believe her: a well-educated lady quite without resources did not enter into his conception of things. But having fetched her a spoonful of brandy in an old cup, he became ruminative and invited Jane into the café where, he said mysteriously, he would write something down for her. Rather unwillingly Jane entered the place which had such happy, out-of-date associations for her. Madame Mouret was nowhere to be seen, but Reine Langlois, noticeably pregnant, was pushing a mop around the floor in a languid manner. Shyly, she and Jane exchanged greetings.

Mouret was writing slowly behind the bar counter in an elaborate looped copper plate, with pauses for reflection. Jane was suddenly reminded of the doll-policeman in the Beatrix Potter tale *Ginger and Pickles*, which Mark had had when he was small, who had 'twice put his pencil in his mouth and once dipped it in the treacle'. She wanted to giggle, and felt better. Mouret only looked up once, to verify Mark's surname with her. Presently he read through what he had written, murmuring the words to himself, blotted it, folded it, sealed it importantly into an envelope on which he wrote in turn, and presented it ceremoniously to Jane. The envelope was addressed to a Dr. Gilbert, at an address in Châtelet-le-Lys.

Jane thanked him effusively and Mouret, with the air of one who has conferred a considerable favour but has been glad to do so, bowed her out of the café. When she got back to the cottage, where Mark had now gone temporarily back to sleep on his rumpled bed, she steamed the letter open over a pan of water. It was disappointing.

'Docteur,' it said, 'Would you be so kind as to attend to Framy, Marc, whose suffering requires treatment? His mother, Leparde, Madame Jeanne, is known to me. Her husband is a prisoner of war. He is a doctor also.'

What real use was that? Silly old stuffed-doll Mouret. She didn't know quite what she had expected, but she almost felt like throwing the note on the stove. Yet when she read it through again, it occurred to her that it was not so inadequate after all: Mouret had signed it with his Gendarme's rank and number, and possibly these days a request from a policeman, however ordinary and semi-retired, was a veiled command. And could 'Madame Leparde is known to me' be code for 'You will realise that this lady is a foreigner in hiding, but that is not your business'?

That was how she and Mark found themselves, later that morning, in Etienne Gilbert's cold waiting room among oil paintings and scuffed, antique dining room furniture. The ride into Châtelet by bicycle had taken all Mark's fortitude and all the brandy: it was the bus-day, but they had missed it. He sat now huddled on a chair, with Jane's silk scarf round his face, looking pale and obscurely furious, as if the developing male within him greatly resented the indignity of pain as well as suffering from it.

When at last they were called into the consulting room, Etienne Gilbert said expressionlessly,

"Your husband, I see, is a doctor, Madame? I should make it clear that I am not a doctor myself – merely a dental surgeon." A brief smile illuminated his passive features, as he added,

"Mouret likes to believe that I am a doctor, and I do not like to disillusion him."

"He said you had treated him many times," said Jane, and he replied in the same quiet voice that gave nothing away.

"I treat the whole Gendarmerie, and also the forces from surrounding districts. Under their terms of service, they are obliged to see me if their teeth are troubling them. Otherwise, of course, they would never come." And again there was that gentle, self-deprecating smile, quickly effaced.

Sitting in that consulting room, a converted drawing room crowded inappropriately with dental equipment but also with signs of a previous family existence – cluttered prints and watercolours against a faded, fleur-de-lys wallpaper – Jane thought,

This man is a friend.

His house, in spite of his air of slightly melancholy disorder, like the litter of past wealth, suggested that he was an educated man, but it wasn't just that. She also detected, from the first, beneath an exterior that seemed deliberately colourless, a current of silent sympathy and support flowing in her direction. Or so she afterwards believed. But then (as she also thought at times) you can believe anything if you want to enough, and by then she needed very badly to trust Etienne Gilbert and to feel that all his actions and his advice were for the best.

So Mark's tooth was examined and Gilbert pointed out that a bit of it had been broken off at the back and an abscess had formed in the gum –

"How did you break it, my boy? Cracking nuts?"

"Yes, actually I did," Mark mumbled, avoiding his mother's eyes.

"Mark *when*? Why on earth didn't you tell me?"

"About – ahh! – about a month ago . . . I thought you'd be cross and that it didn't matter anyway." Temporarily a guilty small boy again, he looked near to tears.

"I'm afraid it ought to come out," said Gilbert, probing with great care. "Otherwise the abscess can't drain properly and infection may get into the jaw." It was to Mark he addressed himself, but his eyes – cold, pale eyes, she noticed now, at variance with his kindly voice – sought Jane's face apologetically as he did so,

"In normal times this would present no great problem, but, as you are probably aware, it is almost impossible to obtain general anaesthetics these days –"

Jane caught her breath: "I didn't realise –"

"I much regret it. I and the two general medical surgeons who operate at the convent hospital spend much of our time trying to negotiate further supplies for essential operations, but without much success recently, I'm afraid . . . Like everything else, it all gets taken off to Germany. My colleagues are even having to remove tonsils and adenoids from young children who are awake and having to be held down. Dreadful . . . Fortunately I have a little ethyl chloride hoarded which I like to use for youngsters like your boy here: it does have some local effect, and so is a great deal better than nothing."

A great deal better than nothing . . . Sent out to walk round the town while the extraction was in process, she repeated the words over to herself and supposed dully that Mark was lucky, relatively, to have that. The amorphous brutality without a name which she had dreaded all along, ever since Pierre had disappeared, seemed to have taken a sideways pace nearer to them. What would the next thing be?

In the Middle Ages, she thought, trying to be stoical herself as if that would in some way help Mark to bear it, this sort of thing was commonplace. Even a hundred years ago, I suppose it was. Everyone had teeth out, when they had to, without anaesthetic. It was just a normal part of life. Like public executions. Now it is as if we are going back in time, not forward. Back to a new Dark Age of oppression under foreign overlords: cruelty and hardship and obscure private suffering too commonplace even for complaint.

Because she had no money to go to a café, she went to walk in the open space planted with stubbled plane trees where once the town's fortifications had stood. A wintry haze hung over the river at the foot of the slope, and the trees were almost bare: the thought that the winter was coming fast, yet another winter of calculation and anxiety and the perpetual hunt for food, was deeply discouraging. How much longer could it all go on? Corsica was liberated already. Surely, as Picard had hinted to her last time she had seen him, something would happen soon, now that what he himself had begun to refer to as 'the Allies' were back on European soil?

Far away over the bald, soggy expanse of what, in summer, was a cheerful promenade, two boys younger than Mark were looking for sticks, picking up an occasional one here and there. They wore inadequate shorts from which their legs emerged long and spindly, to disappear eventually into boots that seemed too big for them. They looked dejected, pinched with cold and maybe with hunger also, scarecrow silhouettes in a dead landscape. It was said that life was much worse in the towns, even small towns like this one: that fuel was in short supply and unrationed food harder and harder to find. For the hundredth time she reflected that she and Mark had had immense good fortune really, being where they were, but this time, watching and pitying the younger boys, the thought was not tinged with resentment. All they had to do, she told herself, breathing in the chilly, clammy air and pressing her arms in her shabby jacket to her side, was hang on just a bit longer. Hang on together –

When she returned, fearful, to the Gilberts' house she found Mark and the dentist waiting for her. "He is a brave, sensible boy," said the dentist gently. Mark looked pale, and bloody round his mouth, and smelt of alcohol, but he was quite composed.

"It's out. It's very sore, but I feel much better. Maman, he's asked me to stay, I can, can't I?"

"I have two boys of my own not much older than Mark," the dentist explained. "They will be home from school presently. Perhaps, as it is a half day, you will allow your son to lunch with us, when he has had a rest, and spend the afternoon here? My boys have table-tennis and other games in the old billiard room we have here, and Mark tells me he doesn't often have the opportunity to play with such things. I will send him home to you before dark."

Riding home alone, Jane thought with pleasure of the afternoon Mark was spending, and wished they had met the Gilbert family before. It seemed so silly: they had been there in Châtelet all the time, and she had never known.

Mark returned just as dark was coming and she was beginning to wonder what had happened to him. He had played ping-pong and draughts, and Paul Gilbert, who was fourteen, had begun to teach him chess. Jacques, who was seventeen, played the violin and had a good collection of birds' eggs which he had said – incredulity entered Mark's voice – that he wasn't really interested in any longer: "So he said I could look through them and maybe have some of them. Not the very rare ones of course, because those are valuable, but some of the ones that are just good specimens that I haven't got. He's *really nice*, Maman. So's

Paul. And they've invited me next Sunday afternoon. I can go, can't I?"

"Of course you can. They sound a very nice family. Kind of them to be so friendly. What's their mother like?"

"She's dead."

"Oh dear," said Jane, disconcerted, and a little disappointed on her own account. "Poor boys."

"Oh, they've got a housekeeper. She cooked lunch. And I think their father takes a lot of trouble over them, if you know what I mean. I suppose he must have thought I would be a good friend for them . . . They're Protestants, Maman, not like everyone else round here, and I said we were too."

"I see. Well I suppose that's more or less true."

"He was asking me about school and that. And I said that Picard was teaching me for the moment, but I hoped to go to High School later, when the War is over. He didn't ask any more, but I'm sure he understood. Because after lunch he was showing Paul and me a map and talking about the conference that's going on in Russia now, and he said something to me about 'your country' so he must have realised I'm English. I'm sure he knows all about us, Maman, but it doesn't matter, does it?"

"No," said Jane wearily, "I don't suppose it does." The thought had occurred to her at that moment that just possibly Etienne Gilbert had known about her considerably before she had heard of him. Perhaps a number of other people in Châtelet whom she did not know were similarly aware of her existence. The idea was so disturbing that she did not, for the time being, speculate on what the nature of their interest in her might be.

Mark had been given some aspirin and a mouth-wash to bring home with him, but declared himself quite well now and seemed almost to have forgotten the drama of the morning. He disappeared shortly afterwards in the direction of the Michards' farm.

That autumn he always seemed to be disappearing in one direction or another. Many days he left the cottage when Jane herself was barely awake and only appeared thereafter at brief intervals to consume whatever food she managed to set in front of him, before going out again. If she asked him where he was going, or had been, he would answer briefly 'doing the cows' or 'to check a trap with Sylvain' or – more and more frequently – 'into town to see Paul and Jacques'.

After the first few times, he was no longer so communicative about what he did during all those hours he apparently spent at the Gilberts'. She fixed the image of him in her mind playing ping-pong and chess and backgammon and having stimulating conversations, for once – all the things she would have wanted for him, in his teens, but had not, in St Laurent, been able to provide. She resolutely prevented herself from minding that she now saw so little of him. At the age he was now reaching, that was probably quite normal anyway.

She could not help but be aware, however, that between his various pursuits he was neglecting his school work more and more. She did not like to enquire too closely into his homework assignments for fear of antagonising him and driving him further away from her; after all, what Picard could offer was not an adequate substitute for a High School course, it probably wasn't worth making a great issue over it at present. But she could tell, from Picard's slightly aloof and subdued manner when she encountered him, that he was disappointed in Mark, and this made her feel guilty and obscurely sad for the little man. He had, after all, done his best for Mark, and considerably more than his duty, whatever Mark himself might say.

In any case there was another reason now why Mark scamped his homework. She had no funds to pay the latest electricity bill, and one late afternoon the light went off and styed off, leaving them with nothing but the glow from the fire to see their way about the room. After a week, she obtained a few home-made tallow candles in the village, but they had to be eked out sparingly, and in any case their light was too poor to read by easily: she wasn't having Mark ruining his eyesight that way, she decided, even for the sake of education. Thank goodness their pump only drew on a nearby well! If the village had been on mains' water that would no doubt be cut off for non-payment too.

When Mark's fourteenth birthday came, early in the New Year, she had for the first time no present whatsoever to give him. She minded this far more than he seemed to. But the following day he came to her, rather shame-facedly, saying that he had something to ask her: he had, he said, been given a little money by the Michards for an end-of-the-year bonus. He had – he insisted – been keeping it to give her as a surprise next time she seemed really worried, but if she wanted to give him a birthday present could he keep it instead? "It would be wonderful," he explained simply, "to have a little money in my pocket. Just to *have* it, like the other boys do."

She agreed at once, telling herself that this was right and proper, that he was growing up fast, that she ought to be glad he was becoming so self-sufficient. In looks and build he was like his father, James: he was now tall and heavy for his age and could almost have passed for an adult, but it pleased her to feel that he was not much like his father in personality. James, viewed in dim and occasional retrospect down a vista of years, now seemed to her a soft creature, both mentally and physically, his assumed strength merely the stiff carapace of the British upper classes. Whatever Mark was – and at times he just seemed to her archetypal Boy, with his fishing lines and birds' eggs, like an illustration in one of the old Annuals they had had at home – she didn't think he was soft. It wasn't true, what idiots like James used to pretend, that a boy brought up on his own by a woman would turn into a mother's boy. On the contrary, occasional things made her suspect that, under his calm and cheerful exterior, Mark might turn out one day to be very tough indeed.

Early in January 1944 Laval, whose authority was now greater than Pétain's, made a speech denouncing 'democracy', which was widely interpreted as a further warning against the Communism which would engulf France if the Germans should be displaced. The same week the Russians entered Poland, forcing the Germans to retreat. This move meant little to Jane, but she was aware that it was being widely said that the Maquis was Communist-run. This made people, according to taste and disposition, either like the Communists more or the Maquis even less, and the rifts that already existed in St Laurent widened and deepened.

She wondered if the bands of young men could still be really living out in those wooded hills that were now white with frost. She asked Mark what he thought, and he replied briefly but authoritatively that most of them were now lying low in people's houses and farms, waiting till the worst of the winter should be over.

"Is that what Sylvain says?"

"Sylvain – and other people too." But he would not elaborate.

The next thing that happened was that the potential call-up of males between sixteen and sixty for forced labour was extended over the whole of Vichy-France to cover all classes and occupations. And at the same time it was announced that all identity cards would shortly have to be turned in and re-application made for new ones from the central authorities.

Vichy-France had been theoretically occupied, of course, since late 1942, but, up till now, the occupation had been much less oppressive than in the north. Now at last, however, the lingering differences between the north and the erstwhile Free Zone were to be abolished. The intruder was moving nearer to them.

"It's very stupid of them," said Picard acidly when she discussed the alarming news with him. "Do they really imagine they will stamp out the Resistance movement by sending all the young men to Germany? On the contrary, this new call-up will simply drive the boys into the Maquis, if I know boys."

She asked him about the new identity card problem, hoping that he would put on his bland, knowing expression and tell her not to worry, but he looked worried himself and said flatly,

"That is a problem to which I have not yet found a solution."

"But – will you still be able to issue Mark and I with ration cards?" This was what worried her most. To her consternation he spread out his hands,

"How can I? I am the Mayor's Secretary: I would be held responsible. If the ration cards only become issuable against the new identity papers – this is the new regulation – and the identity papers in turn can only be re-issued after a proper check ... Frankly, I do not see how ... But don't distress yourself, Madame Leparde. Perhaps a solution may come to me."

She walked home feeling wretched. Bastard, she thought a little later, when she had recovered somewhat – he's up to his usual tricks: beating me down in order to make me really grateful when he picks me up again. But suppose that this time he really did have no answer?

She suddenly thought of seeking advice from Etienne Gilbert. But, rather to her disappointment, she herself had only met the dentist again once, briefly, since Mark had become friends with the family. He had never sent any bill of course for his services, and Mark had had a lot of hospitality and a lot of food there: she hesitated to impose on him further. Though he had spoken as pleasantly as ever to her when she had encountered him one day in Châtelet market, and had assured her that Mark's frequent visits were a great pleasure to his own boys, he had looked tired and preoccupied. A fine skin of exhaustion had seemed to her to lie over his otherwise unremarkable features, veiling his pale eyes as though they were looking elsewhere. He had thanked her for her diffident invitation to call one day if he were passing St Laurent, but she had felt he was unlikely to do so and indeed he had not come. Probably, she thought now, her instant conviction on first meeting him that he was a friend, had been merely the product of her own need: probably he was prudently wary of having anything much to do with her, a clandestine foreigner. A refugee child was one thing, but an adult – she had, after all, no real reason to suppose that he looked kindly on her or on the English at all. He might be merely charitable and discreet ... She prayed desperately to some unknown and eyeless Fate that he was discreet. Mark was there so often.

Three days later Mark told her that Jacques Gilbert had received call-up papers, and was therefore going 'into hiding'. It was just as Picard had said.

"Where's he going to hide?"

"Going into the Maquis, of course."

On a sudden impulse, she put her arms round him and said, holding him tightly to her,

"Oh thank God, thank God that you are not sixteen."

"But if I was," he remarked, smiling and gently disengaging himself, "it wouldn't make any difference because the authorities don't know about me! Like you've often said, we don't exist, officially."

Barely two weeks later as he was returning on his bicycle from Châtelet on Sunday evening, he was stopped by a Militia patrol on the main road. He had no identity papers on him, and the three men therefore accompanied him back to the cottage. They were strangers to the district, with shut, deliberately expressionless faces. Coldly polite, they stood grouped in the firelit kitchen, seeming to fill it.

Trembling, not daring to speak beyond a muttered greeting, she fetched her own worthless identity card and Mark's and thrust them into the men's hands. They seemed satisfied, surprisingly unsuspicious. They were not, she realised after her first moment of panic, Germans, but Frenchmen in military police uniforms, dour shop-assistants or railway clerks who had seen an opportunity to better themselves.

"You see," Mark said to them, with what seemed a nice mixture of firmness and deference, "I am only just fourteen. I know I look more, but I can't help it."

The men excused themselves. Madame no doubt understood: they had their duty to do. So many deserters and runaways now – these new regulations … By the way, Madame realised, did she not, that these cards would soon have to be exchanged?

She nodded, and smiled, and nodded again, feeling like some sort of fairground toy. Would one of them suddenly fling aside his mask of correctness and strike her?

They went, with docile apologies for disturbing her. Their boots were loud on the gravel path as in the terrible moment when they had arrived, with Mark in their midst. Then their bicycles squeaked away into the dark from which they had come.

Mark flung his arms exuberantly round Jane,

"Huh, so much for them, the idiots! They were convinced I was sixteen. Maman, thank *goodness* you kept quiet. I was *praying* you would."

"My – my accent?"

"Of course. Mine sounds just like everyone else – so the Gilberts say – but yours! If only you could hear yourself, poor old Maman –" He rolled up his eyes, flung himself into the basket chair and said, mocking her and all his past childhood, "You're an awful responsibility, Maman! Suppose they had asked you something else you just had to answer? … I think I'd better keep my own card on me from now on, hadn't I?"

"Yes – and you'd better damn well get back from your expeditions in future before dark falls," said Jane furiously, her paralysed fear now melting into anger. After a moment, she began to cry. Mark, not particularly disconcerted, patted her shoulder and comforted her, as if consciously playing the traditional rôle of a man comforting a crying woman, his mind really elsewhere.

He promised not to get caught out after dark again. But she felt that he was promising this for her sake rather than for his own.

Towards the end of February German troops, with lorries and armoured cars, descended onto two large villages near Montluçon. Acting – it was said – on a tip-off, they rounded up some forty refugees from the north, mostly women and children, including a dozen foreigners with false identity papers. They had been taken away in the lorries, no one knew where.

The following afternoon, just as it was getting dark, Jane received a note on exercise-book paper, folded tight, delivered by the cobbler's small grandson. The note was from Picard: she had, she realised, as she hurried to dry her hands and open it, been half-expecting it all day. Would she, it asked, kindly come to the Mairie?

Leaving water heating on the side of the stove in case Mark should return before she did, she hurried up to the village through the dank, fading light. But when she reached the brightly lighted Mairie – it, and the adjoining school-house, were some of the few buildings in the village with electricity – Mark himself was there, clutching his school books, standing uneasily by the door. At the big desk sat Picard, and next to him the Mayor. The unshaded bulb shone down on Monsieur Marceau's balding head, and glinted on Picard's spectacles. It made the margarine-coloured paint with which the walls and doors were liberally coated look yellower than ever, giving the place an air of spurious warmth. Really, it was bitterly cold; like all small Mairies up and down rural France it was normally open one afternoon a week. Why were Marceau and Picard both there tonight? She felt that she had been summoned to some formally convened Council of War.

Ceremoniously they invited her to seat herself, but, as if only existing in their official capacity tonight, did not rise themselves. Mark was told to shut the door and sit down also.

It was the Mayor who spoke first, his country accent even broader than usual, perhaps from embarrassment.

"Madame Leparde, Monsieur Picard here and I are both of the opinion that things cannot continue as they have been ... You have heard the news from over Montluçon way?"

"Yes. It's dreadful."

"Dreadful it is, and for us as well as you," Monsieur Marceau paused, as if satisfied that the dramatic resonance of this remark expressed his deep feelings in the matter, but then seemed unable to find the right words in which to continue. Taking pity on him eventually, Jane said,

"You mean that this means Mark and I are at risk too ... But we have been all along."

"Far more now," put in Picard instantly, and Marceau nodded his head in solemn agreement.

"See here, Madame," he said persuasively, after another pause, holding out his hand, palm up. "It isn't just you and your lad – it's us too. Not just Picard here and myself, the whole village. If the *Boches* come here next and we should be found to have been harbouring you all this time ... You take my meaning? It isn't right, Madame Leparde, or fair."

And, looking down at her clogs, and at the worn, red-tiled floor, Jane said quietly that, yes, she could see it was perhaps not right and not fair, and that the last thing she had ever wanted to do was to put anyone else at risk, or create trouble for them – but what could she do?

She spoke quietly, without indignation or pleading, because (she now realised, sitting in this cold room with these men) for nearly four years she had been waiting for this to happen. At some level, even when lulled by the tedious labour of her life into believing that she and Mark were at least safe, she had yet known that this crisis was coming, was on its way. Now, it had come. She recognised it, and its inevitability, almost as if she had been here before, as if this scene had been enacted before, even many times, and even in the same detail – the same bentwood chairs around the desk, the same yellow light and cold smell of ink and dust.

She looked across at Mark to see how he was taking it. But he was frowning and cleaning his nails with the corner of an exercise book, as if that were his main preoccupation.

She looked back at the two men she had known for years,

sitting there behind their desk like puppets. She tried without success to perceive the private men that might be there beneath Picard's perennial loose-fitting grey worsted suit and beneath Marceau's tight, shiny-elbowed alpaca jacket. Like most of the village men he wore no collar or tie, but a white silk muffler round his bull's neck, beneath his ill-shaven chin. What real humanity or compassion could she expect from him? Or, for that matter, from Picard either? She had never been really sure of Picard all along. She had always known in her heart, without exactly blaming him for it, that he was a coward. If a German officer was driven in a staff-car into the square of St Laurent might it not, after all, be Picard who obsequiously led him to the cottage down the lane, calculatedly sacrificing her and Mark to save all the rest of the villagers, the people with a right to be there and whom he was paid to serve?

Possibly, even, this interview was in the nature of a final warning to her. Get out – or we betray you.

She clenched her hands inside the pockets of her jacket.

"We will go," she said firmly. "I don't know where, exactly, and I don't know how. But don't worry, we will go. Won't we, Mark?"

But before Mark could or would answer, Picard said in apparent surprise, scraping back his chair,

"But how would you go? . . . Have you any money saved?"

"You *know* I haven't, Monsieur Picard. Nor anything left to sell – except my wedding ring, and I can't get that off now. They could file it in the smithy, I suppose –"

Serge Beckman briefly crossed her memory. She thought of his amethyst, long turned into bread, and of his own going into unknown territory, covered only by night and silence. Gone for ever, like Pierre before him.

"Well then," said Picard testily, "you can't very well go then, can you? Don't distress yourself, Madame Leparde: we do not want to drive you out of St Laurent – that would be inhuman, if you have nowhere else to go. It is something other that Monsieur Marceau and myself have in mind to propose to you. A little arrangement – for convenience sake."

So she listened intently, eyes still on the floor, as they told her what they had decided she must do. By the end of the explanation it dawned on her that they were quite pleased with themselves, like two boys setting out to trick a headmaster, ingenious and sly.

After a long final silence she said:

"But what about Mark. Your – your plan for me doesn't seem to take Mark into account?"

Mark looked up and spoke for the first time.

"I'm going to join the Maquis, Maman. I've talked to Monsieur Picard about it. He agrees that it's the best thing."

They walked back together beneath a white full moon, riding above the now-invisible clouds that had darkened the ending of the day. Mark slipped his arm through hers and pressed himself against her.

"Don't worry, Maman," he said. "It'll be all right. Really it will."

She said, her voice sounding tiny and insignificant to her own ears in the immense darkness of the landscape,

"But Sylvain. Of all people . . . Do you think anyone will really believe in it?"

"Of course everyone in the village will know you're marrying Sylvain for an identity card," he said consolingly. "It'll be like Picard and Marceau said – a marriage of convenience, just something to keep you out of harm's way till the War is over."

She said suddenly, crushed by the weight of his apparently superior knowledge of the way life was,

"I only hope Sylvain is happy about it . . ."

"Oh, Sylvain will do what they want him to do – if he knows it will please you too. Sylvain isn't difficult, poor old lad. Identity cards are a bit beyond him, anyway. It's other things that matter to Sylvain."

She remembered the way Picard had said dismissively, almost contemptuously, "Monsieur Marceau and I have come to the conclusion that there is only one man in the village of plausible age and who is unlikely to want to marry anyone else." She resented that they should, with their beady-eyed practicality, dispose of Sylvain's future in this way. She resented the proposal far more on his account than on her own.

"I wonder what Marie Stefan will think of it," she said. Marie Stefan and Marceau were long-term enemies. That much was village tradition.

"I think Picard's already had a word with her – and with Sylvain himself, of course."

"And with you too, I take it?" she said evenly. Her throat was beginning to ache with unshed tears.

"Yes. Actually he did. This morning. They both did. Marceau came up to the school and they had a great session together during break and then called me in there."

"And – and you said I would agree?"

"I said I thought you'd take what Picard is always calling 'the reasonable point of view'. Actually, Maman, it's Marceau more than Picard who's scared. He's petrified, I think, that if the Germans come here and find us then *he'll* swing for it . . . It's a habit the Germans have got into recently, taking it out on village Mayors. Mayors and Curés, Etienne Gilbert says."

She said dully, "Swing for it? You mean –"

"I mean he'd be hanged. It happens."

She thought of Marceau's fleshy neck in its white silk muffler, beneath his unshaven jowl. She thought of the plane trees in the square behind the church. It seemed utterly improbable, ridiculous even. Yet her mind told her that such things took place every week now, in peaceful villages not unlike St Laurent.

"I understand," she said humbly.

They walked a few more yards close together, their feet in unison on the road. When they were under the blackness of the big oak tree at the foot of the lane, the place where long, long ago Pierre had invented the giant that breathed, she said valiantly,

"Why didn't you tell me that Etienne Gilbert is the main organiser of the Maquis in the area? *Is* he? Picard says so."

Mark said quietly that yes, that was so. Close as she was to him, under the tree she could not even see his face. He added after a minute, apologetically,

"I did want to tell you when I first realised, but he and the boys said I shouldn't discuss these things with anyone, and so I practised keeping them to myself with you, and after a while I got into the habit, you see –"

She cried out, as she had already to Picard,

"You're too young! Why should you go –?"

He stopped and clutched her with both hands:

"Maman, this is the right thing – the reasonable thing for me to do. It's like Picard says – and Gilbert says it too – if I stay here with you like a good little schoolboy I could be caught like a rat in a trap. I'm big for my age, I'm sure to get picked up again on the road, or even in the village, now the Germans are moving into the area, and you being Sylvain's wife won't give *me* any protection. I'll have a much better chance fighting with the others in the hills. It's getting very big, you know – the Resistance, I mean. It's highly organised now and arms are being dropped in by parachute and so on. People in this village don't realise how big it is."

She said, finding the possibility almost unbearable even to utter –

"But you might get killed." Or worse, her mind screamed. Or worse, or worse –

"I might anyway. I'll be better off on the move with the rest of the lads ... Boys of my age are safer then men, anyway, Gilbert says so. Paul is going too, we'll go together. Maman you must believe me. *I do know best*. You don't realise – I am more French than you are. I've grown up here. I *know* about these things."

As they went up the lane in the dark, still pressed close to one another, she suddenly recalled, as if from an infinite distance, as remote in space as one of the barely visible stars, the reason for bringing Mark to France in the first place, all those years ago. *God never intended little boys of eight to be sent away from home*, she had imperiously declared, in her youth and her ignorance.

Did He intend a boy of just fourteen to go away for ever? It seemed, by the same argument, that He did.

Part Five

The following Sunday Jane was married to Sylvain behind closed doors in the Mairie by Monsieur Marceau. She had not seen Sylvain all the week till that morning. From tact or embarrassment he had evidently been keeping out of her way, although a message had reached her through Picard that he was 'agreeable to the arrangement'. *'Barkis is willing!'* she had thought, with a tiny flash of amusement.

As if to underline the purely-business nature of the ceremony (at least, she hoped that was the reason) neither of the other Stefans was present. Monsieur Picard and Evangeline Bisset were the witnesses. Evangeline, when consulted, had assured Jane that she was doing the right thing – that she must have confidence in Picard and hope and wait. After the War, when Dr. Leparde reappeared again – as they all so hoped and trusted that he would – matters could no doubt be sorted out, in time. But she nevertheless looked deeply shocked by the whole procedure, on some level where Jane could not reach her. She had in any case been looking worn and tired this last year. The unceasing need to be support and provider for her mother, and to run the Post Office at the same time for a salary blocked at pre-War level, was telling on her. Jane had not seen much of her recently. She regretted that taking Evangeline into her confidence about the marriage with Stefan had necessitated admitting to her at last the irregular nature of her union with Pierre. But she supposed the whole village would realise that, now.

The possibility that they would simply assume, instead, that she must have had definitive confirmation of Pierre's death, did not, then, occur to her.

Remembering how the difficulty in assembling birth

certificates from London and Strasbourg had been one of the factors fatally delaying her marriage with Pierre, she was a little surprised that Picard brushed this aside as being of no importance.

"Sylvain's birth was registered here in this very Mairie – no problem. As for your supposed birthplace – Roubaix, didn't we say? – on the Belgian border, that area was so heavily bombed in 1940 that a difficulty in obtaining any record for you is quite plausible. For this very reason, during the War, many marriages have been celebrated without some of the proper documents. We will make that all right."

She had the impression that he, in a covert way, was rather enjoying himself at his self-appointed task of outwitting Them. Was he enjoying something else too? She had long guessed at a faint sadistic streak in his nature. In marrying her off to Sylvain, could he possibly be taking an obscure pleasure in seeing her reduced to such a level? More intelligent and sophisticated than most of his neighbours, perhaps he had resented Jane and Pierre a little, right from the first – resented them for their free and easy outsiders' way with his school and with the village itself. If so, he had certainly managed to get his own back ... But presently she dismissed that thought as bitter and distorted.

Monsieur Marceau, on the other hand, seemed to be nervous of the whole proceeding. As soon as the ceremony was over, he rapidly shook hands with everyone and then took himself, his Sunday suit and his collar and tie, off to his own house. Jane had the impression that when Marceau actually came face to face with Sylvain, he felt a little ashamed of himself.

Sylvain was also arrayed, surprisingly to Jane, in a tight black Sunday suit of antique cut. He seemed stoical about the whole affair, calmer in fact than anyone else in the room. Only when the time came for him to sign the register did he betray a little tension, handing the pen back to Monsieur Marceau and saying loudly, using the intimate *tu* form of address,

"You know I don't do writing." Monsieur Picard came

to the rescue, with a discreet, ambiguous squiggle in the right place.

If Sylvain felt that he was being exploited by people of better education than himself, he did not show it. As for Jane, she did not feel any longer like someone intrinsically different from Sylvain. She had felt like nothing and nobody, like someone whose life was ended and who was existing posthumously in a blanched emptiness, ever since Mark had left three days before.

He had gone off definitively to the Gilberts in Châtelet on Pierre's bicycle, as the first stage in an unknown journey. He wore Pierre's trousers and the boots that had once belonged to the Chauvins' son, an old waterproof of Picard's and a new jersey pressed into his hands by Madame Marcelle, who said that she had intended it for her nephew Henri but that in the circumstances ... A number of people, notably the Bonnins, had given him money. Jane had not believed, beforehand, that she could bear him going, but when the time came she did bear it, because she had to.

After the formalities in the Mairie they hung about momentarily in the square. Evidently no one quite liked to suggest a celebration drink; that would have made it seem too much like a real wedding. Evangeline Bisset kissed Jane and squeezed her hand, but said with a forced smile that she must be hurrying back to her mother.

Then, abruptly, Sylvain turned to Jane; he spoke in a shy undertone,

"Mother said, seeing as it's Sunday, you'd be very welcome to dinner. My brother won't be there, she said to tell you. He's seeing his girl over in Merserolles. So it'll be just us. We've a chicken."

Later, when the War was over, Jane found that she remembered less of that time after Mark had gone than of any other period since 1940. Perhaps there hadn't really, except for one or two incidents, been all that much to remember?

She had believed, in those four years, that she had

struggled to do her best because of Mark: she had thought that all the efforts she had made had been for him, and sometimes the burden had seemed considerable. Only now when it was abruptly removed from her did she realise that it was not so much she who had supported Mark but he who, in a more fundamental sense, had supported her.

Without him she was lost, without a purpose or an occupation. Her mind seemed to have relinquished its concentration and to have become ineffectual. She would begin some domestic task – re-staking the goat and her kid, say, or mixing the chickens' mash or earthing potatoes – and then drift off to another leaving the first job unfinished. Then later, she would notice the unfinished work and realise dazedly that her thoughts had once more been elsewhere. They had been feebly and obsessionally ranging the mountains, plateaux and forests of southern France, as once they had hopelessly ranged there for Pierre: she had been looking for her son.

Whole days passed when she achieved nothing, and yet was not even aware of it. The vegetable garden did not flourish that spring, but she could not even find the energy to worry about what she would eat that year. One day in March she failed to latch the hutch properly and Colette disappeared, taking an unborn litter with her. Henri, less intelligent and more domesticated, escaped no further than the garden, where he found a hole in the fence and squeezed through to demolish the winter lettuces.

She gave him away to Sylvain after that. She did not enquire what became of him.

She saw Sylvain and Marie Stefan frequently, but few other people. With Mark gone, her regular links with the village were reduced, and she could no longer summon up the resolution to smile at people and make small talk about the weather or the likelihood of being able to obtain a little chicken meal. She was sick of all that, she said to herself; she did not analyse her sickness further nor give it the name of mourning.

She had in any case the feeling that people shunned her

slightly now. However much they understood the common-sense reason for her alliance with the Stefans, she suspected that some of them felt deep down that it wasn't quite nice: she was sure the Langlois were shocked by the business, though none of them had said anything unpleasant to her, and Jeanot had genially wished her good luck when she met him in the road.

Other people, she guessed, were simply relieved at not having to bother about her any more. For the first time, she had a full set of legal ration cards; she had married Sylvain, therefore she existed. She no longer had to be an object of perpetual charity but could buy fats or cheese in the shop like anyone else.

Even the money problem was eased. She had not expected that Sylvain would begin to keep her. She knew that, guided by Marie Stefan, he made quite a lot of money these days, selling rabbits, poultry, game and goats' milk in Châtelet, where prices on the 'free market' were going higher and higher. But Picard had stressed many times that of course the marriage was a mere subterfuge for the authorities, and had insisted that he had explained everything to Sylvain in this light. When, on the first market day after their wedding, Sylvain came to the door of the cottage and presented her with some notes and a handful of change, she was much disconcerted.

"But you didn't sell anything of mine this week. I can't take your money, Sylvain."

"Mother said as now we ought to go shares with you. We got plenty anyway."

"But that's not fair."

"Why not?" said Sylvain sturdily. Jane knew quite well why not and suspected that, for all his innocence, Sylvain did too, but she did not feel equal to putting the matter into words. She and Sylvain did not even say *'tu'* to one another, though he and Mark had.

So she weakly thanked Sylvain and kept the money, which after that appeared regularly. But after three weeks Sylvain said to her,

"About the nanny goat..."

"Yes ... I'm sorry I don't seem to be making much of a job of milking her, these days. Mark usually did it, when he came in from the Michards, so I never got much practice. Also, now the kid's getting bigger, he seems to take a lot."

"He's greedy," said Sylvain shortly. "You did ought to sell him soon."

"I know." She did not like to admit, even to someone as uncensorious as Sylvain, that the thought of taking the nanny-goat's kid away from her was more than she could cope with, now.

The next time he came, Sylvain said, as if testing what her reaction would be,

"I might take the nanny and the kid back to our place one of these days ... Mother'll keep her milk going. She'll dry up if you don't strip the teats properly."

"All right. If you think that's best..."

"I mean," he said slowly, "It's all one now, isn't it – your property and mine? It don't make any difference who has it."

She agreed docilely that this was so.

In spite of Sylvain's money, she still could not afford the luxury of having the electricity re-connected. Now, with Mark gone, she did not bother to beg and scrape to acquire candles any more. Instead, when the still-early dark settled down over her cottage, imprisoning her at the close of yet another lonely day, she simply went to bed. In the dark she lay there till sleep came, her mind revolving in its perpetual theme.

How did they manage in the hill-camps in the dark? They couldn't show lights there, for fear of drawing attention to themselves. Etienne Gilbert had told her, before Mark left, that much of the time the Maquisards – now dignified with the name and organisation of French Forces of the Interior – were sheltered in people's houses or in empty buildings. But she always saw them in her mind's eye camped like a prehistoric tribe round some forest or moorland fire, never really warm, never properly dry.

Please God, don't let him be ill. He's only a child really, whatever they think or he pretends. Don't let him get pneumonia.

Don't be silly. If he's ill they'll leave him in someone's house. They've got supporters everywhere. Dr. Gilbert said so; all France has swung in their favour.

Not *all* France. What about the Militia? And all those collaborators in the towns. Someone tipped the Germans off near Montluçon. And what about those Maquis who were caught last week near Mende – how do you know he isn't somewhere near there too?

She could only debate the matter to and fro with herself, and wonder. There was no one who could give her any answers. One day she called on Etienne Gilbert, hoping for news, but his housekeeper said he was 'away just now'. Even Sylvain could tell her nothing, though he seemed wordlessly sorry for her as if he understood her distress. What the Maquis did and where they went when they moved out of the district, was outside his ken.

And then, one day in spring, they were back again. It was rumoured that a small detachment of men, complete with rifles and berets, had appeared 'as large as life' in the village in the very early morning. Jane heard about it from Madame Marcelle, where she had gone to buy thread for Marie Stefan.

"In my young days it was the Little People you were supposed to see if you got up really early!" declared Madame Marcelle gaily. "Now, it seems, it's the Maquis." She and many other people, even those who had previously been dubious about Resistance activities or openly disapproving, seemed excited and encouraged by their bold appearance in the light of day. They were said to be camping in the woods near at hand. 'Like Robin Hood' thought Jane, pleased at the image from a childhood book that sprang up clear in her mind: noble ideals, and dappled sunlight through the oak leaves.

On an impulse, she went to look for them, taking some food for them with her. She couldn't find them, or Sylvain, who would undoubtedly know now where they were. But in the afternoon, when she was hoeing the vegetables in a desultory way, three strangers came up the lane and, having looked all round, pushed open her gate. They were dressed as farm-workers but she knew they could not be. She ran to greet them.

The older man introduced himself as 'Coppé' and the two younger men by Christian names. They had, he said, been recommended to her by Raoul, of Châtelet-le-Lys.

"But I don't know a Raoul," she said, puzzled.

"Ah . . . But you know a Doctor Gilbert? Etienne Gilbert?"

"Oh yes, of course –"

"To us, he is Raoul," said the man, watching her as if assessing her.

Jane said eagerly, "Oh have you – has he – any message for me?"

"Message?" The man looked surprised, and a little forbidding. He had a fine-drawn, sharp face, and his manner and bearing, beneath his nondescript old clothes, were, Jane realised now, those of a man used to authority. She had the sudden impression that if she were to speak to him in English, he would answer her in the same language. But instead she said humbly, wanting to retain these visitors at her side,

"I meant from my son. He's away with – that is, Dr. Gilbert arranged for him to go away. I thought you might have news of him."

"That's why the lady was so glad to see us!" put in one of the younger men. He spoke in a joking tone, but glanced compassionately at Jane as he did so. The third one was, she noticed now, very young, a round-faced boy in a jersey, only a year or two older than Mark himself.

They could tell her nothing of Mark, but she invited them into the cottage, cut some bread and, despite their polite protests, determinedly opened a pot of chestnut jam. She had, till that day, been mindlessly keeping it for Mark, but it had been one of the things she had put aside for the Maquis this morning.

The younger men ate with good appetite. Over a cup of 'tea' – actually lime-leaves – the leader too seemed to relax, as if he had now made up his mind about her.

"Raoul had mentioned that we might look out for you," he said, "that your – that is, your situation would make you sympathetic to our cause ... But in fact we have come to ask you for something specific. We noticed that the big house next door to you is apparently standing empty, and we were told by the Mayor's Secretary that you have the keys and might let us camp in it? It would be just for a night or two, you understand, while we re-group ourselves. We shall be dispersing and moving off again soon."

She accompanied them round to the Yrieux house. That past winter, Jean Langlois had had back-trouble and had failed to trim the hedges and the ornamental shrubs. Now they were beginning to sprout bushily, and for the first time since Madame Yrieux's departure the primly shuttered house had begun to look empty, not derelict yet but odd and withdrawn from reality, like a place that was not what, at first glance, it seemed.

They had a struggle to get the key to turn in the unaccustomed lock. When at last the heavy front door with its wrought-iron trimming creaked open, the stationary air of several winters, dank and slightly fetid, met them like an invisible wall. Jane had not set foot in the house since that first winter after Pierre's disappearance. Perhaps, she thought now, she should have visited it regularly, but such visits would have served little rational purpose, and a generalised sense of both guilt and resentment toward Madame Yrieux had kept her away from the place.

Every picture and ornament was still as it had been, but it was as if they were lightly sealed in place by the dust that had spread itself silently over them. In the drawing room, the Second Empire couch still offered its hard seats to anyone who would like to sit there – but on closer examination the edges of its tassled bolsters had been gnawed and the stuffing spread around. It was damp and unpleasant to the touch. On the desk in Oncle Ernest's study the yellowed newspaper giving news of the invasion of France still lay, but that too had been much shredded by unseen teeth and claws. Time had stood still here. And yet at the same time its inexorable progression was apparent: rot and decay. On the sheeted dining room table Jane almost expected to find a Miss Haversham wedding-cake festooned with spiders' webs.

Her three companions, however, appeared delighted with the house. It was just the sort of place they had been looking for, Coppé said, to accommodate his troupe of twenty-five or so: they would treat the property with respect, he gave his personal guarantee. They were particularly pleased to find that the hand pump by which water could be raised into the bathroom tank still worked.

"Come round and see us tonight," said the younger man to Jane. He seemed to be the second-in-command. "You'll find us very comfortably installed. We may even offer you a bit to eat!"

"Actually I was wondering about that, earlier today. If you have enough food, I mean?"

"For the moment, we are well supplied. The people round here are very good to us. They even seem eager to give; no doubt they have their reasons." There was a glint of ironic humour in his eye. "It was a rather different story nine months ago. We went hungry, then."

Jane did go round there that night, and afterwards the occasion remained in her mind like a bright, lighted place in a dark countryside. Candles, a dozen or more stuck at different points round the study, dazzled when you looked straight at them but left odd gaps, sudden segments of darkness, between one group of men and the next. All was thrown in sharp relief or black shadow: faces, hands, eyes, raised wine glasses, against the blur of half a dozen different conversations.

Intoxicated partly with wine, but also with pork roasted on skewers at the fireplace, and with the presence and talk of twenty-five strangers, Jane passed the evening in a state of heady excitement. Two or three of the men were local countrymen, not much different from Jeanot Langlois or his brother, but most were from towns and from the north. One, a quiet, shy boy whose looks nevertheless reminded her of Pierre, confided to her that he was a law student from Paris; and 'Coppé', who was also called 'Chief', was apparently a political science lecturer from the University of Poitiers.

She learnt none of their true identities, she realised afterwards: evidently it was Resistance policy for everyone to go under an assumed name, but they talked freely to her and made her feel one of them. They asked sympathetic questions about how she came to find herself in St Laurent; and some of them, to applause and laughter, tried out High School English on her.

They told her things too. Not about their own immediate movements in the area: they were reticent about that. But they confirmed what she had already heard from Picard: it was beyond all doubt now, they said, that the English and the Americans were planning some kind of massive attack on Occupied France. The only uncertainty was where it was to be. Some of the company, including the lively second-in-command who came from near Le Havre, declared that it would be in the north, but others said that, on the contrary, it was sure to be on the Riviera now that North Africa was in Free French hands. Only Coppé did not commit himself to a guess. Perhaps he actually knew.

Mentally famished from four years of living in St Laurent, cut off from knowledge and from the company of knowledgeable people, she hung on their words. On the one hand their authoritative information thrilled her: the English were, after all, her people; it exhilarated her to hear them spoken of by these men with admiration and expectation. She saw them absurdly in her mind, as in a child's history book she had once had called *Our Island Race*, landing on the coast of France garbed as St George and Britannia, light playing round their righteous heads. But at the same time, with a colder, adult awareness, she dreaded the idea that the Resistance was being trained and strengthened now with the immediate prospect of playing its part in such a final, desperate battle. Mark. *Mark* – Was *he* in the north now? Or in the south? None of them could tell her, though several of them memorised his name and promised to give him her love should they happen to meet him. She longed to believe that they would.

Wanting to do something for them, wishing she had done something more, long before, she offered them the remaining guns on the study wall – the Napoleonic flintlock, the eighteenth-century blunderbuss. They smiled, but declined. A year ago, they said, when they had been badly in need of arms, any arms, they would have accepted, but now they were better equipped and these antiques were more trouble than they were worth. But as an afterthought, perhaps sensing her disappointment, the young law-student asked Coppé's permission to take the least ancient gun that hung there, the carbine that had been carried by one of Pierre's great-uncles in 1870. She was to wonder, afterwards, if it had brought him luck. Or not.

When at last she left them, very late, it was a fine moonlit night. Confusing shadows crossed the road, bars of dark and lightness as within. She had almost reached the oak tree at the foot of the lane before she saw something move from the blackness beneath it. She jumped and caught her breath, thinking – an ambush! The Militia – But it was only Sylvain.

"What are you doing here?" she said, cross because she had been frightened.

"I've been waiting for you," he said calmly.

"How did you know where I was?" She didn't want to talk to Sylvain now, to scale her conversation down to his level. The evening had stretched both her mind and her emotions, making her remember the past of real companionship and stimulation and believe again that a future with such things might still be in store for her. She resented being dragged back abruptly, so late, to the suffocating, isolated present.

"As you weren't at home I knew as you must be in there with them," he said with placid conviction. "I met 'em this afternoon, see."

"Did you Sylvain?" She softened towards him a little. "They didn't tell me that." Since it had not occurred to her to mention Sylvain to them, much less to tell them she was supposed to be his wife, this was not surprising.

"I was showing them my hideouts and that," he said. "At first the Chief wasn't sure as he could trust me –" a slight smile crinkled round his mouth as if he was mocking outsiders' assessment of himself – "But then Picard told them I was all right and that Mother and I had helped people before."

It was news to Jane that Picard was such a keen supporter of the Resistance. But, on reflection, their presence in the village in such numbers suggested that he must be – now.

They walked towards the cottage.

"I'm very glad you were able to help them Sylvain," she said, in the tone of one congratulating a child. "They must have been pleased."

"Yes. They told me they'd be moving off again soon – splitting into smaller groups, like – and that my hideouts would be just the thing . . . They said as I should come round to the Yrieux house this evening if I liked . . . But I didn't really care to."

"You should have, Sylvain. They'd have made you welcome."

"I didn't care to," he said obstinately. "I went to the café instead . . . Then I came and waited for you."

She guessed that a mixture of shyness and jealousy, of a lifetime's reserve combined with a longing to join the unprecedented party going on behind the shutters of the Yrieux house, had kept him stationed at the oak tree. Had he really been waiting for her, and if so why? He had evidently convinced himself during his tedious vigil that he had.

They reached the cottage door, but instead of saying goodnight to her as she had expected he followed her in. Inside, it was very dark. The stove was almost out. With his mind evidently still running on the day's events, Sylvain said,

"I'm not to tell my brother about the Maquis using my hides, though. Don't you say anything to him neither."

It was months since Jane had seen Stefan-Postier, to talk to. She said guardedly,

"Doesn't he like the Maquis, then?"

"Well he thinks they're trouble-makers, don't he? Him and his mates in the town . . . And he's got this la-di-da girl over at Merserolles whose father's a corn-dealer, and her uncle's in the Militia."

"I didn't know that," said Jane with foreboding, her heady pleasure in the evening very slightly dimmed. That Sylvain's brother should be on intimate terms with such a family seemed to bring danger unpleasantly near again. "Does Picard know that?" she asked.

" 'Course he does. Picard knows everything, don't he?"

"Yes, I believe he does," she said thoughtfully.

"You don't want to worry," said Sylvain. To her surprise, he put his arm round her and squeezed her almost as Mark might have done. "My brother won't give you away," he said comfortingly. "Not now. Not now you're married to me and Mother's approved of it and all. He knows Mother would never speak to him again if he did."

"Wouldn't she really," said Jane, touched by this proof of Marie Stefan's regard for her.

"Nah, she wouldn't. When Mother says something she means it . . . Though, come to that, 'twouldn't make no difference, for I'd kill him before long anyway. If he went telling tales of you to the Germans, that is."

"*Would* you, Sylvain?" She put her own arms round him. Only then, scenting his breath, did she realise that he had been drinking, just as she had.

So the thing that, once, she would have regarded as out-of-the-question, something which Sylvain himself would not even suggest, became transformed in a matter of minutes into something which it already seemed too late to refuse, impossible to sidestep. She knew that it was Sylvain, fantastically *Sylvain*, this heavy body pressing hers onto the hard, cold tiles, but it might at that moment have been any one of the twenty-five men with whom she had passed the evening. She felt she loved them all, all, and could have laid down with any one of them rather than with Sylvain, and felt in the same moment that she would never love anyone again. Love was in another life, and Mark had taken the last of that life away with him. The happy hours just past had been a mirage of such life, but now it was all gone again and there were only the cold tiles in the obliterating dark, and Sylvain.

Looming above her, fumbling determinedly with his clothes and hers, he said:

"After all – I have been giving you money . . . I have been good to you, like a husband should be . . . It's fair, isn't it?"

Fair. Yes. It was fair. After all, who else, more than Sylvain, deserved her compliance? She had come all this long way, and there was no turning back, now. She smelt the wine on his breath, and the sweaty, animal-skin aroma of his greasy corduroys, and felt his soft, clumsy lips on hers and his work-calloused hands that were like an animal's pads on her skin, and tears trickled from her shut lids. But they were not tears for herself, nor yet even for Pierre or Mark. They were tears for Sylvain himself, because there was really so very little she could give him, just this insignificant trifle, and he ought to have had a wife who could give him so much more.

Abruptly, the weather got warmer. Flowers spotted the ditches. Was it just the season's change that made life seem different and easier? Jane was not sure. Perhaps it was the Resistance. They had disappeared again from St Laurent as suddenly and quietly as they had come. But the feeling of them, an unseen, ever-increasing force permeating the French countryside, remained with her, now that she had seen their faces: the idea of them gave her strength and comfort. At any rate she supposed this was another reason for her new, vague sense of well-being.

Inside the Yrieux house, which was once again shuttered and still, a small pile of wood ash in the study grate and a few empty wine bottles stacked in the dark hall were all that marked their passing. Outside in the garden the lawn, still untended, grew tall and green, keeping pace with the young wheat in the field beyond. Jeanot might have scythed it, perhaps, in his father's place, but his mind was apparently on other things. Since his second child had been born it was common knowledge in the village that his young wife had been tearful and withdrawn, failing to do her share of the farm work and exasperating her mother-in-law. She had even, it was murmured, made a half-hearted attempt to kill herself. Jane would have liked to have said something to Jeanot about it, to sympathise in some way, but there was no opportunity. She never saw him any more these days. If things had turned out otherwise, if he had not been married already . . .? With the warm weather an unfocused sense, which was not so much desire as a general physical awareness, seemed to have stirred within her. She was particularly aware of substances and textures, of scents of earth and water.

Now and again, after night had fallen, Sylvain visited her. At such times he did not come as he did in the day, with a farm-implement or a sack or a message from his mother. He came silently, tapping on the shutter, hardly uttering a word all the time he was there. She found she was glad when he came. He was company and physical warmth, as a dog or a cat might have been. After that first time, she was touched to realise, he always wore his stiff Sunday suit – his wedding suit – on these occasions, though perhaps that was partly because he came on his way back from some café in the neighbourhood. She also thought that he had been washing and shaving more, these days, though it was always dark; she could not really tell.

Once in her cottage he had a fit. It wasn't alarming. He went rigid for a moment, then shuddered, and after that seemed dazed and confused and rolled away from her, as if forgetting what he had come for. It didn't matter, she told him, comforting him and gently helping him to dress again. It was easy to be kind and gentle, she told herself, to someone who did not really matter to you.

When he was not with her, or when she talked to him,

rather self-consciously, in the day times, she continued to tell herself that what passed between them at other times was something purely physical and insignificant. Each episode was separate and undiscussed, without prologue or sequel. Beyond a diffused tenderness, a remote, bruised warmth, he left nothing of himself with her; directly he was gone, disappearing softly into the night, she was alone again. Or so, at any rate, she believed.

Yet as time went by he was more often in the forefront of her thoughts. She looked for his coming. And she no longer lived a life peopled largely by absent faces. It was almost as if, each time she held Sylvain wordlessly in her arms, his hair like rough black feathers against her skin, something of her previous loves was being – no, not blotted out, but dissolved and fused in this new outlet for feeling. Her double bereavement, as a wife and as a mother, now found a minor but real solace in her rueful tenderness for Sylvain.

May slowly went by. The weather was sunny and dry now. One day she was visited by a little boy on a bicycle who said he had a message for her from Monsieur Gilbert. Heart banging, she tore it open. But inside was just a brief, unsigned note saying that he had seen Mark recently, who was well and sent his best love and said to tell her that he was getting plenty to eat and that she wasn't to worry.

'Never write a word that could incriminate you or anyone else if it fell into the wrong hands.' Since the evening in the Yrieux house she knew that that was the first rule of a clandestine existence. She yearned over the brief words, reading and re-reading them, hoping against all sense to extract some further meaning from them, but it was no use. On the surface of her mind, she was pleased and relieved to have the message. But afterwards Mark seemed further away from her than ever, emotionally. It was, after all, documentary evidence that he was leading a new life on his own which she could in no way share. He did not need her now. Perhaps he would never really need her again.

Sylvain pointed out one day that the long grass next door was full of wild rabbits, which would invade the cottage garden. He set traps there. One day he asked her:

"Do you think the lady'll ever come back any more?"

"Madame Yrieux? I really don't know, Sylvain. I suppose she might – when the War is over."

After a while he said,

"Will *you* be here then?"

"I don't know, Sylvain, I really don't know." She did not have the heart to tell him outright that she would not be. And in any case, anything seemed possible in that unreal, brilliant green spring, as the whole of France, both those who were for the Germans and those who were against them, waited covertly for the next event. Perhaps she *would* be here for ever, now, she thought. In some moods the idea was almost a welcome one.

One day Sylvain took her far up into the woods, to a rocky outcrop among the fresh green bracken with a view through branches over the next valley. There, someone – he, she supposed – had erected a roof of woven sticks and turfs between two rocks to make a primitive house. While she rested in it on a pile of dried heather, enjoying the sunshine that flecked between the chinks in the roof, he snuffed about, finding a bottle, a tin, a cartridge case, some crumpled newspaper.

"They've been here again," he said, pleased. "They told me they thought it was a very useful hide and that they'd be here again soon. The Chief said that a lot of 'em would be moving down again, by and by."

"The Chief? You mean the one they call Coppé?"

"Tall man – not very young. Speaks like a gentleman. That's him . . . They're going to try something soon, I think."

"I wonder what?" she said eagerly.

But if Sylvain had any idea, he kept it to himself. He looked, for him, almost secretive and smug. "They said they counted me as one of themselves," he said after a while. "The Chief said they'd remember me – after the War, like." There was a deep, juvenile pride in his voice.

Ten days later, on June 6th, the British-American Normandy landings began. And simultaneously, all over France, a Resistance campaign of action was launched. Bridges were blown up along the main line railways. German troop trains bound for the northern coasts were derailed. Picard was quietly triumphant: he had said that the attack would be made in the north. That week the portrait of Pétain finally disappeared from the schoolroom.

On the Saturday, Jane expected Sylvain to call as usual on his way back from selling things in Châtelet market. She had even prepared some lunch for him. But he did not come at noon, nor yet, more surprisingly, in the evening. She slept badly that night, half wondering through her sleep where he was. She was afraid that he might have had a bad fit in one of the town cafés he liked to frequent when he had money in his pocket.

In the morning, when there was still no sign of him she took the field path for the Stefans' house. Just before she reached it, she came upon Marie Stefan, at the edge of the copse, where a small stream ran down the river. She had dragged out a huge iron pot like a cauldron, which Jane had seen lying about there but had supposed to be a relic of the past, and had built a fire of birch logs beneath it. Now she had something boiling in it. With her flappy clothes and straggling hair she had never looked more like a story-book witch, even though the smell from the pot indicated that the steaming contents were merely washing. Marie greeted her gaily, but seemed fractionally embarrassed for once.

"I know it's Sunday. But I suddenly took a fancy to doing the sheets off the bed, like, and the boys' shirts. The sheets haven't been done in a while . . . My old Mother always said the end of May was the time for a wash, and that's past now."

Jane sat down to watch, enjoying the uncharacteristic sight. It was a beautiful day, like the one on which Sylvain had taken her to the hideout in the feathery green forest. Marie stirred the heavy mass with a wooden paddle: evidently on the rare occasions when she did wash she believed in making a proper job of it. Presently she sat down herself on an upturned pail. She said again,

"I know it's Sunday. But I never set much store by that."

"I should think not," said Jane abstractedly. The cracked church bell was ringing out across the fields. It occurred that, after all this time, she herself had never so much as set foot in the church while a service was going on. She told Marie so, adding "No wonder that fat Curé pretends not to know me when he passes me in the village." Marie chuckled, and squinted sideways at her.

"Where's that boy of mine, then?" she asked presently, as if something was amusing her.

"I don't know, Marie – I thought he was with you?" Her anxiety, momentarily allayed by Marie's cheerful busy-ness and unconcern, returned. "Hasn't he been home all night?" she asked.

"He has not. I thought he was with *you*."

Oh did you! thought Jane. It was the first intimation she had had that Sylvain had confided in his mother about those late night visits. But probably, on reflection, he hadn't – or not in so many words. What words indeed would he use? Probably Marie had just guessed. It would be like her.

She said,

"I haven't seen him, Marie – honestly. I'd tell you if I had . . . You don't think – ? I mean – nothing could have happened to him. Could it?"

"Not 'im," said Marie instantly. "He can look after hisself. He'll have been up all night more like chasing after some beast. And it won't be the first time, neither." But the animation had gone from her lined face, and her mouth had dropped at the corners so that she suddenly looked like a very old woman.

Sylvain was not returned to the village till Monday evening, and then only after Jane had persuaded Picard to telephone the police in Châtelet-le-Lys. He had been picked up by the Militia on Saturday afternoon as he had been leaving the market. They had taken him to their headquarters in the railway hotel and had apparently questioned him about recent Resistance movements in the area. They had been convinced that he knew more than he would say, as perhaps he did. Jane guessed that they were also convinced that he was brighter than he appeared, again with some reason. They didn't believe him when he told them he couldn't sign his name, and that seemed to have upset him more than anything else, though he had clearly been beaten up, probably more than once. He had a black eye and a cut lip and huge bruises on his body, though the two Militia men who deposited him unceremoniously at the Mairie in St Laurent said, before driving off again, that he had injured himself falling in a self-induced fit.

He probably had had a fit, or several, Marie Stefan told Jane sorrowfully, later: when he had been brought down to her house by Marceau himself in one of his carts, his trousers had been stiff with dried urine.

"It was too bad of them to beat him," said Marie, compressing her lips. "Too bad, whatever they thought he knew. He isn't like other people. I know that. They shouldn't have done it – not to him, not with his fits ... They shall pay for this one day."

"Perhaps they didn't realise ... They wouldn't have known him like everyone round here does," suggested Jane feebly, but Marie gave her such a fierce look from under her hair that she said no more. To look for a rational excuse for an act of brutality was, she realised now, the cowardly reflex of someone who has led a life of sheltered ignorance. Evil existed, and not just in some distant place but quite near at hand. She herself had no reason now to ignore this fact.

She minded dreadfully for Sylvain and wondered if, that day when he had been talking proudly about being one of the Maquis, she ought to have tried to warn him. But how could she have? She hadn't been expecting this to happen herself – not to Sylvain, of all people. Her fears had all been for Mark, in his unknown, separate existence. But it was never, it seemed, the things you most dreaded that happened, but something else, a different horror you had not thought to predict.

She dreaded that Sylvain's fragile brain might have been further damaged by the treatment he had received. Poor love, he had seemed so happy recently, too, more assured and communicative than she had ever known him. She grieved over him like a mother over a hurt child. But, after two days of staying in bed at his own mother's house, shocked and miserable, the covers pulled over his head, Sylvain seemed to recover from the incident if anything better than Jane herself. Perhaps, she thought, it was just as well he always tended to live in the present, agreeing amiably to Picard's proposition, spending money as it came to him, seeking Jane out determinedly when physical desire presented itself to him, leaving her casually afterwards. When he had asked her in the Yrieux garden if she would be there after the War, that was the one occasion on which he had seemed to be looking ahead.

She tried to make him promise that he would not have anything more to do with the Maquis for a bit, telling him that this prudence was for their sake as well as his own, now that the Militia had him marked. He 'promised' readily enough, glad to please her, but she did not know how much weight his words carried.

Cherbourg was liberated at the end of June and Caen early in July. The Allied Forces were pushing inwards on the north and west. In retaliation for this, and for more local acts of Resistance sabotage, the German SS made examples of towns far from the battle front. Hostages were hanged in Lyons, in Tulle: there were garbled tales of worse things in a village in the north.

But, in the deceptive green peace of St Laurent the echoes of battle reached Jane in an even fainter and more muffled form than usual. She had something else on her mind, something odd and different. She had not had a period since April.

This had happened once before, the winter before last. It had puzzled her but, knowing there could be no alarming explanation for it, she had eventually gone to consult

Solange Langlois, Jeanot's cousin the village nurse, who lived with her husband and children on an outlying farm. She had mistimed her visit; the family were at their midday meal, and Solange, a strapping woman with a rather intimidating manner, had come to the door chewing. When she heard what Jane had come to consult her about, she had not been rude exactly but she had not wasted any time on her either. She had told Jane not to worry – that it was poor food that was to blame: several of the women in the village had been having the same symptom these thin, wartime winters, particularly those with large families to feed. Their usual 'visitor' would return with the spring vegetables and the eggs and milk of the new season. It was nothing to fuss about.

Jane had cycled home again, relieved, but rather downcast because she felt that Solange Langlois was one of those people who would rather not have had a foreigner in the neighbourhood in these uncertain times, and did not want to be friends. Anyway she had been right: the usual cycle had re-established itself when life got easier again.

Now, when she belatedly realised that it was happening again, Jane tried to tell herself that the reason was the same. But she knew in her heart that it was unlikely to be so. The weather was fine and warm, she had been eating positively well since her wedding with Sylvain – better than for a long time. For the first time in years she had even put on a little weight. Her skin was smoother and softer again. She felt tired and vague as she had for months, but basically healthy.

The possible truth was staring her in the face. During the day, she managed to avoid it, as being too embarrassing and ridiculous to take seriously. But in the nights, lying awake, she knew that it was not merely possible: it was actually so.

Evidently she had been mistaken in believing that in their few, brief, silent encounters, that were so unlike the rest of life, Sylvain could have left no permanent trace of himself within her.

But she still put off thought, let alone action. In July 1944, with the British guns attacking Avranches, the 'future' did not mean months or years, it meant no further than next week, or tomorrow even.

On July 14th, Bastille Day, the village staged a tentative ceremony with a small bonfire in the square, a glass of wine all round and a brief and almost furtive address from Monsieur Marceau, whose manner suggested that he expected a German convoy to come roaring down from the main road at any moment. He spoke, in anxiously general terms, of the good days soon to come, and urged what he obscurely referred to as 'moderation' on his co-citizens in 'whatever struggles Fate may still have in store for our beloved country'.

Jeanot Langlois, who had moved near to Jane in the small crowd, told her in an amused undertone that Marceau and Picard had quarrelled over the wisdom of having this little festivity at all. "Marceau didn't want it," he said, "Said it might 'lead to trouble'. Trust him. But Picard was set on it. If you ask me, he's hoping for a pat on the back from somewhere when it comes to the reckoning up after the War."

"Will there really be a reckoning after the War?" said Jane, not liking the idea in spite of everything.

"You can be sure there will. We all know who's been on Their side."

"You mean – the Militia?"

"And their informers, yes."

"But – there isn't anyone like that in the village, is there?" she asked. It was the question she had been wanting and dreading to ask for years.

"Not in this village, I don't think so, no. But you can never be entirely sure. These are strange times, Madame Leparde."

"Don't call me that Jeanot," she said quietly. "I'm Madame Stefan – for now, if it's Madame anything."

"Yes, I forgot, I'm sorry," he said, embarrassed, so that she wished she had not mentioned it. But after a minute he said softly,

"I really was very sorry about what happened to Sylvain – we all were, even Mother, for all she says about the

Stefans. I'm glad to see he's around again, none the worse for it. Will you tell him that, and give him my good wishes? I can't see him just now."

"I will. Thank you Jeanot." She wanted to say something to him in return, about his own wife, who was not there with the rest of the family that evening. Jeanot himself had his small daughter perched on his arm. The moment did not seem entirely propitious, but she knew there would not be another one.

"I – I'm sorry your wife isn't well."

His face shut. "She's getting on," he said noncommittally. A moment later, as if deciding to confide in Jane, he added, more dejectedly,

"She varies so. Last week I really thought she was getting better – taking more of an interest in the kids, like. But this week again ... She cries a lot. *I* can't do anything for her. And Mother losing patience with her –"

"I'm very sorry," said Jane again.

"I just don't understand it," he said wearily. "She's got everything that she wants – me, the children, all our family – and when I look at people like you, with all you've gone through, managing on your own ... It's so unreasonable."

"I don't think sadness *is* reasonable," said Jane. "For myself – I haven't been nearly as sad most of the time these last four years as I perhaps reasonably should have been. Sometimes I've been really happy." She only knew this was true as she said it.

"Our cousin Solange says I ought to make my wife pull herself together," he said. "She says I spoil her. Do you think she's right?"

"No. No, I don't." Fat cow.

"Nor do I," he said in apparent relief. "My poor lass can't help herself – I do know that really. There's something the matter with her. But I don't know what it is." Jane's support seemed to have cheered him a little. "I've even wondered –" he began: "No; it sounds silly."

"No, do go on?"

"It's just that ... She seems so frightened. I've even wondered sometimes if she sees something that the rest of us don't."

"You mean – in the future?" said Jane uneasily. Her first reaction was to reject this sort of thing as peasant superstition and she would have expected Jeanot to take the same view. But now his face looked odd and different, lighted from beneath by the fire.

"Ah, it sounds daft put like that! I'll be turning into one of the old women next and running after Marie Stefan to read my hand ..." He dismissed the subject, and humped his daughter higher onto his shoulder to 'see the fire'. The proprietor of the smaller café had just thrown on a couple of broken chairs; the flames got to work on the shapely, long-seasoned wood, melting down forty years of purpose. Some young men standing outside the café cheered.

"I never really like to see things, that have once been used, burnt," said Jane, speaking the thought that suddenly came into her head.

"Nor do I, really," Jeanot agreed. "I think to myself of the time when they were made. Someone took care and trouble over those chair legs once ... But that's the way it goes."

Soon after July 14th the Maquis moved back into the district. They had not been seen in the village this time, but everyone knew. They were said to be in the woods quite close at hand and to be planning something in connection with the level crossing fifteen miles away on the other side of Châtelet-le-Lys. An atmosphere of discreet excitement pervaded the village.

The next evening Stefan-Postier called on Jane. She was surprised, but greeted him pleasantly and invited him in. Though she rarely saw him, didn't like him, and knew that he disapproved on some vaguely-defined 'principle' of her alliance with Sylvain, she was always careful to be polite to him.

He would not sit down however, but remained standing by the door. She did not like his expression.

"I've come about the Maquis," he said, breathing heavily.

"Oh yes?" she tried to look helpful but uncertain. Was Stefan-Postier now going to become a fervent Resister, in spite of his girl friend's uncle in the Militia? It didn't seem likely, but you never knew. As Jeanot said, these were stange times.

"You keep away from them this time," he suddenly said, evidently bringing out something he had rehearsed. "You keep your nose out of it. You've caused enough trouble for my family already."

She said, confused by the unexpected attack.

"But Sylvain and your mother were taking food to the Maquis before I ever knew about it – long before Mark went away to joint them."

He probably knew this was true, she thought, but he pretended not to. He blustered, and said something scathing about bloody foreign interference in French affairs and how the British had always been troublemakers – they'd learnt that at school. It occurred to her that he was slightly drunk.

"You make sure Sylvain stays out of it this time too," he kept repeating. "If you lead him into anything again, you and your precious son, I'll tell the Germans in Châtelet all about you . . . I could have, long before, you know, and it would've saved us a lot of trouble. I've been too nice, that's where it is –"

She said, trying not to tremble, hating and fearing him as if he were a German officer in person,

"I've not led Sylvain into anything. In fact I've advised him against it now. He's promised me –"

" 'Promised'," he sneered. "You think his promises count for anything? He's soft in the head – that's the only reason you were able to get hold of him. And let me tell you he's sitting in the café on the square at this very moment talking about his Maquisard friends! I give you *friends* – people who get you into a load of trouble you haven't looked for . . . Not that I care about Sylvain myself, of course," he added quickly, "It's our mother I care about if next time they kill him . . . How d'you think she'd feel if she saw her darling idiot son – your precious idiot so-called husband – dangling in the square by his neck?" And he made the momentary obscene face of the Hanged Man, eyes bulging, tongue out, head lolling.

Disgust almost choked her. "You're tired," she said. "You're tired and it's late. You'd better go home." She had nearly said 'You're drunk. Get out of my house', but had stopped herself. She might as well deliver herself over to the Militia as say that, now.

He remained by the door, half scowling and half leering.

"I tell you," he said. "If any trouble comes to anyone else in this village – anyone I say – after they blow up the level crossing, you just watch it. That's all I can say. Maquisard!" He spat on the tiled floor.

She said, setting her jaw,

"Don't be *silly*. It's nothing to do with me and you know it."

"I just know you're English . . ." he blustered. "I'm just warning you –" In the end she got rid of him, she was never sure how.

She hardly slept that night. In the morning she went over to Marie Stefan to tell her what had happened. To her chagrin, she found herself beginning to tremble as she had not done the evening before, even when she had disgustedly wiped Stefan-Postier's saliva from the tiles. Marie Stefan was consoling, and made her a cup of coffee.

"Don't take on so, my girl, no harm'll come to you, I'll take care of that. I'll speak to that boy when he comes back from his round this afternoon. Like as not, he's ashamed of himself by now . . . He didn't really mean what he said, you know. If he'd really meant to denounce you in Châtelet he'd have done it long before, like any of us could've" – she accompanied this grim reminder by a mischievous nudge at Jane's ribs to show it was a joke. "It's just that he was a bit upset about his brother like we all was," she went on, as if her sons' well-known antagonism to each other was quite irrelevant here, as perhaps it was. "Also, he gets nasty when he's been at the drink, I'm afraid. It's in the family – his father did too. I could tell you some tales –"

A few minutes later she broke off the recital of her younger years to say thoughtfully:

"All the same ... Perhaps it might be safer if you didn't stop alone at your place for a few nights once those boys there in the woods have done their little job ... No point in laying yourself open to trouble."

Jane nodded and looked at the ground. She knew Marie was right. Suppose bloody Stefan-Postier got drunk again, and in Châtelet this time?

"I would say, Come here," said Marie slowly. "He couldn't do nothing then! ... But I'm afraid he wouldn't stand for it." It was clear that 'he' in this sentence was her eldest son.

"No, of course. Don't worry, Marie; I'll think of somewhere." 'Hunted', 'refugee', 'on the run' ... the words, hitherto only theoretical, describing *other* people intrinsically different from herself, trailed through her mind.

"There's always Sylvain's hideouts in the woods," said Marie consolingly. "You could make a little camp for yourself in one of those, couldn't you, and he can come up with things for you? I'll look after your chickens and that while you're gone. Nice dry weather – you'll think you're on your holidays, as they say –

"– Ah don't look so worried, my girl, don't fret yourself. Life lasts a long time. When you're my age, you'll look back on it all and wonder what the fuss was about!"

Part Six

Jane followed Marie Stefan's advice and camped by night in one of Sylvain's hides: not the one high among the rocks where he had taken her in May, but in a nearer one, an abandoned charcoal burner's hut, which he had patched with chicken wire. She did not let anyone but Marie and Sylvain know she was there, returning by day to the village to wash or change her clothes and seek further provisions, just as if she were living there normally. As Marie had predicted, once she got used to being out at night she almost enjoyed it. It was high summer, the woods were very pleasant when she woke each morning, soon after dawn, and if they were lonely when dark closed in she found them no more lonely than her cottage had been in recent months. She discovered that she was oddly relieved to be away from it. Too many failed hopes were bound up for her with the cottage, perhaps; too much fruitless longing.

"Aren't you afraid here all on your own?" said Sylvain when he came to the woods.

"No, I feel much safer here than at home, just now."

"Most of the women would be scared. They wouldn't even entertain the idea."

She thought of the other women in the village, and knew that this was true. Their lives were all of a piece; they would never stray far from home in any sense. Whereas she . . . what a distance she had come. And how far she might still have to travel.

What care I for my goose-feather bed
With the sheets turned down so dainty-oh?

– Not much, not much, and just as well. She felt immeasurably remote from the young woman she had once been. Had she really once lived in a comfortable house in Henley and employed maids and a nanny and had rows with her husband about not playing bridge? Fantastic. But hardly less fantastic was the memory that she had once travelled freely to Paris to meet Pierre, and spent money on a pretty hat to have lunch with him in a restaurant by the Jardin du Luxembourg.

She had lost or forsaken so much that it seemed to her now that this pattern could only continue – that gradually she might detach herself from ordinary society altogether, even from the primitive rural world of St Laurent. She and Sylvain. He was, after all, part-gipsy; the village was not his natural habitat any more than it was hers. Two nights running he spent with her there in the woods, 'for company' as he said. In those nights it seemed literally possible to her that, once the War was over, this might become their way of life for a considerable part of each year. They might travel from one place to another under the skies of France. If they travelled, the world was theirs. Only by staying perpetually in one place did one become a prisoner. She thought that she would never make that mistake again . . .

Off with the Raggle-taggle gipsies-oh –

In the chilly morning she knew that this was just a fantasy, left over from her infinitely distant childhood, songs in the drawing-room at Rottingdean, her mother's hands on the piano. But in the dark, with Sylvain's arms about her and a bottle of inky wine to warm them both, it did seem real.

But you're expecting another child. You know you are. Soon it will begin to show. Some time next January it will be born.

All the more reason to settle for a life with Sylvain. Well, why not? He will like to have a child. He'll be proud of it and look after it. It'll be the making of him. And Marie Stefan will help us. There's no rule, just a silly social convention, that a woman has to make her life with someone of equal education to herself. Countless men marry women far simpler than themselves and it works out all right.

So she persuaded herself, even when she was alone, lying dreamily there, imagining the baby to come, tranquillised by her pregnancy, poised between past and future and not really examining either of them. Even the thought of Mark no longer disturbed her. Perhaps he would join their roving way of life; he seemed to have a taste for that sort of thing too, and he liked Sylvain ... Here in the forest, with the perpetual tiny sounds of its unseen population, she felt nearer to Mark again, as if that lost child and the child to come had fused themselves, for her, into one. Perhaps Mark was lying now, at this moment, in some other wood, not even very far distant from her?

She was peacefully sleeping just before dawn on July 20th, when the Maquis blew up a German troop train that had been bound at high speed for the disintegrating German front in Normandy. A large number of soldiers were killed or injured. The small German force from Châtelet-le-Lys descended on the area, followed a few hours later by reinforcements from Châteauroux and Montluçon, but by then the Maquis had once again left the district, as silently as they had come.

The explosion had not taken place fifteen miles away. It had been on the line on the near side of Châtelet, much closer to St Laurent than they had all expected. Perhaps the other rumour had been deliberately leaked to put the Militia off the scent. There may have been another reason also: the need of the Resistance to keep the local populations on their side. There were some annoyed and anxious murmurs in the village that morning.

The area round the devastated train was at once cordonned off, but people crept over from St Laurent to peer between the trees. Most of the adults had seen Germans before, standing about in Châtelet on market-day making their presence clear, but many of the children had never seen the mythical Them. They gaped in undisguised interest at the monsters in field grey, and with equal interest at the shrouded bundles now being removed from the wreckage and loaded into military ambulances.

Then Monsieur Picard came up and ordered everyone, grown-ups and children, peremptorily away. It wasn't healthy, he said, to take so much interest in what didn't concern them. Some unpleasant result could follow.

That was a Friday. Jane hung about the village much of the afternoon, listening to the gossip, but she returned to the woods in the evening. The next day she stayed there alone, lying hidden, reading and thinking and just dozing. It was market-day in Châtelet, many people were on the roads, and it was rumoured that some reprisal arrests might be made in the district. However when Sylvain visited her at dusk with some cheese and fruit he had nothing alarming to report. He wouldn't stay with her that night, he said: his mother wanted him home to help with things. He'd see her the next day.

So she was there alone early Sunday morning, when a detachment of the German SS from outside the region came driving into it, through towns and villages, through Châtelet-le-Lys and on towards St Laurent. They forked left at the main-road, near the scene of the explosion, hardly slackening their speed, passed the railway station a few kilometres later and then drove down the hill and into the heart of the village. They stopped in the square by the church. There were many of them and they had armoured vehicles with them. The intruder had come.

From her hideout Jane had no view of the village. Even when she ventured out onto the fringe of the wood, the curve of the hill hid the sky above the village from her view. She came out there once or twice and stood listening because, although she had no idea that anything particular was happening, she heard occasional gun-fire. She was not sure where it was coming from. Were the Maquis and a stray German patrol having a shoot-out, she wondered? It seemed prudent to remain where she was, and she returned to her nest among the leaves. Yet the guns reassured her rather than frightening her, and after a little while she realised why. They reminded her of other Sundays in the first autumn and winter of the War, when France had not yet been invaded and cheerful parties used to shoot at weekends, making the woods ring. Could there possibly be such a cheering explanation for the guns now, she wondered? After all, they had dared to celebrate Bastille Day; the German domination really did seem to be breaking up.

After a while everything fell silent again. Towards noon she began to make her way slowly back to thc village. When she saw a heavy smoke cloud hanging over it she thought 'a building has caught fire' and quickened her step. But she still did not understand.

Then, when she reached the corner of the green lane, she found that both her own cottage and the Yrieux house were blackened, roofless ruins, travesties of reality, the stuff of nightmare itself.

Her first wild, horrified thought was that she had slept some sort of unnatural sleep – perhaps gone peacefully mad, there in the forest – and had come back after an infinitely greater time-lapse than she had supposed to find that years of change and decay had taken place.

But no, this could not be true, for this destruction was still in process. The roof-beams of the cottage were still smouldering, its smoke drifted across her face. She began to tremble and leant for a moment against the oak tree, sickened and incredulous.

The murderous personal attack on her, which she had been dreading uncertainly for four years, had apparently come. After the first violent shock she felt no surprise, merely a horror and misery so great that she could not bring herself to approach the cottage. It did not, in that moment, occur to her that any other houses beside these two might have been destroyed. 'The Maquis must have been occupying them,' she thought. 'What Stefan-Postier threatened has come true.'

But after a while she noticed that her own house and the neighbouring one were not the only source of the smoke. The worst of it still seemed to lie ahead of her. And the Michards' farm too, over on the other side of the road, was obscured from her view by a grey miasma. She realised that all the while she had been standing there the cows had been lowing and lowing in their byre somewhere beyond this rolling, evil cloud. They were making a terrible noise, as if in fear, or – something else. Further off again a dog was barking hysterically, in short sharp bursts.

A terrible premonition began to form in her. She told herself it was unthinkable, out of the question. But this billowing smoke, making her eyes smart, those sounds, and now other things too ... Strange odours were now, like the greyness, borne towards her on the breeze. Odours of burnt varnish or paint, a stench of scorched rubber and hot metal. And another sudden whiff, like – like burning meat, momentarily overlaying the powerful wood smoke ... Smells that should not have been. And as she began to walk, resolutely but with shrinking dread, into the smoke, into the main street of the village, her feet began to crunch over still-hot cinders and broken glass, mingled among the drifting blindness; and then she began to stumble over things – broken things, charred things, soft things too – that should not have been there.

But even then she did not fully understand, could not understand, till she had got right into the village, coughing, eyes streaming, half feeling her way past the familiar and unrecognisable, that every single building had been fired. Every small shop, every house, every shed or barn, had been partially or wholly destroyed, with its contents.

It was not until she came upon the fire itself, still crackling behind the broken window of Madame Marcelle's shop, from where a dress-maker's dummy of twisted, blackened wire had fallen into the street, that she began to run. She ran back the way she had come, out of the smoke towards the fields, choking and weeping, and as she ran she called out Marie Stefan's name again and again.

Long afterwards, when the events of that morning were pieced together from sparse and fragmented accounts – for no one who could recount it had witnessed all of them

– it became clear that it had all happened in a short space of time. No one in the village had had a chance to think, let alone organise a mass escape.

First, in the way that was becoming customary in raids, the SS went from house to house, into the cafés where people were having an after-Mass glass, and into the church itself where some were forgathering for the next service. They ordered all the men out onto the square. Some came. Others, however, made off into the fields. The harvest was due to begin there any day: the maize stood high, and they hid among it. Some of them hid in the vines, where a bumper crop was expected that year.

The SS commander was angry. He told Marceau, who was already under arrest, that if all the men weren't on the square in twenty minutes the whole village would pay for it. He knew, he said, exactly how many men ought to be there.

Marceau prayed abjectedly to the German officer to relent. He had no power to force his co-citizens to return to the square, he said – no power whatsoever. He was just an ordinary carter – Mayor almost by accident, you might say – who had never meant any harm to anyone. He wasn't one of those bandits of Maquisards, he cried, who were bringing terror and destruction to the countryside. All he had ever asked was to live in peace with his neighbours – surely *Monsieur le Commandant* would understand that?

The poor man even went down on his fat knees before the officer, clutching at his polished boots, but it was no use. The officer, possibly repelled by Marceau's emotional appeal, calmly had him put up against the church and shot there and then as an object lesson to the village in general.

Unfortunately, however, the shot did not work as an object lesson for those who had run away, for they heard it from where they were hiding out in the maize and it merely encouraged some of them to escape even further off, to the woods and hills.

The account of events, after this, becomes sketchy. Really, only the bald outlines are known, through deduction.

In the course of the next half-hour the Germans decided that they now wanted everyone in the church – men, women and children: the whole village, every last baby and old woman. They advised the people through a loud-speaker that for their own sakes, they had better go quietly. Many of them, people who all their lives had been reasonable and law-abiding, believed what the commander said and did what they were told. Unlike the citizens of northern France, they had no previous experience of German reprisals. The Curé, pale and sweating, prayers silenced, led them in. But others, because they were old or deaf, or still in bed, or were of a more defiant and suspicious nature, remained in their houses. A search was instituted: people were dragged out of doors, protesting. Some more shots were fired. Some more people ran.

The SS ranged the village from one end to the other, and also the nearer fields. Finally, when they had found all they could, the heavy church door was locked with six hundred-odd people inside. The hidden listeners in the fields and woods around waited, straining their ears for another loud-speaker announcement.

Instead, the church was efficiently fired. The rising heat set the bells in the tower swaying, and one or two of them gave out broken chimes, far across the sunlit cornfields.

Then, it would seem, the Germans systematically went up and down the main street with petrol drums, attending to every house in the village.

After that they drove away.

All those in the church died, except one refugee child: a solitary little girl, she had come to St Laurent already wise in the way of escapes. She climbed up on others' shoulders, managed to leap from one of the high windows on the side away from the square, and crawled away with a broken ankle to hide like a cat among the bushes. She did not die.

Some people died before the church was locked: they never knew the fate of their relatives and neighbours. Like Marceau, Monsieur Mouret met his end at an early stage in he proceedings. He had responded to the first order to present himself on the square as an old officer of the law who knew where his duty lay. But also, as an officer, he reckoned he knew the rules of war, and that it was an affair for men, not for children and pensioners. He protested strenuously to the German Commandant that half the males they had managed to assemble before the church were boys under sixteen or grandfathers. It was not correct, he declared. It was one thing to order the Mayor's council and the owners of property to stand-to: he for one was here and waiting, but what was the cobbler's father-in-law, an old man of eighty-three, doing on the square? He was still arguing vociferously when the Germans got tired of him and shot him too.

Marceau and Mouret both died as they had lived, each clinging to their own particular set of values. So did the Chauvins in the bakery. They had been baking, as they did seven mornings a week, fifty-two weeks in the year, when the SS had arrived. If they heard the first call to the square from their hot bake-house, they ignored it contemptuously. Then, when the cry went up that the Germans were searching the village, they barricaded themselves in. They were particularly well-equipped to do this, since the previous year they had had iron shutters put on the bakery to protect it from marauding flour-thieves. The Germans saw that the shutters were fast, and did not waste any time on them. They simply fired the bakery as they passed it the next time, when they fired every other house, and the Chauvins perished with it.

Some others died with uncharacteristic bravery. Bonnin, the butcher, and his young son, Mark's school-friend, had been among those who had escaped into the fields at the beginning of the raid. Hidden, holding onto each other, they listened to the loud-speakers from the village ordering all the inhabitants into the church.

"They'll take hostages when they've got them all there," muttered Bonnin. "Ah, the bastards –" He did not fear too much on his own family's account, for he knew that only his wife and daughters were there and hostages were always men ... But when the first smoke began drifting above the church roof – black smoke fueled by the petrol that was being poured on the flames to get the recalcitrant sixteenth century fabric alight – he cried out again,

"Ah, the bastards!" – and leapt up and began to run towards the village. His son came after him. They ran into the village street at the opposite end from the church: Bonnin was making for his own shop. When a detachment of Germans caught sight of him, he was waiting there for them and even ran towards them. That mild-tempered, cheerful man, who all his life had aimed only to please people, now swung one of his own meat choppers at the advancing enemy with fearsome cries. He had killed one and seriously injured another before he and his son were mown down.

The Stefan brothers died together also. In life, they had disliked and distrusted each other, but were inextricably linked through their separate allegiances to Marie Stefan. In death, they were similarly linked and divided. They had both been in the smaller café when the trouble had first started, and had escaped with some other young men into the Langlois vineyard on the rising ground towards the railway line. A contingent of Germans came up there to flush them out with machine guns. At the first burst of fire some of the other men ran, but Sylvain clutched his brother's arm warningly and lay quite still, flat to the earth, between the green bushes with their blue-rimmed leaves. They might both have survived, had not Stefan-Postier, in a pause during which he could hear the Germans talking among themselves, suddenly leapt upright with his hands above his head. He was babbling – "Don't shoot – I've been working for you. My fiancée's family are in the Militia. Wait! There's an English woman in this village – a Maquisard. Wait –" Perhaps he had been going to say more, but a nervous German corporal, suspecting a trap, opened fire on him, and he died, and Sylvain died also in the same place.

Others did not die in any memorable or significant

way. Or, if they did, no one else survived to record it. They died just because they were inhabitants of St Laurent on July 22nd, 1944, innocently, ignobly yet memorably, gaining in death a lasting collective fame to which in life they never aspired. Madame Mouret and her daughter died, and Madame Marcelle and her sister-in-law and Henri Marceau died, and the Petitjeans died – but not Jean-Baptiste Petitjean, who was hiding in the maize. The Michards died, dragged terrified and lamenting from their farmhouse, and nearly all the Langlois clan died: Madame Langlois had been one of the first to say that if the Germans wanted everyone in the church then they'd better go there quietly. The two grocers died, and the cobbler and his wife, and his eighty-three year old father-in-law who could remember the news of the Prussian invasion of '70, and his bad-tempered mother-in-law who had not wanted Jane in the village. The tailor and most of his family died. Madame Picard and her children died. The Curé also died. Young and old, prosperous or penniless, intelligent or dull, liked or disliked, whether they have figured in this account or not, they all died. Or nearly all.

Some, however, did not die. Evangeline Bisset did not die, because it was Sunday morning and she wasn't in St Laurent at all, but at home in Châtelet rubbing her mother's bad leg with linament and wondering how to make their money last till the end of the month. She knew nothing of the massacre till news of it began to trickle through to the town, and to the appalled villages round about, in the early afternoon. When she did hear it, she got on her bicycle and took the road she had taken every working morning of her life for the past eight years. She did not believe, she kept telling herself as she peddled mechanically up and down the inclines, that it could possibly be as bad as the rumour said: surely even They would not do a thing like that? They were Christians in Germany, after all, even devout Catholics some of them, it was said. But when she reached the top of the rise, and looked out over the known view, and found it transformed into a blackened spectre of itself, she knew it was true, what she'd heard, every word of it and more.

She stood there for some time in incredulous horror, weeping and clasping her gloved hands together; then a detachment of the local police, who had been grimly surveying the scene and bringing the bodies out of the church, came upon her and gently urged her away. It was, said one of them heavily, no sight for a young woman. Nor for anyone, he added. He had known the Petitjeans, and had been related to the Langlois by marriage.

Jeanot Langlois did not die because, for once, he was not in the village that morning. He had woken at dawn beside his still-sleeping wife, and had decided on impulse to walk over the hill to the hamlet of Ourlats, five kilometres distant, and have a quiet talk about things with his wife's mother. His wife had mentioned suicide again this week: he couldn't just sit there doing nothing, could he?

He made his visit and was kindly received by his mother-in-law. He heard for the first time that an aunt of his wife's had been taken strange in the same way after one of her children was born, and had recovered in the course of time and was now just like anyone else. He was much encouraged by this information, and his mother-in-law's apparent confidence in him. He breakfasted there, and lingered for a while before walking back again. The sun was rising high before he reached the top of the field path which wound down again to the river and thence across a footbridge to the road that led to St Laurent. By then the smoke was rising high also, a great black pall over the village, obscuring the sun. He paused for a second – and then began to run. Right down the hill, he went, across the shaking bridge and up the other side. He cut off the curve of the road by running in at the bottom gate of the cemetery, open as usual on a Sunday, leaping and striding over the graves and coming out again at the top gate without pausing for breath. He was panting, his heart was tearing at his chest, by the time he reached the first houses in the village – or what had been the first houses. But he came too late, too late even to die himself. The Germans had just departed in the opposite direction. He was thus the first living man on the scene after the massacre.

But soon he was joined by others – survivors, leaving their hiding places in fields and woods and straggling down to the village in ones and twos, their faces changing as they came nearer and their wary steps breaking into a run, a sudden urgency like Jeanot's, which came too late and was no use, no use at all.

By a fortunate chance, Monsieur Picard also was absent from St Laurent that morning. He too had got up very early as he did most Sunday mornings – no attendance at Mass for him – and had gone to one of the network of local farms he had long ago persuaded to supply him with food at cut prices, on the logical grounds that he was an important person in the community. (He had carefully picked rather stupid but docile peasant farmers, who were half inclined to believe that the schoolmaster might indeed do them or their children some harm if they refused his requests.)

He was on his way back to St Laurent considerably earlier than Jeanot: in fact he was in time to see the German forces go past on their way there, as he stood waiting with his laden bicycle in a side-lane. He too thought of his wife and children. But, deciding that they would in any case be distinctly better off without him there, he turned his bicycle round and rode smartly off again into the green-and-gold countryside to lie low for a few hours.

It was a reasonable decision, for he was a reasonable man. He could not have guessed the unprecedented action the SS were about to take, and if he *had* guessed what point would there have been in him offering himself to them as one more martyr? None whatsoever. Yet, in after years, he sometimes used to say that if only he had been in the village at the time he might, in his capacity as Mayor's Secretary, have been able to lessen the massacre by encouraging people not to file obediently into the church but to scatter in all directions. Many would have been cut down, certainly, but many would have survived. In time, he probably began to believe himself that this is how he would have behaved.

Marie Stefan did not die, because the German search did not reach her farmhouse, well out of sight from the village under the lee of the hill. As Jane struggled towards it over the field path at midday, tears and vomit streaking her face, she could see the house ahead, a lighter blob on the edge of the woods, only a thin filet of smoke rising harmlessly from its tall chimney-stack.

"Marie Stefan," she called again and again, her voice reduced by the smoke she had swallowed to the croak of a child who has cried itself into despair. "Marie Stefan they're all dead – all except you –"

So she was with Marie Stefan, cradled in Marie's scrawny arms, later that afternoon, when she began to bleed. In the next two days, in spite of Marie's efforts and medicines, she lost the baby, Sylvain's child and Marie's grandchild, that she had been going to bear. It seemed, even to her, an almost irrelevant footnote to the catalogue of destruction which was now being drawn up, with ever graver faces, by people from all the country round.

Among others who did not die in St Laurent-la-Rivière was Pierre Leparde, because, of course, he had died long before in Germany, where he had been sent after his arrest on the Zone-frontier in September 1940. Or so those who were related to him or had known him were eventually forced to conclude. In what incriminating circumstances he was caught, and why he was not returned to an ordinary POW camp, were questions that were never answered. He was known to have been deported, but there was never any real evidence about the date or place of his end. Like the central character in *Le Grand Meaulnes*, the book he had so liked in his teens, he just disappeared without trace into the dark. And so there was, after all, never any one day when Jane learnt that he was dead; rather, the faint hope of seeing and touching him again, which rekindled in her at the end of the War, gradually extinguished itself in time and silence. When, long after the cessation of hostilities, she finally received official notice that he had been declared Missing, Presumed Dead, the news already seemed long out of date, a mere rubber stamp on something that had been true for years and years already.

And Mark did not die in St Laurent, because at that time he was safe in the south of France with a different detachment of the Maquis. With another boy, he ran messages for them, while they waited for the Allied landings in Provence in the middle of August. Late that month and through September, as the victorious army moved northwards to meet their allies coming down from Normandy, he followed them, attaching himself to a Canadian battalion because they made him welcome and fed him. Gorged with corned-beef, sardines, jam and chocolate, plied constantly between meals with chewing gum, he rolled towards Paris in their lorries, drunk with the excitement of it all and with the pleasure of speaking his native tongue for the first time in two years. He had felt a passionate identification with his Maquisard companions while the struggle had lasted; but now the Canadians, with their physical size and ebullience and wealth in comparison with the people among whom he had spent the last years, seemed to him like a new and more splendid race of men. Some of them even spoke French, too. Listening to their accounts of life back home, and of a country far bigger and wilder even than France and with far more strange animals and birds, he resolved to go there at the first opportunity.

The Canadians had no idea of events in remote villages in central France, and he had been in Paris for several days, enjoying himself, before he encountered anyone who told him something of what had occurred in St Laurent. Then he went to the new Headquarters of the French Forces of the Interior and hung about there all day till someone paid attention to him. Fortunately they were able to tell him, when he returned two days later, that his mother was in Paris now, and looking for him.

At first, he was incredulous at this news. With the resilience of extreme youth, he had spent the last forty-eight hours accustoming himself to the idea that he was an orphan now, and free to go wherever he wanted for ever and ever. He was delighted to hear that Jane was alive, and flung himself tearfully upon her when he saw her, but mixed with his profound and genuine relief was a tinge of disappointment, all the same. Being an orphaned war-veteran of not yet fifteen had been an awe-inspiring and heady prospect.

Part Seven

By early 1945, Jane and Mark had been repatriated to Britain. Jane was thankful. For her, the whole of France and of her last five years there was now that scorched and blackened territory of nightmare. It was a place of dread, where everyone, even the exuberant crowds in newly liberated Paris, seemed to her to be so many skulls opening and shutting quacking mouths against a background of dark into which one might fall and fall, a sickening descent into nothing and non-being ... A Red Cross doctor at the Headquarters where she had found temporary work urged that she would make a quicker recovery from her 'nervous depression' in her own country; she took his advice.

Mark was not pleased. He had been having an exhilarating time in Paris that autumn, and had made many new friends. England at the end of the War was a drab place, full of tired people more deprived in undramatic ways than many of the French were now. They also seemed to him amazingly ignorant. His grandparents in Rottingdean, whom he had remembered only dimly as large, benevolent beings, had, to his eyes, become old, shrunken and querulous. They deplored the Labour win in the General Election ("Such ingratitude ... Winnie must feel it so ...") and when he tried to tell them about the Marxists who had been his admired commanders in the Maquis, they listened with the forbearing, embarrassed expressions of people determined not to be drawn into an argument. He heard them saying to his mother in undertones that "the boy would get over his dreadful experiences by and by," and that "of course boys of this age often *are* a little difficult, we do realise" – and he raged inwardly, like an exile deprived of his true country.

When James, his father, reappeared on the scene, his

seven-year-old plan to send Mark to Public School was finally put into practice. Winchester declined, regretting that Mark's odd educational background now made him ineligible, but a scarcely less illustrious school was persuaded to take him. James had had what was then being called 'a pretty good War': he had been in the Middle East and then at the Salerno landings and finished up as a Lieutenant-Colonel. It was partly on account of this, Mark gathered with bafflement, that the school was ready to make an exception for a boy with 'little Latin and less Greek' as the housemaster, ponderously jocular, described him. He added in an undertone that they already had several pupils who had recently returned from spending the War in America, and that these boys often settled in remarkably well once they had buckled-to and found their own level. The great thing, was it not, was to get back to pre-War standards as quickly as possible? But Mark did not see matters in that light. A short spell of English Public School life merely confirmed for him anything he had ever heard in France about British vice and oddness. It seemed particularly extraordinary to him that anyone should imagine they could keep him in such a place against his will, and after he had run away – or rather walked away – several times, the attempt to turn him into an English schoolboy was finally abandoned. Jane felt that her battle with James on this subject was long over, for good or ill: it no longer even roused passion in her, she had been prepared to let him try his way: yet ironically it was now won in the end for her by Mark himself.

Mark returned to Paris of his own volition ("taking French leave" as Jane's father wryly described it). He parked himself on Mlle. Yrieux and her sister, with whom he had struck up an unlikely friendship when he and Jane had been in Paris at the end of 1944. And there, except for visits to England to see Jane, he remained for the best part of two years, attending ill-defined courses in French History and Zoology and giving English lessons to fellow pupils. Any suggestion about more serious study for University entrance he resisted politely but firmly. There was something of James's own obstinacy in him. When he was eighteen he followed the plan he had formed three and a half years before during the Liberation of France, and emigrated to Canada.

Mlle. Yrieux and her sister – whom now at last Jane found herself authorised to call 'Tante Madeleine' and 'Tante Yvonne' – were sad survivors of the war in Tante Yvonne's flat in Passy. Their cousin-in-law, Pierre's father, had died suddenly of a heart attack in 1943, and Pierre's mother (so Jane gathered from their discreet, regretful references) had had some sort of collapse herself and was now 'a permanent invalid'. According to the better-informed Mark, she had become an alcoholic: at all events Jane never, after everything, managed to meet her. Perhaps Madame Leparde could not forgive the younger woman, the foreigner, who had borrowed her name illicitly and taken her son, and had possibly – Jane could admit this to herself now – been responsible for his capture and death. If so, Jane could not blame her.

But Tante Madeleine assured Jane tearfully that neither she nor any of the rest of the family had *any idea*, till Jane and Mark reappeared in Paris, that they had been in St Laurent all the time.

"We were *convinced* you had escaped," she told Jane. "I always understood that my cousin had sent you money for that very purpose. We heard nothing, and naturally thought you must have succeeded – either that, or that you had disappeared like our poor, dearest Pierre . . ."

After hearing this on a number of occasions in the late 1940s, Jane came to understand that Mlle. Yrieux had probably found it convenient to believe that Jane and Mark had escaped to England, and had encouraged Pierre's parents to wash their hands of the whole affair. They had, after all, had Pierre's disappearance to worry about, and all the other problems of life in Occupied France. It was all over now, and if it was an aftermath of guilt that made Tante Madeleine so friendly towards them at last, even assuming the obligations of a real aunt towards Mark, so much the better, Jane thought. Perhaps too, like many people of her kind, Mlle. Yrieux also felt a generalised guilt and regret for her earlier support of Pétain, and a need, now in her old age, to placate God and other people by showing herself to be well-intentioned and kind. Because of the events at St Laurent, her brand of religious belief led her to treat Jane, in the rôle of miraculous survivor, as some specially marked creature, sacred repository of God's inscrutable Will. She also liked talking to Jane about Oncle Ernest, now similarly metamorphosed from a tiresome brother with deplorable atheist tendencies into some kind of martyred saint. She was in any case, it seemed, one of those people for whom the past, any past, has a glow and a meaning unshared by any present.

In the end, though embarrassed and faintly amused, Jane genuinely became quite fond of her; she continued to visit the old lady occasionally in Paris long after Mark had gone to Canada and she herself had re-married. When, about 1960, Mlle. Yrieux died, Jane was rather sorry. She discovered to her surprise that she minded the idea that her last link with St Laurent-la-Rivière was thus ended. For the first time in many years she found herself wondering if Marie Stefan were still alive, and feeling sad that she had abandoned Marie on the very day she felt strong enough to hitch a lift to Paris, never, as it turned out, to come back again.

It was from this time on that fragmented and fleeting memories began to assail her, and disturbing, inappropriate dreams; they were like coded messages that St Laurent, however finished and destroyed, was not entirely extinct for her after all. Presently she began to think that, at the time of the holocaust, she had left the scene so soon and in such panic-stricken fear, that she might one day have to return there simply to lay the dead to rest in her own mind.

Its legacy to her had been a lasting slight nervousness, an increased sensitivity akin to some minor physical disability. She, who had been recklessly optimistic as a young woman, now found herself afraid of a great many things, and morbidly aware of the reality of evil. It did not stop her from enjoying what was enjoyable in her life – far from it: she lived through the years of her third marriage and Diana's birth and childhood with a passionate consciousness of her good fortune and of the fact that these, too, would not last for ever. But St Laurent was there as an eternal point of reference, something by which everything subsequent was implicitly measured. Never again would she take security or life itself for granted.

Indeed, through its destruction the village had become, she eventually realised, a permanent place, fixed and immutable as a symbol. What represented death already could not die to her, as other places, affections and periods die to one as life goes by. At my life's end, she thought one day with sudden foreknowledge, there will be nothing else left any more: just myself and St Laurent-la-Rivière, face to face once again. I shall have returned.

So it was that Jane and her daughter Diana found themselves, one day in the 1970s, driving down through the centre of France, past Paris and the great plains, past the Loire, past the Cher and on into that peaceful country that lies towards the mountains.

She knew that the ruined village had been 'landscaped' and left as a permanent memorial. She knew too that a new village – St Laurent-le-Nouveau – had now risen on the fields above the river on the opposite bank. Years ago, she had been sent by Tante Madeleine a magazine photograph of some Government dignitary laying the foundation stone of the new Mairie. The short text had mentioned that the village was being re-established by survivors and by relatives of those who had died, but she had not believed that this could amount to much more than a defiant gesture. So many more had died than had lived, and who from outside would voluntarily come and establish themselves in that place, that place –? She expected to find the symbolic Mairie there, and a few cottages to house those prepared to act as part-time monument wardens and cemetery-keepers, and little else.

However the new loop of road, which branched up-hill and swung round in a curve above the old one, led to a substantial settlement. Before she had properly got her bearings, Diana was driving through a grid-pattern of wide roads edged with uniform, pink-roofed villas. There was a central square with a modernistic Mairie in regrettable concrete, a large building that seemed to be a High School, a sports' centre and even a swimming pool. Money and resources had evidently been lavished on this place, by national or international bodies bent on making reparation to the survivors of St Laurent, however inadequately or inappropriately. Sitting there on its hill in the rural heart of the Berry, the new settlement looked more like a reconstructed suburb in some war-torn district of northern France. But it did look genuinely prosperous. They passed shoe shops, a furniture shop –

"Should we park here?" said Diana, hesitating among the shiny cars near the school. Children in brightly coloured anoraks stood in groups, idling away the last few minutes of the lunch-break before the bell rang. The clatter of metal trays and the hiss of water came from the open windows of a long building marked 'Canteen', biliously gay with frescoes.

"I'm not sure," said Jane, at a loss. "I mean, I don't think there's really much for me here. Not in this new place … Nothing here. We should have taken the other road, back at the fork there."

"O.K., we'll go back," said Diana, consciously forbearing. Only as they moved off again did Jane see the name-plaque: *'Place Marceau'*. It was another moment before eye and memory made the connection.

"That was the old Mayor!"

"Who?" Diana braked, expecting someone on the footpath.

"No, no, go on, just the street name – Marceau was the Mayor who was killed."

"Poor man."

"He was an awful old woman, actually."

Diana looked sideways at her mother, as if relieved to discover that the afternoon did not have to be exclusively conducted in a tone of funeral reverence. "Actually," she said, "I suddenly thought while we were in that square back there: why don't you call on the present Mayor and explain who you are?"

"Oh – he might not like it," said Jane at once. Her long-ago chronic anxiety about making herself conspicuous or importunate reasserted itself.

"Rubbish, he'd be pleased I should think. He must be used to having callers anyway. You couldn't possibly be Mayor of St Laurent today and *not* be used to welcoming people who'd come about the holocaust – so to speak ... They had five hundred representatives of German Youth organisations the summer before last, all beating their breasts together in some huge ceremony."

"Good heavens ... How do you know?"

"I read about it in a newspaper. The trouble with you, Mummy-duck, is that you've been keeping this whole business locked up inside you for so long that you don't realise what a well-known place this is now. It's not just your personal past – it's history." She sat back in her seat, looking faintly satisfied with her turn of phrase.

They returned to the fork. The old road which, within a few yards, would lead them to the crest of the hill and so to the view over the abandoned village beneath, was marked 'No Entry for Vehicles'. This, as Diana defensively pointed out, was why she had not taken it before. Instead, she swung the car into the yard of the station (now apparently disused): it was marked 'Visitors Car Park'.

So it was, that for the second time in her life, Jane made a momentous, long-awaited descent into St Laurent-la-Rivière on foot under a fine afternoon sky.

It was the grass that surprised her most. It seemed to be everywhere. Not the rank grass that grows and grows in a truly deserted site, obliterating stones from view, returning cultivation to Nature, but a smooth-cropped lawn grass. People had been busy here, even if they no longer lived here. Green verges ran between the neatly sanded roadway and the shells of the houses, up to their very thresholds. Green grass carpeted all the segments of land between the buildings, which had once been a patchwork of vegetables, flowers, bald yards and chicken-scratched orchards. Against this uniform smoothness the well-heads, pumps and occasional carefully-tended shrubs stood out like pieces of sculpture on display.

It was as if St Laurent-la-Rivière had been turned into a curious, beautiful English garden, and had thus changed its very substance. The image of permanent devastation, which Jane had carried in her mind for nearly thirty years, turned out to be an illusion. Even while she herself had ignored the place in horror, time had done its work here after all.

And yet as she made her way down the ghostly street, feeling ghostly herself, the English garden turned out to be an illusion also. For, under its calm disguise, it *was* the village she had known after all. The place was fragmented and dispersed as in one of those dreams where different periods of life are confused with one another, and yet it was there. Every few yards some detail – the angle of a wall, a known doorway now opening onto airy space, an enamel advertisement still adhering to a blackened wall – would present itself to her, so familiar that, if she concentrated on it for a few seconds, it was impossible to believe that the whole village was not there after all, complete, behind her and to left and right of her, just as it had always been, and that if she glanced round quickly enough she would find it. Knowledge and memory were at variance with one another.

Yet this in itself was not a new experience. In every sense, not just the literal one, she had been here before. At her age, she had had countless times already, in the normal course of events, the experience of coming to a once-familiar locality and finding it changed or simply destroyed. The London she had known as a young woman had been eviscerated, some of the places she had lived in had been knocked down just as surely as if an enemy had done it, most of the people she had known as a girl were dead. All these experiences she had accepted as commonplace, part of the natural order of things, so that now, oddly, the power of St Laurent either to shock or surprise her was considerably diminished. She could tell herself, standing there: this was different, this was destruction and loss of another order. She knew it. But now, all this time later, the end result did not *feel* so very different. That 'time heals' she had always regarded as a silly idea put about by those with weak memories and nothing much to be healed anyway. But she saw not that time, enough time, changes everything, every context, so that meaning itself is changed in the end, is eroded, dispersed, rendered down into something different.

The oak tree by the green lane was a dead trunk, silvery as bone, a tree from some remote antiquity. The cottage itself had been allowed to sink into an insignificant ruin half buried in rhododendrons which must have invaded from the Yrieux garden next door. A wild cherry was flowering in what had once been the kitchen. No trace of furniture, stone sink or even visible floor tiles remained. It reminded her of an unimportant Roman ruin once seen in southern Italy. Hesitating on the threshold, which was itself half buried in earth, Jane told herself 'here – *here* –' But in what sense was this square of tangled earth still the cottage? In what did the essential element of place exist?

She had said, up the hill in St Laurent-le-Nouveau, 'There's nothing for me here.' But she discovered that, after all, there was really nothing much for her here either.

They retraced their steps to the car. Diana, far more affected than her mother, said with a break of emotion in her voice: "It seems a very peaceful place now –"

"It always was."

"I – I really can't imagine it ... On that day in 1944, I mean ..."

"Nor can I – now. Although I've had that picture in my mind all these years. Funny, it's everything else I remember now. Or no, not really funny because of course the ending didn't really happen to me. Really, I missed it. I never even saw the Germans come or go. What counted for me was the life here. Not the end of it."

As they began to climb the road again to the new settlement, Jane suddenly said:

"Oh – could we stop here a moment? There's another house I want to see. It's not on a road, it's by a field path. We must be just above it here. We may be able to get down."

"If you think the house is still there."

"Oh I'm sure it is. It – it wasn't destroyed like the rest."

A gate led into the damp field where Charollais cattle, white as beasts in a fairy story, raised their heads to look at the intruders. In the past the cows had been brown. The lumpy pasture dipped down to a hollow where a path ran, then rose abruptly up into heather and bracken and woodland, bright green now with early leaves. A small brook issued from the woods making its way towards the river. It was the exact point where the France of the plains met the France of the mountains; Jane recognised the place clearly.

But the house itself was quite gone. The building that had survived after all the others, the one remaining repository of life when all the rest had been smoking ruins, had now vanished it seemed from the face of the earth. Jane searched diligently, knee-deep in last years' dead bracken through which the new, curled fronds were already pushing, but found almost nothing – a few boulders, moss-covered, that might or might not have been foundations, some brickwork that could have come from the chimney, a rusted iron pot, a few hunks of timber as rotten as cheese … Nothing that was recognisable. The village itself had been preserved almost artificially, petrified like a fossil in grass and flowerbeds because people had cared. But no one had cared about this house and so it had simply gone. Jane found that she minded that, in a way she had not, after all, minded the rest.

"Ah, it gives me great pleasure to see you here today.

Really." The Mayor of St Laurent-le-Nouveau had ushered them into his front room and provided them with tiny glasses of sweet liqueur. The room was crowded with upholstered chairs similar to those in the furniture shop across the street. A large television set with an embroidered cloth draped over it held the central position. The Mayor fussily twitched the cloth into place and re-arranged a pot-plant: evidently, in his widowhood, he had become house-proud. An old man, white-haired, thin and slightly stooped beneath his loose-fitting suit, genial, almost a dear old boy – would she have recognised Monsieur Picard if she had not known it was him? Jane was not sure. Luckily the young woman secretary in the Mairie had mentioned his name when they enquired for the Mayor, and had assured her that, yes, he really was the old schoolmaster 'from the time of the disaster'. 'The disaster' appeared to be the accepted modern way of referring to the events of July 22nd, 1944. Evil perpetrated by identifiable individuals had been transformed by distance into a horror without partisan overtones, almost an Act of God.

She supposed there must have been long years of bitterness on the one hand and expiation on the other before this transformation could take place. Through how many summers had young Germans needed to come, as Diana had said, to beat their breasts here, before the principle of Revenge was appeased? Had the SS perpetrators of the crime been traced and executed after the War? She was not even sure. She had missed out the whole long process of retribution and eventual reconciliation that had evidently taken place. Nor, as she had said to Diana, had she even seen the crime committed at the time. She had not, finally, come face to face with Them. In the end, her perception of the existence of Evil could only remain, it seemed, what it had always been – theoretical. It was both a relief and an anti-climax.

"I was so glad when I heard you had survived," said Picard chattily. "So glad, naturally ... I had assumed, of course, that you had perished like everyone else, and not till definitive lists were being made out by myself and the other authorities did I realise that you were unaccounted for. Then someone told me you were staying with Marie Stefan. But by the time I tried to call on you there you had already left – for Paris, I heard. Of course, it had just been Liberated."

Jane moistened her lips. "I went to look for Marie's house just now," she said. "I thought it would have survived. But it isn't there any more."

"Ah yes – derelict now, I know."

"Not even that. Just gone."

"Really? Dear me. Of course it's a long time since I've been down that way. I don't get about as much as I used to, and the land-owner who farms all that land now has closed off a lot of the old paths to keep his livestock from straying ... Gone, you say? Well, well."

"When – when did Marie Stefan die?"

"Die? I don't know. She went away, you know – oh, quite soon after the disaster. Soon after you left yourself, I suppose ... No, I don't know where she went. She had nothing to stay here for any more. Several of the other people who had survived also left afterwards for that reason. Ah dear me, those were sad times!" Monsieur Picard made the remark easily, as if time had gradually turned it from a heartfelt expression into his standard uncontroversial comment, brought out for all visitors whatever their nationality.

Jane said, wanting only now to cry,

"I feel badly about Marie. She was so good to me when I had lost everything and I was ill, and as soon as I was better I just left her and never saw her again. I didn't mean it to be like that. I was desperate to find Mark, you see, but then I thought that, later, I'd come back to Marie, make sure she was all right, see if she needed any money or anything ... I wrote to her from Paris, but I don't know if she got my letter. She didn't write back but I suppose I shouldn't really have expected her to. Then I wrote again – we were actually back in England by that time, I think: so far away ... That letter eventually came back to me marked 'Gone Away'.

I thought it might be a mistake – that the central Post Office was just returning all letters addressed to St Laurent – but I didn't do anything more about it. I wish now I'd tried to keep in touch with her ... Oh dear, do excuse me, I know it's no use saying that now."

"Don't distress yourself my dear," said Picard comfortably. "Marie Stefan would not have held such a thing against you. She understood that you came from a different world and that, had it not been for the War –" Before Jane could object to this view of events, he hastened on:

"But you had not lost quite everything, I hope? Your boy: you mentioned him just now ... Yes, Mark. I hope – ?"

"Oh yes, he survived! You're quite right, Monsieur Picard, I hadn't lost everything. Though Marie had lost *her* sons ..."

"Mark is working for the Canadian Government now," put in Diana helpfully in her halting French, as a pause followed this. "In the Forestry Department."

"In Canada. Well, well! But you see him from time to time, I hope, nevertheless?"

"Yes. I stayed with him and his wife and children when I was there last summer. Next Christmas they're coming to England." It was still Diana who spoke. Jane, momentarily overcome with memory, was silenced.

"A nice lad," said Picard reminiscently, "A bright boy, too ... I always like to hear of my old pupils doing well." From his tone of generalised satisfaction Jane guessed that he did not, in fact, remember Mark particularly clearly, in spite of all those special lessons. He was an old man, after all. His acuteness had no doubt softened with the years along with his asperity. And surely his accent had broadened and softened also, so that he sounded less like the northerner he was and more like a local peasant landowner?

Jane found her own voice,

"Did you – that is, have you any children born after the War; like Diana here?" she asked. It was the nearest she felt she could decently get to mentioning Eulalie Picard and their pinched-looking little girls. Picard had expressed conventional but apparently sincere pleasure at the idea of Mark's life continuing successfully. How could she politely mention his dead children in return? The pit was there before them: there seemed nowhere for their conversation to go. She saw that he was relaxed and happy, his grief and loss evidently long transmogrified into the satisfying identity of chief citizen and survivor, but she could not emulate his ease of manner: she hadn't his practice.

"No, no children," he said briskly. "But my life has been a very full one. So many deputations and pilgrimages come here – more and more in recent years. I did remarry, but unfortunately my second wife died the other year at a relatively early age, although she was considerably younger than me. That is her photograph over there. Come, I believe you may have known her! She was the eldest daughter of the Petitjeans, the garage people. She missed the disaster because by that time she was boarding with an aunt in Châtelet and working for a dressmaker."

"Oh yes, I know who you mean! Mark was friendly with the youngest one. But I suppose that he . . . ?"

"Jean-Baptiste? No indeed, he survived too. He owns a big garage on the main road south from here, near Limoges. He got the capital for it from the Reparations, of course. I shall be seeing them soon – they always invite me over at Whitsun."

It was safe, it seemed, the pit was covered in and grassed after all; it was now and not *then*. In weak relief and anticlimax, Jane said,

"You know, I'd supposed that virtually everyone had been killed that – that morning. Everyone except Marie and I. It was stupid of me really. I just didn't think . . . I didn't even know *you* were alive, Monsieur Picard, till this afternoon."

"Then I trust it has been a pleasant surprise for you, Madame!" he said, with a little bow and a hint of his old schoolmaster's sarcasm.

He had been decorated after the War, he told her with ingenuous pride, touching the small ribbon in his buttonhole, as if he had come to believe after so many years that his own survival had been an achievement rather than a lucky chance. Later the Government had given him a pension "in recognition of my efforts to re-establish this place, you understand". He and Solange Langlois – "you remember her? The nurse. They lived outside the village, luckily for her and her children –" had been the first of the inhabitants to return.

And her husband?

No. He unfortunately had been in the Mourets' café at the time of the disaster. Jane suddenly realised, from Picard's placid, matter-of-fact tone, that he had established afterwards the whereabouts of every single person in the village on that fatal morning, and would carry this pointless knowledge to his own life's end.

And the rest of the Langlois family – ?

Gone. All gone – Ah! Except for Jeanot. A look came over Picard's brown, wrinkled face which might almost have been described as tender. He said,

"You remember Jeanot? He came back to see me last year. Such a pleasant surprise! I hadn't set eyes on him since 1945. I had hoped then that he would stay and help us re-found the village. I always had a high regard for that family. But he wanted to make a fresh start somewhere else, as several of the young men did, and I couldn't blame him of course. We all have our own lives to live ... And he's lived his most successfully, I can tell you."

"He was intelligent," said Jane, remembering. "I liked him a lot."

"Yes indeed." An expression of almost malicious glee passed over Picard's face, and he said quickly,

"He would have been a much better match for you than that poor Stefan boy, Madame, I did think that at the time and he might well have liked the idea too, but unfortunately he was already married to that tiresome, weepy girl from Ourlats."

"Monsieur Picard, you were a schemer!" said Jane, surprised, laughing. Diana was looking from one to the other of them, trying to follow this rapid interchange, puzzled at their sudden gaiety.

"Of course I was!" he agreed. "I needed to be, to help you – and others. Ah, those were difficult days, my dear Madame ... But I was about to tell you: Jeanot Langlois came back here to visit us. Driving one of those big Peugeots. After the war he went to work for a manufacturing company in Angers, farm machinery it was, and apparently he did very well and when the Reparations came along he started up his own business. He's got a large factory now, it seems. He was quite the gentleman – you'd never think he'd been reared here as a peasant. A nice lady-wife too, younger than him I'd say, and he told me their eldest boy is in Paris training to be a lawyer and their daughter is working for – a fashion magazine, I think he said. I *was* pleased to see that he had done so well – made the most of his chances, you might say. What I always say, Madame Leparde (excuse my calling you that, but that's how I've always thought of you) – what I always tell visitors, when they come here and see what a fine new place we've built: it's an ill wind that blows nobody any good. Isn't it?"

He insisted on taking them to see over his Mairie. Recalling the many times when he had dismissed her firmly at the end of an interview, Jane was amused to find that old age had rendered him garrulous and eager to retain her. Diana was becoming restive, tired no doubt with vicarious emotion and with listening to a language she only understood imperfectly; eventually Jane managed to ask him the question that, for so many years, had nagged at her consciousness. In a way, she realised, it was to ask Picard this that she had sought him out.

"Monsieur Picard, forgive me, but – I have to ask this. Why do you think the Germans came to St Laurent? Why?

The animation went from his face. For the first time that afternoon he looked pained.

"Oh my dear, you must know that. Surely? It was a reprisal raid. That Maquisard sabotage on the railway line so near the village ..."

"Yes. Yes, I know. But –" she licked her lips: "Are we sure that was the reason? The only one?"

"What else? They were losing France fast and were angry and frightened. They decided to make an example of us. To France and to the world. They succeeded! But not in the way they intended." This was clearly another remark from his set repertoire.

"I have sometimes wondered," said Jane carefully in the pause that followed, "if it could possibly have been something to do with me."

"With you? How could it have been?"

"Just by my being in the village. That, coupled with the Maquis activity, I mean. If they were looking for a scapegoat and discovered I was there ..."

"How could they have discovered?"

"Well ... someone might have told them. It is *possible*, Monsieur Picard, you must admit that. I was, however hard I tried, separate. Those who were wary of me from the first were right, after all. I was, unknown to myself, a harbinger of the village's fate. And yet I did not even participate in that fate. Separate to the end."

There was another pause, and then Picard drew himself up to his not very great height and spoke with firm dignity:

"No one," he said, "would have denounced you. Not one of us. It was out of the question."

"Of course I know that most people wouldn't have. You were all so good to me. But surely you will admit that among several hundred people there must be one or two ..." Her voice trailed off uncertainly. She was intimidated by his gaze.

"*No* one," he said. "Whatever their failings or limitations, they were not base in that kind of way. No, no. My dear Madame Leparde: surely you realise that if – *if*, I say – anyone had felt inclined to draw the attention of the authorities to the village, they would have done so long before. You would not have survived a year. No, no. We were all loyal to you. Anything else would have been unthinkable."

Was that really true? He seemed to believe it but, after

all those years, who could say? He had clearly re-made the whole sequence of events to some extent in his own mind, honing away the rough edges, the inconsistencies. And perhaps she had also, in her own way.

The faint suspicions would just have to remain in the bottom of her mind for ever. There had been people she had trusted and liked less than others. One of the two grocers. The cobbler's mother-in-law. Stefan-Postier –

It came to her that possibly Picard had arranged for her to marry Sylvain partly because he himself did not trust Sylvain's brother and wanted a means of shutting his mouth. Now that she had thought of it, it seemed entirely likely. But she could not ask Picard if that was so. Not now, after what he had said.

Come to that, there had been many times when she had not entirely trusted Picard, either. Yet in a way, in spite of the constraint that had always been between them, her deepest relationship of the whole War had been with him. Picard, the profoundly straight and decent, doing his best for all? Or the archetypal survivor, infinitely adaptable to time and change? She would never know. And perhaps the two alternatives were simply different versions of one truth anyway.

She said goodbye to him with a warmth that was heartfelt, and promised, speciously, to call and see him again some year 'when she was next in the district'.

"Are you passing through Châtelet now?" he asked.

"Yes, I think so."

"Do call on Evangeline Bisset. Yes, the Post Mistress – she's retired now. She would be so pleased. She still lives at the same address. You see, not everything has changed here as much as you thought."

She leant from the window of the car to wave goodbye and was aware of the slight figure, standing as if fixed to the pavement, watching the car until it was out of sight.

Except for the number of cars, Châtelet-le-Lys seemed to have changed much less than might have been expected. It still rose as abruptly as a medieval burgh out of the fields and hills. The Bazaar in the main street had been split up into several shops, one loudly selling records, but the big chemist's in the market place seemed unchanged even to the porcelain jars in the window. Only one substantial block had been rebuilt, near the Post Office, among them the dentist's house. A small supermarket now stood on the site. Jane did not know whether to be glad or sorry that she would not thus be tempted to knock on Etienne Gilbert's door and see if he were still alive. Mark had told her after the War that Gilbert – 'Raoul', as his Maquisard name had been – was a far higher figure in the organisation than most people had then realised. Had that, too, been a reason that the SS, knowing more than the French themselves, had struck so hard at this particular patch of countryside? And had he been shocked and grieved at the terrible reprisal his forces had unwittingly brought upon St Laurent, or had he, long before that, schooled himself to the conviction that such things were the necessary price of victory? He who had been so gentle in his professional capacity, who had been so apologetic about the lack of anaesthetic . . .

She left Diana mulling over some record sleeves in the new music shop, and went to see Evangeline Bisset on her own. There was no obvious logic in this, the Post Mistress had always been the kindest of people, the readiest to rejoice at another's good fortune. And yet when Jane found herself in the unchanged flat with its chilly family furniture, clasped with momentary, almost violent fervour in Mlle. Bisset's thin arms, she was glad she had come alone.

She was about Jane's own age, Jane knew. She had become one of the innumerable old ladies of provincial France, in a black cardigan and grey cotton stockings. Jane would have passed her in the street without a second glance: surely just another old maid, eking out an empty, genteel existence with preoccupied excursions to buy the day's food and vague, timid intimations of mortality. And yet she was Evangeline Bisset. And she suddenly clasped Jane to her a second time in spontaneous emotion, saying,

"Oh, I knew you'd come back! I *knew* you would."

Looking at the black clothes, Jane said: "Your mother . . . I suppose that she – ?"

"No, no," said Evangeline hastily, as if to prevent Jane saying more. "She is still alive. She's asleep just now." She added, "I've been very lucky that she's been spared to me for so long. She's eighty-eight now. It's a great age."

Jane could not detect anything in her tone but spontaneous gaiety, and that touch of crude pride with which people traditionally mention especially-old relatives, as they would speak of an unusually large pet cat or an extra-big vegetable marrow. But Evangeline Bisset did not look at Jane as she said it, so Jane could not be sure of the feeling behind the cheerful words.

Evangeline made weak tea with lemon ("I always regretted not being able to offer you English tea in the War!") and produced some rather stale sponge biscuits in a decorated box. "I shall have to go and see if Mother is awake soon," she said, "but first I have something for you. Just between ourselves. I have never told anyone else about it, you understand. Not even Mother."

She disappeared for a moment, and Jane sat there with the thin china in her hands, listening to the modern traffic in the street below rattling the old window frames. She had a suffocating sense of expectation, momentarily convinced that what must have come into Mlle. Bisset's hands was a letter. From whom, ah from whom ... Serge Beckman? Pierre? No, no impossible.

Then her friend returned. She had something which was not paper, but which she held in her cupped hands as if it were a bird's egg. Or perhaps a fledgling bird, for she opened her fingers cautiously to show Jane as if it might fly away. It was, in a sense, from Pierre after all. It was the gold chain he and Jane had bought together in 1940 in the Place Vendôme, and which she had given to Mlle. Bisset to sell in 1943 along with Serge Beckman's amethyst ring.

"I did sell the ring," Mademoiselle Bisset explained apologetically. "As I told you at the time. I was sorry to do it, but you said you didn't attach any great importance to it and it fetched a good price, didn't it? But the chain, now ... You'd told me how it had been your husband's gift to you, and it didn't seem right ... I saw you wearing it once, on a black dress, when you came to celebrate New Year's Eve with us. I've kept it for you, all these years, hoping you would come back for it. I'd heard you were alive, but I didn't know where to send it to you, you see."

"But you told me – you gave me the money for it," said Jane, aghast. "Hundreds of francs. I remember it clearly. I must repay you –"

Embarrassment suffused Evangeline Bisset's thin, unlovely face.

"Please don't, don't speak of it," she cried in evidently genuine distress, almost in anger, "You must understand. I felt it was something – *one* thing – I could do. I had a few savings, just in case I should ever marry myself ... I was *glad*. Particularly afterwards ... But you'll think me very stupid if I tell you –"

"Of *course* I don't think you're stupid," said Jane. "But I'm shocked that you should have done this for me."

"As I say, you'll think me very stupid. But afterwards, after the disaster and when the War was over, I was appalled – yes, I think that *is* the word – appalled to know that, for no reason I could see, I had been spared ...

"Oh yes, that was a terrible responsibility for me. You don't understand, I can see, and I don't really expect you to, for you haven't lived my kind of life. But for me, with my beliefs ... To know that everyone else in the village had been called upon to face this supreme test, and I had just – missed it. It was terrible, my dear Jane, terrible! I felt so empty. As if my life was worth nothing, not even worthy of sacrifice, and now nothing would ever happen to me again. And I had done so little, and never would. I hadn't even saved anyone – not one of those children, no one ...

"I got very low for a while. And in the worse times – oh, I know it was conceited of me – but I used to get a little comfort, just a little, from the thought of you, and the idea that I had after all helped you: one specific instance, you understand, nothing grand or far-sighted, but something *done* – and that one day I might be able to complete it by giving you back your chain unsold, and that it would be a nice surprise for you –"

Her speech ended on a note of interrogation. Realising belatedly that she must make some response, Jane said,

"Of *course* I'm pleased. It *is* a nice surprise. But oh, Evangeline! What a shame."

"How? What do you mean?"

Jane really meant something like: what a shame that, all these years, you should have been supposing I should still attach importance to a gold chain. Never, after July 22nd, 1944, have I attached any importance to physical objects. I was freed from that violently, once and for all. And whatever Pierre means to me now, he does not mean a piece of jewelry. But she said weakly,

"I mean ... oh, what a shame I didn't realise. I would have come before."

She was assailed by this unguessed responsibility that, all these years, she had apparently been carrying. If she, the outsider, had unwittingly played such a key part in Evangeline Bisset's personal version of events, what potent image of her might have been preserved through time by Marie Stefan? Or by Jeanot? Or by others she could scarcely recall, each of whom had their own individual realities? Others, like herself, had had to continue their fractured lives with the daunting burden of being survivors, but, unlike her, had had no ready escape-route; for them there had been no amnesiac repatriation to another life, an alternative identity.

'You must do your best to become invisible' Picard had told her once, and because this obligation had become an obsession with her she had fallen into the trap of thinking that she had succeeded. She had believed, because she had wanted to believe it, that any stake she had had in the place had perished in the fire – that, just as she had lost every-

thing here, so nothing of herself remained either. Clearly, however, it had not been true.

She laid a hand on Evangeline Bisset's shoulder, bony as a bird's beneath the worn cardigan and the grey silk blouse, and squeezed with all the tenderness she could muster.

"I *am* glad you still have the chain," she said. "Very glad. I could not have wished for anything that would have made me happier."

She would have liked to tell Evangeline Bisset to keep it, after everything. But this would not have been right either. It was hers and she must accept it, just as she must accept the knowledge of everything else that had been real also: Pierre's life and death, Sylvain's, everything that had been – and those other things that might have been, too, had the Germans not come to end it all so abruptly, so artificially.

For a generation, dazzled like everyone else by the glare of the fire, she had accepted only that view of St Laurent: the public one, the martyred village, the blackened archetype. Only today had the irrelevance of this ending, to everything that had been real before, come home to her.

With a hint of conscious ceremony, she held her hands cupped in her lap and Evangeline Bisset poured the chain into them. It shifted slightly as it settled, its scores of tiny links disposing themselves like molecules in a chemical process, and then lay there, cool and heavy and real against her warm skin. Irreducible, unchangeable gold.

Also available in Pavanne

Gillian Freeman
An Easter Egg Hunt

On Easter Sunday morning in 1915, the girls of a select academy in the country were to go on an Easter Egg Hunt. One of them never returned . . .

She was seventeen and deeply in love with a young airman already marked down to die.

Her name was Madeleine, and no one would ever see her alive again . . .

'A brooding, haunting, highly-charged story . . . don't miss it' COSMOPOLITAN

The Marriage Machine

In 1947 the Marriage Machine stands in a New York bar. For a nickel it dispenses a truncated version of the Christian marriage service, a cellophane packet of confetti and a miniature marriage certificate. Prior to their real wedding in a Berkshire village church, seventeen-year-old Marion on a visit from England, marries G.I. Johnny Hartman in front of the machine. Twenty years later Marion returns home to England on the collapse of this marriage and looks back on her initial infatuation at the age of twelve with the infiltration of wartime American soldiers and her fantasy that life as a war bride would fulfil some kind of teenage dream – a dream which was constantly shattered until both she and Johnny became the victims of the artificial machine which married them.

'A splendidly sophisticated exercise in Anglo–American misunderstanding written with a lot of wit and humour and knowledge, but above all with a delicious British streak of malice' DAILY TELEGRAPH

)avid Littlejohn

;oing to California

. witty yet moving novel about the repercussions during the honeymoon rive across America of two mismatched romantics who marry within x weeks of meeting.

immy is forty – a big, macho, impulsive, raunchy, open air type with ne broken marriage already behind him. Audrey is in her early twenties petite, demure, an Irish Catholic home-body. They are in love, they ay, but reality collides constantly with their romanticism. He envisages ndless sex with a firm young girl as well as rediscovering his own lost nocence which he believes he sees in her. She dreams of soft vomen's-magazine love with a big, strong man.

've seldom read a story which so wittily exposes the compromises, the nismatched moods, the private loneliness, the moments of tenderness, laustrophobia, lust and grace which combine to make a marriage. This ch, human book shows exactly what it's like' DEBORAH MOGGACH, AILY MAIL

:. M. Peyton

)ear Fred

. captivating novel from the creator of Yorkshire TV's long-running *lambards* serial.

ı Newmarket in the 1880s, young Laura cherishes (along with the rest f England's female population) an ardent attachment to Fred Archer (still ıe greatest jockey of all time who tragically committed suicide aged venty-nine), spending more time in her uncle's stable where he trains ıan in her own somewhat Bohemian home.

. M. Peyton has taken the drama of Fred Archer's real-life achievements nd mixed with it some beautifully interpreted fictitious characters to ıake a magnetic and finally heart-breaking story.

Varm-hearted, richly-endowed with exciting scenes and with utterly elievable characters' SUNDAY TIMES